I confess I might have missed out on many a good book because of the fact that if the first page does not grab me. I put it down. Russ Snyder's book grabs you and holds you from one page to the next. He is an all action writer. And sends you to wishing those characters could step out in the real world and do their public service.

—A.L. WHEELER
Author of upcoming "YOU CAN CALL ME KARMA"
and "THE FINAL OBSCENITY"

The President's Weapon is absolutely addictive! Once I started reading it, I knew at once it'd be one of those chosen few that I'd wonder about the characters, during my day, which to me, means, it's a winner. It jumped right in, grabbed my attention immediately, and kept me hanging on for dear life through to the final sentence. Russ Snyder will become America's *number one drug of choice,* for sure!!

—BARBARA JEAN COUTTS
Sunnyside Library Book Group, Oregon

Read with breathless anticipation—Russ Snyder's work "The President's Weapon" is a perfect blend of action and innovative characters creating a masterful story that is entirely believable. The characterization throughout the book was extremely well done; I was absolutely and completely drawn in and found myself constantly cheering for Sergeant Marvin Styles and his team. Russ has a gift for making his stories both very easy to read, extremely suspenseful and completely enthralling—I literally inhaled it. I can only hope there are more stories to follow. GREAT job...

—CHERYL ANN LYCANS,
Sarasota Book Club

The President's WEAPON

RUSS SNYDER

abbott press

Abbott Press books may be ordered through booksellers or by contacting:

Abbott Press
1663 Liberty Drive
Bloomington, IN 47403
www.abbottpress.com
Phone: 1-866-697-5310

Because of the dynamic nature of the Internet, any web addresses or links contained in this book may have changed since publication and may no longer be valid. The views expressed in this work are solely those of the author and do not necessarily reflect the views of the publisher, and the publisher hereby disclaims any responsibility for them.

Any people depicted in stock imagery provided by Thinkstock are models, and such images are being used for illustrative purposes only. Certain stock imagery © Thinkstock.

ISBN: 978-1-4582-1847-6 (sc)
ISBN: 978-1-4582-1848-3 (hc)
ISBN: 978-1-4582-1849-0 (e)

Library of Congress Control Number: 2015900086

Printed in the United States of America.

Abbott Press rev. date: 01/21/2015

CHAPTER 1

AKBAR AL HAMID stepped casually through the employees' entrance of Madison Square Garden—something that he had been doing for almost fifteen years. He was a senior maintenance technician at the facility, where he was known as Gino Salerno. "Gino" had been smuggled into New York at an early age—fifteen, to be precise. He was held in state care until he turned eighteen and then released. He was quiet, minded his own business, and had shown an interest in mechanics. He caused no trouble and seemed eager to please. His story was that he'd been abandoned by his mother and had never known his father. A police officer had found him sitting on a street curb, trying to hide the fact that he was crying. He was a boy that everyone took a shine to. After his eighteenth birthday and his release from state custody, he secured a job as a construction laborer. He worked in this capacity for three years, during which time he observed, quite intently, the work of other, more skilled, workers. He had a natural aptitude for electrical work. This would serve him in good stead later on.

Gino had the complete trust of his supervisors and enjoyed the run of the place. He would be painting hallways one day and mopping floors the next. He would do any task asked of him and never complained. He was always smiling. He tended to be a bit of a loner but was never standoffish. He rarely socialized with any of his coworkers outside the workplace. No one would have ever guessed that for the past two months he'd been Though his antisocial ways seemed odd to some of them at first, they soon accepted him smuggling in components to make a bomb. A piece here, another stashed there; most made their way inside hidden in his lunch box. Directly after 9-11, all workers were searched upon entry each day, but that had relaxed after five years. Now the guards merely waved Gino through, never giving him a second look or thought. For the last week Gino had been bringing a new lunch cooler with him. The guards and his coworkers had joked with him about it.

"Yeah, the old Igloo finally wore out," he always said, grinning. Actually, he had two new lunch coolers: one that held his lunch, snacks, and cold packs; and a second, which was designed much heavier. This morning he was carrying the lead-lined unit, trying, with difficulty, not to give away the obvious weight difference. His intention was that this would be his last day, as he was planning on calling in sick the following morning. By then, he would be far away.

"Hey, Gino, morning; how's it going?" one of the guards, Eddie, called out.

"Not so great. Didn't sleep much last night. Feel like I'm coming down with a cold or something."

"That sucks. Well, don't sneeze in my direction." They both chuckled, then Gino walked down toward the time clocks, punched in, and headed down to the maintenance locker room.

"Hey, Gino, we got a bad GFI breaker in the panel box for the women's bathroom up in the offices. Check that out when you can," Chuck, his immediate supervisor, directed.

"Sure, boss. Get to it shortly. Gotta finish up some crap from yesterday first." Then Gino went to retrieve his tools, which were all placed in an organized manner on a rolling cart. Today, however, he hid his lunch cooler on the lower shelf, out of sight, by two tool chests, a coil of multiple extension cords, and boxes of assorted supplies. He took a service elevator down into the bowels of MSG. There he made his way into an area where few people ever had cause to go, an access region, where the cooling system piping for the ice rink was housed. He entered and quickly grabbed one tool box along with his lunch cooler. Walking toward the rear, where the piping was most congested, he set to work. An hour later he was finished. The dirty bomb was completed, and the timer set. It was an ingeniously designed device; there was no risk of radiation exposure to him. There was to be a playoff game between the New York Rangers and the Washington Capitals the following evening. The bomb was set to go off at 7:35 p.m., the time the puck would be dropped to start the game. He then made a quick retreat back to the locker room, where he signed out a GFI breaker. He went to make that repair as he'd been instructed. Upon conclusion, he signed the original work order, signifying that the task had been completed. Then he went to find his boss.

"Chuck, I'm really starting to feel bad; I'm afraid I'm going to start puking. I'm going to pack it in and hope I feel better tomorrow."

"Ouch. That's too bad. Yeah, sure, go ahead. You don't get sick hardly ever. Hope it's nothing too bad. I'll make a note. If you still feel lousy tomorrow, don't worry about having to call in. I got you covered," Chuck offered.

"Thanks man, appreciate it." Then Akbar al Hamid walked out of Madison Square Garden for the last time, and he never looked back.

CHAPTER 2

T HE TROOP TRANSPORT had landed. All of the soldiers had disembarked and were walking with excitement and anticipation toward the large crowd that had gathered to welcome them home. Banners were flying, a band was playing, and people everywhere in sight were cheering, screaming, laughing, and crying. There was uncontrolled happiness and elation that beloved family members and friends were home at last. Had someone looked closely, he or she might have noticed that one soldier stood out from the others. He wore a slightly different uniform as a member of the US Marine Corp, while the other soldiers were all US Army. The decision to be on this particular flight home had not been of his choosing. He had been ordered. He had spent just over twenty years in the Corp and now found himself being forced out. An incident in Afghanistan had precipitated this.

Sgt. Marvin Styles was unique among all other marines. No one else did what he did in quite the same manner. He was a sniper. He had been a sniper for over fifteen years during both wars in Iraq and two campaigns in Afghanistan. He worked completely alone—no spotter, no supporting unit. He *was* his unit. His mission was simple:

kill the enemy by any means available. He would go out on his own for months at a time, only to reappear at his base, where he would write up a report and send it onward, as no one at that base would ever read it. For all practical purposes, he was not under the command of the base commanding officer, something that the base CO absolutely hated. Styles kept to himself, which created a certain mystique that surrounded him.

This was his method of operation, and he liked it. Over the years he had acquired the nickname "Ghost." When he returned to base, no one would ever see him. Suddenly he was just there, usually found sleeping in his rack. No one would dare wake him, ever. While not a big man, just over six feet tall and weighing a buck ninety-five, he was without question one of the deadliest men alive. Not only was he extremely skilled with various firearms, but he was also an expert with edged weapons and was over the top in his hand-to-hand fighting capability. His father had enrolled him in a martial arts dojo when Styles was only seven. By fourteen he had earned two black belts. By age twenty he had efficiently incorporated several different styles, easing in and out of all of them effortlessly, depending on what might be desired. His hand techniques made it virtually impossible for anyone to grab him. Anyone who tried always heard his or her own bones snap. His physical training was insane. He could do 2,500 push-ups in two hours. He would hang by his heels upside down on a horizontal bar, hooking his feet around the vertical bars to the sides, and proceed to do two hundred inverted sit-ups, touching his chest to his knees. He would then do five hundred pull-ups. He would finish by doing a split, pivoting himself forward at his hips to touch his forehead on the ground, then pivoting backward and touching the back of his head to the ground, all the time keeping his feet pointed straight up. He would repeat this particular exercise one hundred times. On alternate days he would run twenty-five miles with an eighty-pound pack strapped on his back. Carrying his sniper rifle. This was his main routine, though he worked out on both heavy and speed bags constantly. He had also mastered isometric exercises that he could employ when he was in stealth mode. Seeing him in clothing, one would never guess that underneath was a walking rock.

On this particular morning, his dark brown hair was a bit on the long side for a soldier and he hadn't shaved for a few days. This had been pointed out to him by several superior officers over the course of the last three days, to which he had simply replied, "So?" He had less than forty-eight hours left in his military career; he was getting the shaft, and he was *really* pissed about it. He was in no mood to listen to some jackass complain about his appearance. After having spent more than twenty-seven of the last thirty-six months in-country, tracking and killing members of the Taliban and al-Qaeda, then witnessing a completely avoidable, by his own warning, clusterfuck that had cost the lives of nine American soldiers, the result of sheer arrogant stupidity exhibited by one certain army captain, he'd had his fill of orders.

The darkly tanned soldier was more comfortable alone than with large groups of people, one of the many attributes that made him such a successful sniper. His twenty-ten eyesight and natural skill with a rifle were also strong assets. He was looking forward, albeit with some concern, to spending time with his father. Accompanying him home were a few more scars, reminders of a mortar attack. One, on his left cheek, added to his hard looks.

Sgt. Marvin Styles paused for a moment to survey the scene ahead of him. He set down both the bags he carried, for a moment, and just watched. He rarely smiled, but he could feel himself doing so now, seeing the joy unfolding before his eyes. His own father didn't know he was coming home. There would be questions that his father would ask that Styles did not want to discuss over the phone; therefore, he was planning on returning unannounced. He had spent most of his life arriving unannounced, and as often as not, someone died as a result. He had no qualms about what he did or who he was. It was a job that needed doing, and he was extraordinary at it. He lost no sleep.

He picked up his bags and headed for the large hangar to complete some paperwork and receive instructions on where he was to report. He had mixed emotions about leaving the military; it was the only home he had known as an adult. He and his father had never been particularly close, and his mother had died when he was a young child.

He had no siblings. Growing up, he was used to being alone. He spent much of his youth in the woods, hunting, not realizing how much he was honing the tracking skills that would be so vital to him later in life. Starting a new journey down an unknown road, he strode toward the hangar.

CHAPTER 3

T HERE WAS SO much hoopla still going on outside with the soldiers and their families that Styles was able to walk straight over to the area designated for processing. Two government types in civilian dress, including the mandatory sunglasses, approached him. Instinctively Styles's guard went up.

"Sgt. Marvin Styles?" the older of the two asked.

"Yes," Styles replied curtly.

"Would you come with us, sir?"

"Why?" Styles demanded.

"We asked you to," replied the second suit.

"Means I can say no if I want," Styles replied.

"Sergeant, we are asking you to come with us now only for the sake of time. We know you still have forty-eight hours left in the Marine Corp, and if you don't want to come now, you'll be with us shortly." He handed Styles a manila envelope. "Inside this you'll find orders for you. Please examine them closely."

He paused for a moment, putting down his bags, and opened it to read that he was being instructed to accompany Agents Banks and

Rutherford. Everything looked kosher, so Styles asked them for ID. They looked at each other with resignation and showed their Secret Service badges and their photo identification cards. "What the hell does the Secret Service want with me?" he asked.

"That's above our pay grade, Sergeant. We were just told to come down here and pick you up. Other than that, we are supposed to deliver you to Washington, DC."

"Washington? What am I going there for?" he asked, fuming.

"Sergeant, we honestly don't know. We are to deliver you and set you up in a downtown hotel; from there you're not our problem. Now it would be easier if we could just get going, but if you want to call someone, you can use my cell."

Styles reread what was in the envelope, and the orders were clear. Included was a handwritten note from one of his former commanding officers, the one man he undoubtedly felt closest to in the entire military. He recognized his handwriting. "Let's go," he said flatly. He caught what looked like relief on their faces and followed them to a waiting Ford Crown Victoria, typical government-issue transportation. Dark blue, plain steel wheels with dog-dish hubcaps, and multiple radio antennas across the back.

"You can put your bags in the trunk," offered Agent Banks as he popped the lid.

Styles tossed his duffel bag inside but carried the second with him toward the rear passenger door. "This will stay with me," Styles said with finality.

"Why? What's in it?" asked the younger agent, Rutherford.

"That's above your pay grade," he shot back.

The two agents looked at each other and shrugged, then climbed into the front seat while Sergeant Marvin Styles made himself comfortable in the rear.

CHAPTER 4

STYLES HAD BEEN ordered to fly into Ft. Campbell, located in Kentucky, as it was the first plane back to the States. Certain members of the military command in Afghanistan wanted him out ASAP. Sitting in the backseat staring out the window, he found himself reflecting on the events that had taken place over the past four days. *Hell, all I did was smack some dipshit captain,* he thought. *He gets nine good soldiers killed because of his stupid ego, and I'm the one getting bounced. What the fuck is up with that!* He pondered how the whole structure and concept of the military had changed over the last ten years, and he caught himself thinking, *Maybe it's a good thing I am getting out.* It seemed to him as though "we" really weren't interested in winning the war anymore. *Too much bullshit politics and not enough soldiering.*

"How long to DC?" asked Styles.

"Eight hours, give or take," Agent Rutherford answered. "You hungry, Sergeant?"

"I'm good for now."

"Well, let us know if you need anything," added Agent Banks, who was driving.

Styles decided to try to relax and thought some music might help, so he dug into his bag and retrieved an iPod. He noticed that the movement seemed to make Agent Rutherford anxious.

"Hey, what are you doing?" he asked with a note of alarm in his voice.

"Relax, it's just an iPod. Look, Agent Rutherford, let's get something straight right now. If I didn't want to come with you, I damn sure wouldn't be sitting in this car. So just do your damned job and get me to DC so whatever shit this is I can get it over with."

Agent Banks looked over at his junior partner and simply said, "Hey, Jim, tone it down. This man is no more concerned with us than you are a housefly."

That comment caught Styles by surprise, and he wondered just how much they knew about him. He wasn't exactly the poster boy for enlistment offices. If anything, he would be the one they would want to be kept hidden on the back shelf in some locked closet somewhere. For years he'd had a seven-figure price tag on his head. Even his own troops tended to steer clear of him. *Having a reputation as an ice-cold killer does have its advantages*, he mused to himself. *Keeps the wannabes at bay.*

Around five that afternoon, about three hours out of DC, Styles piped up to say that he could stand to take a piss.

"Might as well get a bite to eat too, that okay?" Agent Banks offered.

"Fine by me."

"Any problem with Cracker Barrel?"

"Nope."

"Got one about eight miles up the road. We'll stop there."

"Fine," Styles replied.

Six minutes later they were exiting off Interstate 81, headed toward the restaurant. Soon Banks was parking the car. Everyone got out and stretched his legs. Styles took a moment and, bending over at the waist, held the palms of his hands against the pavement. He could feel the others staring. Without looking at them, he said, "Just loosening up a bit, boys, no need to worry," then reached in the car and grabbed his bag.

"Why not just leave that? I'll lock the car," Banks offered.

"This bag stays with me."

"Do you really think—"

"It stays with me!" he stated firmly, interrupting Rutherford in midsentence.

Again, they both shrugged. All three walked inside.

"Gonna take a leak; I'll find you," Styles said.

Forty-five minutes later found the trio back on the road headed toward Washington. This time Styles left the iPod in his bag and just stared out the window. They were in the mountains, and the view was nice. He was still wondering what in the hell the Secret Service could possibly want with him. Maybe it wasn't about them at all, but then if not, why was he being taken to Washington? *Guess I'll find out soon enough*, he thought. He decided to let himself just zone out, drifting into a place where he wasn't asleep, but rather in a deep rest; yet he was totally aware of everything going on around him.

It didn't seem long before they were entering the outskirts of Washington. Traffic wasn't bad; everyone else was headed out, while they were headed in. In a short while, Styles could see the Capitol Building, all lit up. Eight minutes later the car pulled up to the downtown Hilton, catching Styles's attention. "Well, this isn't Motel 6."

"Not our choice," Rutherford snapped. Styles guessed he'd never stayed at the downtown Hilton.

All of the guests at the hotel were dressed in suits and expensive dresses. A dedicated follower of fashion he wasn't. "I'm gonna fit in real well," he quipped.

"You're not going in. Wait here with Rutherford and I'll get you checked in," Agent Banks answered.

"Fine by me."

Seven minutes later, Banks returned and handed Styles a key card. "You're in room 821; we'll walk you up."

Styles and Rutherford got out of the car as Banks reached in and popped the trunk lid, allowing Styles to retrieve his duffel bag.

The trio walked through the reception area to the elevators. Styles stopped.

"I'll take the stairs," he announced.

"What?" Banks and Rutherford exclaimed together.

"I said I'll take the stairs."

"Why in hell would you want to do that?" Rutherford demanded to know.

"It's what I do," he answered, and he started walking toward the door marked "Stairway."

"Wait a minute," barked Banks as he came hustling up to Styles. "We're not supposed to let you out of our sight until you're checked into your room."

Styles looked at him sternly. "Guess that means that either one or both of you are climbing stairs. Don't worry; if you can't make it, I'll carry you."

"Jesus Christ," he heard Rutherford swear as he started up behind him. He guessed Banks had opted for the elevator.

Pausing at the door that led out to the eighth-floor hallway, Styles had to wait on Rutherford. He was at least three floors down. By the time he reached Styles, he was puffing. Styles just looked at him and shook his head. *Wouldn't last ten minutes in-country*, he thought.

Room 821 was just a short distance down the hall. Banks was waiting. "Let me have the key card," he said.

Styles handed it to him without saying anything.

"Stay here," he stated. He then walked into the room with his hand on his gun, a fact that Styles picked up on before his fingers had closed around the butt of his Glock.

"Clear," he announced loudly thirty seconds later. Rutherford and Styles then followed him into the room.

"Mind telling me what that was about?" Styles asked.

Agent Banks just replied, "Standard procedure, nothing more."

"Right ..."

Rutherford turned toward Styles and gave him another large envelope. "In here is a cell phone and an ATM card. Password is your first name. It has five grand on it. Don't spend it all tonight. You'll be getting a call at 0900 in the morning, sharp. Answer it." Both agents then turned and left.

CHAPTER 5

S TYLES LOOKED AT his watch. It was shortly before nine in the evening. He was restless. He walked over to the large picture window and pulled back the curtain. The view of Washington, DC, was spectacular at night. *Probably looks nicer now than daytime*, he thought. Styles walked back over to the bed and went back through everything in the two envelopes he had been given. Not surprisingly, everything looked the same. He glanced over his orders and read every word again. Nothing jumped out at him that meant anything. Simple and to the point, just what anyone would expect of the military. Then he studied the note written by his previous CO, Captain Richard Starr. Styles had known Starr for over fifteen years and had stayed in touch until Starr retired from active service three years earlier.

Starr had been instrumental in creating the position that Styles had occupied for longer than he really cared to remember. It had been a reversal from standard sniper operation. Modern warfare sniper teams are usually composed of two men: the sniper, who actually fires the rifle, and his spotter, who calls out distance and other relevant information. Either man is fully capable of doing either job. Styles had a knack for being able to do both instinctively. He knew growing up in the woods was the basis for his ability to learn to track, read the wind, and, most of all, exercise simple patience. He once holed up for sixty hours, less than four hundred yards from a suspected al-Qaeda safe house, in a ghillie suit he had made himself. He had three specific targets. Countless times the enemy had passed within thirty yards of his position, but had never been made. Then, late in the afternoon, two cars pulled up. All three targets were suddenly right in front of him. Less than four seconds later, all three targets were down. Four seconds after that, the other three masked men were also down. The sound suppressor on his rifle made it all but impossible for the enemy to accurately acquire Styles's position. He stayed right where he was, hidden, until well after dark. With his night goggles in place, he easily made his way out of the area and back to his campsite, a small hole dug out of the hillside and covered with his ghillie suit. Anyone could walk right past it and never make it for what it was.

Styles read Capt. Starr's note again. It simply said, "Marv, go with these men, no questions asked. All will be explained." Starr called Styles "Marv." Styles called Starr "Starr." It was their own way, friendship, grown from respect. So Styles had agreed to his friend's request.

Now, alone in his hotel room with no idea at all of what was about to transpire, Styles decided he wasn't going to waste time and energy wondering about it. He would find out soon enough. He decided to get some exercise. He took some clothes out of his duffel bag and spread them across the bed. Shorts, T-shirts, fatigues, blue jeans, underwear, and socks. What he would need for that evening and tomorrow. The blue jeans would work fine for tomorrow. On a hunch, he picked up the phone and rang the service desk, inquiring about laundry service. Of course they had it. He informed them he had some laundry he'd like done and would set it outside his door by midnight. This would allow him to toss in the clothes he would wear for his exercise session that night, as well as the fatigues he'd been wearing for two days now.

He then unpacked the second bag. The most important item was his custom-built sniper rifle based off the M40A3, featuring a two-inch-longer barrel and full rail system for fast scope interchangeability. He would change from his Leopold Mark 4 ER/T day scope to the AN/PUS-10 night vision scope, with a clarity so high it seemed surreal. He stripped half the bed and put the rifle, the scopes, the ammunition magazines, bipod, and all other related items, including his three knives, between the mattresses. Then he remade the bed exactly as he had found it. The rifle was in a soft case, which was why he was so damned particular about not letting it out of his sight. Normally he preferred a hard case, but that would prove to be too recognizable, while the soft case fit easily into the smaller duffle bag. Finally, with everything placed where he wanted it, he changed into his shorts and T-shirt, threw on some socks and running shoes—a welcome change from his usual combat boots—and headed for the stairs. Before closing the door behind him, he tucked his room key card, his military ID, and two twenty-dollar bills inside his right sock.

CHAPTER 6

P RESIDENT ROBERT WILLIAMS, from Texas, was four months into his first term. He had been elected on a platform promising change in the strategy to restore the US economy, and to take the fight to Islamic Jihadists. He was having a discussion with his chief of staff, Andrew Ladd.

"Andy, I'm going to do this."

"Sir, I understand your frustration. Hell, I think just about everybody is frustrated, but we still have to respect our laws, respect our constitution."

"Those damn psycho bastards don't respect anything. Children, women, innocent people, anything. I'd nuke 'em if I thought I could get away with it, but even I know that's out of the question. But don't think for a second I haven't spent time thinking about it. I'm tired of the same old shit. Something has to, and is, going to change how we fight these maniacs."

"Mr. President, I couldn't agree more. I just think this road you're talking about could end up being a one-way street to disaster. What are you going to say if this *ever* gets out? That you not only condoned but actually conceived the idea of a president-sanctioned assassin?"

"Andy, half the world knows the CIA assassinates designated targets. So does Mossad. The Brits. However, since the CIA is, by law, not supposed to work within our own borders, I want an alternative choice. Plus, the liberals in Congress are always on their ass."

"But sir," an exasperated Andrew Ladd argued, "a presidential assassin? Think of the problems that could cause. Not just for your presidency, but the entire party."

"Andy, when those damned terrorists start playing by some kind of civilized rules, then so will I, but I am not going to fight a war with these bastards with my hands tied behind my back any longer. Look, I believe in the Constitution as much as anyone, but I don't think our Founding Fathers had this situation in mind when they drafted it. If these suicide bombers are so hell-bent on killing themselves, then I'm going to help them along. My sworn duty is to protect this country and its citizens, *not* the legal rights of these bastards. To borrow a line from a TV show I like, *NCIS*, this man is going to be the sharp end of *my* spear."

Chief of Staff Andrew Ladd sat down with resignation. He knew he was not going to win this one. His boss was too pissed off over recent events. Few people were aware that a dirty bomb had failed to explode in New York three weeks previously. It was sheer dumb luck; the detonator had failed. Had that not happened, the casualty list would have been countless. "Sir, do you have someone in mind?"

"A close friend of mine does. I'm meeting with him tomorrow. Andy, only four people are going to be aware of this action. Myself, you, the joint chief, and my friend. Obviously, the individual chosen will know."

"What if you offer to someone who won't accept? Wouldn't that cause an issue?"

"No individual will be asked unless it's certain he will accept. This is going to take a very specialized man. Unique not only in skill but in personality. My friend has assured me that he knows the perfect man for the job. He commanded him in the Marine Corp. This man is just now getting out—forced out, actually. Apparently, a particular Captain over there issued some dumb-ass order that got nine of our soldiers killed. This guy smacked him one. They didn't want to court-martial him because of his service record, but he was pushed out. My friend thinks that will work to our advantage in recruiting him."

"Who is this man?"

"Let's wait until he accepts, then you'll meet him. Like I said, only four of us will know of his existence. My friend will become his handler. We both will communicate directly with my friend." President Williams came over and sat down across from his advisor. They went back a long way together. "Andy, I know that you are only looking to cover my ass, and we both know that, at times, it needs covering. This is something I feel I really need to do. I need to know that you're on board with it."

Chief of Staff Ladd was quiet for a moment, then looked his boss squarely in the eyes. "I'm not going to lie to you, sir, and say I agree, because I don't. My job is, however, to serve the president, and that I will do whether I agree or not. So, if this is the course of action that you wish to chart, I will support it fully. That you can count on."

The two men eyed each other for a moment. Then President Robert Williams leaned over and slapped his friend on the shoulder. "Andy, that's all I ever hoped for. Your honesty with me, over the years, is why I have come to trust you as I do. The last thing I want as a chief of staff is a yes-man. For all you've done, and will do, thank you."

Andrew Ladd had phone calls to make. After his meeting with the president, he returned to his office. First he called the head of the Secret Service and was informed that the gentleman that his service had been instructed to pick up had arrived. Ladd thanked him and hung up. He called his boss. "Sir, the man you are expecting has arrived. I'll set up the meeting for tomorrow."

"Excellent," the president replied. "Let me know the particulars as soon as everything is in place."

The next phone call was to Captain Richard Starr, retired. Starr picked up on the third ring.

"Captain Starr," Ladd said. "Your man has arrived. He's over at the Hilton in room eight twenty-one."

"Thank you, sir, I'll have a talk with him and get back with you ASAP."

Starr called the Hilton. "Room eight twenty-one please." He waited to be connected.

"I'm sorry, sir, there's no answer at this time. Would you care to leave a voice message?"

"Yes, I would."

"Speak after the beep please." The operator transferred the call to room 821's voice mail.

God I hate these damned beeps. Just once I'd like to hear a bop or something, Starr thought to himself as the beep sounded into his ear. "Hey, soldier boy, this is Starr. Call me at this number when you get back." He then recited his cell number into the phone. Had Starr called fifteen minutes earlier, he would have caught Styles before he went out for his run, and possibly saved someone from having a very bad night.

CHAPTER 7

STYLES WALKED BACK down the stairs and out into the lobby, attracting quite a few odd looks in his workout attire, which consisted of typical khaki shorts and a green military T-shirt. He ignored the stares and headed out the front door. The doorman looked at him and said, "Have a nice run." He looked as if he expected a tip; if so, he was disappointed.

Styles turned left, starting out at a slow, easy pace. He hadn't done much but sit for the last thirty-six hours, so he decided to take it easy and let the rhythm come to him. He was about four miles into the run when he noticed a definite change of scenery. Gone were the hotels and restaurants; pawn shops and liquor stores had taken their places. Styles had a natural sense of direction no matter where he might be, so getting lost was never a concern. He also had ingrained in himself to *always* be aware of anything and everything. He noticed that an older Chevrolet sedan, with those idiotic wheels that spin all the time, had passed by him three times. *Don't bother me, I don't bother you*, he thought. He kept running. He had first noticed that the car contained three young adult males; but on the last pass, it had contained only two. In his profession, the flag doesn't get any redder. He continued, crossing the street to run on the other side, and could see an alley coming up a block ahead on the right. He crossed back. If these clowns were going to make a move, it would be there, at that entrance. As he approached the alley, he slowed his pace. Ten feet from it he slowed to a walk, acting as though he were tired. Nothing could have been further from reality.

A man in his midtwenties stepped out of the dark and turned to face him. "Hey man, you got some cash you could front me?" he said with a smirk.

"No," Styles responded calmly.

Two other men, roughly the same age, were crossing the street toward them. Within five seconds they were just off to the right of the man standing in front of Styles.

"Answer the man's question, running boy," one of the new arrivals spat out.

"I did," Styles answered.

"But dude, like, it was the wrong answer. Now, you got money? It cost money to run on our sidewalks."

One of the men standing next to the street started to circle around to get behind Styles.

Styles looked at the first gangbanger, figuring he was in charge of these three punks. Looking him squarely in the eyes, he simply said, "Leave *now*."

"Hey, we got us a funny one here, Leroy," the one still standing by the street said. Then he pulled a knife. He walked toward Styles without a care in the world. Styles turned, just barely, so he was at a slight angle to the man approaching him. "Last chance," he told Styles.

"You're right!" Styles noticed the other two had not moved closer. He figured that the one with the knife must've been the "hitter" of the three. Knife Man stopped four feet in front of Styles.

"You gonna die, motherfucker."

Styles said nothing. He just waited. The attack came. Knife Man lunged toward Styles with the blade extending out from his arm. He had stepped forward and thrust forward, almost like a move one would expect to see in a sword fight.

Styles stepped forward into the man, catching his hand just above the handle of the knife, then snapped the hand completely over to the outside, shattering the wrist bone. He instantly spun around back to his left and drove his left elbow into the man's left temple. He was out cold, and quite possibly dead, before he hit the sidewalk. As the man's body hit the walkway, Styles took one step toward the leader of this little bunch of thieves and delivered a brutal side kick straight into the man's solar plexus. The blow was so powerful that something snapped as the man was driven backward; he was literally parallel to the pavement when he crumpled onto it. The entire incident had unfolded in less than three seconds. Styles spun around to face the third man, who was already running across the street. He felt no emotion watching him run away. He continued observing for a couple of seconds, then continued his run without even looking down.

Seventy-five minutes and approximately twelve miles later, he was back at the entrance to the Hilton.

"Have a nice run, sir?" inquired the doorman.

"Couldn't have been better," Styles answered. After going through the doors, he headed to the stairwell and went back to his room. He saw the message machine blinking and punched the button to listen. As he listened to it the second time, he grabbed a pen from the desk and jotted his former CO's number down on the pad by the phone. He decided to take a quick shower before he returned the call. After drying off, Styles put on a clean pair of fatigues. He called Captain Starr, who answered on the second ring. "Hey, Captain, glad to see you made bail again," Styles greeted his friend.

"Don't 'bail' me, sonny boy; you're the one whose ass I'm always having to pull out

of a sling. Weren't for me you'd be on your way to Leavenworth by now. What in the hell were you thinking?"

"Starr, that fucking idiot got nine good boys killed, and all because his arrogant ass wouldn't listen to his LT. I should've slit his fucking throat."

"Tell me how you really feel," Starr replied, chuckling.

Styles calmed down and said, "It was time for me to get out anyway.

23

I got my twenty in, and the way those fucking politicians are running things over there, only been a matter of time before I got in real trouble."

"So tell me, Marv, what you got planned?"

"Hell if I know, but since I got picked up in Kentucky by two Secret Service agents and got a note from you, maybe you ought to tell me what I've got planned," Styles answered.

"Let's meet for breakfast, there at the hotel, and we can talk. There's something that's come up, and I think it just might be something you'd take an interest in. That is, if you're still the same soldier I've known all these years."

"I guess so, maybe a little more jaded."

"Jaded is good for this, son. I'll see you in the restaurant around zero seven hundred."

"See you then, Starr." He hung up.

Wonder what he's got going? Styles thought.

He turned on the television and tuned to the Leno show and watched for about fifteen minutes, then decided to crash. He snapped off the lights and took one last look at the evening view of the city before crawling into bed.

CHAPTER 8

STYLES WALKED INTO the restaurant at five minutes before seven. He still hadn't shaved yet, enjoying the freedom of it not being required. Plus he didn't think Starr would mind. He was wrong. Styles chose a booth near the door, so Starr could spot him easily enough. Thirty seconds later a rolled-up napkin hit him in the back of the head. He didn't need to look to know. Styles got up and headed back, and sure enough, four booths back sat Captain Richard Starr, his favorite CO he'd ever served under.

"What'd you do, forget your damned glasses, as well as shaving, Sergeant?" snapped Starr.

"Nice to see you again too, *sir*. Sorry, I didn't know we were playing hide-and-seek."

"Don't give me that "nice to see you, sir" shit. You're still in the marines, and I damn well expect you to act like a marine, soldier."

Styles snapped to and gave Starr an exaggerated salute, adding, "Sir, yes, sir, you can get in line and kiss my ass, sir."

Starr burst out laughing, then said, "Well son, I'd consider that, but I'm kinda hungry, and I'm sure that's a very long line." Then he stood

25

and grasped Styles's hand. "How you doin', Marv. Damned good to see ya." He was one of the two people on Earth who could get away with calling Styles "Marv."

"I'm doing okay, Starr; still a little pissed, I guess, but okay," Styles answered.

"Yeah, I heard you got kind of a raw deal over there. Should've known better though, smacking a captain, especially in front of a colonel."

"He was a fucking idiot, Starr; got nine good men killed. He had bad intel, and I told him so myself. I spotted a whole shitload of bad guys moving in the exact direction two days earlier, on my way in. I heard about the mission and got my ass over there big time and tried to tell that no-balls sack of shit, but he wouldn't listen. Kept pointing toward drone pictures, said I didn't know what I was talking about. Told that bastard I'd seen more ragheads carrying AKs than any damned drone and he was sending those boys to die. He told me to shut the fuck up and speak when spoken to, and that's when I backhanded that arrogant little prick. If we'd been in-country, I'd have fragged that asshole."

"Yeah, Marv, it's tough when you got brainless morons calling shots, but that's the new and unimproved military, I guess. Glad I got out when I did. Hell, I probably would've hit 'im too. So what's the final call on you?"

"Getting bounced, like you know. Guess I'm gonna get my pension, but some of the brass made a stink about it. Finally decided on an honorable discharge with pension. My record saved that for me, I guess. Couple of 'em didn't like it, though. Thought that little bastard was going to lie right down on the floor and have a baby, he was squalling so much," Styles fumed.

"Pretty much what I figured," Starr agreed.

They both slid into the booth. A waitress came up and asked if they were ready to order. Styles hadn't even looked at a menu, but breakfast was pretty brainless. "Three scrambled eggs, cheese in 'em if possible; some fried potatoes; a couple of biscuits if you have them, otherwise toast; also a large water and coffee."

Starr asked for a short stack of pancakes with bacon and coffee.

After she walked away, Styles looked at Starr and asked, "So what's up?"

"Not here, son. Let's eat, then we'll talk."

"Okay by me."

"So they sent you through Fort Campbell huh?"

"Yeah, first plane out. Brass wanted me outta there."

"Have any company?" Starr asked.

"Nah, everybody else was army. They stayed clear."

"Not surprised." Starr was thoughtful for a few moments and then added, "Wonder if anybody will take a look at that screwup of his?"

"No idea, not my problem anymore."

"Well, you're right about that."

The food came and it smelled good, so they both dug in, eating pretty much in silence, Styles wondering, and who knows what was going through Starr's mind. The waitress came by and refilled their coffee cups twice. Finally they finished and asked for the check.

"Relax, son; this one's on your old CO."

"Now why does that make me nervous?" Styles said with a grin.

"Son, you've got no idea, at least not yet," he said seriously.

Chapter 9

"MEET ME ON the sixth floor." Starr turned and walked toward the elevators knowing that Styles would take the stairs. There was no need to ask any questions. Styles double-timed it up the stairway and beat the elevator. He waited just inside the door that led out into the hallway. The elevators were seventy feet away. He heard the ringing tone, signaling its arrival, and stepped halfway through the door opening, waiting on Starr.

Starr got out and looked over at Styles, and he ever so casually signaled him with his fingers—six-two-four. Room six twenty-four. Automatically Styles checked for security cameras. One was mounted directly over the elevator doors. Starr also had noticed them, which explained why he had signaled Styles tight against the wall. Starr also motioned for him to hold up. Styles let him get inside the room before moving. He kept tight to the wall and made his way to where Starr was waiting for him. Starr opened the door for him just as he arrived, and motioned for him to be silent. He closed the door and reached down into a bag directly at his feet. He retrieved a radio frequency finder, a device used to locate any electronic bugs in a room. He carefully made his way around the entire area, checking everything: curtains, light fixtures, table, chairs, the bathroom. He spent ten minutes checking every conceivable place someone might have planted a listening device.

"Okay, looks like we're clear," Starr confirmed.

"You want to tell me why you're checking for bugs, or don't I want to know?"

"If you had any brains, you wouldn't want to know. But since you don't, let's sit down and talk turkey." That was Starr's slang for letting Styles know that the subject was serious. Both sat down at the table.

"Marvin, what do you have planned?"

"Since you just called me Marvin, maybe I'd better get a will made up real quick."

"I'm serious here, Sergeant, what do you have planned now that you're out?"

Styles could see immediately that Starr was in CO mode, so he responded in kind. "I really don't know, Starr; probably go back home for a while and try to spend some time with my father. Other than that, besides buying a truck, I really don't have anything planned, why?"

"What I'm about to tell you goes with us to our graves. Agreed?"

"You don't have to tell me that."

"I know, just making sure."

"Okay," Styles said. "What the hell are you getting me into?"

"Make yourself comfortable, son; it's a bit of a story. You know our new president, Williams, is from Texas, right?

"Starr, I've been in Afghanistan, not on the fucking moon."

He nodded. "All right. Here's the deal. We've had us a new president for four months now. Not a lot of people know, but he and I go way back. I've met with him three times over the last month. He's come up with an idea, one that I happen to agree with. His chief of staff, guy named Ladd, doesn't like it, but he's a college-bred pussy. Williams ain't. He's run this by me. We've talked it through from one end to the other. We both agree that it warrants being tried." He paused for a moment, thinking, then continued. "This plan he's come up with, only four people in the world are going to know about it. The president, his chief of staff, and me. It requires one more person."

29

"Why do I get the feeling that this last person is me?"

"'Cause it's your lucky day, sonny boy, because it's your lucky day."

"Yeah," responded Styles, though not entirely convinced.

"Anyway, our new president is pissed. He's been pissed for a long time. But now he's in a position to do something."

"What's he pissed about?" Styles asked, feeling he already knew the answer.

"Terrorists. He's tired of us having to play by some sort of civilized rules while they don't. Don't get me wrong; he believes in the Constitution, he believes in due process, but he don't believe that our Founding Fathers had terrorists in mind when they wrote up the Constitution. Plus you've got all these bleeding-heart liberals screaming about *rights*. Where are the rights of these kids they strap bombs to?"

"Starr, you don't have to convince me, I been over in that shit pile for going on fifteen years. I've *seen* what those fanatics do. I got no problem at all in saying I'm glad I shut off the lights in way more than I can count. I figure for every one I shot, I kept one of ours from getting shot or blown up. They don't fight a conventional war, and they don't give a fuck about innocents; they just want to kill us. Makes me want to kill them, and I damn sure did that. I've gutted them with a knife, and with their dying breath, they're cursing America. Or praising Allah. That is one sick society." Styles paused for a minute, then looked Starr straight in the eyes. "I'm gonna tell you something that I never told nobody, and I'm the first to say this might be my own personal shit. These bastards claim that they blow themselves up for virgins right? Well I'm telling you, here and now, that there's a whole bunch of them who might get to those virgins, but they ain't gonna have no dicks. I shot 'em in the balls whenever I had the chance, after the kill shot. And it didn't bother me one fucking bit."

Starr looked at Styles, eyes wide, and said, "Jesus, no wonder they wanted you dead so bad. That must be the biggest damned secret that psycho bunch has ever kept. At least from us." After pausing for a moment to digest what Styles had just told him, he shook his head and continued. "The president wants to play dirty. He strongly believes that as long as we play by one set of rules and they play by another, we're going to stay stuck in this sand pile. So he wants to try something new. He wants to try a new weapon."

"What do you mean?" Styles asked.

"Well, thanks to your old commanding officer, he wants that new weapon to be you."

They were quiet for a minute as Styles looked out the window and thought. Finally he turned back and looked at Starr. "Just exactly what do you mean?" he asked, although he already knew the answer.

"Marvin, he wants you to do what you do. We both know the CIA performs assassinations outside the country—and, on occasion, inside. Regardless, it takes a lot of shit to get someone taken out. Especially if it's here. The president wants to be able to act on confirmed information without having all the bullshit."

Styles asked, "Just how would this little idea work, Captain?"

"This is how we've pretty much laid it out. The president will obtain confirmed information from all his resources. He, and he alone, will make the decision about a target. Once he decides in the affirmative, he will contact me. I will be your handler. The chief of staff will be the one who physically hands me all the info that's required for you to do your job. Your designated contact will be me. Except for the initial meeting with the president, you will have little, or no, contact with him. He wants to meet and assess you. That is just a formality. He's studied you. He knows your capability. Your reputation. The chief of staff referred to you as a two-legged animal. The president responded, and I'm quoting here, "That's exactly what I want.""

Again Styles looked out the window for a few moments. When he turned back to Starr, he said, "Guess with what I've done, doesn't appear as though I've got much of an argument on that issue. I can say I never killed anybody that didn't need killing. And I damn sure don't feel bad about what I've done. I don't know, Starr, maybe I'm just wired a bit different. I mean, I know right from wrong, at least I think I do, and maybe shooting off their dicks was a bit over the top, but—and this is no bullshit here—the only reason I did it was so just in case they did make it to those virgins, they'd damn sure be miserable because of me. So I guess if that makes me sick, I'm sick. Want to know something else? If I am, fuck it, I don't care. What I've seen of those fucking bastards, ain't nothing I ever did that compared to them. Anybody else don't like it, well fuck them too. They haven't seen what I've seen." He was visibly angry.

Starr looked at him for a minute, then just smiled and said, "Yep, you'll do just fine. I knew you wouldn't disappoint me. And about that shooting thing—I only wish I could've done it myself."

CHAPTER 10

CAPTAIN STARR WAS speaking into his cell phone. He'd been talking for about five minutes, listening more than talking. Finally he hung up, went back over to the table, and sat back down across from Styles.

"You got any decent clothes, like a sport coat, that kinda shit?" Starr asked him.

"No, just my dress uniform, fatigues, jeans, that kind of stuff."

"Well, we're gonna have to dress you up a bit to meet the president of the United States."

"Yeah, I suppose so," Styles agreed.

"You got money?" he asked.

"Yeah, those Secret Service guys that picked me up gave me a couple of envelopes; one of them had an ATM card with five grand on it."

"Good. Go out and get some clothes. Don't go overboard; just make yourself presentable. Don't forget a razor either."

Styles gave him his drop-dead look, but Starr just smiled.

"Can't have you looking like some kind of animal, now can we?" he replied, starting to laugh.

"Guess not," Styles said, somewhat sour. Coats and neckties were not his thing.

"All right, go pick up some clothes. I'll be back here around three. We're going to be picked up at three fifteen this afternoon. We'll be standing out front, and a limo will roll up for us. Then to the White House." With that Starr got up and left. Five minutes later Styles followed and went back up to his own room. Styles hated general shopping. Absolutely hated it. An idea came to him. He walked back down the stairway and found the concierge, some guy named Maurice.

"I have to get some decent clothes to wear to an appointment. Is there some way I could just call somebody and tell them what I need? I know all my sizes," Styles inquired.

Maurice spoke up quickly, probably thinking about a good tip. That seemed to be the standard procedure in DC. "Certainly, sir. If you would just make up a list of what you require, I'll have them delivered to your room. Just write down what you'd like,"

"Good. I'll go make up a list and get it back down to you ASAP," Styles told him.

"ASAP, sir?"

"As soon as possible," Styles explained, trying hard to keep the annoyance out of his voice. He still had to watch himself dealing with civilians.

He went back up the stairs, sat down at the table, and made up a list of the crap he thought he should get. He had all the personal stuff; it was just the clothes he needed. So Styles just wrote down his sizes, suggested a blue blazer and whatever else would go with that. Seemed pretty safe. He also asked for a belt and shoes, noting that he was not a fancy kind of guy and would just like to keep it straightforward. Twelve minutes later he was back downstairs, talking to Maurice. "This should pretty much cover it." He handed over the list.

Maurice looked it over and asked, "How much do you care to spend?"

Styles quickly saw where this was going. "Decent, but not real expensive. I don't wear this shit often." Styles swore he saw Maurice grimace.

"Certainly, sir. Shall I just have the clothes sent up, or shall I send for you?"

34

"Just send 'em up. I'll be paying for this with a card," Styles replied.

"I could just add it to your hotel bill, sir."

"No. Just have the store call me, and I'll pay for it over the phone," Styles answered. Maurice was visibly crestfallen. *Probably gets a percentage of everything he sells*, Styles thought. He walked away, leaving Maurice disappointed. Near the front entrance, he paused to check on Maurice, and he watched as he immediately went to his station and picked up his phone. Styles strongly suspected that someone could place an order for a frozen elephant with him and he would know who to call.

CHAPTER 11

NINETY MINUTES LATER Styles' phone rang. He had been doing push-ups. It was the store telling him what they were sending over, and the amount due. The total was $842. He was glad he'd told Maurice to go cheap. Otherwise he might have needed another card. *Almost a thousand bucks for a fucking pair of pants, shirt, tie, belt, socks, shoes, and sport coat. Just another reason I hate this shit*, Styles thought. He read his card number over the phone, and in less than a minute the transaction was completed. Twenty-five minutes after he hung up the phone, it rang again. On the other end was Maurice, telling him that he was sending his clothes up. "Thank you." Short and sweet.

Four minutes later there was knock at his door. Opening it, Styles found a young lady with one of those rolling baggage carts. The sport coat, shirt, and what appeared to be expensive dress slacks had all been carefully placed on hangers. He guessed the shoes, belt, and tie were in the boxes. She rolled the items in and placed them in the closet and on the table. He thanked her and gave her a ten-dollar bill as a tip. She thanked him in return but made him feel as if the ten wasn't enough. Too bad. Styles looked at her and asked, "Is there anything else, miss?"

She got the hint, turned around, and walked out, closing the door behind her. He had been in DC for less than sixteen hours and already could not wait to leave.

Styles turned the TV on to a local twenty-four-hours news channel and went back to doing push-ups. Shortly a story came across about two suspected muggers who had been found the previous evening. One was dead, and the other badly injured, in what appeared to be a robbery attempt gone bad. Styles allowed himself a small smile. It sure had. He didn't have time to complete his full regimen of 2,500, so he stopped at 2,000. It was time to shower and get ready for his visit with the president. Styles had never met one before, hadn't thought he ever would. He really didn't care one way or the other if he ever did or not.

Can't be too much of a stiff if he goes back with Starr, he thought as he headed toward the bathroom. First he shaved, and then he showered. He toweled off, then sat at the table for a few minutes, just looking out over the city. He had been correct the previous evening; the city did look much nicer at night.

"Might as well put this shit on," he said aloud. He got dressed and struggled with the necktie for fifteen minutes. He *hated* neckties. *Whoever thought them up had to have been a masochist and should have been shot at the damned thing's introduction.* Finally he had tied the closest thing to a reasonable knot that he was going to achieve. It looked pretty bad.

Just then the phone rang. It was Starr. "I'm on my way up," he said, and he hung up before Styles could say a word. Three minutes later, more knocking.

He let Starr in and the first words out of his mouth were, "Take off that damned tie. Hell, a tree stump could do better."

"Don't give me any shit about this stupid fucking necktie," Styles shot back, taking it off and throwing it at him.

Starr took off his own coat and tie. In thirty seconds he had taken Styles's tie, retied it, slid it over his head, and given it to him. He then retied his own and put his coat back on.

Styles slipped his tie on and straightened it. It did look better. "Nobody likes a smart ass," he snapped at Starr.

"My, what a change," Starr said to him sarcastically.

"Fuck off."

"Well, let's get going; time to meet the big man. Try not to embarrass me too badly, okay? I told him you were fully capable of chewing with your mouth closed."

As they walked down the hall toward the elevator, looking at Starr, Styles said, "How about I chuck your ass down the elevator shaft?" He heard a slight chuckle.

Together they took the elevator to the lobby and headed out to the sidewalk. All the while Starr was laughing to himself.

CHAPTER 12

P RESIDENT ROBERT "WILD Bill" Williams was madder than at any other time in his life. His director of the National Security Agency, Elliott Ragar, had just dropped a bombshell on him, almost literally.

The president and his chief of staff were in an emergency meeting with Ragar. How in the *fuck* did this happen?" he screamed at Ragar. This was the first time Chief of Staff Ladd had ever heard the president use the *F* word. He instinctively backed up a couple of steps.

"We're not exactly sure, sir. We think we know how the device got into New York, but we do not know exactly who was responsible. We have a few leads but nothing concrete. There was absolutely no chatter anywhere concerning this event. Not anywhere." Ragar was equally upset, but his anger was focused in other directions.

"Run me through this one more time so I don't have any misconceptions here," the president demanded.

"Sir, the short of it is just what I told you. A dirty bomb was smuggled into New York. It was placed at Madison Square Garden and set to explode during a New York Rangers hockey game. Against the Washington Capitals to be precise. There is no other way to say this.

We just got lucky. The detonator failed. I don't know the exact specifics of what, or how; I should have that information within the hour, two at the most. We didn't even know it was there. It was found by accident. They were having a problem with the cooling system for the ice rink. A technician found it. He didn't even know what it was. He just reported it to his supervisor. The supervisor contacted the NYC bomb squad. Luckily, we intercepted the call and were able to contain the situation. We invoked national security to keep the NYC boys out of there. The technician and his supervisor have been temporarily detained until they can be apprised of the overall situation."

"In other words, until you can persuade them to be sure to keep their mouths shut," the president fumed.

"Ah, that would be correct, sir."

For the first time, Chief of Staff Ladd spoke up. "What exactly is the situation now, Elliott?" He purposely used the director's first name in an effort to calm the scene.

"The device is on its way to Quantico. Obviously it's been rendered harmless. We will have forensics go over it with a microscope for any leads. Bomb makers usually leave some type of signature. Every aspect will be compared in the data banks to see if it matches up to anything previously found," Ragar answered. He was openly sweating now.

"Do we have any idea whether this is an isolated incident, or are there more bombs out there that we don't have any idea about?" the president asked, his voice dripping with sarcasm.

"Sir, I hate to admit it, but we just don't know. The general feeling is that this is an isolated incident. I'm sorry; we just don't know."

The president picked up a book that was on his desk and hurled it across the room in anger. He walked over to the window, stared out for a few moments, then turned around. He stared daggers at Ragar, then finally spoke. "Four hours. You've got four hours to bring me something, or bring me your resignation."

"Yes, sir," Ragar replied, immediately turning and leaving.

The president and his chief of staff were silent. Finally Andrew Ladd spoke. "Sir, you will not hear one more word against your idea. I don't even want to think about the consequences should that bomb have gone off. You're right. We have to get dirty to get these fanatics out of our country. I apologize for not getting on board with you quicker."

President Williams walked behind his desk and sat down. He looked tired. He motioned for his chief of staff to sit. "Andy, no need to apologize; you were doing exactly what I expect of you—offering me your objective opinion. That's why you are in the position you are in. I swear to Christ I'm about ready to nuke that whole damned region of the world. They've been fighting for so long over there they don't know any other way of life. Damn, wouldn't it be nice if they'd just go ahead and kill each other off."

Chief of Staff Ladd wasn't exactly sure what to say, so he just kept quiet. The president spoke first.

"I'm with you that I can't even begin to imagine the consequences of that bomb. A Stanley Cup playoff game. Hell, I can't even begin to imagine the nationwide, even worldwide, repercussions. Good portion of New York gone, would've sent our entire financial market into the ground. Who knows who would have been screaming what. Jesus, what a mess. If there was ever a time for the 'better to be lucky than good' saying, this was it." Still no response.

The president looked at his watch. "Andy, I meet this guy in two hours. I will say I'm glad you feel a little stronger about this new approach. I'm going to take this meeting alone. I want you riding herd on everybody, and I want to know something concrete by the time I'm out of that meeting. I want you to coordinate with all the involved agency heads. Make it crystal clear I expect nothing but the most complete cooperation between all agencies; otherwise, heads will roll.

"And I damn sure don't want this getting out. Matt Sanderson is on his way back from California," the president added, in reference to the director of the FBI. "I'm going to call him now and bring him up to speed. This is going to be a long night."

"We will get these bastards," Ladd said, with determination.

"You bet your ass we will," the president agreed.

Chief of Staff Ladd got up and left the room. He had many calls to make and a lot of ass to chew. He also had to set up a cabinet meeting to read everybody in, although the president had made it clear that he wanted only certain secretaries in attendance. The president felt strongly that he wanted to keep this in what one might refer to as the inner circle.

Once his chief of staff had departed, President Williams picked up and acquired a secure line to his director of the FBI. "Matt, keep a straight face over what I'm about to tell you." The president went on to explain in detail what had happened. He was surprised that Matt Sanderson had already heard about the bomb. Silently the president swore to himself about how people seemed incapable of keeping their mouths shut in this town. "Matt, I cannot stress this strongly enough. I'm uncomfortable that you already know about this. I see both sides of the fence, though. However, there *has* to be a lid kept on this. I can't have a mass panic on my hands right now. It would only compromise horribly our ability to investigate this matter. You make it clear to your people that if I catch anyone talking out of turn, I'll bury their asses so deep, light won't find them." The only words the president heard back were the occasional "Yes, sir," but then again, Sanderson wasn't the most talkative individual under any circumstances. The tense conversation ended.

He had been off the phone for two minutes when his secretary buzzed in. "Sir, the director of Homeland Security is here for you."

"Bring him in, Alice."

Charles Rockford entered the room. The president motioned for him to sit. There was no exchange of formalities.

"What have you got?"

"Sir, I've just come from a quick meeting with Ragar. We've concluded that the bomb was probably smuggled down from Canada via automobile. Perhaps a van. Ragar and I both agree that any other manner would have set off flags somewhere. There's just too much security, and we've always felt that Canada was the weak link. So for the present, we are going to concentrate in that direction. We discussed putting in radiation isotope detectors at the border crossings, but odds are these people are not using the main roads, so that probably won't help that much. We agree that installing detectors at toll booths on the interstates might have a better chance of picking up something. We feel that once inside our border, the perpetrators would want to get to their destination quickly, plus with all the traffic on the interstates, they would blend in easier. This, of course, is strictly conjecture on our part, but in the time given, we feel that until something more definitive comes to light, this is at least a solid shot."

"In other words, it's your best guess," the president said, staring hard at Rockford.

"Yes, sir, but we feel it's stronger than a guess. We've run the scenario through the computers, and this is what they're spitting out. Kind of like weather computers trying to track a hurricane. Some will say this, some that. However, a very strong majority are indicating a Canadian course is accurate."

"How long to get the detectors in place?" asked the president.

"We're scrambling now to transport them to blanket the northern border from coast to coast. We should be setting up within seventy-two hours. Of course, there're literally hundreds of state roads that will be unprotected, but we still feel they'll be traveling the interstates. I know that if I were in that position, I wouldn't want to chance being pulled over by some local LEO for some stupid reason."

The president was quiet for a few moments. "That's pretty solid reasoning, Charles. I know it's a guess, but it's a good one. How are you explaining the radiation detectors?"

"We're saying they're traffic counters, that we're conducting a study. Bill Cochran is handling the details of installation," he said, referring to the secretary of transportation. "Every unit will feed via satellite directly into a real-time program in NSA. Multi-angle cameras will be installed so that if any signal is picked up, the target will be photographed from all four sides, plus two cameras will be directed toward the windshield. We want to be able to identify any vehicle that might be suspect."

President Williams sighed audibly. "Good work. Question: is there a way a detector can be installed inside a van or something? A rolling detector, so to speak? I'd like to get as many as possible up and rolling, and out on patrol."

"Yes, sir, you're reading my mind. That wheel is also rolling forward."

"Good. Keep me informed every step of the way."

With that the Director of Homeland Security left the room.

The president looked at his watch. He was hungry but had one more meeting to take. "Alice, has Director Backersley arrived?" the president asked his personal secretary.

"Yes, sir, about ten minutes ago. Should I send him in?"

"Yes."

Seconds later Bernard J. Backersley, Director of the Central Intelligence Agency, entered. Backersley could walk past a thousand people without one ever guessing he headed up the CIA. A diminutive man, barely five feet six inches tall and weighing around 145 pounds, he had an oversize head and was comical in appearance. He also possessed a photographic memory and an IQ that was off the charts. President Williams had met him eight years earlier when he had proposed a radical new method of border security between Texas and Mexico. The president had been impressed by how quickly the man could recognize, dissect, strategize, and implement solutions to a variety of problems. He was the president's first choice to head up the clandestine agency when he took office. He was also capable of verbal warfare on an unprecedented scale, something several senior members of Congress had discovered the hard way.

"Mr. President," Backersley greeted the president.

"Please, take a seat, Bernard. We have a critical situation to discuss."

"You are, of course, referring to the bomb under Madison Square Garden," Backersley stated rather than asking.

While President Williams should have been surprised, he wasn't. Bernard J. Backersley always seemed to know everything in advance. "I suppose there's no point in asking you how in hell you know that?"

"No, sir. I'm CIA at your request. Not knowing would not be doing my job."

The president unconsciously rolled his eyes ever so slightly, which did not go unnoticed by the CIA Director. Then the president said, "Is there any place where I can talk without you hearing it?"

"Of course, sir, you just don't know where they are," he said, allowing himself a small smile.

The president smiled back. He couldn't help but like the man. Then

President Williams got serious. "Since this is out of your supposed jurisdiction, you are going to have to keep a low profile. I do want you working your magic on how this happened. I do not want the CIA taking action. Any intel you can gather I want you to bring directly to me, personally. Theories, ideas, anything, bring it to me and me alone. You are the one man who is going to play outside the envelope. Officially, you are looking outside the country, but I want you on all of it. I've laid down the law to Ragar and Sanderson about interagency cooperation, but you are officially outside their loop. Feed them what foreign intel you need to so they don't squawk too bad, but I want your input kept inside this office. Any questions?"

"No, sir. One thing though. Right now I firmly believe the device, or the materials used to build the device, came through Canada."

"Sanderson and Ragar agree."

"Maybe there's hope for them yet." Backersley smirked. He was openly disdainful of both men, who had difficulty thinking outside the proverbial box.

The president looked sternly at Backersley. "I don't want this to get into a pissing contest, Bernard. I need your help here, but just as importantly, I need it in my own manner. So again, any questions?"

"No, sir, I'll be on my best behavior," replied Backersley.

"Maybe I'd better get that in writing, Bernard," the president retorted.

"I'll be good." He stood to leave. The president stood with him.

"Bernard, we need to get a handle on this, and quickly. I want you to concentrate on foreign circumstances. If you get any information, though, call me, and me only. Don't even talk to Ladd. Me, and me alone."

"I understand perfectly, sir, and I won't disappoint." Backersley turned and went back out the door.

The president buzzed his secretary. "Alice, have a roast beef sandwich sent in with some iced tea. Throw some chips on the side, but don't you dare tell my wife."

"That might cost you, Mr. President."

"If it does you'll find yourself in Cuba." He heard her laughing.

45

CHAPTER 13

STARR AND STYLES were standing on the sidewalk in front of the hotel. For the second week of May, the weather was spectacular. Temperature in the high sixties, and bright brilliant sunshine, the kind of day postcard manufacturers pray for.

Starr nudged Styles in the ribs and said, "I think these are our boys."

A black limo pulled up curbside, and they got in the rear doors. The glass partition between the driver and the passenger compartment was completely blacked out, matching all the windows in the vehicle. The Rolling Stones could've been inside that vehicle, and no one would ever have known. No words were spoken from the front. For a while they rode in silence.

Finally Starr spoke. "I'm not sure who's going to be at this meeting; I'm guessing the president, probably his chief of staff, and us. I'm sure we'll be going into the underground parking area, where they'll let us out. Don't speak to anyone. Not a word. Try not to look anyone in the eyes. The less of a visual anyone might get of you, the better. This may well be your only visit to the White House."

For the remainder of the trip they remained silent. Then the limo turned into a drive with the White House in the background. The car was waved through a security gate. They continued on into an underground parking area and pulled up near a pair of entrance doors. There were heavily armed guards visible throughout the area. The vehicle stopped, then Starr and Styles got out.

A Secret Service agent took a pass that Starr handed him and motioned for them to follow. They went through the doors and were handed off to another pair of agents. Again they followed in silence to an elevator. Always to an elevator. One of the secret service agents pushed an unmarked button, and the door opened silently. He stepped inside with Starr and Styles following. He pushed another unmarked button and then quickly stepped off before the door closed, leaving them alone. It was so smooth that it was difficult for them to tell if they were going up or down. Six seconds later the door opened and they got off. More agents, although this time four. Starr and Styles fell in between them and walked down a hallway. The group passed through another armed security point and continued left, where four hallways came together. Finally they came to a door that was opened, and Starr and Styles were ushered through. Inside were two more agents. They opened up yet another door on the far side of the room. Styles followed Starr as he walked into a small conference room. The agents did not follow. The door was closed behind them. The room was austere. A counter ran along one side with some cabinets and a refrigerator. Glassware was laid out on the counter, and a round table stood in the middle with eight chairs around it.

"Take a seat, Marv," directed Starr. "Just remember to stand when the president comes in." His demeanor had changed; he was all business.

Styles glared at Starr and said, "No shit." He sat down and waited. Thirty seconds later a door on the far side of the room opened. The president of the United States, Robert Williams, entered. Immediately Styles stood. Starr had remained standing.

"Sit down, please, gentlemen; sit down," said the president. "Good to see you again, Richard." He leaned over and shook Starr's hand.

"Always good to see you, Mr. President."

"Richard, in this room, for this meeting, call me Bill."

That caught Styles totally by surprise. He had no idea that Starr was that close to the president. He could tell there was a genuine friendship between the two men. Then President Williams leaned over and offered Styles his hand, saying, "President Bill Williams. I've been looking forward to meeting you, Sergeant Styles."

He shook President Williams's hand, saying, "Sergeant Marvin Styles, sir. It's an honor to meet you."

Everyone sat down.

The president looked at Styles and said, "I understand that you are getting out of the marines very shortly; is that right?"

"Yes, sir. I'm officially out tomorrow. It was kind of a rushed departure, you might say," he answered.

Then the president looked at Starr. "Richard, how much have you told Sergeant Styles?"

"I've pretty much laid it all out on the table, sir."

The president looked back at Styles and was quiet for a few moments. Then he got up and started pacing. "Sergeant, I'm going to give you the short version here. First and foremost, I know I have your word that nothing that is said goes outside this room, ever—and I mean ever. Understand?"

"Goes without question, sir," he replied strongly.

"Good. Let me get to the point. If you have two boxers in the ring and one has his hands tied behind his back, he's at a rather large disadvantage, wouldn't you agree?"

"Yes, sir, no doubt."

"Well, I'm going to untie the hands that are behind Uncle Sam's back. I'm going to tell you something that fewer than fifteen people in the world know about. Two nights ago, a detonator on a dirty bomb failed to function. That is the only reason that Madison Square Garden and a large portion of New York are still here. The bomb was smuggled in, or perhaps assembled there, and was found only by sheer accident. A maintenance worker at the complex, checking a problem in the cooling system for the ice, discovered it. A playoff game between the Capitals and Rangers was being played. The bomb was timed to go off at the puck drop. For reasons I don't know yet, the detonator failed. Otherwise it would have exploded, and we wouldn't have known a damned thing until it was over. That terrifies me."

Styles and Starr remained silent.

"I'm going to drop the Marquis of Queensbury rules. I want someone who will get his hands dirty; someone who will do whatever needs to be done, without hesitation; someone who is willing to ensure that who I say has to go ends up gone. Do I make myself clear?"

"Yes, sir."

"Your former CO and I go way back. When I started getting this idea of mine, I asked him his opinion on whether it could make a difference and who I might be able to place in this position. He immediately recommended you. How do you feel about that?"

"Sir, Captain Starr is responsible for sending me into more shit holes than all of my other COs combined."

Styles heard Starr audibly groan. The president almost contained his grin—almost.

"Well, Sergeant, that's good to hear, I think."

"Yes, sir. That was meant as a compliment, sir."

Starr spoke up. "Don't try to be so damned flattering." That brought a grin from everybody and seemed to relax the tension in the room a bit.

"Obviously there are some ground rules. Under no circumstances are any innocents ever to become involved, accidentally or otherwise. Same goes for any law-enforcement agencies. You will have a free hand to do what you do. How you do it is up to you. I'm not going to be so smug as to actually believe I could ever hope to tell you how to do your job." He paused, then continued. "I have a world of information at my fingertips. I have access to intelligence agencies all over the world. I have no problem in admitting to you that the CIA, on several occasions, has taken out targets, almost always on foreign soil, though occasionally in our own country. That gets way too risky, and the CIA has many political enemies that would use that as an excuse, if they were to be caught, to really cause a stink. I've got enough problems without having to deal with a bunch of bleeding-heart liberals who are more interested in protecting the rights of these damned bastard maniacs than protecting our own citizens. Hell, I can think of half a dozen politicians that I wouldn't really mind if you shot. Of course you won't, but it damn sure wouldn't bother me.

"There will be times you will go abroad. You'll go anywhere you need to go. Richard will be your handler. He will get his orders and information from me or, in an emergency, my chief of staff. You and I will seldom meet. You understand so far?"

"Perfectly, sir. You point, I shoot."

The president looked over at Starr. "You were right, Richard, I like him." Then he looked back at Styles. "I want you to know that I've got your back. I'll do all in my power to protect you, but I also need your help. I need you not to get caught. Still with me on this?"

"Yes, sir," Styles answered firmly.

"Good. Now, when you get back to your hotel room you'll find a briefcase. Inside there will be assorted paperwork including a special federal firearms license that allows you to purchase any type of weapon you may want. It also allows you to carry any firearm anywhere in this country. No questions asked. It is signed by the director of ATF. There will be several different sets of matching IDs, driver's licenses, passports. Use them at your own discretion. Again, I will not suggest how you do your job. You will also find various forms regarding financial paperwork. Combined you will have, for a start, fifty million dollars at your disposal. I don't expect receipts, but I expect you to use the money wisely. Get yourself a place to live, vehicles, whatever you require. Keep Richard in the loop. You don't need permission, but I expect responsibility. Richard has sworn his life to me on you, and I could never ask more than that."

Another audible groan from Starr. "Did you have to say that, Bill? Shit, I'm never going to hear the end of it." He just sat there, shaking his head.

"Do you have anything to say, any questions?"

"Yes, sir, I do. I'm glad we finally elected a president with some balls. What are your directions if I end up butting heads with the FBI or some other agency?"

"Good question. Normally, I will send you on a mission after a designated target has been acquired. I'll feed the other agencies some bullshit reason for holding them back, to allow you to take care of business. However, if unforeseen circumstances should arrive, your top three priorities are as follows: first, take out the target; second, don't cross swords with any of our other agencies, at least not lethally; and third, don't get caught. Those three requirements are mandatory, as well as ensuring no innocents are involved, much less hurt or killed. I would also like it if a target sends a message. You'll have access to phosphorous grenades, which should burn any and all evidence should that be necessary. I understand that you are proficient at manufacturing your own ammunition."

Styles replied, "That is correct, sir. I have come up with some pretty interesting combinations. There's one other thing, sir. Since I have spent so much time over in the sandbox, I have learned to speak Arabic reasonably well—good enough to get me past a casual observation."

Starr spoke up for the first time. "I didn't know you'd learned the language."

Styles glanced over at Starr and just shrugged.

The president spoke up again. "That is excellent, Sergeant. I don't honestly know how long this little operation may last. Through my presidency, obviously; after that, it would depend on the incoming administration. One more thing: I may throw another element into the mix; however, I'm not at liberty to say just yet."

"Yes, sir," Styles responded.

"Sergeant, you're also going to have to trust me that if I give you an assignment, you will know it is for the good of our country. That is the only reason."

"I would think so, sir."

President Williams grinned and leaned over to shake Styles's hand again. "Don't let me down, marine; I'm depending on you."

"I won't, sir. You can depend on it. Besides, Captain Starr would never let me forget it."

"Damn straight, soldier. And don't even think you're gonna go out and buy some fancy Ferrari or something," Starr snapped.

"Kiss my ass, Starr, the president said I don't need permission."

The president paused on his way out and looked back. He grinned and said, "Yeah, you two are going to do just fine."

CHAPTER 14

AFTER THE PRESIDENT left, Starr and Styles made their way, via escort, back to the waiting limo. Styles started to say something, but Starr gave him the "we'll talk later" look, so he kept quiet. Back in front of the hotel, they got out and the limo took off. They were standing out front, and Starr suggested they go up to Styles's room.

Per the routine, Starr took the elevator, while Styles took the stairs. Again Styles beat him. He was standing by the door he'd already unlocked, and Starr followed him in. Sure enough, sitting there on the bed was a large briefcase. They ignored it, went over to the table, and sat down.

"Sent me to more shit holes; *that* was nice," grumbled Starr.

"Credit given where credit is due," Styles quipped back.

"Yeah, okay."

"So what do you think?" Styles asked.

"Well, although the president didn't talk about it specifically, I guess I'm kind of a silent partner in all of this. I'll give you intel, backup when needed, and pretty much anything else you need me for. There is no captain, and no sergeant, in this new deal. We're a unit—equals. You

52

have final say on anything operational, no questions asked. I'm more of the nuts-and-bolts guy. I've got an idea. Why don't you go visit your father for a week. I'll give you a call and tell you where to meet up. I'm gonna scout for a place for you to live. I'm thinking country with some land. That way you can set up a training field along with firing ranges. I know how you have to shoot and run. Hell, maybe I'll get a four-wheeler and tag along. It's important to get a place big enough that you can shoot without drawing a lot of attention. Redneck country would be best. Also, maybe a place with four seasons so you don't get used to one climate. You've been in the sand too long already, and we have no way of knowing where you'll be going. Probably be a good idea to pick up a normal truck of some kind. Or a car. Whatever you want. Start composing a wish list of armory components. If something comes up quick, we don't want to have scramble for something. If you think you might ever need it, get it. Better do some shopping, pick up clothing for year-round use. That means a couple of suits, too, and don't give me any shit about that. I'm sure there'll be a time or two you'll need them. This isn't going to be military; this is civilian, and you gotta be able to blend in. Other than that, I can't think of anything at the moment. Got it?"

"Yeah."

Starr got up, went over to the bed, and came back with the briefcase. He opened it and handed Styles a cell phone. "There are four others in there that are burn phones, but this is your main one. Numbers you'll need are already programmed in. I'm first on the speed dial. At some point you'll get a satellite phone, but we don't need that yet. Spend the rest of the day, and tonight, going through everything in the case. Your father still in Florida?"

"Yeah, still in Sarasota. I hate Sarasota—nothing but gated communities and pink flamingos."

"Well, go down and take him fishing or something. Maybe he can teach you how to tie a necktie."

Styles winced.

"Okay Marv, I'm gonna take off. I got a lot of shit to do. Normally I'd hook up with you for dinner, but not tonight. I'll probably be out of DC within a couple of hours. So you're on your own. And if you go running tonight, try not to hurt anybody."

Styles just looked at him and shrugged. Wasn't anything to say.

Starr stood up. "All right, I'm gone. Glad you're on board with this. Isn't anybody else I would trust." He started toward the door.

"Starr, how do you think that shit with the garden went down? That bother you as much as it does me?"

"Sure does, sonny. Shit like that is why we're gonna do what we're gonna do. Don't kid yourself here, Marvin; you're gonna get your hands bloody. I know Bill Williams, and he's a Texan through and through. And he's gonna *want* you to send a message."

Styles barely nodded at Starr, and then he was gone.

Styles pulled the briefcase closer. He liked that everything was so separated and organized. Still, it was going to take a while. He got to it.

When it was nearing eight in the evening, Styles found himself getting hungry. Normally he'd go out for dinner, but he knew Starr would expect him to familiarize himself with everything contained in the briefcase, and it was taking him a hell of a lot longer than he'd thought. So he ordered room service. He figured he was still on the government's dime, so he ordered a filet mignon, baked potato, asparagus, and a small salad. He also asked for a pot of coffee. Then it was back to the paperwork. Styles had turned on the TV at low volume, just for background noise.

Half an hour later his dinner arrived. He was eating at the table, watching the tube, when a commercial came on that actually caught his eye. An advertisement for a new model of Jeep. A Wrangler, Black Ops edition. He hadn't given a single thought to acquiring a vehicle, but this stood out immediately. He turned the sound up a bit, grabbed a pen, and wrote down the local dealership's phone number. He liked the looks of it. He thought about checking one out the following morning. Then he turned his attention back to the dwindling pile of paperwork.

His new cell phone rang, and he picked it up. "Starr" came up on the face, and he answered. "Yeah."

"How you coming with your homework, soldier?"

"Pretty much through it," Styles answered. "Think I found a Jeep to go look at. I was eating, saw a commercial, and liked it. Gonna check one out tomorrow."

"Sounds reasonable," Starr replied. "Have you called your father yet?"

"No, thought I'd just surprise him."

"He know you're out yet?"

"Nope."

"You gotta report anywhere, or anything?"

"Nope, all done. They wanted me out *now*."

"Their loss."

This was about the closest thing to a compliment Starr had ever given him. "Is what it is."

No response. Then Starr continued. "Think I found a property that might work out. I'm flying out in an hour to Nashville; at the airport now. I'll call you and let you know what I find."

"Got it." He hung up.

Styles turned back to the pile of paperwork, hoping it was for the last time. There were four different sets of fake identifications. All photographs were different—various shirts, mustache, beard, longer hair, military cut—and he had no clue as to how they had made them. He didn't need to know. *Computers*, he thought.

Each set consisted of a driver's license, various credit and ATM cards, passports, federal firearms licenses, Social Security cards, and even library cards. He had no doubt that each would easily pass muster. Even the exclusive American Express black card. Finally, he felt comfortable that he'd had studied the material sufficiently, and he packed it back into the briefcase. He placed it in the closet, on the floor. He then retrieved all of the items he'd had stashed between the mattresses, and placed them in the closet as well.

He turned and looked out over the city. *Wonder if I'm going to be living in Tennessee?* he thought. He'd once driven through it on Interstate 40 but had never spent any time there.

It was still pretty early, around ten, so he called down to the service desk and requested a laptop computer. He had the thought to go online and check Tennessee out.

Four minutes later a knock on the door signaled its arrival. After tipping the bellboy five bucks, he opened it up on the table, and Googled Tennessee. Forty-five minutes later he knew much more than before. He'd had no idea there was a National Hockey League team based in Nashville. He had heard of Dollywood. Then he decided to Google the Jeep Wrangler, and he learned more about that vehicle. They were more expensive than he would have thought. Finally, having had enough of staring at a computer screen, he logged off and closed it up. He wasn't tired yet but really didn't want to go for a run either. Then he remembered the hotel had an indoor pool. It had been quite a while since he'd been swimming, so he thought he'd give that a try. He grabbed a towel, a pair of shorts, and a T-shirt, and headed back down the stairs. He found the pool area and went into the men's locker room to change. Leaving his street clothes (which he had changed back into after the meeting with the president) in a locker, he headed out to the pool.

"Sir … *Sir*," somebody was hollering. It took Styles a couple of seconds to realize the voice was directed at him

"What?" Styles asked, annoyed.

"I'm sorry, sir, but you're not properly dressed," someone dressed in a bellhop's uniform said to him.

"And just what the hell am I supposed to be wearing?" Styles asked, getting more irritated by the second. *Preppy little jackass.*

"You are wearing gym shorts, sir; that's not allowed."

"It's all I have. Besides, what's the difference between shorts and a bathing suit, for Christ's sake?"

"Well you can't use the pool unless you are properly attired," insisted the little man.

Now Styles was mad. "Well, you're not properly 'attired' either."

"What do you mean, sir? This is my hotel-supplied uniform."

He looked at him and snarled, "For swimming." Styles grabbed him by his collar and belt, and threw him in the pool. Then Styles stormed out.

CHAPTER 15

S TYLES WAS SITTING in the office of your typical showman car salesman. "I'll have to check with my manager, sir," seemed to be the only words that came out of his mouth. Styles had taken a taxi from the hotel, after breakfast, to the Jeep dealership he'd seen advertised on the TV. There were three Black Ops edition Jeep Wranglers out front, all of them equipped with a six-speed manual transmission, which was what he wanted. He certainly didn't let the salesman in on that information though. Styles had led him to believe he wanted an automatic. The salesman had already checked other dealerships in the area and found two with automatics, but they wouldn't part with them. Styles finally told the sales guy that he'd accept the six-speed manual if he discounted the price of the vehicle a bit. He was stalling, and they both knew it. The Black Ops edition Wranglers were nice, but they weren't cheap. The last thing Styles had told him was "Look, if you can't do this deal, fine. There's a black Hummer H3 with an automatic transmission that I looked at yesterday that will work for me. I'll be paying for it now, no financing bullshit. Just decide yes or no; I don't have all day." That was what sent him running to his manager. He saw his easy commission walking out the door.

Three minutes later the salesman returned. "I can meet you halfway, but that's the best I can do. There just isn't that much meat on the bone," he said as he walked back to his desk.

"Okay, thanks anyway." Styles got up to leave.

He was one step outside when he heard, *"Wait."* Inwardly, Styles smiled. He had him.

"I can do this, but it's coming straight out of my pocket," the salesman said with resignation.

Styles turned to face him. "Nobody is putting a gun to your head. Either yes or no."

"Yes," he replied sullenly.

Styles gave him one of his new ATM cards. The salesman instructed Styles to follow him over to his manager's office. The manager wasn't there. Styles wondered if he'd ever been. He swiped the card, and the Jeep was his.

He then called an insurance agent he knew through his father, and in ten minutes it was insured. Fifteen minutes later, after the dealership-provided temporary tag was affixed, he was driving his new Jeep. It rode much smoother than Jeeps he remembered but still had full off-road capabilities. Of the three available, only one had the cloth interior and that's the one he took. He hated leather interiors.

Next was a drive over to a mall, and Styles headed toward a Belk's department store. As quickly as he could, he bought more jeans, socks, underwear, T-shirts, four polo shirts, four dress shirts, four pairs of casual slacks, two hooded sweatshirts, two lightweight denim-style overshirts, a baseball cap, another pair of athletic shoes—or sneakers, as he would have called them—and two pairs of dress shoes. As an afterthought he also got another belt. With bags in hand, he made a hasty retreat to his Jeep. He hated shopping.

By now breakfast had worn off. He spotted a Steak 'n Shake, a semi-fast-food restaurant he used to love going to before he went overseas eight years earlier. He swung in and went inside, found a table, and sat down. He was wearing blue jeans and a white USMC T-shirt with one of his new long-sleeved blue denim overshirts. The waitress was right there and took his order: two double steakburgers and, of course, a chocolate milkshake. He hadn't even bothered to look at the menu. The food was up shortly, and it was as good as he'd remembered. The check was what he had not remembered. Hell, he could've eaten a steak for what it cost. After leaving a reasonable tip, he was quickly out the door and headed back to the hotel. He had packing to do and wanted to get started toward his father's place, in Sarasota, before it got dark. After signing for the hotel bill, he carried everything to the Jeep. Twenty-five minutes later he was on I-95 headed south, on his way to Florida, completely comfortable with the feeling of his .40-caliber Beretta, with three spare magazines, in his shoulder holster, hidden under his denim overshirt.

CHAPTER 16

AKBAR AL HAMID was out of his mind with fury. All the planning, all the time, all the danger—for nothing. The bomb had not detonated. He did not know why and didn't care. The only thing that mattered was that the bomb had not exploded. He would have been a hero. Sure there were others involved, some much more important than he. But it was he who had placed the bomb. It was he who had smuggled it in, right under the noses of the arrogant infidels. The glory should have enveloped him like an aura of light. Now there was nothing but failure. He was sure he would be blamed. It was not his fault, of course; he had not built the bomb. But there was no way to know just exactly what had gone wrong. There was no mention of the incident anywhere—not on the televised news, not in the papers, not anywhere. Others would simply blame him, accusing him of failing to find a proper hiding place. No one could've possibly known the detonator had failed. Had that fact been established, he would've been off the hook. That information, unfortunately for him, was not forthcoming; nor would it ever be.

He was hiding out in a rental house that he had lived in for two years. He had been a maintenance worker at Madison Square

Garden. He'd been in the States for over fifteen years, hating every minute of it.

He had received a text message with instructions on where to meet two Afghanis and a Saudi Arabian, who were his partners although he despised them—at least the Afghanis; the Saudi was okay. Akbar al Hamid was a surprisingly educated man. He considered himself far superior to the two Afghanis, and the equal of the Saudi. Those feelings were *not* returned.

He was to meet the men at a Thai restaurant in Fairfax, Virginia. They had used this spot before. It was located in a low-end strip mall frequented by many ethnic groups of people. No one would stand out there.

Akbar arrived early, something he always did. He found a table in the corner of the restaurant, ordered a cup of coffee, and told the waitress he was waiting for friends. She smiled at him and nodded accordingly.

Ten minutes later the door opened and three men walked inside. Both Afghanis were wearing dark sunglasses; they were rarely seen without them. They looked very angry. The Saudi looked concerned. A vast difference. Akbar was scared.

The Saudi greeted Akbar like an old friend. "Akbar, how are you? You are looking well," he said in perfect English.

"I am good, but greatly disappointed Saheeb, thank you."

The Afghanis did not speak.

The three men joined Akbar at the table. They all picked up menus and pretended to study them.

"Akbar, as you know, something failed."

"I am well aware of that."

"Do you have any idea what might have happened? Nothing has even been reported. It is like nothing was there. The Americans must have found it. Are you sure you hid it well?"

This was exactly what Akbar was afraid of—that the blame would be placed on him.

"I spent four days looking for the perfect place. I cannot believe that it could have possibly been found before the time. I placed it there only six hours before the start of that stupid game. I think that something failed within the device. To me, there can be no other explanation. No one even goes down where I put it. It had to have been a mechanical or electronic failure. It had to be."

"That is a possibility," admitted Saheeb, his voice not entirely convincing. "Yet the possibility also exists that it was merely found and disarmed. We have no way of knowing."

"Saheeb, you have known me for a long time. I have never failed you. This failure was not my fault."

The two Afghanis leaned close to each other and spoke very quietly. Their English was bad, and they rarely spoke aloud in public. They both looked directly at Akbar and scowled. Their displeasure could not have been more evident.

Akbar merely held his arms out, with his hands up, in a gesture of helplessness. The Afghanis were not convinced.

Luckily Saheeb was willing to give Akbar the benefit of the doubt. "Akbar, you have done what you have said. We cannot place blame on you without knowing. Be warned, though, that you will be watched closely, and should you fail again, you know the penalty. We will have another chance. Possibly within a month, maybe less. We will have to choose another target. Do not go back to New York. You cannot be questioned. I will be in contact." With that, the three men got up and left. One of the Afghanis paused to look daggers at him, then went through the door.

Akbar felt lucky he had not wet his pants. He knew how close to death he was. The waitress returned and asked about the other three men.

"They had unexpected business come up. I would like your number-eight combo please, with a large glass of water." As she left to place his order, he saw that his hands were trembling. He hoped the waitress hadn't noticed.

CHAPTER 17

STYLES WAS ENJOYING the drive south through Georgia on I-95 with music. He couldn't have known that halfway around the world, eight top terrorists, on everyone's most-wanted list, were screaming at once. Their perfect plan to blow up New York City had failed. It had cost them an unimaginable amount of money, but it was their pride that had taken the hit. They had bragged to others how they were going to make the 9/11 attacks appear weak. They were going to bring down half of New York City. Yet it was still standing. For two hours, screaming had ensued, with nothing resolved.

Finally, Sheikh Ami al Hadid, the acknowledged leader, had to fire a shot through the ceiling from a pistol he kept in his robes, to get everyone's attention. In retrospect, he realized that with everyone on edge, he was probably lucky it didn't start a firefight between all of them. Everyone was quiet and looked at him. His message was short. "We will have another chance; we shall succeed. We have the chance to obtain a Russian nuclear device, much stronger than the one that failed. We need to cooperate between ourselves to make this work, not scream accusations at each other. What is done is done. We move forward or we go home with our tails between our legs. What shall it be?"

The grumbling continued, but the maniacal screaming was gone. Finally one spoke. "It is as you say. Allah will see to our success. Praise Allah." Then everybody joined in, saying "Allah Akbar" (God is great). Slowly the eight men ventured out and went their separate ways.

Halfway around the world, Starr had made an appointment to look at property in middle Tennessee. It was a large renovated farmhouse with two barns on 280 acres of land. Approximately thirty acres were rolling hills and pasture, and the rest, woods. He had Googled the area and been able to download some pretty good pictures of the property. The two back sides were bordered by sheer bluffs. The front part of the property was where the buildings and open land were located. In between, virgin Tennessee woods. He was able to obtain the GPS coordinates of the property and had chartered an aircraft out of Nashville to fly over so he could see it from the air. He liked what he saw. Inexplicably, there was a newly paved road in the front. The nearest neighbors were over five miles away. He was even able to make out some natural trails through the woods, probably from deer over decades of use. Upon his return to Nashville, he was anxious to see the property, the appointment scheduled for ten the next morning. He decided to see it before he called Styles, who had jumped over to Interstate 4, headed west toward Tampa, where he would then turn south onto Interstate 75. That would take him straight into Sarasota.

Styles was hoping that his father would not be upset at his unannounced visit. He could be peculiar about such things. *Guess I'm gonna find out*, he thought. He then changed the CD and started listening to the Beatles' *Abbey Road*, his personal favorite piece of music. It had been a nice drive down, with good weather. Styles had stopped for a two-hour nap in South Carolina. He knew he really needed some exercise; sitting for so long over the last few days was making him a bit stir-crazy. He found it odd that in-country he could remain still for three days if necessary but sitting in a vehicle too long really got to him.

He was really hoping that the visit would be relaxing. His father had some strange quirks. Styles never did exactly understand what made him tick, he just accepted that sometimes his father seemed tuned to a different channel. Their relationship had always been respectable; however, Styles knew that in the later years, his father had resented him being gone so much. It's just where Styles's life road had taken him.

A signpost told him that Sarasota was forty-seven miles away. It wouldn't be long now.

CHAPTER 18

IVAN KOVESKY WAS all but licking his chops. His brother-in-law, a captain in what was left of Moscow's military, had actually succeeded. He had stolen a nuclear bomb. Petr Pevosky was in charge of the transportation of nuclear devices destined to be dismantled under the recently signed treaty with the United States. This treaty was designed to reduce both country's arsenals. He had been able to doctor the paper trail quite easily, thanks to how badly the Soviet record-keeping had degenerated.

Pevosky had texted Kovesky. The message was brief: "All is good." Kovesky was already dreaming of what he would do with his share of the money that was about to be made—$10 million. First, get the hell out of the Soviet Union and go someplace warm. He had made a deal to sell the bomb to an obscenely rich Saudi. He was perfectly aware of what the bomb would ultimately be used for, but he didn't care. He would not be anywhere in the world where there was conflict. He had seen too much in his life, and now wanted a peaceful, albeit privileged, lifestyle. Kovesky had spent most of his adult life in various criminal enterprises, but establishing contacts with the Arabs was finally going to be his big payday. It had been no problem bringing his brother-in-law on board. He went months at a time without getting paid. His take would be $5 million. They often talked together of the good life, which they were about to enjoy. Life would finally be looked forward to rather than endured. He picked up his cell phone and sent a text. Again, simple: "Your horse has arrived."

Nakhan Zazar felt the phone vibrating in the pocket of his robe. He quickly strode away from others and retrieved it. He read the message. *This should please Ami al Hadid*, he thought. He went to find him to tell him the news.

Finding al Hadid in his office, he smiled broadly. "I have very encouraging news. The acquisition is complete and will be on its way here shortly." He beamed with importance.

"Yes, yes, that is very good. Sit down, Nakhan." He gestured toward a chair. "Perhaps this will allow us to focus on our destined path. Recent events have taken a toll. Too many are too occupied with blame; we need to focus. This should help."

"A question if I may?" asked Nakhan Zazar.

"Certainly, my friend."

"Shall we tell the others?"

Ami al Hadid pondered that question. "I think not for the moment. We will inform them that progress has been made, but no more. I have no wish to increase any chance of more disagreement and blame. If something unfortunate should happen, it could splinter our group. We must not allow that to happen."

"That appears to be wise," Nakhan Zazar agreed, knowing full well he would have supported anything that might have been suggested.

"Convene the others for a meeting this evening. Inform them there is positive news."

CHAPTER 19

S TYLES PULLED UP to the security gates at the entrance to the golfing community where his father lived. This in itself was a mystery, since his father did not play golf. Whispering Pines was a typical gated Florida community, with tyrannical homeowner associations and equally dictatorial rules. You had to get permission to paint your bedroom, and even then, the color had to be approved. Styles, for the life of him, didn't know how anyone could possibly stand it. But then, he didn't live there; his father did. He had never remarried after the loss of Styles's mother, when Styles was only six—an event he had never recovered from. Neither had Styles. His father had gotten him involved in karate and other martial arts as both a distraction and a coping mechanism. Styles thought it worked. It helped him to positively channel his anger and frustration. He was convinced that he would otherwise have ended up in prison, or worse. He'd been shot, stabbed by shrapnel, but nothing ever hurt like the loss of his mother. His father became emotionally closed. Styles knew that his father loved him, and he certainly took good care of him, but his outward signs of affection became virtually nonexistent. Styles never blamed him for anything, because he knew his father was hurting worse.

Finally, the car ahead of Styles pulled away and he pulled up to the gate. A security guard in his early thirties came out to greet him, complete with clipboard. He was big, probably six foot four, maybe 250. A gym rat. Styles lowered his window. The guard quickly scanned the lower left section of his windshield—for a decal, he suspected.

"Who are you here to visit, sir?"

"My father, David Styles."

He looked over his clipboard. "I don't see any notes of your visit, sir."

Styles felt his temper waking. "You wouldn't. It's a surprise. I just got out of the Marine Corps yesterday, and he doesn't know I'm here."

"I'll have to call him to verify."

"I can make this easy. I have all my IDs handy; I'd still like to surprise him."

"Sorry, sir, but it's our policy. Our residents don't want surprises."

Now Styles's temper had stretched and was wide awake. *"Come here,"* he said to the guard, his voice changing from pleasant to hard.

"Yes, sir?"

"I've just spent the better part of fifteen years with sand blowing up my ass, chasing and killing terrorists. I just drove over a thousand damned miles to surprise my father. I don't give a fuck about your *policy.* I've offered to show you my ID, you have my plate number— although I do realize it's a temp—and I'll gladly have my father call you to let you know that it was perfectly okay to have let me in. But now I'm out of patience. If you don't shut the fuck up and let me in to see him, I'm going to get out of this Jeep, fold you in half, and shove your head up your own ass. *Get it?"* Styles had removed his sunglasses so the guard could clearly see his eyes. He wanted to leave no doubt as to just how serious he was. Styles could tell the weight rat wasn't used to someone talking down to him. He tried to stay in control of the situation.

"Sir, I don't like threats, and I'm paid to enforce our policy."

That was it. Styles was out of the Jeep in a flash. He walked up to within three feet of the security guard and stopped. "Listen, I'm trying real hard to keep my cool. What I'm asking is not unreasonable. I also see the Mace and the Taser on your belt. If either hand goes for either one, I'll shatter your knee before you touch it. So unless you want your ass handed to you hard, open the gate *now.*"

He stared at Styles hard for two full seconds, his hands perfectly still. Then he very slowly triggered a remote on his belt and the gate swung open.

"Smart move. Thank you. I'll be sure to have Dad call you," Styles snarled. He drove through the gate. He had been here nine years earlier, but it had changed. More security, more flowers. An odd combination. Two minutes later he was parked in the driveway. He got out and could faintly hear music coming from the backyard—classical music, his father's favorite. Styles walked around, and there stood his father, painting. Styles didn't know his father painted. Not the house or anything, but with an easel setup. He was painting flowers he had arranged atop an ornamental black stand. He had aged considerably. Styles was thirty-nine, his father sixty-six. His father had not seen him. Styles stood there for a few moments just watching him. A flood of memories came back. Finally his father sensed him and looked over.

"Hi, Dad."

CHAPTER 20

STARR HAD MET with the realtor at the appointed time, and he'd liked what he'd seen. As far as he was concerned, it was perfect. The farmhouse on the property had been restored, with attention directed toward the preservation of the house. Updates had been made, of course, but nothing that detracted from the flavor the home offered. Starr, of course, had already planned many upgrades, such as a state-of-the-art security system, for starters. The property was secluded. That was a strong point, in Starr's opinion. It would work out well, and importantly, he felt that Styles would approve. He'd received permission to walk the property, although he'd thought to bring a four-wheeler with him. He offloaded the off-road specialty vehicle and spent four hours scouting the property. The closest town was Clarkrange, with Interstate 40 about forty minutes away. He drove back to Cookeville, where the realtor's office was located.

He walked in. Twenty minutes later he walked out. He had made a cash offer, and it had been accepted. Starr had the keys, although it would take a few days for the paperwork to be completed. It would ultimately be impossible to determine who this property belonged to. From the parking lot he made several phone calls. Within fifteen minutes wheels were rolling that would result in all the changes and upgrades Starr wanted. With that settled, he called Styles.

Styles and his father had finished bringing Styles' gear into his father's spare bedroom when his cell phone vibrated. He wasn't big on ringtones. He saw that it was Starr.

"Yeah."

"We have a house. It's outside of Clarkrange, Tennessee. It's nice, and it has everything that we need. I've already begun making some mods I want. Here's the GPS info."

Styles wrote down the coordinates. "When do you want me up there?"

"Take your time. It'll take at least a week to get done what I want. Figure on being up here in a week or so. Just be sure to call first."

"Got a hot tub?"

"Of course." He hung up.

His father was standing in the doorway. "Anything important?"

"Not really," replied Styles. So far his father seemed genuinely glad to see him. Styles had already told his father of his discharge from the marines. He had seemed relieved at the news. "One of my old COs is involving me with a security firm he's starting. I don't need to meet up with him for a week. So guess you're stuck with me."

"Well, I'll try to make the best of it," his father replied, smiling widely.

Styles stowed his gear and looked at his watch. He had time to work out. He went out to the kitchen and found his father. "Dad, I think I'm gonna work out for a while. Being cooped up in a car gets to me."

"Sure, son, we've got over three hours until dinner. Knock yourself out."

"There any kind of a gym here?"

"Yeah, out the drive, down two streets, take a left, and it's about two hundred feet down on the left. Can't miss it. Probably not your type, though. Remember, this is a golfing community, not Parris Island."

"I'll make do. Thanks."

"I'll call down to their service desk and tell them to expect you."

Then his father walked over to him and ran his finger over a scar on Styles' left cheek. "What's this?"

"Piece of shrapnel. Nothing serious. Got a couple more from that night."

"You know, son, you've never really talked about what you did over there."

He just looked at his father and said, "I fought."

His father smiled at him and patted his arm. "Have a good workout, and try not to kill anyone." Styles wasn't sure if he was joking or not.

Styles changed into some khaki gym shorts he'd bought and, of course, a USMC T-shirt. Low-cut socks and athletic shoes and he was good to go. "Be back in a few hours, Dad," Styles said.

"Okay."

He made sure he had his driver's license and military ID with him, stuffed in his sock. He also stashed a twenty-dollar bill, although he didn't anticipate needing any money.

He jogged easily over to the gym.

"Mr. Styles?" the receptionist asked as he walked through the entry door.

"Yes."

"You father called. Help yourself. If you have any questions, we have two trainers available to help you."

"Thank you, I won't need them." She gave him a certified plastic smile, and he went into the gym, if you could call it that.

He stopped, looked around, and laughed. He didn't even really recognize what he was looking at. It looked more like a virtual reality workout station. He double checked the time and decided he would have to make do with an abbreviated workout. One of the trainers approached him. He gave Styles a once-over.

"You're not our typical guest."

"Probably not."

"Any questions or need any help?"

"Nope."

"Didn't think so." He walked away.

Styles went over to a corner and did some quick stretches, then stretched out and snapped off a thousand push-ups. He caught the two trainers talking out of the corner of his eye. *Guess they don't know what a push-up is.* When he was finished he walked over to them. "Okay if I use one of your machines a little differently? I won't hurt them."

They looked at each other, and then back at him. "Sure," one of them said.

He walked away and went over to a machine that he had absolutely no clue how to use. Didn't matter. He pulled some cables out of the way, which enabled him to hang upside down on a bar and curl his feet around two supports. He was in business.

He then proceeded to do two hundred inverted sit-ups, arcing up, touching his chest with his knees, pausing a moment, then lowering himself straight down. When finished, he did two hundred pull-ups with first his right hand, then his left. After that it was time to get back to his father's house, shower, and get ready for dinner. He put the cables back as he'd found them and started to leave.

One of the trainers approached him. "Excuse me, I've been a trainer for fifteen years and I've *never* seen anything like that. Not even close. How do you do it?"

"Repetition." Then he was out the door.

CHAPTER 21

A FISHING TRAWLER SLOWLY made its way into Chaleur Bay from the Gulf of St. Lawrence, located in New Brunswick, directly north of Maine. It was flying the Canadian flag. Seventy-two hours earlier it had rendezvoused with a similar boat flying a Russian flag. A large crate had been clumsily transferred from the Russian trawler to its Canadian counterpart. If the seas had been any rougher, the transfer might not have been possible. No one aboard either boat, including the captains, knew what was inside the crate. They were being paid to transport only. The payment was sufficient to keep curious noses in place. The presence of two extremely cruel-looking men that accompanied the crate also deterred anyone from thinking about snooping. This Canadian trawler, named *Sea Spirit*, was a familiar sight in these waters, where it had been plying its trade for over twenty years. No one paid any particular attention as it plowed toward its home port of Bonaventure; it just received the usual waves from the crews of other boats. The two unusual men kept a low profile during this final leg of the voyage. They did not want to stand out, which in this part of the world, they certainly would have.

The *Sea Spirit* arrived earlier than anticipated. They had planned on coming back under the cover of darkness, but sundown was still an hour away. The captain thought it might look suspicious to just wait out the small amount of time; any fishing vessel returning would be expected to do just that—return.

Captain Jean Ricard grabbed his cell phone and sent a text. It read, "Arrival in ninety minutes." Three minutes later he got an answer: "Understood." Along with the mystery crate, the *Sea Spirit* also carried a load of fish. It would offload the fish first, with the crate securely hidden. Once the fish were removed, and the boat hosed down, the four regular crew members would go home, which left only Captain Ricard on board along with the two crate-sitters. They would anxiously be awaiting their bonuses, which they expected to receive the next day.

Unknown to anyone else on board the *Sea Spirit*, one of the two extra crew also texted a message. "Arrive in one hour. Instructions."

Three minutes later Dimetri Kozloff got his answer. "Kill everyone." He looked over at his brother, Antrolov, and ever so slightly nodded. Antrolov understood perfectly.

By nine that evening all the work was done. The crew was cheerfully drinking beer and smoking cigarettes, relaxing before heading out. Two were married and would be going home to their wives and children. The two bachelors would be headed to a local bar where they were well known. Captain Ricard was speaking to his crew when they were surprised by the emergence of the two Russians. During their time on the boat they had kept strictly to themselves. The crew became quiet. One of the Russians, Dimetri, walked among them and handed them all heavily wrapped packages, smiling at each of them, then stepped back to stand alongside his brother. The men were all busy opening their parcels, expecting money. None noticed the two Russians had drawn pistols equipped with silencers. They had purposely chosen American-made Smith & Wesson nine-millimeter weapons. They did not want a ballistics team to trace the bullets that would be recovered from the bodies back to a Russian gun. Besides the silencers, they were also loaded with subsonic rounds. The only noise came from the cycling actions of the guns as one bullet was discharged and another one loaded. Just fifty feet away, nothing could be heard. Three of the five crewmembers were shot while they were still unwrapping their packages. The last two had only enough time to look up to see themselves being shot at. When all five bodies lay on the deck of the trawler, a final round was administered to the head of each crewmember and the captain.

In under a minute the two Russian brothers were joined by two Middle Eastern men. The mystery cargo was offloaded from the boat to the dock, then carried up to a waiting van. In less than three minutes, all that remained was the silent boat.

CHAPTER 22

S HEIKH AMI AL Hadid entered the room that previously held a screaming match. Today it could not have been more different. He surveyed the scene before him, enjoying the anticipation. Nakhan Zazar looked particularly pleased. He was the one who had delivered the good news that Ami al Hadid had been so anxiously awaiting. "Allah is being kind and rewarding us for our patience. The latest device has arrived safely in Canada and will be transported soon to its final destination. I have requested this be a slow and careful journey. We desire no more problems. Once the destination has been achieved, I shall inform you. Allah Akbar." Sheikh Ami al Hadid allowed himself to enjoy the looks of confidence that were beaming in his direction. Then, as regally as he could, he turned and left. He could barely contain his own excitement, at the thought of the suffering the Americans would soon be forced to endure.

∞

The week that Styles had spent with his father had passed quickly. They had rented a boat and gone fishing twice in the Gulf of Mexico. More than anything, though, they had talked. Undoubtedly, these were the most meaningful conversations they had ever enjoyed. Styles lightly broached the subject of his missions while overseas, without getting into specifics. Styles's father informed his son of a lady he had met and was becoming involved with. She, as it turned out, was the source of his newly acquired interest in painting. This brought a solid laugh from Styles. They had finally formed a solid relationship. The father had questioned his son about his new business enterprise, and Styles had managed to satisfy his father's curiosity without revealing anything meaningful. Styles met his father's girlfriend and had immediately liked her. He found her to be witty, with one of those personalities that one just couldn't help but find enjoyable to be around. She was obviously very good for his father, and he told him so.

On the sixth day of his visit, Styles' cell phone rang. He had finally found a simple ringtone that didn't annoy him. As expected, it was Starr.

"So, Marv, how's the visit going?"

"Really good, Starr, really good. I think it's been the best time that we've ever really spent together. It's like we became friends."

"That's good to hear. If you're ready, why don't you head up. I'll text you the address. If you get lost, just keep on going. You been working on your wish list for your little armory?"

"Yeah. Some of the stuff we may never need, but if we do, nothing else would work."

Starr replied, "Good. When you get up here we'll go over it and start acquisition. Anything that we can't get ourselves, the Man will get for us."

"So what's this place you got me?"

"Big spread. It's located in what is called the Cumberland Plateau. Just under three hundred acres, restored and updated farmhouse, two barns. Two sides of the property are sheer bluffs. More than enough privacy. I've already had work done. I think you'll like it. Got, or gonna have, everything you might want."

"Sounds good, Starr."

"When you gonna head up?"

"I'll head out early tomorrow. That'll put me up there late afternoon.

"Okay, I'll see you then." He hung up.

Styles went to find his father.

Chief of Staff Andrew Ladd knocked on the door of the Oval Office and walked through. President Williams looked up. Ladd rushed over and sat down. It had been agreed between them that the subject of the president's latest plan would never be discussed in the Oval Office. They had employed a sign that would signal a meet, where there was no chance they would be overheard, by accident or otherwise. Ladd handed the president an envelope with his fingers extended in a V.

"Let's walk, Andy."

They walked out into the lawn of the White House and sat on a bench surrounded by shrubbery that had steel walls concealed within.

"Sir, we've had a hit on one of the moving patrols housing a radioactive isotope identification device. It was picked up forty miles south of Bangor, Maine, on Interstate 95. It's being tracked by both ground and air units."

President Williams could hardly conceal his emotions. He was hugely relieved that this plan had worked, but terrified of what it might mean. "How long ago was it picked up?"

"Approximately forty-five minutes ago. A naval aircraft was scrambled from Brunswick Naval Air Station. We've got ten different vehicles on the ground tracking it visually. It was suggested that a GPS tracking unit be placed on it, but I nixed that because I don't want the chance of their having an identifier aboard. The absolute last thing we want is for them to know we're on to them."

"Good thinking, Andy. Are we sure it's a bomb, or the material to make a bomb?"

"These devices are calibrated to pick up a certain level of radiation. It's ninety-five percent certain it's some sort of nuclear device, or material for one," Ladd answered.

"Andy, I want an update on its position every half hour. Under no circumstances lose that vehicle."

"It's in a plain-Jane white Ford cargo van. Just one of tens of thousands out there."

"Keep me posted."

The two walked back to the White House in silence, deep in their own thoughts.

CHAPTER 23

INSIDE A NONDESCRIPT 2004 white Ford cargo van, two men who could have easily passed for natural-born Americans were driving south on Interstate 95. Both could have been mistaken for New Yorkers of Italian descent. Their accents were perfect. And they should have been; they had practiced for nearly ten years.

They had crossed the Canadian border into Maine just north of Van Buren. "Tony" and "Joey" had driven down from Bonaventure, New Brunswick, by skirting around Chaleur Bay and Tracadish Bay via Route 132. At Matapedia they had gone south on Route 17, to within twenty miles of the border. At that point, they had turned off onto a logging road that wound around and joined others. It took them almost sixty miles on land to travel what would have been twenty miles as the crow flies. It was very slow going; they sometimes traveled only five miles per hour. The roads were muddy, and the driver, Tony, was glad that the van had heavy-tread "mudder" tires mounted on the rear. Otherwise they surely would have gotten stuck several times. In the rear of the van was a pair of street tires mounted on rims; they would swap these over once they were safely across the border and back on solid pavement.

They would then simply dispose of the mud tires after wiping them clean for any fingerprints. "Tony" (real name Johazza Tahaah) was an Iranian who had taken up residence in New York fifteen years earlier. His best friend "Joey" (actually Cyrus Jafarri) was an Afghani. They were two sleepers who had volunteered for this mission when they were teenagers. Brainwashed by the Taliban, they would eagerly sacrifice anything in the name of the Islamic Jihad.

They had a very long journey staring at them. They did not know what was in the big box in the rear of their van; they only knew it was more important than their own lives. Their destination was nearly 1,500 miles away—Indianapolis, Indiana. The van in which they were traveling was completely legal, registered to an antique business operating out of New York. The paperwork on the crate identified the contents as Civil War artifacts. They were being shipped out to a well-known collector. As long it was not opened up and emptied, it would hold up under the closest scrutiny. Even then the crate had been packed with Civil War objects around the real package, though Tony and Joey had no way of knowing that. Their mission was clear: get the crate to Indianapolis without being pulled over for any reason. They were both very clean-cut and well dressed. The two were armed with a Valentine One radar detector just to warn them of speed traps, though they had no intention of speeding. On the interstate they were just one of a seemingly endless line of vehicles. The windows had purposely not been tinted dark. No suspicions were to be aroused. Anyone looking at them would see only a couple of guys droning along on a delivery.

CHAPTER 24

STYLES BADE HIS father good-bye, promising to stay in close touch. The visit had been remarkably refreshing for both. They had parted feeling closer than at any other time of their lives.

He had crossed over the Tennessee border on Interstate 75, then looped over to pick up State Highway 127 north, bringing him within ten miles of his new home. He was more curious than excited about just what he would find. Knowing Starr like he did, he was certain that the new digs would be sufficient.

He'd finished up his armory wish list the previous evening. He laughed out loud imagining what Starr would think when he read it. As he would tell Starr, "Better to have it and not need it, than need it and not have it." It was definitely a who's who of any armory. Styles's cell phone rang, and "Starr" showed on the screen.

"Yeah," Styles answered.

"Whereabouts are you?"

"Hour and a half, give or take."

"If you're hungry, don't bother to stop. I've got us stocked up here pretty good."

"Okay."

"We'll have a few army construction guys around for a day, maybe two, finishing up some changes I had done."

"No problem," Styles replied.

"See you in a bit." Starr hung up.

One hour and thirty-two minutes later, private citizen Marvin Styles turned onto Bluff Ridge Road. He was surprised that the road was in good condition. He followed that back almost seven miles and came upon a freshly paved drive on his right. Turning in, he slowed way down to look the entrance over. He wound his way back almost half a mile before he popped out of thick woods and into a large clearing housing three buildings. There were three large flatbed trucks parked in front of one of the barns, with at least ten uniformed construction workers running around like mad. He spotted Starr among them, giving instructions. He approached the front of the house, parked his Jeep, got out, and stretched. Starr started walking toward him.

They shook hands, and Starr asked, "So, how does it feel to be a civilian?"

"I don't know; haven't given it a lot of thought," Styles replied.

Starr merely nodded at him. "Well, let's get your gear into the house, and I'll start giving you the high-dollar tour," he said with a grin. "You want to eat something first?"

"Nah, I'm good."

"All right, well let's get you squared away." The two men walked to the rear of the Jeep and began to unload it.

"Hey, this is nice, Marv. Don't think I've seen a Jeep rigged like this."

"New model, called Black Ops Edition. I like it 'cause it ain't fancy."

"How's it drive?"

"Nice. Imagine anything drives nicer than what I'm used to."

"Yeah, probably right about that," Starr agreed.

The two men walked through the front door, and Styles was surprised at what he saw. Past the doorway he was standing in was a large country family room with a sizeable stone fireplace on the far wall. It was an open floor plan, and he could see a dining area beyond.

"First floor has this family room, the dining room, big country kitchen, pantry, bathroom, study, and a security room, where all the goodies are, including twelve monitors. Four bedrooms upstairs, two bathrooms, and a very secure room we can use as a second armory. There are decks on both floors and lots of attic space. We got two barns out there—one for an armory and a gym, and the other for vehicles and toys."

"Lot nicer than I thought it'd be, Starr. Nice job."

"Wait till we get on the four-wheelers and take a jaunt around the area. You've got plenty of trails to run. I've set up three different ranges, including one for fifteen hundred yards. We'll have state-of-the-art communications, computers—even have access to spy satellites."

"You're kidding," Styles exclaimed.

"Nope. The big man wants us to succeed, and to do that we've got to have tools."

"I'm impressed."

Starr continued. "We've got state-of-the-art security here. If it's made, we've got it. Motion detectors, infrared, laser, you name it. Nothing bigger than a small dog can get on this property without us knowing about it.

Styles couldn't help himself. "That mean you're moving in?"

Starr just looked at him and deadpanned, "Yeah, and I don't know how much your rent is yet." After a second, both men laughed.

"Well let's take a ride," suggested Starr.

"Following you."

For the next three hours, the two men scoured the property, with Styles stopping several times to survey the area. When they got back to the barn and had parked the four-wheelers, Styles walked over to Starr.

"Starr, you outdid yourself with this. Far as I can see, it's perfect. This should work out real well." Styles could see Starr was pleased.

"You hungry yet?"

"Yeah."

"Well come on in, and I'll cook dinner. Tomorrow is gonna be a big day."

"What's on for tomorrow? Styles asked.

"Your first flight lesson," Starr answered with a chuckle.

CHAPTER 25

P RESIDENT WILLIAMS, ALONG with his chief of staff, Andrew Ladd, came striding into the Situation Room. Standing as one when they entered were the director of the FBI, Matt Sanderson; the director of the CIA, Bernard Backersley; Elliott Ragar, the director of the NSA; Charles Rockford, director of Homeland Security; and John Clayton, the joint chief.

"Have a seat," said the president. "Right now we are tracking and have visual contact on a cargo van that we believe contains some type of nuclear device or the material to make such. The van crossed into the United States from Canada. We have aircraft and ground support involved. It is apparently headed away from the Eastern Seaboard. We do not know its destination. The question we must answer is, do we pick it up now, or track it through and try to dismantle more, if not all, of this current operation? My personal feeling is that it is part of the group that tried to take out New York. Of course, I could be wrong, but I think that two different factions acting this boldly at the same time is improbable. I need your input."

Backersley of the CIA spoke first. "Mr. President, I agree with your opinion that it is more than likely that the same group is responsible. For that reason, as long as we can be reasonably assured that the damned thing won't go off—which is unlikely while it is in transit —I believe we should, within established safety standards, follow and apprehend. We stop it now, we get the bomb and the driver or drivers. We follow it, and we possibly get the cell, and maybe the ability to trace its origin."

Several heads nodded in agreement.

Charles Rockford, of Homeland Security, was the next to speak. "Sir, I have to question whether it's prudent to allow an acknowledged nuclear device to remain in a terrorist's hands one second longer if we now have the capability to capture it."

"It's a valid question, Charles," replied the president.

Elliott Ragar, of the NSA, spoke next. "Sir, if we take down this device now, we take down the one device. I'd bet that this driver isn't going to be able to provide us with adequate information to track its origin. I feel it's just as important to acquire the intel to determine whether there are more coming after this one. We take it down now, we risk losing that chance and continue to invite risk. As long as we are confident we can keep this one under surveillance, I believe it's imperative to do everything possible to determine the origin and the group behind this attack."

Again heads nodded in agreement.

Then Matt Sanderson, of the FBI, spoke. "I agree with Elliott. I think the risk factor of not taking it down immediately is relatively low. Certainly within acceptable limits. I think it's vital to learn as much as possible about this new group. This is certainly the boldest move since 9/11, and we must make every attempt to squash it. If we don't, the way these fanatics think, if this attempt is at all successful, we may have a rush of zealots trying to get in with bombs. I think it's absolutely critical that we get to the bottom of this, then destroy it."

There was a light murmur in the room. After a few seconds the president spoke. "Gentlemen, it appears that we have a consensus. I think it would be foolish, if not irresponsible, if we did not make every attempt to stop this entire operation. That's what we're supposed to do, so that's what we *going* to do. This absolutely cannot become public knowledge. I want you to use only your most trusted resources on this. If this goes public, we're not only going to have mass panic, but we'll also completely blow any chance of getting these bastards. And gentlemen, *I want* these bastards. If we can track them back to any certain mainstream group or country, there will be extremely serious consequences. I vowed to make this country safe, and that's what I'm going to do. Quite frankly, I don't care who I piss off to accomplish that. Now get to work, but do it quietly. I want updates from all of you every three hours, or less. Immediately as any knowledge becomes available. Gentlemen, it's time to do our jobs." With that, President Williams and his chief of staff got up and left.

Walking back to the Oval Office, the president and his chief of staff were speaking in hushed tones. "Andy, keep an active eye on everyone. Don't crowd them, but be aware. Let them do their jobs, but keep me informed every step of the way. I've got calls to make."

"That's fine, sir. I have some other business to attend to as well. I'll catch up with you within the hour. Sooner if necessary." With that the two went their separate ways. The president went back into the Oval Office, picked up his secure line, and dialed a new number. On the third ring it was picked up.

"Starr here, sir."

"Richard, it's me. I've got something to fill you in on." He proceeded to bring Starr up to speed. Starr remained silent, just listening.

When the president was through, Starr said, "Jesus Christ. This is getting to be some serious shit. Uh, sorry, sir."

"That it is, Richard; that it is. I'm filling you in because as of right now we have too many open doors in front of us and I'm not sure which one I'm going to want to walk through. You and your operation are one of those doors. So I just want you to keep it in your forethought that you may have to act fast should you be needed."

"We'll be ready for whatever you require, sir. That you can count on. We are putting together all of our necessities as we speak. You give the call, we're good to go."

"That's what I wanted to hear. I'll keep you posted, Richard." He disconnected.

Styles looked at Starr and asked, "Was that the President"

"Yeah, seems we have another problem like the one we narrowly avoided in New York." He then proceeded to relay the information that the president had just laid out.

Styles listened intently. When Starr finished, he whistled softly. "This is some fucked-up shit, Starr. We gotta shut these clowns down hard."

"That is exactly what the president intends to do."

CHAPTER 26

T HE RUSE HAD apparently worked. The last thing the Kozloff
brothers, Demetri and Antrolov, had done before departing the
Sea Spirit, was to throw a brick of cocaine onto the deck of the fishing
trawler, making sure it broke wide open, spreading the powder all over
the deck.

For the next two days, the main topic of news around New
Brunswick was the slaying of the entire crew of the fishing boat *Sea
Spirit* in what appeared to be a drug deal gone bad. This had stunned
the entire immediate community. No one ever suspected these men of
being involved in this type of activity. They were all homegrown, and
although the downturn of the economy had adversely effected them
along with almost everyone else, it just seemed so hard to believe they
had turned to this answer. The funerals were held, families torn apart
forever. Life, never quite the same, went on.

Demetri and Antrolov were giddy—as giddy as Russians ever get.
They had pocketed the money that was supposed to be paid to the crew
for themselves. Between that and the amount they had already been
paid, they now possessed more money than they had ever dreamed of

having. Now the question that faced them was whether to go back to Russia or just disappear.

Demetri looked at his brother and asked, "So, Antrolov, what are we to do?"

"I think we say fuck going home and we go our own way. We have money—more money than we ever thought we'd have—and we know that crate is going to be very dangerous for everyone involved. I say we run like hell and enjoy what we have."

Demetri Kozloff was quiet for a minute. Finally he looked at his brother and agreed. "I think that you are right. The Americans will spend time looking for the Muslim fanatics when they discover what was in that crate. The Canadians think drugs killed those fisherman. No one should be looking for us. We go." With that, Demetri and Antrolov Kozloff walked away, never to be heard from again.

Akbar al Hamid had been given instructions to go to Indianapolis, where he was to meet up with Saheeb and the two Afghanis that scared him to death. He had never even been told their names. He had thought about running but realized he had nowhere to go and not nearly enough money to just disappear. Sick to his stomach, he had made the decision to comply with the directions he'd received. "If they wanted to kill me, they would have done so," he kept telling himself, over and over. So he was taking a bus cross-country to his destination. He would have felt even more ill if he had known that Saheeb and the two Afghanis were thirty thousand feet above him in a private jet.

CHAPTER 27

"*F*LIGHT LESSONS!" STYLES blurted out.

"Yep," Starr replied. "I've been taking them for about three months now, and the president and I thought it might be a good thing for you, too."

"*Flight lessons?*"

"Yeah, you know those things called airplanes? Well, flight lessons are how you learn to fly 'em."

"Why?"

"Christ, Marv, no wonder you never got past sergeant. Think about it. What're you gonna do? Go up to some commercial carrier, and ask whether or not you have to check your fifty-cal Barrett? We don't know from one hour to the next where we might have to go, and we damned sure can't fly commercial. So the president thinks that it'd be good for us to be able to fly ourselves. That way we can take whatever we want to, with no questions."

Styles was quiet for a moment. Then he looked at Starr and said, "Yeah, makes sense, I guess."

"Ya think?"

"What kind of plane?"

"Business jet."

"A jet?"

"Yeah. When we have to go, we'll have to move fast. No sense in fucking around in those little civilian Cessnas. So we ain't gonna waste time with those right now. I'm close to getting licensed, and we're gonna really work you to get you up to speed. If we have to move before we can fly ourselves, we'll get a military pilot. With what we got told today, I got a feelin' we'll be moving sometime soon."

Starr looked at Styles and changed subjects. "I got started on acquiring your armory list. It raised an eyebrow, but we're gonna get it all. Be a truck here day after tomorrow that should have just about everything you asked for. Hell, some of it made me wonder. But this is all your call."

"I know some of it we may never need, but if we did, it ain't something we can go to your local gun shop and get. At one point or another, I've had to use everything on the list, that's why I asked for it. You been keeping up on your shooting?"

Starr grinned and said, "Yeah, little bit. Could always be better."

This time it was Styles's turn. "So you mean now you can hit the water from the end of a dock?"

"Smart ass," Starr came back with.

"All right, so now we've established that maybe, with luck, you can hit something. Good. Now, how much longer are these guys going to be around here?"

"Two days max. Why?

"I want to start using the ranges, but I don't want to do that in front of them."

"Yeah, I figured as much. I know that you go through gunpowder withdrawal if you don't fire a weapon after a while," Starr quipped.

"I won't deny that."

"Well, they'll be done soon enough. I've got to run over to Cookeville to pick up some stuff we're gonna need. Want to go?"

"Nope, I'm gonna take a run around the property, burn off some of this restlessness I've got going on."

"Okay, Marv, you go run, I should be back in a few hours. Don't socialize with those army guys. They may start asking questions as to what this place is."

"I've pretty much ignored them."

"Good. All right, catch ya later." Starr turned and walked toward his dark blue Suburban.

Styles started walking back to the house to change into fatigues and combat boots. He actually had a hint of a smile on his face.

CHAPTER 28

SAHEEB AL KAZHED was using his laptop while aboard the private jet that was flying him and his two Afghani associates to Indianapolis. He had reserved two rooms at the Holiday Inn nearest the world-famous speedway. He had been in the company of the two Afghanis now for almost six weeks and didn't think he'd heard a hundred words spoken between the two of them. He knew they spoke little English and that they did not want to stand out. He also knew that by mere appearance, probably the only place they would not look out of the ordinary might be an underground fight club. They had made it clear from the very beginning that they did not want their names said aloud. He would merely nod at whichever one he might need to communicate with. He might as well have been working with mutes, which, given the circumstances, he didn't mind. He didn't have to waste time answering questions he did not want to answer. Their role was to oversee, and protect, Sheikh Ami al Hadid's interest. He thought it curious that Afghanis had been placed in the position rather than Saudis, but then again, that was none of his business. All had been made clear at a meeting with Ami al Hadid nine months earlier in Saudi Arabia. Saheeb al Kazhed was married to one of Ami al Hadid's daughters. While the marriage had been arranged, it had worked out well for Saheeb. He had access to wealth and power he'd never dreamed of. His own father was an influential businessman, which was the main reason he'd been considered as a marriage prospect. Saheeb often wondered what Ami al Hadid would think if he knew just how much of a sexual tigress his daughter was. Saheeb could barely keep up with her. The thought of her brought a grin to his face and a bulge to his pants. He'd not seen her in almost two months and found himself getting very horny. Yet again, he had to go to the men's room and relieve himself.

Returning from his business, he walked up to the Afghanis. "I've obtained two rooms for us at the local Holiday Inn near the Speedway. I've also rented us a car. It will be at the hotel. We will keep a very low profile until time. Understand?" He received little more than stares from two men. He just nodded at them and walked away, not knowing if they had any idea what he'd been talking about. He had learned to just say things and ignore the lack of reply. Saheeb himself spoke only English when in America. So far, there had been no problems. Saheeb knew the others understood English much better than they could speak it. They were not there for their language skills. Almost as an afterthought, he rented one more room at the Holiday Inn, using a different company credit card. This room would be used for whatever Saheeb deemed necessary. He wanted an extra meeting area that could not be tied to him. That task completed, he then sent an e-mail to Tony, one of the two drivers in the van. He directed him to call in on his cell immediately upon their arrival in Indianapolis. Saheeb had secured a storage facility on the outskirts of town, in a low-rent district. He had scouted the area previously, and had picked this particular one because of its low security. There was a video camera at the gate, but it was the only one he'd seen. He intended on installing his own surveillance camera to keep watch on the unit he'd leased. He'd paid cash for six months in advance, which the manager had eagerly accepted. He spoke broken English, as Spanish was obviously his primary language. When Saheeb had flashed the cash in front of him, he hadn't even bothered to ask him for ID. He had merely taken the money and let Saheeb fill out the paperwork. Saheeb laughed to himself at how easy it had been. He then called the captain, asking him how long before they would arrive in Indianapolis. He was told less than two hours. His choice of seating arrangements on the plane allowed him privacy when on his computer. With some time to kill, he did what he always did. He brought up some porn, specifically bondage, on the Internet.

CHAPTER 29

P ETR PEVOSKY, THE captain in the Russian Army who had stolen the nuclear device currently being driven toward Indianapolis, was meeting with his brother-in-law, Ivan Kovesky, who had brokered the sale of the bomb. They were seated in a back booth in a Russian tavern, enjoying finishing off a bottle of vodka. When it was empty, there would probably be another. The Russians, like the rest of their nation, enjoyed their vodka. Kovesky, talking in a low murmur, informed his brother-in-law that there was a request for a similar device. "They have offered even more money if delivery can be arranged in a short time span."

Captain Pevosky was quiet for a few moments, swirling the vodka in his glass. The bottle itself was sitting in a small keg of ice, but no ice ever touched either glass. Finally he spoke. "It is tempting, Ivan, very tempting. I have concern that maybe it is too soon. I can falsify paperwork, but not on a constant basis."

"Petr, if we sell one more, we have more than enough money to go anywhere in the world."

"Yes. That, however, will not stop those who may wish to find us, should it be discovered what we have done. Only one person was aware of our deal before, and I personally took care of him. He is reported as missing, but he will never be found. He will be thought of as nothing more than another deserter. We have much money now, probably enough should we decide to leave."

Ivan was quiet for a minute, then looked at Petr with a crooked smile. "I have an idea. What if we only pretend we sell a second device. We could demand half of the money in advance. When we receive that, we run. It will piss off those sand fleas, but they do not have the resources to be able to ever find us. You think the first device will never be missed. If that is so, your superiors will think of you only as a deserter. One of many thousands. They will not look for you."

Petr responded, "You might be right. In my position, though, it may create more than the usual suspicions. It would all depend on whether they could ever discover a bomb was missing."

Ivan pressed his brother-in-law. "Do you think they will find out?"

Once again, Petr Pevosky was quiet for a minute, looking hard into his half-full glass. Then he spoke. "No, I do not think so. On the original lading document, there was one bomb too many. Otherwise, I would have never thought about taking it. There was a mistake before me. If the mistake is ever caught, the attention should be above me." Then he smiled. "It would be a great satisfaction to fuck the sand fleas. They are butchers. How much more money do you think they would be willing to pay?" Ivan grinned again. "I think they would pay double. Only their egos are larger than their bank accounts."

Peter then acknowledged, "That would give us both double the money we now have. That would be a great amount." He was quiet again, looking at his glass for answers. Finally, he looked up and told his brother-in-law, "See if you can arrange it. Say half the money is needed in advance for payoffs. Then tell them that it will be at least three weeks, once we receive the deposit, before we can deliver the unit. Both of these conditions are nonnegotiable. Should they try, tell them to go to hell and walk away."

Ivan nodded. "I'm sure they will argue, but they will do it."

They raised their glasses and toasted each other. They were sure they would never have to endure another miserable Russian winter. They had no idea how right they were.

CHAPTER 30

T HE PRESIDENT HAD convened his small council to assess the newest terrorist threat. He stood and addressed them as a group. "Do we have any solid intel as to what might be the next target?"

For a moment the group was silent, then Elliott Ragar spoke up. "Mr. President, I don't have solid information on that yet, but I do have an educated guess."

"Go on," directed President Williams.

"Well, sir, given that the first bomb was intended to take out a playoff hockey game, I think that it's safe to say that they will look for another large gathering of people. Maybe even some type of national event. This latest device, we believe, is much stronger than the one found at MSG." He paused for a moment, then continued, looking around the room. "What is the largest event going on in this country during May?" he asked the group as a whole.

"Well, obviously Memorial Day," answered Matt Sanderson, the director of the FBI, displaying outright annoyance at what he thought was a stupid game that Ragar was playing.

"Correct, Elliott," he said, not letting Sanderson's sarcasm bother him in the least. "And what's the biggest Memorial Day celebration we have?" Ragar was stunned that no one said anything.

"Well, we don't really have a national celebration," answered Charles Rockford, the director of Homeland Security.

"No, but we have the Memorial Day classic, the Indy 500," answered the director of the CIA, Bernard Backersley.

"Bingo, which is exactly where that van appears to be heading. Now, of course, there is a chance that van will just keep on going, but I think it's going to Indianapolis."

"That's a damned good educated guess, Elliott," the president said to his director of the National Security Agency. "A damned good guess, and it makes perfect common sense. That would not only kill a great number of people, but it would also attack one of this country's great national events. I think you're on to something here. Let's go with this theory for the moment, at least until proven that it's wrong. Start putting together a response, and get the pieces in place should this hold true. Bernard, I'm sorry, but you're going to have to take a seat on the sidelines for the moment. As soon as we can track back anything beyond our borders, you'll be in charge of that aspect. Gentlemen, the clock is ticking; let's get our asses in gear." With that the president left the room.

Charles Rockford, who had never been a fan of Elliott Ragar, approached him. "Elliott, that was some good reasoning. I hate to admit it, but I never gave that a thought."

"Charles, this isn't some stupid competition about which director shines the brightest; it's about working together to stop this threat."

"You're absolutely right, Elliott, absolutely right." And for the first time in his life, Charles Rockford extended his hand to Elliott Ragar. Ragar took his hand and shook it warmly. He smiled and said, "Let's not disappoint the president."

"Let's not" was Rockford's reply.

The group got up en masse and left, each man's mind whirling with what he had to do to hold up his own end of this imperative investigation.

Curiously, no one seemed to take notice of the absence of the president's chief of staff, Andrew Ladd.

CHAPTER 31

THE PRESIDENT HAD been back in the Oval Office for barely ten minutes when his secretary, Alice, buzzed in. "Sir, Michael Shoshan is on the phone for you." Shoshan was the assistant director of Mossad, the Israeli intelligence agency. President Williams had met Shoshan on one previous occasion. He had barely learned the proper protocol with Israel.

"Shalom, my friend," the president greeted Michael Shoshan.

"Shalom, Mr. President. I have news for you. We have ascertained that a Saudi prince, Sheikh Ari al Hadid, has acquired one nuclear device, possibly two, from a Russian captain, one Petr Petrovosky. He is in charge of part of Russia's nuclear arsenal disarming program. This information is correct. We believe that at least one is already in your country. We also know that it was smuggled into Canada, and we believe it was taken from there into America. We have other suspicions, but they have not yet been confirmed."

"Michael, we already know about the devices being here. One was taken out; the other is being tracked as we speak. We wanted to track the origin, but this information you have offered me saves us a great deal of time. I cannot thank you enough. We suspected the Canadian connection, but you have confirmed that as well. Any other information you can relay to me would be greatly appreciated."

"We are side by side in this war against the radicals, Mr. President. Mossad is always willing to help where we can."

"I cannot thank you enough, Michael. Be sure to pass along my best to your father. I will keep you apprised as this situation unfolds."

"Thank you, Mr. President. Shalom."

"Shalom, my friend."

The president then buzzed his chief of staff. "Andrew, get in here if you can."

"Be right there, Mr. President."

Less than two minutes later, there was a knock on the door, and Andrew Ladd entered.

"Andrew, sit down. I just spoke with Michael Shoshan of Mossad, and he's given me some vital information." The president then conveyed to him what he had learned.

Andrew Ladd looked at the president and stated simply, "It's amazing what Mossad is able to acquire and accomplish."

"You're not kidding about that."

"So what are you going to do about this Russian captain?"

The president just smiled. "I think I have the solution."

"Yes, sir," Ladd replied. "If that's all for the moment, sir, I've got other issues I'm addressing at the moment."

"By all means. I just wanted you to know the latest."

"Thank you, sir." Ladd left the office.

President Williams then made a phone call.

Richard Starr had just parked at an electronics store in Cookeville, Tennessee, when his cell phone chirped. He saw it was the president.

"Yes, sir," Starr answered.

"Richard, I just spoke with Mossad, and they had this for us." The president then updated Starr about what he had learned from Michael Shoshan.

After the president had finished, Star responded with "So they're certain of this Russian captain, sir?"

"When Mossad says they're sure, they're sure."

"What are you going to do about it?"

"Start boning up on your knowledge of Russia." with that, he hung up.

Starr went inside and picked up what he'd ordered, which included a sixty-inch flatscreen LED television, complete with a Klipsch surround-sound system powered by a Yamaha amp, a top-of-the-line computer system complete with a printer/fax/copy/scan unit. Though both Styles and he already had laptops, he thought it'd be a good idea to have a home-based desk unit as well. He paid for the items with one of the provided credit cards, packed everything up in his Suburban, and headed for home. He had decided to call home "the Ranch."

An hour later he was back and unloading the 'Burb. Just as he was walking through the front door with the last package, Styles came running up. "Hey Starr, what you got there?"

"Everything already unloaded. Where were you, up in the trees watching?"

"Nah, got a natural ability for that shit."

"Wouldn't surprise me."

"So what'd you get?" Styles persisted.

"A flatscreen with a good surround-sound system, and a computer with a printer that does everything."

"You're gonna make somebody a fine wife someday," Styles quipped.

"Shut up or I'll put the flatscreen in my bedroom."

Styles grinned and quipped, "Might as well have some type of entertainment in there."

Ignoring the barb, Starr continued. "Got another call from the president. Mossad came up with some info. Guess we know where the shit came from. Russians. Some asshole prince in Saudi Arabia is behind it all. Williams told us to bone up on our Russian. I've got a feeling we'll be going somewhere soon."

Styles was quiet. Then he looked over at Starr and motioned for him to follow him over to the dining room table, where they both sat. "I was approached by them. Guess it was about five years ago, after I got hit by that shrapnel."

Starr looked at him with surprise and asked, "Who, by Mossad? I didn't know they brought outsiders in."

"They don't. Wanted me to contract for them. I'd been out of the hospital and was in Italy recovering. Figured that'd be a safe place for me. How they found me, I'll never know. Those boys are damned good. Anyway, I told them I was happy where I was, and they let it go. Told me who to call if I ever changed my mind."

"Who was it?"

"Can't say. Told 'em I wouldn't."

Starr didn't bother to press. He knew that if Styles told them he wouldn't say, he wouldn't say, and that was that.

Styles continued. "Listen, there's something I've been wanting to talk about. This flying thing. I don't think I want to do that. I got enough to keep in my head, don't need to try to learn flying jets. At least not right now. I don't see any reason you can't fly us around. You won't be going in-country with me; I don't operate that way. If something should happen, well, we'll deal with it then. Or the president can give us a pilot. I don't care which. I just don't want to take flying lessons right now."

Starr looked out the window for a bit, then back to Styles. "Yeah, I guess I can see that. Okay, you're off the hook for now. I'll keep going, and I can't really think of any reason to disagree. You do what you do. That's hard enough. I'll take care of it."

"Thanks. Thought you'd probably pitch a fit about that."

"No reason to; I can't argue against it. Besides, I've known you long enough that I know not to even try—wouldn't get me nowhere."

"You're right; it wouldn't."

CHAPTER 32

NAKHAN ZAZAR WENT to find Sheikh Ari al Hadid. He found him in his office with two of his family members. Immediately Ari al Hadid dismissed them and motioned Zazar inside.

"What news do you bring me, Zazar?"

"I have contacted our Russian friends. They will sell us another device, but it will be double in price. I argued, but to no avail. They will require half the funds in advance, to cover payment costs on their end. Again I argued, but it did no good. If we want the device, those are their terms. I told them I had to confer and would get back with them. I need direction, al Hadid."

Ari al Hadid was obviously not pleased. "Why do these Russian pigs insist on money advanced? Have we not kept our obligations?"

"That is what I asked. I was told that there were more people who had to be paid. I was told that there would be no more available for the foreseeable future. I was also told there were others who were interested, but because of our current successful relationship, he was offering us first chance. We have forty-eight hours to decide. Then the decision will be made, and it will not be in our favor."

"That is much money, Zazar. We shall play on our brothers' allegiance to the cause and tell them that the device will cost us three times as much. Then we shall allow them to make up the difference. They will howl and curse the Russian pigs, but they hate the Americans more, as do we. In the end, they will concede to pay the money. Only you and I will know the real amount. Agreed?"

Zazar said with triumph, "I believe that is a wise plan, al Hadid. They will never know."

"Call a meeting for the council, for tomorrow morning. We shall ask our brothers if they believe it to be a wise choice. Contact the Russian pig, and tell him we accept."

"I shall do it immediately."

Al Hadid interrupted. "Wait until tomorrow. We do not want to appear too anxious, or they may start thinking they can always raise the price on anything we may want in the future."

"That is wise, al Hadid. I shall do as you say."

Little did al Hadid know that Zazar had *already* accepted the terms. He also did not know that the Russians were giving him a kickback as a finder's fee. If al Hadid ever found out that piece of information, it would cost Zazar his head.

CHAPTER 33

T HE FOLLOWING MORNING, a nondescript box truck pulled up the long drive to the Ranch. A man dressed in military fatigues got out and knocked on the door. He noticed several workmen packing up and getting ready to leave. He looked around and could tell that a lot of work had just recently been completed. He knew better than to ask questions.

The door opened before he had a chance to knock again. "Yes?" the man standing inside asked.

"I'm looking for a Mr. Jordan?"

"That's me."

"I have a delivery for you. I guess you have the key; I don't. I'm supposed to wait somewhere while you unload the truck."

"Wait here." Starr turned around and was back in a flash. He tossed the driver the keys to his Suburban. "Take that 'Burb and be back in an hour and a half."

As the driver for the box truck left, Styles came walking up. "What's going on?"

"I think your arsenal has arrived. I'll drive the truck over to the side, and we'll offload it through the deck doors. No need for the boys over there to see any of this stuff." Starr walked out to the truck and moved it around to the side yard. Then he unlocked the rear slide-up door and stepped back in amazement. The truck was damn near full. "Well, if the fucking national guard ever runs out, they can always come here," Starr lamented.

It took over an hour and fifteen minutes to unload all the hardware. It was literally a wish list of the latest in military armory. If they made it, Styles had it. Ten minutes later the 'Burb was coming back up the drive. Five minutes after that, the box truck was going back out the drive. Fifteen minutes after that, the last of the workmen were leaving. Finally it was just Starr and Styles.

"Well, let's go see what they did," Starr said.

They walked over and went into the barn on the left. Styles was amazed. Per Starr's request, he had not even been near the area while the work was being performed. Now he was impressed. Inside was a simple gym that held everything he would want, an indoor shooting range, and a handball court.

"A handball court?" Styles asked.

"I like handball. You know, there's nothing wrong with me getting something out of this deal," Starr griped.

Styles just shook his head. "Jeez, you're getting crotchety."

"Well I'm learning from the best," Starr shot back, but with just a hint of a grin. "Come check this out." Starr walked down to the far wall and stopped. Styles followed. "Now pay attention, gun-hopper." Star reached over to the wall and pressed a switch hidden in the woodwork of the wall. A five-foot panel slid aside, revealing an elevator. "Going down?" Starr grinned.

They both got on, and the door closed. Three seconds later the door opened back up and they both stepped out. Styles's jaw dropped. To the left was an armory, just waiting to be stocked. To the right was a communications center that rivaled anything he'd ever seen. He didn't even know what most of it was. "Who's gonna teach us this shit?" he asked.

"Well, believe it or not, your old CO knows some of it. The rest—well, I guess we'll get us some kind of tutor."

Styles walked inside the communications half of the building and just looked. "Man, somebody outdid himself here."

Starr motioned for Styles to follow him over to a console that featured twelve video monitors. "This is our video security. There will also be twelve monitors in the house. All sides of the house are covered, the driveway entrance at the road, and all sides of the barn. Hell, we've even got the grounds covered out to about three hundred feet, give or take. Each monitor is hooked up to four cameras, giving us forty-eight shots at any given time. Over here"—he motioned to another bank of computers and light boards—"we have motion sensors and infrared detectors, like they use down along the Mexican border. Same light boards in the house. The entire perimeter of the property is now protected."

Styles just looked at Starr in disbelief. "Do we *really* need all this shit?"

"Probably not, but hell, if he's gonna offer it, I'm gonna take it. We gotta remember here, Marv, what we're doing is highly illegal, at least according to the Justice Department. We're fighting an enemy that refuses to wear a uniform designating him as a soldier, so the president has decided to throw away the rulebook. He has no intention of asking Congress for permission. When I brought that little detail up, specifically mentioning Senator Hoover from New York, the president's response was, and I'm quoting here, *"Fuck him."*

"Well, I guess if anybody can pull this shit off, we can," Styles offered. "He's sure given us the stuff to do it with."

"Yeah, now all we gotta do is show the president it was justified."

"I don't think that will be a problem, as long as he holds up his end. Listen, I got another question for you."

"Shoot."

"Is the vice president in on this?" Styles asked.

"No, I don't think so. Bill Williams hates Herbert Lamar. He thinks he's a spineless liberal that the Republican Party stuck him with. They felt that adding Lamar to the ticket would guarantee them taking California's electoral vote, something that was felt necessary to win the election. I know the president threw a fit over it but finally agreed, although he damn sure wasn't happy. JFK went through the same shit when he got stuck with Lyndon Johnson. Democrats weren't sure they could win with a Catholic. So Bill Williams is doing pretty much with Lamar as JFK did with Johnson. You notice that Lamar is out of the country most of the time. Well, JFK made Johnson a goodwill ambassador to keep him out of the way, and that's pretty much what's going on with Lamar."

"You think Lamar will get the nomination in eight years? And if so, and if he wins, and if we're still doing this, would 'this' keep going?"

"Marv, my gut feeling is that Lamar couldn't win the nomination. But that's only my opinion, and we all know what those are worth." Starr was quiet for a few moments. "If—and that's a big if—he did get the nomination, and won, I think he'd shut us down faster than shit going through a goose. He's such a fucking weenie, I don't know how he's a Republican. That's something we'll deal with, though, when the time comes. For now we serve the president."

"Yes we do, Starr, and the American people. Most of them just don't know it."

CHAPTER 34

ONY, AKA JOHAZZA Tahaah, and Joey, aka Cyrus Jafarri, had arrived in Indianapolis. Per their instructions, they pulled off and parked at a combination gas station and variety store. They were both hungry and were tired of eating sandwiches they had been making on the trip. Cyrus Jafarri, who spoke excellent English, went inside and ordered two pizzas to go, while Johazza Tahaah picked up a burn phone and prepared to call Saheeb al Kazhed. Abruptly he closed the phone and decided to wait until after they'd eaten. *Half an hour won't make any difference*, he thought. Fifteen minutes later Cyrus came out with the pizzas and two bottles of Gatorade. *The one thing the Americans can be proud of*, he thought. Cyrus loved the stuff.

Climbing back into the van, Cyrus asked Johazza, "Did you call Saheeb?"

"No, I thought we would eat first. He can wait a few more minutes. I'd like to eat one meal without driving."

"Good idea, Johazza, Saheeb is always in such a rush."

For the first time since they'd left Maine, the two men were able to eat in peace and quiet, in a vehicle that was not moving. It was relaxing for them. When they finished, Cyrus took the pizza boxes and dumped them into a trash can, while Johazza called Saheeb, who picked up on the third ring. "Saheeb, it is Johazza. We have arrived."

"Excellent, Johazza, excellent. Where are you?"

"We are at a Shell gas station at mile marker 117 on Interstate 65."

Saheeb thought for a few seconds, and then said, "Stay there. I will come, and you will follow me to where we shall store the van. I should be there in half an hour. You have done well indeed, Johazza. Tell Cyrus the same."

Johazza was feeling very pleased. "Thank you, Saheeb. The journey went well. No trouble anywhere."

"That is good, very good. I will see you shortly."

Saheeb quickly went to the room next door and notified the Afghanis of Johazza's arrival. "We leave immediately," Saheeb ordered, and the three men went to Saheeb's rented GMC Yukon.

They were at the Shell station in twenty-eight minutes. As they were approaching Johazza's location, Saheeb called him. "We are in a silver GMC Yukon. We shall drive by, and you will follow us. We will drive slowly so as not to lose you. In case we should get separated at a traffic light or something, we will pull over and wait. Be careful." And he hung up.

Less than thirty seconds later, the silver Yukon passed slowly by the white cargo van, which fell in behind the Yukon. They made their way over to the storage facility, to the unit Saheeb had leased. They arrived without incident. Saheeb punched the security code into the keypad, and the big sliding gate opened. Both vehicles passed through. They drove to the rear of the facility, where the unit was located. Saheeb got out and walked over to the van. "Drive the van inside." He then walked over to unlock and then raise the door. Saheeb quickly motioned for Johazza to enter. As the van cleared the entrance, the Yukon pulled right up to the opening, effectively blocking any view inside. The two Afghanis got out and joined Saheeb, standing off to one side. Johazza and Cyrus got out and stretched.

"It is good to be here, Saheeb."

"It is good to have you here, both of you."

Cyrus and Johazza looked around and noticed three large barrels off in one corner. Cyrus asked, "What are the barrels for?"

Saheeb smiled and replied, "To hide. They are made of lead so no heat signatures can be revealed. With the technology of the Americans, we cannot take chances."

"That is wise, Saheeb," Johazza offered.

Cyrus was mildly curious as to why there were three barrels, so he asked.

"Because we have three items that need to be hidden."

At that point the two Afghanis stepped up and shot both Johazza and Cyrus in their heads with their silenced .22-caliber pistols. Because they were loaded with subsonic rounds, anyone walking outside the door would not have heard the shots.

"I am sorry," Saheeb said to the two bodies lying on the floor. Then, looking at the Afghanis, he stated, "Put them each into a barrel and be sure it's airtight. We do not want odors. Put the device into the third. Be sure it's latched thoroughly. Then throw that lead blanket over the barrel. We'll leave the cargo van in place. Throw some bleach on the blood. Then we go."

CHAPTER 35

P RESIDENT WILLIAMS CONVENED another meeting between all his directors of the various agencies that were in the loop, with regard to the bomb that had now arrived in Indianapolis. Bernard Backersley, director of the CIA, was not currently present.

FBI Director Matt Sanderson had just finished briefing everyone on the status of the surveillance on the cargo van carrying the device. "We have five different sources of observation currently in place. We have photographs of the three men who led the van to the storage facility. They are being run through facial recognition as we speak. We have the plate number of the GMC Yukon; we know it's a rental leased out to Petroleum Consultants, Inc., which we believe to be a shell company. We have people tearing this company apart. We have interrogated the manager of this storage facility and believe him to be an innocent. We have replaced him with one of our own. The lease agreement information is completely false; however, we are going over the original paperwork for prints or DNA. We should have an identification of the individual within the hour. We have a team that has located a video feed of the storage unit in question, but we know it is not one from the storage facility. We are going to install our own camera at the exact same angle and boost our signal beyond the strength the suspects are using, which will enable us to override it. Then we will make a video loop that will take the place of the live feed and allow us access to that unit without being seen. After that, we will return the original feed signal. We also have six other cameras set up for our own surveillance. The Yukon was tracked back to the Holiday Inn located near the racetrack. There are two rooms registered under this Petroleum Consultants outfit. Curiously, there is a third room registered to Eastern Global, which is a large oil company based out of Saudi Arabia. We are checking for any connection as we speak." With that, Sanderson passed around copies of the entire report to everyone in the room.

President Williams was silent for a few moments, and no one else spoke. Finally he stated, "That's good work, Matt. So we expect to know the identity of this suspect quickly?"

"There are three total, sir; the one who drove the Yukon had two passengers. We know the two men who were driving the van are still inside the storage unit; they did not leave with the others. We are going to insert a microfiber video camera inside the unit before we go in, to see where they are and what they are doing."

At that point, Bernard Backersley of the CIA entered the room. "Sorry I'm late, but I've just finished an intel report that I believe is accurate."

"Sit down, Bernard," directed the president.

"Yes, sir." He began arranging paperwork in front of him and then looked up. "I've got a story to tell. Much of it is speculation, but based on solid fact. It's a little out there, so I'd appreciate you let me finish before asking any questions."

The president nodded and simply stated, "Go on."

"Okay, back in the late sixties there was an oil company in Saudi Arabia called Eastern Petroleum Products. According to our research, it was always on the up-and-up. It was a minor-league player that sold the majority of its product to Japan. Then, four years ago, three wealthy-beyond-belief Saudi princes bought it lock, stock, and barrel and renamed it Eastern Global. They have interests now in most of the world. They are definitely major league. No doubt. Now this is where it gets interesting. The principal owner is one Sheikh Ami al Hadid, a man worth more than Manhattan. The other two owners are, uh, silent partners, for lack of a better phrase. They've been checked inside and out; the only thing we haven't done is given them a colonoscopy. They check clean. Sheikh Ami al Hadid, on the other hand, has some serious question marks. He has family members, albeit distant family members, who are very strongly believed to be tied to al-Qaida. This was confirmed by two of our 'friends.' They believe there is no doubt. They are also convinced that al Hadid has some connection to someone, possibly al-Qaida or, more likely, a splinter group, possibly from Hamas. Either way, it is believed that he is sponsoring a major terrorist cell.

"Here's where it really goes off the path. Eastern Global is currently building a massive refinery in Saudi Arabia. When complete, it is supposed to be the most modern, state-of-the-art facility of its type in the world, bar none. This new refinery is designated for gasoline production. Eastern Global has also commissioned four new supertankers to be built, designed to carry gasoline, not crude oil. The holds of these new tankers are rumored to be virtually impenetrable. Eastern Global is claiming that they can provide refined gasoline anywhere in the world for sixty cents on the dollar that it would cost us to produce. In other words, they can bring these supertankers into Tampa, Galveston—anywhere—and offload gasoline ready to use at forty percent less money than we can produce it for ourselves. That cost difference completely rewrites the chart. Global Eastern has stated that they would build a second refinery and commission as many tankers as needed, which theoretically would allow them to take over the entire industry of gasoline refinement."

Backersley paused for a few moments to let the information settle. He then resumed. "Now, this could be the best thing, or end up being the worst thing, in the history of refining. The best because if it worked, gasoline prices worldwide would drop tremendously. The worst because down the road, if they did become the principal refiner of gasoline, what could stop them from hiking the price through the roof? Think about it. Our own refineries are in need of repair, we don't have enough, and suddenly this company comes charging in on a great white horse and appears to solve problems with gas prices, then they stick it up our collective asses. See my point?"

Elliott Ragar started to speak, but Backersley merely held up his hand to stop him. "Wait just a moment, please, Elliott. Where was I ... okay, got it. Now, I started thinking about all this from every perspective I could come up with. One question kept coming back to me. With the attention that is being paid to alternative fuel sources, why would Eastern Global gamble all this money—and gentlemen, I'm talking perhaps as much as half a trillion when said and done—just for the startup. What for? The damned gas business? They claim they are two years away from becoming operational; however, they have a representative that for the last six months has been meeting with the appropriate people in several different companies around the world, trying to gauge feedback on their proposal." Backersley glanced at Elliott Ragar.

Ragar asked, "Okay, why would they?"

Backersley grinned and stated, "I was hoping you'd ask me that."

"So why would they?" echoed Bill Cochran, the secretary of transportation.

"Simple answer. They wouldn't. It's all bullshit," snapped Backersley emphatically. "It's all a facade, a giant theatre set. They want the world to believe that is what they're doing."

"But why?" asked Elliott Ragar. "What about those tankers, what about the refinery?"

"Oh, they're building the ships and the refinery all right, but the story about it being all for gasoline is pure bullshit. Has to be."

Now the president spoke up. "Why this pretense, Bernard? What is their purpose?"

"They want unfettered access to different countries around the world. They want to come and go without raising suspicion. Hell, they're being welcomed. I believe that this company rep is actually targeting for this new terrorist cell headed by Sheikh Ami al Hadid, head of Eastern Global."

This time it was Matt Sanderson of the FBI who spoke up. "What makes you think all of this?"

Backersley sat down and leaned back in his chair. "Because this company rep is named Saheeb al Kazhed, and I believe that he is the gentleman you are watching at the Holiday Inn located in Indianapolis."

CHAPTER 36

STYLES STOOD BACK and looked at his armory. Even he was impressed. He hadn't really thought that he would be able to procure everything that he'd requested. Not only did he get all of that, but he got a few other surprises thrown in as well. President Williams certainly was holding true to his word to give him everything he needed. He had everything from laser distance finders to laser scopes. There were RPGs, several types of land mines, and pistols, including a Desert Eagle .50-caliber semiautomatic. His own personal handmade sniper rifle was there, of course, as was his other favorite, the Barrett M82A3 .50-caliber rifle which was able, with the right ammo, to stop a tank in its tracks, or blow a man in half from two miles away. When armed with the Raufoss Mk II 687-grain bullet, which has a tungsten carbide penetrator that creates a mini shape charge and then bursts like shotgun pellets, you could take out multiple targets behind a concrete wall. This was one of the most feared weapons available, and in the hands of someone like Styles, it became a tool fit for a surgeon who needed to amputate large amounts of "matter."

Styles had spent the last two days rigging his multiple shooting ranges for both rifles and pistols, including a "pop-up" range. He also had his knife collection, including a custom set of throwing knives he could strike with accurately out to fifty feet. He was just about to take the Barrett out when Starr came walking in.

"That is one hell of a gun. I've never fired one; how hard is it?" Starr asked.

"Not something you'd go plinking with, but not as bad as you'd think. I was just gonna take it out; why don't you come try it? Be good for you to get comfortable with this bad boy."

"Yeah, I guess," Starr replied, less than enthused.

"I'm telling ya, it ain't that bad," Styles insisted.

"Okay, we taking the four-wheelers?"

"Yeah, we'll set some targets up at one thousand yards, get her sighted in."

"What we gonna use for targets?" Starr wanted to know.

"I mixed up some concrete in five-gallon pails. It'll give you a good show at what this beast does. Let's go hook up the trailers behind the four-wheelers."

Together they got the vehicles rigged and loaded up the trailers with the Barrett, ammo, and the targets. They placed the concrete pails, then headed up to the head of the range. Styles attached the bipod and set the big gun down on the ground. He handed Starr a spotting scope and a pair of earmuffs. "You definitely want to put these on. And be sure to stand behind me, not just off to the side. The concussion on this thing is brutal."

Starr put on the muffs and took up a stance ten feet behind Styles and five feet off to the side. Styles put on his own muffs, loaded up the magazine, and inserted it into the rifle. He racked the bolt and chambered the first round. He turned around to grin at Starr. Then he put his eye to the scope. Even through the muffs, Starr heard what sounded more like an explosion than a rifle shot. He could feel the air compression from the blast. Looking through the spotting scope, he saw the pail of cement explode into dust. Styles stood up and said, "It's not bad. Try it."

Starr had fired many a gun in his time, but nothing like this. He approached it with a bit of trepidation.

"Go on, it doesn't bite," Styles chided him.

Starr stretched out behind the big gun, took a firm grasp, centered the scope sights on the cement pail, and touched it off. It definitely let him know it was there, but the recoil was not as bad as he had feared. He looked back through the scope at the target he had aimed at and saw it was gone. "I wouldn't want to put thirty rounds through this thing, but you're right, it wasn't that bad."

"Told ya." Then Styles exchanged places with Starr. He had set up twelve pails of cement, which left ten. He ejected the magazine and replaced the two spent rounds. He then placed a spare magazine, already loaded, next to him. "Time me." He sighted in on the first target and quickly, but smoothly, dispatched the final ten buckets of cement. All of them disappeared into a cloud of dust. When he was finished, he sat up on his knees and said, "Well?"

"Twenty-six and a half seconds. Not bad considering you had to reload magazines."

"Nah, that's slow. I was expecting around twenty since the targets are preset and I know where they are, plus they're still. I'll have to practice more. Problem is finding targets for this beast."

"I'll say," Starr readily agreed. "Guess you could start shooting some trees."

CHAPTER 37

SHEIKH AMI AL Hadid, accompanied by Nakhan Zazar, walked into the council chamber. The muttering within immediately gave way to silence. Zazar took a seat at the table, and then al Hadid sat. He looked at everyone slowly, then cleared his throat.

"We have a decision to make. One of utmost importance. It is established that we may purchase a third device, but it will cost us greatly. Three times the amount of the last one. This will be the only one available for some time, and I'm told we are not the only group interested in this. We have thirty-six hours to reach this decision. Also, we have to give half the amount in advance. We have a good relationship with this particular Russian. I do not believe there is danger in giving him the money. The deal cannot be done any other way. So you must decide, do we purchase this device, or do we not?"

Immediately the rest of the council began squabbling among themselves. "Outrageous" ... "Why so much?" ... "Foolish to give this man this much money."

Ami al Hadid merely watched and listened. After six or seven minutes, he was finally asked his opinion. He gave it. "To me, there is only one question. How committed are we to bringing the Americans to their knees? If we act on what we say we will do, we will purchase the weapon; otherwise, we go home like cowards." Strong words from a strong leader, who hit the group right where he needed to. Their egos. There was silence for maybe ten seconds. Then one stood and said, "Death to the American dogs." There were immediate nods of approval that quickly escalated to cheering. Ami al Hadid let them continue for a minute; he then stood, which brought immediate silence. "Then is it decided. Zazar will instruct you on the immediate transfer of funds. I think we have chosen wisely. Allah Akbar." Then the leader left the chamber, with a smile on his face.

Nakhan Zazar remained behind and met with others one by one to exchange account information for their money to be wired into Ami al Hadid's bank account. It took less than thirty minutes to complete all transactions. Then Zazar left and went back to Hadid's office.

Hadid looked up and stated, "I trust everything went smoothly."

Zazar answered easily, "I've never seen so much money given up so easily. They could not give me their information fast enough."

"That is good, Nakhan, that is good. Now we wait for word from the Russian."

"I'm sure that will be soon, very soon," Zazar offered with a glimmer in his eye.

CHAPTER 38

THE RACE CARS had started running practice laps, the track was alive. Qualifying laps were constant now, each team trying to obtain that magic balance between control and disaster. A few spectators were already in the stands watching. Some even had stopwatches to record lap times for themselves.

The FBI had thirty-two agents directly involved in the surveillance of Saheeb al Kazhed and the two unidentified men with him. Though excellent photographs had been taken of the two strangers, for the facial recognition programs, and fingerprints had been collected off their door handle and sent through every print ID system in the world, their identities still remained a mystery. This fact was giving FBI Director Matt Sanderson fits. His voice had become hoarse because he had been yelling so much—not at anyone in general, but mostly, in fact, at his cell phone after ending calls that always seemed to end without results. He was frustrated at having to relate this to the president: "No, sir, not yet, but we expect their names shortly." Finally the president, not bothering to hide his anger, had told him not to call back directly until he had those names. "Go through Ladd," he'd ordered Sanderson, who hadn't taken the rebuke well.

Sixteen of the agents made up four different sniper teams. Set up in four locations approximately three hundred yards out to cover the Holiday Inn from all sides, they rotated in six-hour shifts. Each team consisted of the standard two-man team: spotter and shooter. The rest of the agents were dispersed in different areas in and around the motel. They did an excellent job of blending in. No one, including guests or the motel's staff had any suspicion that anyone was being watched.

Since returning from the storage facility two days earlier, the three had not left the motel, either eating in the motel restaurant or eating take-out in the rooms. The FBI had multiple state-of-the-art listening devices set in place, including one that could listen for vibrations from the pane of glass in a window. So far, only routine noise had been observed, including porn from the cable TV, though that had been heard only from Saheeb al Kazhed's room. The two unknowns seemed to prefer Westerns. Al Kazhed's choices led all to believe that he was much more Western than he might want Islamic followers to believe.

On the fourth day, a different type of conversation was unveiled. The two cell phone towers in the immediate area, were under close observation. It was a combination of listening to what was said in Saheeb al Kazhed's room and matching it to a recorded conversation from the cell tower. Once a match had been established, the computer whiz gang had determined that a cell phone from the Holiday Inn, established as al Kazhed's, was in communication with a cell phone in Saudi Arabia. What was heard raised goose bumps on everyone who later listened.

Sanderson, looking somewhat ragged, was about to tear his hair out. He called Andrew Ladd, the president's chief of staff. "Andrew, we've intercepted a phone call between al Kazhed and Saudi Arabia. He was informed that a deal has apparently been made for the purchase of another device, from a Russian source. We believe that money has not yet exchanged hands but will—sooner, not later. He was instructed to wait for further instructions. "Has any progress been made, from any other source, as to the identity of these other two men?" He felt it would be better for him to ask rather than be asked and have to answer no.

"No, Matt. Everyone, and I mean everyone, is locked in trying to

ID these two. So far, nothing. At least you're not alone in that boat," Ladd offered.

"Doesn't make me feel any better; in fact, worse. Hard to believe that the spy agencies across the world can't find out who these bastards are," Sanderson snapped back.

"Trust me, Matt, the president is a hell of a lot madder than you are. He's about to start chewing on his coffee cup."

"Yeah, okay. Let me know anything that might come up. I'll keep you posted." He then broke off the phone conversation.

He looked around. He had a mobile command center set up in two interconnecting rooms at the Ramada Inn, directly across the street from the Holiday Inn. The rooms were full of equipment; he had no idea what the hell most of it was. Luckily, he didn't need to. "Okay people, let's move. I want to know exactly where in Saudi Arabia that phone call originated from, I want to know who it was from, and I want to know yesterday," he barked at his agents. He stormed out to get more coffee—just what his stomach needed. He was thankful he still had a large bottle of Rolaids with him. He was starting to chew them like candy.

CHAPTER 39

P RESIDENT ROBERT WILLIAMS had reconvened his intimate war
council. FBI Director Sanderson was absent, as he was personally
heading up the surveillance on the suspects in Indianapolis.

With Bernard Backersley of the CIA leading the way, along with
Elliott Ragar of the NSA, the dots were connected.

Backersley was finishing up. "So what we have is that this new
oil consortium, Eastern Global, appears to be the front for this new
terrorist organization. We don't know what they call themselves, as they
have not claimed any responsibility for anything as of yet; however, we
are certain they have ties to al-Qaida. Sheikh Ami al Hadid, the Saudi
prince, appears to be the head of this group. His right hand is Nakhan
Zazar. Zazar does the actual negotiations with the Russians who are
supplying these devices. Captain Petr Pevosky, who just happens to be
partly in charge of Russia's nuclear stockpile, is the brother-in-law of
Ivan Kovesky, a well-known black market supplier who is the one in
direct contact with Zazar. We believe that after financial transactions
are complete, the device is then loaded aboard a boat, probably a Russian
fishing trawler, and then smuggled into Canada. From there the device

is then smuggled, using logging roads, by cargo van across our border. We have Mossad to thank for helping us connect these dots. So we now have the supplier, the buyer, the way they are getting them here. I believe we are in the position to shut these bastards down."

Everyone looked around, nodding in agreement.

The president spoke. "Gentlemen, you have done your jobs well. You've found out the information required to stop this flow. Matt Sanderson has kept me informed that no attempt has been made to reacquire the device from the storage unit where it has been concealed. The race is in five days, next Sunday. I'm going to order the FBI to neutralize the bomb immediately. The suspects will not know we have done so, because of the video loop the FBI has installed that is overriding their own surveillance system. After the bomb is secure, I will decide on taking down the suspects. I will keep you informed." The president and Chief of Staff Ladd left the room.

"Why do you suppose he's waiting? You know, on taking out those assholes in Indy," asked Charles Rockford, the director of Homeland Security.

"Probably doesn't want to take a chance that they've got a remote detonator in place. If the bomb doesn't work, it can't explode," answered Backersley without even bothering to look up. Backersley thought of Rockford as a complete idiot.

That answer brought the meeting to its unofficial close.

Back in the Oval Office, the president made a phone call.

"Yes, sir," answered Starr.

"Richard, you boys are about to get your first assignment. You have that encryption device installed correctly?"

"Yes, sir," Starr stated firmly.

"All right. You will be receiving a brief. Study it, plan for it, then make sure it's safe."

"Any specific instructions, sir?"

"Yes. Do what you do. And don't get caught. When you're ready to move, I'll send a plane for you. It's yours for as long as we, uh, continue this operation. The pilot will be assigned to you. Military fighter jock. I'm pulling him out of Topgun. I'm going to form a new, very exclusive, very small group. The Department of the Presidential Office. No one else will know of this for now, not even Ladd."

"Sir?" Starr asked, somewhat surprised.

"We'll talk later, Richard. Just be ready to act. Stage one will have to be completed rather quickly. You'll have your intel within the hour." The president signed off.

Starr went out to the gym, where he knew Styles was working out. Walking in, he shouted, "Hey, slow down for a minute."

Styles was in the middle of his inverted sit-up routine. "Yeah, okay. He flipped himself off the bar and walked over. "So what's up?"

"Just got off the phone with the Man. We're getting ready to head out. We'll have our instructions in an hour. Be ready to brief." Starr turned around and left.

Styles felt a small surge of excitement. He didn't know what he was about to do, but he knew he'd be doing something. He went back to the chin-up bar and finished his inverted sit-up routine. Then it was off to the shower.

CHAPTER 40

S TARR HAD JUST finished reading over the decoded material when Styles came downstairs, still toweling off his hair.

"'Bout time for a haircut, isn't it?" Starr asked gruffly.

"You talking about me or you?"

"Well mine sure as hell doesn't need cutting, so who the fuck you think I'm talking about?"

"Seein' as I ain't in the military anymore, I don't figure my hair's anybody else's business, especially yours. You don't like it, tough shit," Styles snapped right back.

"You never were real good at taking orders, Marvin."

"Probably the main reason I got as good as I got, because I learned a long time ago most of the guys who give orders don't know their ass from a hole in the ground."

"You referring to me by any chance?"

Styles grinned at his friend and threw his wet towel at him. "What we got here?"

Starr threw the towel back at Styles and said, "What we got here is an interesting proposition." Starr then picked up the papers that he had stacked in three separate files and put them together, cross-stacking to keep each independent of the others. "They've ID'd the main bastard who is in Indianapolis. He met the guys who drove the bomb there. Those two have gone missing and might be dead inside the storage unit. We should know that by end of today. They've tracked this guy, name is Saheeb al Kazhed. He's got two guys with him, but we don't know who they are yet. Tracked the bomb back to a Russian Captain named Pevosky, who stole the bomb. He's in charge of some of the Russian nuclear devices that are being dismantled. He's got a brother-in-law, guy named Ivan Kovesky, who is a known black market supplier. They stole the bombs, then sold them to a prince in Saudi Arabia, guy named Sheikh Ami al Hadid, the head of a big-ass oil company called Eastern Global. Eastern Global is a front for a terrorist group; don't know exactly what they call themselves, but it's believed they're tied to al-Qaida. Our mission is to take out the targets in Indianapolis first, then the two Russians, then the Saudis. Not sure yet on just how many Saudis. The Man will let us know."

"Mind if I look at the papers?"

"Just don't screw up the order."

"Screw this, Starr." He reached over and slid the stack of papers toward himself.

"Gonna make some coffee; want some?" Starr asked.

"Yeah, thanks."

After ten minutes, Styles pushed the paperwork back, stacked the way Starr had it, and looked up. "This will be fun, popping these guys right under the noses of the FBI."

"I'm sure that's the first priority on the president's mind—you having fun," Starr quipped back. "One more thing. Looks like this whole operation is going to upgrade a bit."

"What do you mean?" Styles asked.

"The president is forming some new type of intel group. It sounds like he's expanding our role a bit. Right now it's top secret; even the chief of staff doesn't know yet. He's calling it the Department of the Presidential Office."

"Better than 'Killers Are Us,' I guess."

"Well, for starters, he's assigning a military fighter jock to haul us around. I think there might be more, but he hasn't said yet. I think he wants to talk to us before we go to Indiana, but that's just a gut feeling."

Almost as if on cue, the phone rang. Starr answered and listened without saying a word. Then he clicked his phone shut. He looked at his watch, then turned to Styles and instructed, "Pack an overnight bag just in case. We have to be in Knoxville in three hours. We're flying up to Washington."

Styles looked at Starr with suspicion. "Did you plan that?"

"No, but that was one hell of a gut feeling."

"Right," Styles replied sarcastically, and he went upstairs to gather his gear.

CHAPTER 41

PRESIDENT WILLIAMS, SURROUNDED by his Secret Service security detail, walked briskly toward the waiting helicopter that would fly him to Camp David. He was contemplating the meeting that lay ahead. Ducking his head, he entered the chopper that was already running, awaiting only the president before taking off. Once aboard, he buckled in, and the aircraft immediately lifted into the sky.

Starr had received a text message identifying the hangar at the Knoxville airport that he and Styles were to report to. They had just left the Ranch, and were on their way. Knoxville was less than an hour away, which would put their arrival shortly before three in the afternoon. It was a crystal-clear day. They were driving up in Starr's Suburban. Traffic was light, and surprisingly, so was their mood. They had each packed a small overnight bag.

Starr, driving, was enjoying the music on the radio, currently a Charlie Daniels tune. Styles, letting his mind drift, was looking out the window, at nothing in particular. They both knew what to expect—a briefing of what the president wanted and, more importantly, expected.

Arriving at the airport, Starr steered the 'Burb toward the designated hangar. He had Googled the area and familiarized himself, so he knew just where to go.

"Looks like this is it," said Starr, pulling up in front of a sign that read, "Evan's Hangar." It advertised mechanical work and a flight school. He parked right out in front. He and Styles got out, grabbing their bags. Walking through the front door, they were greeted by a man in his midthirties. He looked up at them, then pointed at a door in the rear of the office. "Through there," he said.

Without a word, the pair walked through the door and out into the hangar. Another man in his late forties looked at them and said, "Captain Starr?"

Starr nodded in acknowledgment.

The man walked up to them and introduced himself. "I'm J. C. Christman, your pilot. Follow me please." He led them out of the large sliding doors and onto the flight apron and toward a sleek business jet. Starr thought the jet engines looked particularly large for a plane its size. Starr and Styles fell in line behind him, and they climbed up the boarding stairs.

"Pick a seat and strap in," directed Christman as he turned, retracted the stairs, and closed the entry door.

Starr thought the interior of the plane was rather spartan compared to the few other private jets he'd been on previously.

"Not the fanciest plane I've been on," he commented to Christman.

"This one's not built for fancy. She's built for speed," Christman declared. When we've got more time, I'll show you her goodies. Right now we're a bit pressed. Just sit back and enjoy the flight." He disappeared up into the cockpit. Starr noticed he did not close the door. The motors started spooling up, and within a minute, the jet started to roll. Styles and Starr could hear Christman conversing with the tower on the radio, and they were cleared for immediate takeoff. They taxied out to the end of the runway, turned onto it, and felt, more than heard, the surge of the big engines. Styles and Starr looked at each other as the plane rolled down the runway, picking up speed much faster than either of them had anticipated.

Styles looked over at Starr and exclaimed, "Man, this baby's got some balls."

"You ain't lyin'."

In no time, they were airborne and accelerating even harder. They were both pushed back into their seats with surprising force. The ground below fell away quickly. The plane leveled off, with Starr guessing they were around thirty thousand feet. Even at that altitude, he could tell the plane was moving along at a higher rate of speed than he would've expected.

Forty minutes later they could feel the plane start to descend. They had not spoken since the takeoff. Twenty minutes later they touched down at an airport they were not familiar with. The plane taxied up to a military helicopter that sat parked next to a large hangar. They stayed in their seats as Christman shut the jet down. He then came out of the cockpit and instructed, "Follow me, guys."

They did as requested, and the three of them boarded the military helicopter. The chopper's rotor blades immediately started to turn—very slowly at first, then quickly rotating faster. The men soon found themselves in the air once again.

"Where are we heading for?" asked Starr.

"Camp David," Christman answered.

CHAPTER 42

SAHEEB AL KAZHED was getting frustrated. His two associates, the Afghanis, were starting to go stir-crazy. They were not used to being cooped up in a hotel room. They were beginning to complain vehemently. Al Kazhed kept telling them over and over, "Just three more days. We shall park the van at the racetrack, set the timing device, and leave. Then it will be up to Allah." He had satisfied them for the present, but still, three more days were three more days. He didn't dare let them out in public for long, because of their physical appearance and their horrible English. They would instantly arouse suspicion. Their entire aura screamed "terrorist." So Saheeb was required to keep them all but under lock and key.

Al Kazhed was also distraught because the responsibility of the next target had been placed directly on his shoulders. He knew Sheikh Ari al Hadid expected the same perfect location as his present choice. Al Hadid wanted maximum exposure, for number of casualties and for the audacity of attacking a national American event.

Al Kazhed had already been researching the Internet for the next major American celebration. He thought about some type of Fourth of

July event, but there was no real national event associated with that. He thought about a baseball game, but which one? Finally he caught an article on the web news that attracted his eye. A new casino was to be opened over the July Fourth weekend in Las Vegas, the capital of American vice and debauchery. The more he thought about that locale, the more he liked it. He felt certain that Ami al Hadid would agree. Yes, that was it. That entire city would be the next victim of Allah's wrath. He smiled, as he felt Allah was smiling upon him.

The mood in the room next door could not have been more different. The two Afghanis had been talking in low voices to be sure they were not overheard.

"Jafarri, I do not trust this Saudi. He will put a bullet in our heads when we are not looking, as we have done for him," growled Tahaah

"We have known him for a long time. He has never cheated us."

"Not yet, Jafarri, but this time everyone, except for those two Russian drunks, has been killed," insisted Tahaah.

"Saheeb told us that he was ordered to kill Johazza and Cyrus by al Hadid. It was not his choice," Jafarri continued.

"How do we know that the same order won't be placed on our heads?"

Jafarri looked at the floor with concern. "Yes, we do not know that. What would you have us do?"

"We know al Kazhed has money on his plane. We could go get the pilot and make him fly us home," Tahaah suggested.

"Then that is something maybe we should do," agreed Jafarri, not completely convinced. "Let us both watch al Kazhed closely. We will decide if we think he is not to be trusted."

CHAPTER 43

THE FLIGHT TO Camp David took less than twenty-five minutes. After landing, Starr and Styles disembarked, followed closely by Christman, the pilot who had flown them from Knoxville to whatever airport they had landed at. They didn't know what it was called. Starr and Styles were a bit surprised that Christman appeared to be joining them, but they didn't say anything about it.

The three of them were led by a Secret Service team consisting of six agents to one of the entrances. The door was opened smartly for them as they approached, and the group of three were waved through. Four different Secret Service Agents joined them, leading them down a hallway to an office, and ushered them in. "Take a seat," one of them instructed.

The three sat down at a round conference table with the capacity to seat eight. It was a warmly appointed office, paneled in burled walnut with very comfortable chairs. One wall was shelved and full of books. Scenes of early naval sea battles were on the walls. There were no windows. The room was surprisingly well lit, considering the indirect lighting utilized. There was no conversation.

A door opened on the far side of the room, and President Williams entered briskly. Immediately the three men stood. President Williams motioned for them to sit back down. "Richard, good to see you, as always. Sergeant. And you must be Christman."

"Sir," they answered in unison.

The president sat down and placed a large manila envelope off to the side. "Richard, I want your input on something. It involves all three of you, but for the moment I'm speaking to Richard."

"Yes, sir," Starr confirmed.

"Okay. I am inclined to take a slightly different approach from what I started with you and Sergeant Styles. I want your honest opinion. Don't hold back. I actually started down this path when you informed me of Sergeant Styles's reluctance to train as a pilot. That got me to thinking about expanding this into a little more of a team concept." He paused and looked at each of them. Starr and Christman were staring directly at him, while Styles, he noticed, appeared more relaxed. He had no doubt that he was catching every word. He continued. "After I thought about that, it made sense to assign a pilot to you. Christman is a naval aviator, flying F-14 Tomcats off of carriers primarily, with a few other planes thrown into the mix. Recently he's been an instructor at Topgun. Is this correct, Mr. Christman?"

"Yes, sir."

"Good," the president stated firmly. "I also understand that your private jet was modified a bit."

"Yes, sir," Christman answered again.

"How does it fly?" the president asked.

"Well, sir, I don't have that much time in it yet, but it seems to be on target, from what I was told to expect."

"Excellent." The president glanced around the table. "I'm in the process of putting a new group together under which you three will operate. Officially it will be the Department of the Presidential Office. I'm walking a fine line here, but believe I can do this under my executive powers. As before, you will answer to me, and me alone. I know some of the Justice Department may have a shit fit, but they can shit themselves for all I care. Richard, if this team consisted of you three, who, if anyone else, would you might consider adding?"

Starr was quiet for a few moments, thinking. Then he spoke. "Maybe a really good computer geek. I mean a kick-ass hacker, one who can get in anywhere. That way we wouldn't have to be involved with the FBI for our computer requirements and accessing information that we might need in our assignments. I can't really think of anyone else who would be necessary. Christman flies, Styles does his thing, I make the coffee. A hacker, maybe fluent in some of the foreign languages we'll have to deal with, would be a plus. I think that would about do it."

The president sat back in his chair and gave his wide Texas smile. "Richard, sometimes I think you can read my mind." He leaned over and grabbed a telephone handset. He punched one button. "Send in Ms. Phillips."

The same door that the president had entered opened again. Starr, Styles, and Christman all subconsciously straightened up a bit in their chairs. Darlene Phillips was a tall, slender, dark-haired beauty. Styles guessed her to be maybe in her midthirties, with a definite attitude about her. Her eyes appeared to be glossy black jewels. Styles also guessed that somewhere in her heritage one would find a Native American ancestor. She was obviously athletic; Styles could tell by the muscle tone in her arms, as she was wearing a sleeveless black blouse atop black jeans. She also wore little makeup, and her only accessories were a silver necklace with a small turquoise stone, and a matching bracelet on her left wrist, but no rings on her fingers. Styles couldn't see, but he guessed she was also wearing black athletic shoes.

"Please sit down, Ms. Phillips," the president directed.

"Yes, sir," she said in a firm voice.

"Ms. Phillips, this first gentleman is Captain Richard Starr, USMC retired. Next to him is Sergeant Marvin Styles, USMC retired; and the third is Captain James Christman, United States Navy. Boys, this is Darlene Phillips, probably the best damned hacker on the planet, at least of all the ones we know," the president offered.

The four nodded at each other.

The president continued. "Ms. Phillips, as I've explained, you'd be working with these three roughnecks as part of an extremely specialized team. You've assured me you're up to the job."

"Without a doubt, sir. I was the youngest, with four brothers. I don't think they knew I was a girl until I had my first period."

Styles thought Starr was going to fall right out of his chair.

The president just grinned and continued. "Besides her computer skills, Ms. Phillips is also fluent in five languages and can understand four others reasonably well. Is that correct, Ms. Phillips?"

"That is correct, sir."

The president turned to the three other men in the room. "Any of you have any problems working with Ms. Phillips?"

No one said anything for about five seconds, and then Starr spoke up. "No, sir, I don't believe so, but I'm wondering how this is all going to work. If Styles and I are at the Ranch, where are Christman and Phillips going to be stationed? I mean, if we have to roll fast on something, how will that work?"

"Easy, Richard. When you get back to the Ranch, pick out two spots for two cabins to be constructed. They will each have their private quarters, while you two will enjoy the main house.

Styles unconsciously let out a "Huh?"

Darlene Phillips looked Styles straight in the eye. "You got a problem with me on the property, Sergeant?" Her voice dripped with attitude.

Styles was going to set her straight. "Not at the moment. If I do, you'll be the first to know."

"I warn you, Sergeant, I have a fifth-degree black belt in Taekwondo and a third-degree black belt in Jujitsu."

Styles simply returned her stare and smiled, ever so slightly.

The president spoke up again, quickly. "Let me clarify. I don't mean that I expect Christman and Phillips to live at the Ranch permanently. I know they both have homes. I just want them to have their own space for when your group receives an assignment."

Starr could have sworn he heard Styles sigh in relief.

President Williams continued. "Ms. Phillips has given me a list of computer requirements, which I'm having brought to the Ranch. She'll set it up. I've also got two manufactured cabins being brought down, and these should be set to go within three days. For the time being, I want each of you to study these intel packets. You'll stay the night down in the guest cabins. Get to know each other a bit. Richard, I know I'm springing this on you a bit suddenly, and if you have strong objections, this is not cast in stone. I do think, however, it is the best way to deal with out problems."

"I see both sides of the fence, sir; I'm willing to give it a try."

"Sergeant?" the president asked.

"Got no problem … sir." The "sir" was almost an afterthought.

"Good. Now, the agents will show you where you're staying. There is an excellent dining room there; try to enjoy yourselves. I don't expect you to start strategizing tonight; I just want you to look over the details, familiarize yourself with the facts—that's all. I understand that I'm throwing you all together unexpectedly, I know you will make it work. Thank you." With that, the president stood up and left the room.

CHAPTER 44

THE FOURSOME HAD decided to meet for dinner, after the Secret Service agents got them squared away. Everyone agreed on seven p.m.

Each of them had a room, which was quite comfortable. Decorated in a rustic country style, the accommodations offered all the modern conveniences of a topflight hotel room. Styles had gone over to Starr's room to confer. "You have any idea this was coming?" Styles asked.

"None, and I'm not thrilled about it. This whole idea that Williams and I hatched up only involved you and me. Now we got us a three-ring circus," Starr complained.

"Well, I kinda feel the same way, but like you said to the president, I can see both sides too. I really don't want to fuck around flying airplanes; that ain't my job. I can also see that having our own computer whiz might be a good thing. I'd rather have somebody up close and personal than count on some FBI dickweed when the time comes."

"Just what do you mean by 'up close and personal,' Marv?"

"Don't give me that shit, Starr. You know what I mean."

"You got a crush on Little Miss Hard Ass?"

"Nope. She is cute, gotta give that to her, but if she can run a hack job on anybody, plus speak those languages, she could help. That's *all* I think," Styles snapped back.

They were both quiet for a few moments, then Starr spoke. "Yeah, I can see your point. I guess part of it is I don't really want to be part of some special group. I liked the idea of it being just the two of us, but they could help—that's a fact. I'll just shut up and give it a go."

"I think that's our best choice for now," Styles agreed. If something becomes a problem, we'll deal with it."

"Fine by me. Guess I'll grab a shower before dinner. That'll give us a chance to get to know a little more about our new partners."

"Good idea. See ya at dinner," agreed Styles.

As soon as Styles had departed, Starr called President Williams.

"Yes, Richard, did you talk to Sergeant Styles?"

"Yes, sir. He was surprised at our additions, but he can see where they make sense. I made out like I was a little pissed cause I wanted his own reaction. I didn't let on that we'd discussed this change. I gotta be honest, sir; at first I didn't really like it. I don't like surprises pulled on me at the last moment. I can understand, though, how these additions may make the whole operation run smoother. So we're both on board. If any problems come up, we'll deal with them."

"Richard," the president said, only half joking, "I hope that doesn't mean that Styles will take care of them."

"No, sir, as long as they don't turn out to be bad guys."

Starr heard the president chuckle on the other end of the phone before he heard the click.

CHAPTER 45

SAHEEB AL KAZHED was feeling very satisfied with himself. Akbar al Hamid had arrived in Indianapolis and was taking a cab to the Holiday Inn. He was the man, as in New York, who would arm the bomb and set the timer. Once that was done, he could go back home to the accolades he was certain would be waiting. He would send Akbar to Miami and have him await further instructions. He also wanted to discuss with Sheik Ami al Hadid what was to be their next target.

Saheeb had been checking his video monitor that watched over the storage unit where the van concealing the bomb had been hidden. His security camera was motion-detector operated, and so far only he had observed only the occasional walk by of the storage facility manager. He had noticed that it was a different man, so he had called the facility and asked to speak with the original manager who had leased him the unit. He'd been told that the man had gone on his scheduled two-week vacation. Saheeb al Kazhed had not been concerned over that answer. He should have been.

The FBI had already been inside the storage unit three times. On the second visit, they discovered the bodies of the two drivers inside the barrels. On the third visit, they removed the plutonium and replaced it with a trace of a much lower grade radioactive substance. Unless the bomb was completely dismantled, any Geiger counter used to check for the device's "heart" would make it seem as though everything were normal. The President had decided to disable the apparatus as soon as access was available. No one was willing risk any chance of a nuclear event.

Saheeb al Kazhed's cell phone rang. It was Akbar al Hamid. He'd arrived at the Holiday Inn and had already checked in.

"Akbar, I am pleased you have finally arrived," stated al Kazhed with feigned sincerity. "Did the registration desk ask you many questions?"

"No, Saheeb. I asked them for a schedule of the race, and they seemed pleased I was here. The woman was quite friendly."

"Good. We will travel tonight, and I will take you to the device so that you may inspect it. In two days we move the van to where I have chosen to park it. There you will arm the device. Then we shall leave immediately."

"Saheeb, I must tell you I am not looking forward to another bus ride so soon. There was a horrible pig of a woman sitting behind me, who I would swear shit her pants. Her odor was worse than foul."

"Do not worry, my friend; you will not be riding a bus this time."

"Thank you, Saheeb, thank you. Praise Allah."

Al Kazhed then asked Akbar al Hadid his room number and told him he would pick him up at midnight. Then they would travel together to the storage facility.

"I will be waiting, Saheeb."

CHAPTER 46

STARR AND STYLES walked into the dining room together and found Christman and Phillips already seated at an oversize round table. Christman looked up and motioned them over. Menus had already been placed on the table. Starr sat down next to Phillips, placing Styles between him and Christman, across from Phillips.

Christman started the conversation. "So what do you guys like to be called?"

Starr answered for both of them. "Call me Starr, and him Styles."

"All right," Christman responded. "I go by J. C., and she goes by Phillips." They all nodded in agreement.

Christman continued. "Starr, I guess you're pretty much the top guy here—at least that is what the president indicated."

Starr answered, "Well, I don't know about that. He and I sort of hatched this scheme together a while back, but I don't consider myself the boss. I'm sort of the strategist of the group, the nuts-and-bolts guy. You obviously fly us where we've got to go, Phillips here is the hacker and linguist, and Styles here, well, let's just say he's the, uh, surgeon who will perform the extractions."

Phillips looked at Styles and stated without reservation, "I knew you were the sniper. So how many targets have you taken out?"

"Why?"

"Because if I'm going to put my ass on the line, I want to know that you're up to the job."

"Why? Think I'll have to protect you from one of your fucking keyboards?"

Darlene Phillips's dark eyes began to glow. "I don't need protecting from anybody."

Styles had heard his fill. "Listen, Phillips, you can take those black belts of yours and shove 'em up your ass. They wouldn't be worth shit in my world. If you think I'm kidding, I'll have Starr tie my hands behind my back, we can go outside and spar, and I'll have that ass of yours on the ground before you get halfway to me. And it'll hurt. Now, the president picked you to run computers for us, not put me through some kind of fucking inquisition. Now, you do your job, and I'll do mine. This isn't some kind of competition between any of us, so lose your fucking attitude; otherwise, I'm gonna put you through a wall." Phillips's was seated with her back against the wall. Styles looked at her hard and snarled, "Can you do this?" and before anyone could even react, he had grabbed two steak knives on the table and thrown them past Phillips's head, missing her by half an inch on either side, with the knives sticking solidly in the wall behind her.

Phillips, her eyes on fire, stood up and said, "Fuck you," and stormed out.

Christman looked at Styles and Starr, smiled, and said, "Well, that went well."

Starr quipped back, "Ya think?"

The three men had been engaging in small talk and were halfway through dinner when Phillips returned. None of the men paid her any attention.

Starr spoke first. "If you're not a vegetarian, the filet mignon is as good as it gets."

Phillips nodded. "That sounds good. Let me get this out of the way. I don't apologize very often. I grew up the youngest of five, with four brothers. They were hard on me, hell, my whole family is hard. I went to school to get away from the bullshit. I guess I haven't gotten far from the tree. Found I had a knack for computers and language. Spent most of my time in the CIA. They're pissed that I got reassigned. Not blowing my own horn, but I guess they think I'm as good as I think you are," she said directly toward Styles. "Look, we got off on the wrong foot, and it's my fault. I don't know how I can love men and hate men, but I do. Always feel like I've got to prove myself. I tend to go overboard, and I went way overboard with you, Styles. Won't happen again."

Styles looked at her for a few seconds, not saying a word. He merely picked up his water glass and raised it toward her, nodding. He then said, "You got nothing to prove here. The fact you're sitting with us says all that needs to be said."

The group spent the next two hours finishing their dinners and getting to know each other a bit. Styles gave up the least amount of information, just indicating he'd done tours in Iraq, Afghanistan, Grenada, and South America. None went into great detail about their personal lives; they just joked about pet peeves and such. Christman had stated that on his next vehicle, he wanted photon torpedoes installed, with everyone in agreement.

All of them had just gotten up from the table when a Secret Service agent handed Starr a note. He read it, then said, "Hold up, guys. The president has asked us to meet him for breakfast at oh seven hundred. We'll meet at the entrance to the main building." He received nods of acknowledgment from the others.

Later, after the four had adjourned to their rooms for the night, the two busboys cleared the table. They never noticed the two steak knives stuck in the wall.

CHAPTER 47

THE NEXT MORNING, the president was informed by Director Sanderson of the FBI that the device in Indianapolis had been rendered harmless. "With the exception of a complete teardown, it'll pass any test, though it's doubtful that would be done at this stage," Sanderson offered. The president directed Sanderson to keep him closely informed of any other details and then signed off, as he had a meeting with Starr's group for breakfast, where he was going to give them explicit instructions on the status of their assignment.

At exactly five minutes before seven, Starr and his group assembled at the front entrance of the main building at Camp David. Secret Service agents escorted them to a conference room and instructed them to take a seat. Two minutes later President Robert Williams entered.

"Good morning," he said to the group as they stood as one.

"Sir," they all replied.

"Sit down. We'll be served breakfast shortly. I want to give you the assignment as I see it. I assume you all looked at the intel packets I gave you yesterday. The assignment is simple. I want you to take down the perpetrators in Indianapolis first. Then I want you to take down the two Russians who are responsible for supplying these devices. Then I want you to take down that Saudi prince, al Hadid, and his right-hand man, Zazar. Any other members of that group that you can eliminate, so much the better, but I especially want Hadid and Zazar out of the picture. How you do it is strictly up to you. I don't need details; I need results. I need you to not get caught. When you get back to your rooms, you will all find your official DPO IDs and badges. By this afternoon, the directors of every federal agency will be aware of this new assemblage. You people answer only to me. No other agency will have any jurisdiction over you, federal or state, in any manner, nor you them. You will have complete authority to go wherever you need inside our borders. No one will have command of you. However, as you can understand, it is absolutely imperative that you not get caught at illegalities that you may have to execute during the completion of your mission. Any questions?"

Starr spoke up. "Sir, how do we respond if we should come into conflict with any other law-enforcement agency?"

"On your official ID there is a phone number. Have anyone questioning your authority call it; he or she will get the Justice Department. It will be taken care of. If this conflict should take place during the actual operation of your assignment, neutralize the offending agent or agency, but you are *not* to use lethal force. Is that clear?" the president answered.

"Yes, sir, perfectly," Starr confirmed.

"No other questions?" the president asked. After receiving no response from anyone, he smiled and said, "Let's enjoy breakfast." He pressed a button on his phone, and seconds later a door opened and a buffet was wheeled in. Two servers made up plates for everyone, and for a while the war on terrorism was not openly discussed.

CHAPTER 48

TWO AND A half hours later found Starr and Styles, with Christman piloting the plane, on their way back to Knoxville. Christman had been telling Starr and Styles about the plane they were aboard.

Christman stated, "It was confiscated by the DEA about a year and a half ago. Then the idea came about to modify it. It still looks like your typical jet, but trust me, it's not."

"I thought the jet engines looked bigger than usual when I first saw it," Starr observed.

"You are correct. Power-wise we've got about sixty percent more thrust than normal. We can cruise all day long at seven hundred miles per hour. If we have to, we can crack eleven hundred mph. There's heavy reinforcement in the wings, tail—anywhere that's going to take the additional stress. I haven't really tried it yet, but I'm looking forward to really getting it on. If we get into a situation where we're being chased, it'll surprise a lot of fighters. We can't outrun one, but we might be able to hold one off long enough to get back to friendly airspace, if we get caught where we're not supposed to be." He finished grinning and continued with "It has a good communications center on it, decent computer gear, though Phillips will probably bitch. Plus we've got good cargo room for your toys—and check this out." He flipped two switches and, unseen, two panels on the leading edge of each wing opened to reveal four thirty-millimeter cannons. He fired a burst and just laughed. "Can you imagine a fighter having a civilian jet open up on him?"

Styles whistled softly and said, "Now that *is* a surprise."

"It's got one more surprise; care to take a guess?" Christman asked.

"Damned if I know," Starr responded.

"The landing gear has been modified as well. If I push these two buttons"—he pointed to two switches located above him and to the left—"part of the landing doors open up and we can drop and fire six Sidewinder missiles. Of course, I have to ID the target on this little computer right here, but all I do is put the dot on the spot and boom, no more spot."

Styles was shocked. "You're telling me we're armed with fuckin' Sidewinders?"

"Yep."

"Infuckingcredible. Who did all these little modifications?" Styles asked.

"I don't really know—above my pay grade. But they did a damned fine job, whoever they were. I've actually test fired four Sidewinders, and they work like magic. Somebody wants to pick a fight with us, they've got a hell of a surprise coming. The best part is that the guidance systems on the Sidewinders are both heat seeking and radar operated. They work in tandem with each other. The onboard computer tells the brain that if countermeasures are taken that hinder one system, the other one automatically intercedes. Is that cool or what?"

"No shit!" Starr and Styles exclaimed at the same instant, as if they'd rehearsed the answer.

"The president is also going to give us a chopper to keep at the Ranch so that when we need to go we don't have to drive to Knoxville," Christman added.

Styles looked over at Starr and acknowledged, "Man, the president wasn't kidding when he said we'd have everything."

"Everything except a pizza parlor," quipped Starr.

"Hell, who needs a pizza parlor when we've got DiGiorno," joked Christman, which got all of them laughing.

∞

Darlene Phillips was not a woman with a tremendous amount of patience even when everything went smoothly. Her check-in with the FBI complex at Quantico had been anything but smooth, and the little patience she had was rapidly disappearing. She had been held up at the security desk for over half an hour and was close to decking the asshole standing in front of her. "For the last time, either check with whatever idiot is in charge here or call the number on the ID badge. That gets you the Justice Department. Somebody here is expecting me. Now get off your ass and do whatever it is you have to do to get me to my workstation," she snapped.

"I'm sorry, ma'am, but I've never heard of any Department of the Presidential Office, and I have protocol to follow. If you like, you may have a seat at that desk, and I'll authenticate your presence," the FBI agent informed her.

Phillips turned around and whipped out her cell phone and dialed the number. "This is Darlene Phillips. I'm at Quantico, and some boneheaded ass is dragging his feet on giving me clearance to get to my workstation. Can you straighten him out?" She walked over to the agent and handed him the phone.

"This is Special Agent Eric Jansen," the agent said into the phone.

Phillips, from five feet away, could hear profane screaming coming through the earpiece.

"But sir, you have to understand I need to authenticate her presence."

More screaming through the earpiece.

"Yes, sir, right away." Special Agent Jansen handed Phillips back her phone and walked over to a phone on his own desk. He punched a button, spoke a few words, hung up, and returned to Phillips. "Just a couple of minutes, ma'am."

Phillips thought that steam would start blowing out of her ears at any second. Luckily, less than a minute later, an older man came through a door and walked up to her.

"Ms. Phillips, I'm sorry about your delay. We received confirmation of your arrival only a short while ago, and I apologize; it was my fault the desk was unaware. Please come with me." Phillips noticed that the man did not identify himself. At this point she didn't care, so she just followed as requested.

They got on an elevator and went up to the fourth floor, got off, and walked three doors down to the right and entered. Phillips looked around and was not overly impressed. "This looks like a decent setup. Not nearly as advanced as I'm used to, but it should do for now."

The older agent said to her, "An agent will bring you a guest pass so you don't have any more problems. This guest pass will allow you to access to this office, besides the common areas." He gave her a card. "That is my extension should you need anything. Welcome to the FBI." He turned and left her. She spent five minutes just walking around and digesting the equipment she had to work with. After studying everything, she just shook her head sadly and thought, *No wonder these clowns can't find anything.*

CHAPTER 49

ARRANGEMENTS HAD BEEN made to hangar the plane, after which Starr, Styles, and Christman had driven back down to the Ranch in Starr's Suburban. They were home by 11:40 that morning.

"Why don't you give J. C. the tour?" Styles suggested to Starr. "I'm going to do a full workout."

"Yeah, I thought you'd want to," Starr agreed. "Come on, J. C., I'll give you the fifty-cent tour." He led J. C. toward the barns first. Styles headed over to the house to change.

Starr and Christman were just coming out of the second barn when Styles approached them, heading for his gym. He looked at Starr, and Starr shook his head ever so slightly. Styles knew that to mean that Starr had not shown him the armory.

"Marv, you gonna want lunch or wait till dinner?"

"I'll wait. This will take a while."

"Say, Styles, you mind if I use your gym? I like to try to keep my weight down."

"Help yourself." Styles disappeared into the gym and began stretching.

Right then Starr's cell phone rang. He didn't recognize the number. "Starr here."

"Captain Starr. This is Evan Beyer of the Army Corps of Engineers. I've got two modular cabins coming your way tomorrow morning. I've got two full crews with me to set them up. We should be out of your hair in two days."

"Sounds good; see you then." Turning to Christman, he said, "That was the Corps of Engineers; the two cabins are coming tomorrow. Says he'll have them up and done in two days."

"That's pretty fast."

"Yeah, says he's got two full crews with him, whatever that means. Well, let me show you the main part of the house and explain the security system. We've got two security consoles: the one in the barn, and the other here in the house."

"I'm impressed. You say you've got the entire property zoned?" Christman asked.

"Yeah, it's quite the structure."

"I'll say."

Starr suggested they use the four-wheelers to take a look around the property. Christman was all for that idea.

Walking over to the barn to grab the ATVs, Starr stuck his head in the gym and yelled at Styles, "We're gonna go take a spin around the property. Be back later."

Styles was in the middle of his inverted sit-up routine and hollered back, "Gotcha."

Starr started to walk away and realized that Christman was staring open-mouthed at Styles.

"Problem?" Starr asked.

"Uh, no, I've just never seen anyone do *that* before. How many does he do?"

"I think two hundred."

"*What!*"

"Yeah, he's the one guy on the planet you do not want to piss off. I've known him for fifteen years now, and I haven't met the man yet that I'd put up against him. And J. C., that's straight."

They walked over to retrieve the ATVs out of the barn, Christman shaking his head.

CHAPTER 50

STARR, STYLES, AND Christman were eating dinner in the dining room. Styles was feeling refreshed from his workout. It had been the most intense routine he'd put himself through in weeks. Christman was still thinking about all he'd been shown that afternoon. Starr was busy congratulating himself on the beef stew he'd whipped up, complete with homemade biscuits; he'd mentioned this to the others no less than three times.

"Starr, we said the biscuits were good. You're starting to sound like a commercial," Styles griped.

"Just nice to know I'm appreciated, sonny boy."

Christman piped up. "Sonny boy?"

"Makes up for his infantile insecurities," Styles replied, not looking up from the stew.

"My, sounds like somebody's been keeping up with their crossword puzzles," Starr retorted.

"Crossword this, Starr," Styles popped right back.

Christman looked confused and somewhat concerned. "You guys serious?"

Styles looked over at him and cracked a grin. "Nah, it's just him being the father that, thankfully, I never had," he said, bringing a chuckle from around the table.

Christman got serious. "Starr, do you know just exactly how the president is going to explain this—I mean this whole new department he's cooked up? If we do what he's expecting, isn't that going to draw attention to him?"

Styles added, "Yeah, I've kinda been thinking about that too."

Starr put his spoon down and looked at them. "The three of us are silent members of the DPO. Officially, the DPO is a team that will deal only with terrorism the president has put together for the purpose of information gathering and dispersion among the other intelligence-gathering agencies, including those abroad. He figures that one group serving as the 'motherboard' will work smoother, and keep him informed sooner, rather than having to wait on the other boys to play nice. He'll have a four other members involved. We three are under cover, so to speak. Only two others, besides the president, will be aware of us. Phillips will have complete access to everybody. Officially, she's a coleader. If she's half as good as the president says she is, hell, you could wake up circumcised, and never know she'd been there."

"Nice analogy, Starr, nice," exclaimed Styles.

"Yeah," agreed Christman.

"I'm just saying the chick is good. She should be able to feed us information before the people that know it, know it."

"Well that would certainly be handy," Christman agreed.

Styles looked at Christman and asked, "J. C., just how do those sidewinder missiles actually work? Every one I've seen is mounted to a launch platform."

"Well, when the landing gear door opens, a hydraulic system lowers the platform. The only flaw in the system is that we have to be below four hundred miles per hour to do that. Any higher will disrupt the airflow around the plane too severely and cause control loss. Once down and locked though, we have no speed limitations. Funny part is we can retract the system without any problems. One of those freak laws of nature, I guess, or as the big boys say, aerodynamics."

Styles continued. "When the landing gear doors open, does the whole rig lower automatically, or is that a separate operation?"

"Separate. Why?"

"Means I should be able to squeeze through, and jump if need be."

CHAPTER 51

DARLENE PHILLIPS PICKED up the card the older FBI agent had given her. Special Agent Timothy Scribe was prominently displayed under the words "Federal Bureau of Investigation." Two telephone numbers and an in-house extension number were also provided. No other information was present. She dialed the extension.

"Scribe here."

"Agent Scribe, this is Darlene Phillips, DOP. I need a decent couch brought into my office."

"Expecting company, Ms. Phillips?" Scribe inquired.

"No."

"Then why do you need the couch?"

Phillips could feel her fuse starting to light. "Agent Scribe, it is my understanding that your position here is to provide me what I need, not ask why."

"Ms. Phillips, my position at this agency, inside this location, is to assess what requirements are necessary."

"Fine, Agent Scribe. Perhaps you'll make the same statement to President Williams when I inform him of your lack of cooperation. I suggest you not leave. You will be hearing from him within ten minutes, I would imagine," and she slammed the phone down.

Fifteen seconds later her phone rang. She smiled. "Yes, Agent Scribe?" She didn't wait for him to identify himself.

"I'll have one sent down right away. Do you prefer leather or cloth?"

"Definitely cloth. And be damned sure it hasn't been smoked on. If I smell cigarettes, you'll be changing it out." She hung up. She knew she was going to be putting in an extensive stay at the beginning, and she wanted the couch for some sack time. She didn't see herself leaving for the next twenty-four hours minimum.

President Williams had provided her with all the intel that he had been previously given. It was her job to find, and connect, all dots that were currently not in play. She sat down in front of one of the four computers in the office that had been assigned to her. She got to work. Fifteen minutes later there was a knock on her door. She minimized the open windows on all four of the screens before she unlocked the door.

Two agents were standing outside next to a nice dark green overstuffed sofa. "This for you, ma'am?" the taller of the two men asked.

"Yes. Put it along that wall."

The two men brought in the piece of furniture and placed it where she had pointed.

"Will that be all, ma'am?"

"Yes."

The agent seemed to be lagging a bit. "Don't talk much, do you?"

"No." She walked over to the open door and held it as if she were going to close it. The agent took the hint and walked out without saying another word.

She went back and brought her screens back up. *Okay, let's see where the money went.* She started running her fingers over multiple keyboards.

CHAPTER 52

FBI DIRECTOR MATT Sanderson had telephoned the president. "Sir, Saheeb al Hamid just left the storage unit we have under surveillance. He was accompanied my another man. We don't know his identity yet, but we are running him through facial recognition and are gathering fingerprints. By all appearances he has no idea that we've infiltrated or have been watching him. The device has been fitted with a detonator and timing device. The timing device has not been activated. I believe that indicates he is planning on moving It. I also believe he intends to detonate at the racetrack, to make a statement. What are your instructions?"

"Have you passed this information along to Darlene Phillips?"

Sanderson bristled inside. He *hated* having to share intel with someone he considered an outsider. He hated sharing with anybody. "Uh, no, sir. I wanted to tell you first."

President Williams was quiet for a second before continuing. "Okay, for the moment I'll buy that, but Matt, make no mistake, Phillips is coheading my new group tasked to gather and relay information from everybody, and that includes you. If I find out that you are not keeping her in the loop immediately, I am going to be extremely pissed off. Do you understand what I'm saying here?"

"Yes, sir. Permission to ask a question?" Sanderson replied, struggling to keep civility in his voice.

"Of course."

"I guess I don't see the reason for this new group. We were instructed clearly that all agencies should keep in constant communication with each other. Why the need to change direction?"

"Matt, it is not meant as a slam against you, or anyone else, or any agency. We both know that it's no secret that you boys don't particularly like to play nice. While all of you will comply with my explicit guidelines, I'm not so naive as to think that, at times, foot-dragging will not present itself. This new group avoids that, plus it puts the responsibility on their shoulders to gather the information for me, which they will do with each agency's cooperation. Should I be informed that someone is not cooperating, there will be severe consequences. I absolutely do not expect Phillips to have to ask for anything. I demand that as any information is discovered, she immediately be included. Make no mistake, anyone who drags their feet with her *will* be replaced. Phillips is an absolute magician with computers. When I asked around for the best we had, her name came up eight times out of ten recommendations. I have shouldered her with the job of keeping me on top of everything to do with this war on terrorism. Anyone who is not on board with that, or fails to inform her of pertinent information in the most timely manner, will have my boot up their ass. Any other questions?"

"No, sir, you can count on my complete support."

"I know, Matt. I also know you don't like it, but I know you'll do it. Keep Phillips posted." The president clicked off.

Sanderson was angry about the glaring redirection of the information process.

CHAPTER 53

D ARLENE PHILLIPS WAS tired. She had not left the FBI office for thirty-six hours. She couldn't help but laugh at the uproar of the security desk when she had pizza delivered to her the night before. By the time the delivery man had actually been able to convey the pizza to her desk, after the checkpoints, it had cooled. Of course she had requisitioned a microwave from Agent Scribe, whom she imagined was biting his nails off. After a four-hour nap on her couch, she had gone to the dining room and had a good breakfast and three cups of strong coffee, and she was now back at her desk. She was reviewing all her findings. She had tracked the entire money trail, knew all the participants, knew everything about them she needed to know, and was now printing out her report, which she would hand deliver to the president. There was a knock on her door. She walked over to unlock it.

Agent Scribe was standing there. "Why do you find it necessary to lock the door, Ms. Phillips?"

"I don't want to be bothered."

"You do realize you are in FBI headquarters. We are not used to this behavior."

"You mean you're not used to not calling the shots. Look, Agent Scribe, I'm here on a temporary basis; this will not be my home. I'll be set up elsewhere as soon as the equipment I've requested has arrived at its destination. Then I'm out of here. In the meantime, I don't answer to you, only to the president. You got a problem with that, take it up with him. I thought that issue had been resolved."

He looked over at the two printers, which were both busy. Pointing toward them, he stated, "This is what you'll be taking to the president." It was not a question, but a statement.

"Agent Scribe, that is beyond your concern."

"Ms. Phillips, you are not the most pleasant woman I've worked with."

"We do *not* work together. You happen to work in the same building that I'm temporarily housed in. 'Pleasant' is not in my job description. While I'm here, your sole purpose is to provide me with what I need. That has been made more than clear to you, yet here you are wasting my time, unless there is some valid purpose for your visit."

Scribe pulled a manila envelope from underneath his suit jacket and gave it to her. "This is a report on Saheeb al Kazhed. He and another man went into the storage facility and installed a detonator and timing device, which has not been activated, in the device we are watching. Director Sanderson wanted me to make this available immediately. As of yet, we have not identified the second man, but we will have that information soon."

Phillips tossed the envelope onto her desk. "Thank you. I already know that, plus I already know the identity of the second man."

Scribe was stunned. "How in the hell do you know that?"

"That's a question only the president can answer, if he wishes to. I do not share my intel with you, only with President Williams. That's the way the DPO has been set up. Any questions, once again, talk to the president."

Agent Scribe just looked at her for a moment and then, without another word, turned around and left. Phillips retrieved her satellite phone from her desk and punched in the number she had memorized. "Phillips here. I need to brief the president ASAP on the situation."

A voice that she did not recognize informed her that the president would be calling her back shortly.

"I'll be expecting his call," replied Phillips, and she hung up.

CHAPTER 54

LATER THE FOLLOWING morning, Starr received a call from the president on his scrambled satellite phone. "Starr, I want your group to head out to Indianapolis immediately. A fourth man has joined the party. I want all of them. Phillips is ahead of the curve on the intelligence she has been able to provide. I think it would be helpful to bring her along. Pick her up in DC and head out. Call her and tell her where and when. Keep me posted." He hung up. Starr never said a single word during the conversation.

He walked over to the gym where he found Christman. "J. C., the Man called and wants us up and moving. Where's Styles?"

"He said he was going for a run."

"Thanks. Meet in the dining room in an hour," Starr instructed.

Starr returned to the house and retrieved a semiautomatic twelve-gauge shotgun. He walked out to the side yard and fired four shots in a prearranged sequence. He knew Styles would hear them and head back to the house.

Christman came running out of the barn that housed the gym, looking wild-eyed. "What the hell was that?"

"Sorry, J. C., should have told ya. If Styles is out on the property and we need him, we fire the twelve-gauge in that sequence. The 'not-so-secret' signal."

Ten minutes later Styles came running up, breathing evenly. "What's up?"

Starr answered, "President called, wants us up and running to Indiana. We gotta pick up Phillips in DC, told Christman to meet in the dining room in an hour." Looking at his watch, he said, "Make that fifty minutes."

"Okay."

Forty-five minutes later all three were seated around the dining room table.

Starr started. "As I told you, the president called and wants us to move on the targets in Indianapolis. They are now a party of four. Phillips will read us in on all the logistics when we pick her up. Right now I think we just need to decide what to bring, and that's your call, Marv."

"Got it. I've been thinking about that already, and considering the circumstances we're under, I've got a plan loosely mapped out. Depending on exactly what we find when we get there, I'm probably going to have to take them out from a good distance behind the FBI sniper teams. I don't want to take any chance of them getting in the way, or having enough response time to get a location fix on me."

Christman spoke up. "Styles, okay if I ask you a question?"

"Sure, J. C. Hell, we're all the same team here."

"How far out can you set up? FBI could be three hundred yards out, maybe more."

"I'm pretty comfortable out to about two thousand yards."

Christman thought for a second and then blurted out, "That's over a fucking mile."

"Yep."

Starr just smiled. "That's why we've got sonny boy here." He turned to Styles. "So you got your gear pretty well lined up?"

"Yeah, I'll take my own rifle plus Bertha." That was the nickname he'd given the big fifty-caliber Barrett. "And the usual stuff. Back the

'Burb up; I'll have the weaponry packed in fifteen minutes. I've already got two bags packed for personal gear."

"Starr, what do I need to bring?" asked Christman.

"Just your flying skills, buddy boy. Ten-day supply of clothes should be good."

Styles allowed himself a smirk. "Well, that makes it official, J. C.; you're part of the group now. He's stuck you with one of his asshole nicknames," he said, causing a chuckle from all three.

"All right, we head out in half an hour to Knoxville," Starr directed.

The other two nodded in agreement.

CHAPTER 55

THE SPECIALTY JET containing Starr, Styles, and Phillips, with Christman at the controls, was banking away from Washington, DC, headed for Indianapolis. No pleasantries had been exchanged when Phillips came aboard, just the customary nods. Phillips had immediately retreated to the rear of the plane and started spreading paperwork about the tables on board. Starr and Styles left her alone until they sensed she was ready for them to join her.

Phillips started the conversation. "Okay, guys, here's the short version. Most you already know. Here's what you don't that's pertinent. The ID of the man who joined Saheeb al Kazhed—he's the frontman for Eastern Global—is one Akbar al Hamid, a.k.a. Gino Salerno. Until recently he was a maintenance worker—highly thought of, actually—at Madison Square Garden. He was responsible for the device that was planted there but failed to explode. The reason appears to be just pure dumb luck. The detonator was faulty. Otherwise, we'd be missing a shitload of New York City." She paused before continuing, with a small grin. "The FBI and CIA still don't know al Hamid's identity, though they should before the day is out, unless they're even slower than I think. I swear they've got people at Quantico that can't find their asses with both hands." It was obvious that Phillips had been less than impressed by Quantico. Then her face turned to one of puzzlement. "The one thing even I can't find is the IDs of the two men with al Kazhed already at the Holiday Inn. I'm fairly certain they're Afghanis, but nothing positive yet. I have four searches continuing as we speak. Whoever they are, they have kept one hell of a low profile.

"Currently the bomb has been rendered useless; you may already know that. However, al Kazhed and al Hamid entered the storage unit yesterday. The device has been armed, and a timer installed but not yet activated, which leads to the credible belief that they intend on moving the van containing the bomb to the racetrack itself. It appears that these bastards want to make a statement. The race is Sunday, so it is believed they will move the van Saturday. Plus, I intercepted a communication from someone in Indianapolis. No names were mentioned, but I think it must've been the pilot flying al Kazhed's private jet. He said 'they' would be on their way home Saturday night. No flight plan has been filed as of yet. My guess is they don't want to attract any undue attention by leaving Indianapolis before the biggest event of the year. I think they will file just before departure. Any questions?"

Starr nodded and said, "Good work, Phillips. Sounds to me like you've got it center punched."

Styles looked her straight in the eyes and merely gave a nod, which was returned.

Phillips sat down, and the two men joined her. She then asked, "So you guys got a plan yet?"

Starr answered. "Not defined. We need to recon the area, see what we have to work with."

Phillips pushed a stack of paperwork toward him. "You might find these useful. It's a complete set of satellite photos covering a four-mile circumference around the Holiday Inn positioned in the center. You'll have to tape the photos together, but it gives you a highly detailed overhead view of what you've got there."

Styles reached over in front of Starr and picked up a few of the photographs. He looked very carefully at them, then put them down and looked at Phillips. "Nice, Phillips, real nice. These will help. Good forethought."

"See, Styles, I can be more than just a pretty face or pain in the ass." For the first time, Starr and Styles saw her smile. Then she added, "And I'm not done yet," as she tossed Styles a new roll of Scotch tape.

This time it was Styles and Starr's turn to smile.

Right then the cabin speakers came to life. "Excuse me, this is your captain speaking," Christman said. "Any chance somebody could fill me in on what the fuck is going on?"

Starr winced. "Jeez, it's hard to find good help." He went forward to talk to Christman while Styles and Phillips remained at the table.

Phillips stated, "Let's turn all the photos over. Each one is numbered, so all we gotta do is count and tape."

Styles looked at her with newfound respect. "Seriously, Phillips, you really came through here. He reached over and offered her his hand. She looked at him for a second, then shook it firmly.

"Least I could do for being such an ass last time. Besides, I couldn't lose face in front of such a hard case as you," she laughed.

Styles just grinned and started pulling off short pieces of tape, and within ten minutes they had a nice complete picture of an aerial shot of the Indianapolis racetrack and surrounding area.

Just as they'd finished, Starr returned from filling in Christman. "Christ, I don't believe it; you two actually got something done without being told."

As if they'd rehearsed it, they simultaneously snapped "Fuck you" to Starr, and all three laughed.

CHAPTER 56

SAHEEB AL KAZHED was feeling very satisfied. He had taken Akbar al Hamid to the storage facility and watched as al Hamid had armed the bomb with the detonator and installed the timing device. He even had al Hamid instruct him on how to set the timer, which would not be readied until after the van had been moved over to the racetrack. The idea of driving with a nuclear bomb behind him, with the timer's electrical circuits complete, did not sit well with him. "We shall drive the van over Saturday afternoon; I have already chosen the location. One of us will follow."

"That is good, Saheeb. As you saw, I used a different type of detonator than in New York. I do not want another failure."

"If, indeed, the detonator was a failure," Saheeb said.

That statement made al Hamid cringe. It was a declaration that al Kazhed was still not convinced that the New York failure was not his fault. He had made his case already and thought it better to say nothing.

"What of the Afghanis?" al Hamid asked.

"After we move the truck, we shall pick them up at the motel. Then we drive to the airport and go home. I will have you go to Miami and await instructions for the next event. I need to discuss this with Ami al Hadid. You will have a flight ticket so you do not have to ride a bus. You will also be given an amount of cash to help you settle. It is important that you blend in and not arouse suspicion. That should be easy in Miami." "Thank you for the plane ticket. I shall do as you say."

The jet containing the president's group was descending into the Indianapolis Airport. Christman had been vectored in and was scheduled number three to land. He received instructions on which hangar was expecting their plane. Arrangements had also been made for two vehicles—one Ford F-350 windowless cargo van and a Ford Crown Victoria sedan—for their use.

The flight had lasted less than an hour. Styles was amazed at how fast their jet was.

Once again, Christman's voice came over the speakers. "This is your captain speaking; please be kind enough to park your asses in the seats while I land. Thank you for flying 'Presidential Air.'" The three in the cabin could hear him laughing to himself as he clicked the mike off.

Styles and Phillips could hear Starr grumble, "Great, next he'll be doing stand-up."

Christman executed the landing perfectly, and in five minutes they were shutting down outside a hangar at the far end of the airport. As Christman opened the door and the departure stairs automatically lowered into place, two agents from the US Marshall's Service were waiting for them. One of them asked, "Which one of you is Starr?"

"Here."

The Marshall handed him a manila envelope and two sets of keys, and both turned and walked away without speaking.

"What's in there?" asked Styles.

"The only thing I know for sure is the directions to a safe house the marshalls operate," Starr answered.

"Didn't look real happy with us using it," Styles remarked.

"Get used to it. We're gonna get that a lot."

"I've gotten that most of my career."

"Well, you probably deserved it," Starr chided.

"I tried."

"Probably not too hard," Phillips added.

At that point the airport's maintenance crew was wheeling the jet inside the hangar.

"Thanks guys," yelled Starr as they were leaving in their cart. When they were out of sight he said, "Marv, back the van inside and we'll offload the gear," and tossed the keys to Styles, who caught them while walking toward the vehicle. He climbed up into it and proceeded to back it up next to the jet. He then got out and opened the back doors. He was pleased to see shelving had been installed in the back. The van was dark blue with heavily tinted windows, and it was impossible to see inside. Twenty minutes later the van was loaded and they were ready to roll. Christman double-checked to be sure the plane was locked up, and he then joined the group.

Starr stated, "J. C., you and Phillips follow us in the Crown Vic. This house is about ten miles outside of town. It's supposed to be pretty private. We'll go check it out and decide what we need."

Twenty-five minutes later they pulled up into a long driveway that led to a nice-sized ranch-style house. They parked the two vehicles out front of the two-car garage, and the first thing Styles did was walk the perimeter. Starr and Christman unpacked the weapons and brought them into the living room, placing everything on the floor so that Styles could sort them as he wanted. Phillips unloaded the personal bags, placing them in individual bedrooms. She decided to take the bedroom with a bath complete with tub.

When Phillips got everyone's bags in their bedrooms, she quickly checked the kitchen and, surprisingly enough, found it well stocked. Then she went back into the living room and informed Starr of her discovery. "The kitchen's got about everything we need. Coffee, food, basic staples. Somebody was thoughtful." Then she took a look at the small armory on the floor. "Holy shit, we going to war?" she asked abruptly.

"Marv likes to be prepared," Starr replied.

"What in the hell is that?" she asked, pointing at the big Barrett.

Starr grinned. "That's Bertha, a fifty-cal Barrett. He loves that thing. His personal rifle is inside the unopened case. No one is allowed to touch that. Seriously folks, don't fuck with that one. He'll tear your arm off if you do. He may throw a bitch fit at me just for bringing it in. It's custom made to his own specs, and he's *real* touchy about it."

"Damn straight I am," Styles snarled as he entered the room. "Next time leave it in the fucking truck. Starr, I'm not kidding. Nobody touches my rifle. Or the case."

"Settle down, Marv; I was just explaining that little item. Sorry, I should have left it alone; didn't think you'd be upset about just bringing it in. Won't happen again."

Both Christman and Phillips were outright stunned at Styles's harsh outburst. Starr realized he'd fucked up and wanted Styles to realize it was certainly done unintentionally.

Styles just looked at him hard for a moment, then let it pass. "We got bedroom assignments?"

"Phillips took care of that," Starr answered swiftly.

"You're down the hall, second on the left," Phillips added just as quickly.

Styles grabbed his gun case and went to his bedroom.

Christman said softly, "Jesus, Starr, you're right. I would not want him pissed at me."

Phillips only nodded in agreement.

CHAPTER 57

FOR THE NEXT forty-five minutes, Styles went about transferring his armory into his bedroom, arranging it as he saw fit, in complete silence. When he finished, he went back into the dining room. He saw that Phillips had pinned the taped-together overhead photograph to one wall. He walked over to it to study it. "Thanks for putting 'north' at the top," he said, addressing Phillips. She just nodded in return. "I'm serious, thanks. For whatever odd reason, I read maps easier when north is at the top."

"Yeah, I'm the same way."

He just nodded in acknowledgment without looking at her.

Starr walked in from the kitchen and gave Styles the keys to the Crown Victoria sitting in the driveway. Styles nodded in acknowledgment. He spent the next fifteen minutes studying the photograph, then abruptly turned and walked out the door. Then he started the car and drove away.

Christman walked into the dining room from the backyard, where he'd been sitting. "Styles is some hard case, huh?" he said to Starr.

"Yeah. Let's all sit for a couple of minutes."

Phillips and Christman joined him at the table.

"Let me explain a little about Styles. He's pretty much a one-man show. Always been that way. The whole time he was a sniper in the Corp, he never had a spotter. Hell, the last few tours he didn't even report to the camp CO. Styles was a sort of special one-man operation. His mission was to kill the enemy, any means necessary. And nobody, I mean nobody, does or did it better. Don't get me wrong; he's not fucked in the head—a psycho who gets some kind of thrill out of it. He just happens to be the best at what he does, and he recognizes that. He also has a pretty strong hatred toward these zealots that like to blow up people. But I don't want you two thinking that killing people floats his boat. To him it's a job that needs to be done. And his internal wiring allows him to do that and sleep comfortably at night."

Christman spoke first. "I gotta tell you, Starr, when he came in and steamed about his rifle, he scared me."

"He can have that effect, J. C., no doubt about it."

Phillips added, "So you're telling us that he is 'all there,' right?"

"Absolutely, Phillips; no need to worry about that."

"Then why did he get so pissed about you bringing in his rifle?"

"Those are the tools of his trade. His life depends on them. He needs them to do his job. A carpenter might have certain tools that he doesn't want anyone else using. He's no different."

Phillips nodded, understanding.

"Starr," Christman said, "so you're saying, with no question, that Styles would not 'go off' on us, right? I want that made perfectly clear."

"J. C., trust me on this. I've known this man over fifteen years. There is no one I respect more. Or trust. All the joking between us— that's just our way. I do want to make one thing crystal clear, though. If you guys ever think about selling this country out for any reason, don't. He has acknowledged you as part of 'his' team. To betray our country would be personal for him. He is definitely the deadliest man I've ever known, and I would put him up against anybody. He's done things that would sound like pure fiction—scenes from a writer's imagination."

Christman and Phillips were silent for a few moments. Then Christman spoke. "Hell, Starr, his fucking workouts are straight out of science fiction."

Starr continued. "There's something else I want you to understand. Right here, right now, is the most structured undertaking he's ever attempted. Even as a child, from what he's told me, he was pretty much a loner. He spent a lot of time in the woods and a lot of time in martial arts schools, or whatever they call them now. I will also tell you this: he has accepted both of you. It surprised me that happened as quickly as it did. I think he followed my lead in that. If he hadn't, you damn sure wouldn't be here."

"Does he trust us, Starr?" Phillips asked.

"I trust you because the president trusts you. He trusts you, or is at least willing to try, because I trust you. So I guess you could say he does trust you, twice removed."

"Huh?" Christman blurted out.

"Let me make this easy, okay? Styles is either your best friend or your worst fucking nightmare. There is little in between with him. He does not have casual friends. Has no need for them. But the people he trusts, or maybe even more importantly accepts, he would walk through hell and back for. I've seen him do it more than once, and hell was sorry that he visited."

Everyone was quiet for a bit. Then Phillips spoke. "That night at Camp David, when we all had dinner … When he shot me down, I saw something in his eyes that I've never seen before. Hell, I can't even tell you what it was. I don't scare easily. But those eyes, those eyes scared me—even more than those fucking knives flying past my ears. I'm glad you told us this shit, Starr. I know it'll make me feel more at ease with him."

"Yeah, me too," added Christman. "Where'd he go anyway?"

"Recon. Phillips, you made big brownie points with him with those aerial shots. He was positively giddy." Then the table erupted with laughter and the tension disappeared.

CHAPTER 58

STARR'S CELL PHONE rang. It was Styles. "Yeah."

"I'll be back shortly. See if pizza is good for everybody, and how they want it."

"Hey, Styles wants to bring back pizza. What do you guys like on it?"

Christman answered, "Meat lover here."

Phillips, back in her bedroom, hollered out, "Everything."

"We got two meat lovers and one everything."

"Got it. Be back soon."

Forty-five minutes later Styles came through the front door with four large pizzas. "Got these from a family joint; looks like they'll be good." He threw packets of red pepper and parmesan cheese down on the table.

"Smells good," Christman said, walking into the dining room with Phillips right behind him.

"I'll say; I'm starving," she said.

Starr came in carrying four dinner plates and silverware. "Anybody up for a beer? We got Bud Lite or Heineken."

"Bud Lite for me," said Phillips.

"Same," answered Christman.

Starr looked at Styles, and he just nodded. Starr came back with four bottles of Bud Lite.

Soon all four were devouring the pizza with everyone agreeing how good it was.

Styles turned the conversation back to their assignment. "I did a recon of the area. Phillips, you've done a damned good job of recon yourself. That info packet you had helped. I saw the rooms where the targets are. Two rooms side by side, second floor, and one on the other side of the building, bottom floor. I've got my primary FFP picked out for the first two rooms, and a backup if necessary. About a thousand yards out. Those FBI clowns might as well be wearing hunter orange, they stick out so bad. Starr, call whoever and tell them to hide those idiots better. I'd be amazed if they haven't been made. Like I said, the third room is on the other side of the building. Best way would be to try to catch the fourth guy meeting the others. Not sure how we can do that. I'll use my rifle with the suppressor. There's an abandoned building that will work well for the FFP. Once I'm set in place, Starr, you have everybody and everything packed and ready to go. When I signal, you pick me up. Because of the suppressor, the FBI won't know where the shots are really coming from, other than from somewhere behind them. By the time they can get choppers up, we'll be long gone." He paused to eat more pizza.

Phillips asked, "What's an FFP?"

Starr answered, "Final Firing Point."

She nodded and then interjected. "I think I can handle getting the fourth guy out. I can send him a text message on his cell, bring him over to the other rooms. Would that work for you?"

Styles nodded and said, "Yeah. I'd like to take them at night. I got one of those new An/Pus-10 night scopes. It mounts directly in front of the big Leopold. Damn thing is HD quality. Plus I got a new toy." He purposely waited to make Starr ask.

"Well?" Starr finally said.

Styles grinned. "I've got a new prototype infrared night scope. I want to try it out tonight. I'm told it can 'see' through walls, including standard concrete block. After dinner I'm going to go out, and I want you guys to position yourselves in different places. I'll call Starr and see if I can pick up your heat signatures. If it works, it'll work out to fifteen hundred yards, maybe more."

"You're shittin' me," exclaimed Christman.

"Nope. I've never used one before, but I'm told it really works."

Phillips piped up. "Well, when I'm in the shower, you give me that thing."

"Don't worry, Phillips; it only gives a basic outline—more of a blob, really."

Christman started chuckling and said, "Hey Phillips, nice blobs." That got everyone laughing as Phillips threw a piece of pizza crust at his head.

When dinner was over and the dishes squared away, Styles took his new scope outside and walked down the driveway to the street. He picked a spot where he could see through the trees. He wondered if the shrubs out front would interfere. He dialed Starr and said, "Okay, I'm checking it out." Three yellowish-reddish images appeared in the scope. One in the kitchen, one in a bedroom, and Phillips, he guessed, hunkered down in the bathtub. *Nice try, Phillips*, he thought. He heard Starr ask over the phone, "Well?"

"Tell Phillips that if she's gonna take a bath, she might want to take her clothes off."

CHAPTER 59

PRESIDENT ROBERT WILLIAMS had just finished with a briefing from Director Bernard Backersley from the CIA. They had identified the fourth man who had joined Saheeb al Kazhed in Indianapolis. During this meeting Backersley had been directed to start feeding his information, in real time, to the president's new group, the Department of the Presidential Office. Backersley had not been happy.

"With all due respect, Mr. President, it just seems one more mouth to feed. I understood your initial direction of sharing with the FBI and Homeland Security, but now this new task force? I don't see the need."

"That's because you see so far ahead of everybody else, Bernard. Unfortunately, that same ability of yours at times disallows you to see what is to the side of you. If all the agencies wire into the new DPO in real time, none of you will actually have to stop what you're doing to inform me of developments. That enables you to focus all your attention, and time, on the purpose at hand. It takes all responsibility off your shoulders to keep me informed. It will be done on an automatic basis by this new staff. It is not intended as any type of affront to you or anyone else. It's about efficiency, Bernard, just efficiency. You should be able to understand that easily enough. Remember, presently it only involves terrorism. All other CIA concerns remain within the CIA and are related to me only when necessary."

"Sir, if I may ask, what was the reaction of the others?"

"Same as you, bitching like hell about it. Luckily for me, this is not a debate; it's an order. This is how it will be done. And exactly like I told everybody else, if someone doesn't like it, there's the door."

Backersley knew he wasn't even going to come close to winning this argument. He had thought he could keep the CIA exempt from this new group, but that wasn't going to happen. Not while this president was in office anyway; that was clear. "All right, sir, but for the record, I don't like it."

"Noted, Bernard, but then, for the record, you don't like anything that isn't your way."

"Yes, sir." Backersley got up to leave. "I hope you're right."

As soon as Backersley left, the president picked up his phone and dialed a new extension number that only he had.

"Merritt here, sir." Coverley Merritt had been handpicked by the president to be the public lead of his new DPO. Merritt had come over from the intelligence section of the FBI. Merritt's old boss, Matt Sanderson, had been incensed when the president had tapped him for the position.

"Are you getting the intel from all the agencies in an appropriate manner time-wise?"

"Not bad considering this department is forty-eight hours old and all of them hate my guts."

"It's not you; it's the department."

"Guilt by association, sir."

"Yeah, unfortunately," agreed the president. "They'll get used to it."

"Eventually, sir. So far, though, I can't realistically expect any more for the moment."

"All right, Merritt. Let me know immediately if you suspect anyone of dragging their feet."

"Absolutely, sir." With that, the conversation ended.

President Williams grabbed another phone and called Starr on his secure satellite line. Starr answered on the third ring. "Yes, sir."

"Starr, we've a little more intel for you. Merritt will be sending it to Phillips. We've got the identity of the fourth man at the hotel."

"Sorry to disappoint you, sir"—Starr grinned since the president couldn't see him—"but we've had that information since this morning."

Silence. Then, with a hint of irritation in his voice, he just said, "Phillips?"

"Yes, sir, she's as good as you said she was. Anybody that pisses her off might find pizza for all of Yankee Stadium billed to their credit card account."

The president just sighed audibly, which Starr clearly heard.

Finally President Williams spoke. "So what is your timetable?"

"Day after tomorrow, early evening, sir."

"Evening?"

"Yes, sir. Styles's decision. It's his call. He'll change that if necessary."

"All right. Keep me posted."

"Sir, there's one other thing."

"Yes?"

Styles scoped the area this afternoon and wanted me to tell somebody to have the, and I'm quoting here, 'FBI clowns pull back because they might as well be wearing hunter orange,' or something like that." Starr could hear the president openly groan.

"He does have a way with words, doesn't he, Starr?"

"Yes, sir, he certainly does."

CHAPTER 60

THE NEXT MORNING, Styles was up before dawn and went on a quick fifteen-mile run. On his way back to the safe house, he stopped at a Hardee's fast-food restaurant and grabbed breakfast for everybody. He got back to the house and walked in just as Starr was making coffee.

"I figured you went out for a run."

"You should've come with me."

"Yeah," Starr deadpanned.

Styles threw the bags on the table. "Breakfast. Others up yet?"

"Yeah, both in the showers."

Right then, Christman came walking in. "One of my very favorite smells. Hey, who got breakfast?"

"Guess," said Styles.

"Thanks, Styles, you're gonna make a good husband to somebody someday."

"Bite me, J. C."

"Styles is getting married?" asked Phillips as she walked in feigning total surprise.

Without looking up, Styles just flipped her off, which brought a chuckle from the other three.

When the four had sat down and were spreading out the food, Styles told them he wanted to go over the basic plan. "I need you guys to know that I've always worked alone, so this is a bit of an adjustment for me. I've got something worked out, but I want anyone to feel free to speak up." He looked around and received nods from everyone. "I'm going to get what gear I'll need together, then, later, we're going to take the rest back to the plane. I'm going to set up at the FFP tomorrow after lunch. After that, you guys come back here and clear out the house. Be sure to wipe for prints. Thoroughly. Starr got us radio headsets, so we'll be in constant touch. We'll switch channels every fifteen minutes. Starr, you make up the schedule. Once the house is cleared, J. C. and Phillips will go back to the plane. Phillips, I need you to monitor FBI communications. Anything that comes up, let me know. Also I'll have you text the fourth guy over to this Kazhed character's room. Figure around seven. We'll anchor that down later. J. C., you file a flight plan to New York. We'll figure wheels up around seven forty-five, maybe eight. Starr, I'll show you where I want you to park. Have the Crown Vic. J. C., make sure the van is cleared of prints, and vacuum it out thoroughly. There's a Shop-Vac at the hangar. Phillips, when I give you the signal, after the last guy's joined the party, I want you to trigger the fire alarm. This should get the four outside. I'll be shooting the Lapua 6.5 × 47 round; should be like fish in a barrel. Once the targets are down, I'll book it along to Starr and we'll meet up with you back at the hangar. Once we get there, as I'm stowing my gear, you three clear the Crown Vic, including vacuuming. Once the vehicles are clean, we leave. When J. C. thinks it's time, we'll divert to DC. Phillips, pay particular attention and see if the FBI determines where the shots came from. Like I said, I don't think they will, but best not take chances. Starr, we'll take it nice and slow back to the hangar; don't need to get pulled over by the local LEOs. We're going to be stirring a up a hornet's nest here, so Phillips, draft J. C. to help in any way he can. Feedback, anybody?"

The other three looked at each other, then back at Styles, shaking their heads.

Starr spoke up. "It sounds pretty basic, Marv. Either of you got any questions?" He looked at Christman and Phillips.

"No," they answered in unison.

"All right then. Once we get breakfast squared away, let's all take a drive in the Crown Vic, and I'll show you guys around. I want you to get a feel for what's involved, on my side of this operation. This afternoon I'm going to do a workout. Phillips can monitor FBI chatter. Starr will make up our radio frequency channel schedule and J. C., you can do whatever. Tonight we'll take the rest of my gear back to the plane." He paused. "Oh yeah, tonight dinner is on somebody else."

CHAPTER 61

PHILLIPS HAD FOUR laptops set up in a semicircle on the coffee table in the living room, allowing her to watch all four simultaneously. She was studying one intently when Styles walked past her heading out to start his workout. Noticing her concentration, complete with a frown, he stopped and asked what was interesting her so intently.

"Not sure, Styles, something weird."

Styles sat down across from her. "Whaddya mean?"

"These laptops are feeding from the computers back at Quantico, which I set up to monitor different communications. Well, three of them anyway. The fourth is my designated hacker. In the last hour, I've had two cell phone communications originate in Saudi Arabia from Global Eastern's corporate offices—same number that I linked to al Kazhed."

"Where are they going?

"To a burn phone in DC. I've already tracked the phone; it was purchased from Walmart and paid for with cash. Four others were also purchased, but they haven't been activated."

"Washington?" he said surprised.

"Yeah. Something isn't right. Signal's being bounced around, but I got a lock on it. Right now I'm pulling up the GPS coordinates on the phone's location."

"You can do that—actually find the damned phone?"

Phillips just looked at him.

"Sorry, I'm just not that up on cell phone technology," Styles said.

"No problem. Yeah, a cell phone is many things, one of them being a tracking device. Lot of people don't realize that. As long as the phone is turned on, I can track it. If it's shut off or the battery pulled out—or the memory card, for that matter—I can't. But this one's on, and I'm almost there."

Styles sat silently, watching her work, amazed at how fast her fingers were flying over the keyboard.

Suddenly Phillips straightened up and exclaimed, *"Shit!"*

"What?"

She looked up at Styles and simply said, "The White House—that fucking call is going into the White House."

"What?" Styles exploded.

"Yeah, somebody in the White House is talking to Global Eastern."

Styles immediately got up and yelled for Starr, who came running in from the backyard deck.

"What's up?"

"Tell him, Phillips," Styles directed.

"We've got somebody in the White House, on a burn phone, talking to somebody at Global Eastern on the same number that I linked to Saheeb al Kazhed. It's happening right now," she informed him, never taking her eyes off the screen.

Starr didn't waste a second. He raced into his own bedroom and grabbed his satellite phone and dialed the president. The phone rang at least ten times before President Williams picked up.

"Yes, Richard, what's going on?" asked the president.

"Sir, right now, this very second, someone inside the White House is talking on a burn phone to the same number at Global Eastern that Phillips linked to Saheeb al Kazhed. I find that odd, to say the least. Not trying to overstep my responsibility here, but can you think of any reason anyone in your administration would be speaking with Global Eastern?"

"No. Richard, are you certain of that?"

"Absolutely, sir, no mistake. Phillips is tracking the call as we speak. Wait a minute; she just signaled the connection's been cut."

"Starr," Phillips stated emphatically, "Absolutely no doubt. The call originated from Global Eastern to the White House."

"Sir," said Starr, addressing the president, "Phillips just confirmed that the call came from Global Eastern to the White House."

"Richard, I don't even want to think of what that means."

"Sir, I don't know if it would be best to try to flush out whoever made that call now, or even if that would be possible. If someone in your administration is using a burn phone, chances are he won't be carrying it on him, and it's probably shut off. Sir, hold on just a second; Phillips is gesturing to me."

"Starr, I can fake a phone call from Global Eastern to the burn phone. If it's turned off, obviously it won't be answered, but I could leave a message. It would make sense that the caller would check for messages sooner or later, which means the phone has to be turned back on. I can run a program that would let us know immediately when that occurs. 'Borrowing' GPS tracking satellites, I can nail that phone down to within three feet of its location if it's powered up for forty-five seconds. I can overlay the point on a White House sectional plan and tell them exactly where it is."

"Sir, Phillips can fake a message to the burn phone, know when it's turned on, track the damned thing to within three feet, and tell you exactly where it is. The phone has to be on for forty-five seconds though."

"How the hell—"

"It's Phillips, sir. She's better than you said."

"Do it," the president snapped. "And this obviously stays between us."

"Done." He hung up. Turning to Phillips, he said, "Do whatever you gotta do, but get it done."

"Already on it. Do me a favor; get me the blue bag out of my bedroom. I've got to put these things on power adaptors; don't want to lose the batteries at a bad time."

Starr retrieved the bag and handed it to her.

"Here, take these two extension cords and plug them into two separate house circuits. Bring me the ends," Phillips instructed.

Styles was impressed. Phillips's eyes had never left the four screens; nor her fingers the keyboards.

"There," she stated with finality. "Soon as that burn phone turns on, the program will automatically track it. It won't matter if I'm watching. If that thing stays on for forty-five seconds, if it's in a closet, I'll tell him which shelf it's on."

Styles got up, walked over to her, and lightly punched her in the arm. "That's some serious ass-kickin', girl, serious ass-kickin'."

Phillips just looked up and grinned. "These assholes don't have a chance."

CHAPTER 62

B Y TWO O'CLOCK the following afternoon, Friday, Styles was in place. According to his laser range finder, he was exactly 1,080 yards away from the Holiday Inn. He had set up on the fifth floor, which allowed a perfect sight line to the target—the abandoned building. According to the paperwork on the door, it was scheduled for demolition the following week. *Perfect timing*, Styles thought. The foursome had spent the previous late afternoon and early evening reconnoitering the area, going over the plan repeatedly, transferring all the extra gear back to the plane, and eating dinner out at a chain steak house. Starr had picked up the tab.

Styles was reflecting on a conversation from the previous evening. Christman had asked him why he would set up in the early afternoon if the plan wasn't to start until around 1900. "Want to keep an eye out. Plus, if the opportunity comes up before, I'm there to take it." Christman, nodding, had understood the point.

When Starr calculated the radio frequency schedule, he had also assigned everyone a simple call sign. Styles was designated Point One; Starr, Point Two; Phillips, Point Three; and Christman, Point Four.

"How come Phillips is three, and I'm four?" Christman complained humorously.

"We don't want her whining about discrimination," Starr quipped.

"If brains counted, I'd be P-One," Phillips said, giving it right back to Starr.

Presently, Styles was set up with his spotter's scope mounted on a tripod and his modified M40A3 marine sniper rifle next to him. Seeing as how lit up the motel had been the previous evening, he doubted he would need the night scope. He felt his big Leopold would work just fine. He was twenty-five feet inside the exterior wall, looking through a broken-out window. He could not be seen from the outside. Now it was just a matter of patience, something that much of his life had been about.

Styles's radio headset crackled to life. "Point One, no pertinent chatter," Phillips stated curtly.

"Copy," Styles confirmed.

Phillips had provided Styles with some excellent photographs of his four targets. *Wonder if the FBI would mind if they knew she'd borrowed these,* he thought. He had seen each of the two unnamed Afghanis come out of their room, just standing and looking around from the handrail of the second-floor walkway. He had also seen Saheeb al Kazhed twice: once going down to the motel's office, and once to the restaurant, from which he emerged with three bags of food. Upon returning, he went inside the Afghanis' room, and he came out forty minutes later holding a large take-out drink container. Afterward, he went back into his own room.

"Point One, just intercepted a cell call. Kazhed wants al Hadid to come to his room at six thirty. No reason given," Phillips informed him.

"Copy. Once Hadid is inside with the door closed, I'll have you activate the alarm. Two out of each room is easier."

"Copy, Point One," Phillips replied.

The weather could not have been cooperating any better. It was a crystal-clear day with little to no breeze. When traffic was light, one could clearly hear the racers at the track dialing in their cars. At six-thirty there would be ample sunlight with the sun just setting at Styles's back. The afternoon wore on with little conversation. Starr had reported every time a local LEO cruised past, as well as that there was no helicopter activity.

Phillips contacted Styles. "Point One, update. Sanderson is having a shit fit 'cause they can't get the glass-vibration listening devices to work They think the curtain is too heavy and muffling the voices. Also, reports are that all aircraft is to be strictly monitored."

"Copy."

"Point One, you've got two gangbangers entering the building from the east side," Starr reported.

Shit, Styles thought. He looked at his watch. Ten minutes of six. He did not need these guys here. Styles had chosen the fifth floor to avoid any potential overhead utility wires in his shot path. He could hear their voices from below; they seemed to be heading for the stairs. He quietly made his way over to the stairs and listened. The intruders were definitely walking upward. From the bits and pieces he could hear of their conversation, they were there to indulge in their apparent drug habit. This was not going to work. He thought about what the president had said about innocent civilians, and in Styles's mind, these two did not qualify. He made his decision. He traveled down to the third floor landing silently and passed through a doorway, leaving it slightly ajar. Within seconds, the two were climbing right toward him.

"We go up to the roof, nice and quiet there. Won't be nobody to bother us," the taller of the two said to the other.

"Uh huh," the second man slurred.

As they passed Styles on the landing, he pulled his silenced .40-caliber Beretta and shot both men in the back of the head. They never knew what happened. Styles quickly approached the bodies and went through their pockets. He quickly found a baggie of heroin, and he spread it around to make it look like a drug deal gone bad. Less than two minutes later, he was back in position, feeling no remorse.

"Point Two, all clear," Styles reported to Starr.

"Copy," Starr returned, with no doubt the men were dead.

"Point One," Phillips broke in. "Cell phone interception indicates take-out food to be delivered to Kazhed's room. ETA is seven-thirty. Food for four."

"Copy. Stay with the plan."

At six twenty-five, Akbar al Hamid turned the far corner of the exterior walkway of the motel and approached Saheeb al Kazhed's room.

"Point Three, subject two approaching subject one. On my mark, trip the alarm."

"Copy, Point One."

Styles was now watching through his rifle's scope. He watched al Hamid knock, and he saw the door open wide, the two men greeting each other. The door then closed.

Styles was set. His rifle was set up on its bipod, resting atop an old wooden crate he'd found. He gently swung the scope back and forth between the two rooms. He finally concentrated on al Kazhed's room. "Point Three, *mark*."

"Copy, mark now."

Styles watched and waited. Without actually seeing, he could sense activity transpiring at the motel. Six seconds later al Kazhed's door opened and the two men stepped out, looking around. Styles sighted on Saheeb al Kazhed first, one inch above the bridge of his nose. He squeezed the trigger. He smoothly racked the bolt action on his rifle, placing the second bullet in the firing chamber. He sighted on Akbar al Hamid in the exact same location and gently squeezed the trigger. He swung the rifle to the Afghanis' room and waited. Several seconds passed, and then the door opened slowly. He could see one of the Afghani men peering out, with a puzzled look on his face. Opening it completely, he walked out, with the second man close behind. Styles lined up on the second man first, who was actually still inside the room, but in the doorway. He had decided to take this target first, as that would not allow the first man anywhere to hide. After placing the crosshairs of the scope in the familiar position, he squeezed the trigger. The man disappeared back into the room. He easing his rifle slightly to the left, and the fourth target filled the scope. One final squeeze of the trigger, and this assignment was complete. He lowered his rifle and grabbed his spotting scope to survey the scene: three blood splatters on the wall of the rooms, three bodies on the ground, and one body lying backward across the threshold of the motel room.

"Point two, assignment complete," Styles radioed Starr.

"Copy."

Styles quickly swung the bipod of his rifle to the up position, placed his rifle in the aluminum case, and quickly picked up his four brass cartridge shells. He placed those back inside his box of ammo and then placed that and the spotting scope assembly, along with the gun case, in a duffel bag and snapped its flap cover shut. He then carried it over to the stairway to go meet Starr. Two floors below, he walked around the two bodies of the men he'd shot. He didn't even pause to look at them, as he had already displaced them from his mind. Upon reaching the street level he paused and looked around carefully before leaving the building. As he approached the street, Starr came driving up and stopped. Styles opened the rear door and placed the duffel bag on the backseat, closed the door, opened up the passenger door, and seated himself beside Starr. As previously arranged, no communication via the radio headsets was to be initiated except for an emergency. Wordlessly the two headed for the airport.

CHAPTER 63

MATT SANDERSON, DIRECTOR of the FBI, was screaming maniacally. His entire surveillance operation of the four terrorist suspects had just literally been blown away, right in front of him.

"Who took those shots? Goddamn it, who took those fucking shots?" he was screaming at the top of his lungs. He was yelling into his own radio headset and yelling at the three agents beside him in his quickly set up command post. His own voice was so loud it overwhelmed the voices coming back to him through his earpiece. Finally he had to stop to breathe, and that's when he heard, "Sir, we did not take any shots. Repeat, we did not take any shots." Sanderson recognized the voice of his leader of the FBI's own sniper squad.

"Then who the fucking hell did?"

"Unknown, sir," was the answer. "Repeat, we did not take any shots."

"Where did they come from?"

"Somewhere behind our position, sir. No shots were heard."

Sanderson took off his headset and slammed it to the floor, then stormed out of the room. Across the street, the Holiday Inn was in turmoil. Alarm bells were ringing; people were running out of their rooms and down into the parking lot. Sirens could be heard in the distance, closing fast. Turning around, he barged back into his command post. "Get the scene taped off *now*. I don't want any locals involved. Tell them anything you want, but do not let them near that scene," he ordered. "Give me a cigarette," he shouted to one of his agents.

"But sir, you quit ..."

"Give me a fucking cigarette!" he screamed.

Without a word the agent handed him his pack. Storming back outside, Sanderson watched the scene unfold. "What a fucking mess," he swore aloud. He retrieved his cell phone and dialed the White House.

"Ladd here."

"This is Sanderson. Someone just took out all four suspects in Indianapolis."

"What? What do you mean, 'took out'?"

"Somebody just shot them, Ladd, right in front of us. We had twelve sets of eyes on them. The fourth had just entered Kazhed's room, the fire alarm went off, the four came outside, and in five seconds all four were dead. Professional. No doubt. It was not us. We have sealed the scene from the local LEOs. Inform the president; I'll be expecting his call." He snapped the phone shut to end the conversation. He was in no mood to answer Ladd's questions or listen to his drivel. He knew he was in for an ass-chewing, and he wasn't going to listen to Ladd's shit.

He took five minutes to smoke the cigarette and try to collect his thoughts. The fire trucks had arrived, with firemen spreading all about. He watched them and suddenly realized there was no visible smoke. *Son of a bitch*, he thought, returning to his agents inside. "Find out about any fire over there. Get right back to me. *Now!*"

Six minutes later Matt Sanderson's cell phone rang.

"Sir, no sign of any fire. Something else is odd too. The fire department can't find anyone who admits to pulling the alarm. Everybody flat denies it."

"Then how the hell did it go off?"

"Can't answer that, sir. They're trying to determine that now. It's been suggested it was a prank."

"No, it was not a prank; it was a setup, used to get the suspects out of their rooms," Sanderson stated emphatically.

"By whom, sir?"

"That is what we need to find out." He snapped his phone shut. Ten seconds later it rang again. Sanderson saw it was the president.

"Yes, sir, we've had a development here. All four suspects were shot to death in what appears to be a well-planned operation by professionals. The fire alarm was set off at the Holiday Inn, and when the suspects left their rooms, they were shot and killed. My first guess is a sniper, though that has not been confirmed. There were twelve sets of eyes on the suspects when they went down. No one saw any sign of a shooter. No shots were heard."

Silence. "Was any attempt made to finalize procedure on the device?" the president finally inquired.

"No, sir. As you know, the device has been neutralized, and no one has gone near that unit. We also have the crime scene secure from any locals. Local PD is having a fit, but I invoked 'national security.' They're not happy."

"They'll get over it," the president stated. "I want that device secured. Keep a team on it at all times. I'll make arrangements to have the military pick it up. As soon as I have details, I'll get hold of you. Matt, you did a good job of keeping that device safe. None of us could have known that someone else was watching these bastards. Have forensics go over their rooms, and the storage, unit thoroughly. Have the bodies taken to Quantico. Also, see if it can be determined where the shots might have originated from. I'll be in touch." Sanderson heard the president click off.

That went better than I thought. Guess I'd better slow down on the coffee, Sanderson thought.

Back at the White House, President Williams allowed himself a smile. *One group down,* he thought. *Starr, I damn sure hope you hid your group well, or we'll all be in jail.*

CHAPTER 64

S TARR AND STYLES arrived at the hangar, where Christman and Phillips were waiting for them. Styles got out of the Ford Crown Victoria, went to the backseat, and retrieved his duffel bag. Without so much as a glance at the others, he boarded the plane and secured his weapon in the storage area. When he exited the plane, Starr and Christman were busy cleaning the Crown Vic. Phillips walked up to him with her earpiece in place.

"Shit's hit the fan, Styles. The FBI is going nuts. They know it was a hit, but they've got no idea who, and no location. Matt Sanderson has already talked to the president."

"Did you hear their conversation?" Styles asked.

"Not yet. It should be downloaded, but I figured we'd listen to it together on the plane," Phillips answered.

Right then, Starr yelled over, "We're all clear here. Let's go."

Christman was already aboard, and the threesome joined him.

Christman said, "Everybody down and buckled in. We're outta here." Then he was talking to the control tower, following directions to take off. He taxied out, waited on two commercial flights, then was cleared for takeoff. Again, everyone was impressed at the sheer power of the jet. They were airborne in seconds, then climbing up and away from Indianapolis. Christman leveled off at 35,000 feet, en route to New York. He figured that he would need to divert to Washington when Starr instructed him. Over the speakers, he announced, "We're all set on our flight plan to New York."

Starr went up to the cockpit and instructed Starr to fly to DC to drop Phillips and then head back to Knoxville. There was equipment they needed to pick up before starting phase two of their operation. "J. C., put the coals to her; we gotta make some time."

"I can do that." Grinning, he upped the throttles, and the jet began to whine louder.

"How fast we going?"

"Subsonic, a little over seven hundred miles per hour. We go supersonic and it'll draw attention, since we're not military. Probably some curious about us now, but it won't matter. They'll just think we're some rich assholes with a fast plane."

"Good," Starr commented, returning to his seat. Just then his satellite phone rang. It was the president.

"Richard, I understand phase one is complete."

"Yes, sir."

"Any unforeseen difficulties?"

"None, sir." Starr saw no reason to mention the two dead gang members.

"That's what I wanted to hear."

"Sir, I understand the FBI has their panties in a wad."

That brought a chuckle from President Williams. "That's putting it lightly. They know it was an orchestrated operation but have no idea who pulled it off. I'm going to keep Sanderson out there until the military can pick up the device. Then I'll bring him back. Glad to see you didn't screw up your first mission."

"Sir, never assume. Never assume at all. Assume is spelled a-s-s-u-m-e, which translates to 'ass out of u and me.' I know we got out clean, but never ever assume."

"I get your point, Richard, well taken," the president agreed. "I'm just encouraged that this first assignment appears to have gone smoothly."

"Much better way to say it, Mr. President."

"What is your plan right now?" the president asked.

"We're hauling ass back to DC to drop Phillips off. She's got some nerd stuff to do. We're heading straight back to Knoxville. Styles has some shit he needs back home. Then we'll arrange to pick Phillips up, probably tomorrow morning, afternoon at the latest, and we'll begin phase two."

"Sounds good, Richard. Keep me posted." He signed off.

Starr walked back to Styles and Phillips, who were staring out into the blackness of the night.

"Phillips, the president confirmed just how nuts the FBI is right now. He wanted to know our plans, and I filled him in. We'll be in DC in under an hour, drop you off as planned, then we're headed for Knoxville. Sunshine here has some gear to pick up. How much time do you need to be ready for phase two?"

"I should be ready to go by lunchtime. There are some language programs I need to upload that might help Styles in the field, plus a few other tricks I have."

"Sounds good. Call me in the morning to let me know what time you'll be at the airport; we'll go from there."

"Starr, just how are we going to get Styles into Russia?"

"That, young lady, is a work in progress."

"Which means he hasn't got a fucking clue," retorted Styles.

"Sergeant, you know as well as I that this has to be properly conceived."

"Like I said, he hasn't got a fucking clue."

CHAPTER 65

PRESIDENT WILLIAMS WAS extremely concerned. He was sure that he had a traitor in his group. The problem was, he had no idea who. Ever since Starr had told him the phone call to Global Eastern had been traced back to the White House, he had been in a near rage. This new plan was threatening to blow up in his face. He had to find out who this traitor was.

He decided to call Phillips. He dialed her number.

"Yes, sir," she immediately responded.

"Phillips, as you can understand, I am seriously apprehensive of this phone call you traced back to the White House."

"As you should be, sir."

"Besides what has already been discussed, what other, if any, measures can we take to try to identify the individual who was on that call?"

"I could track the serial number of the phone number that Global Eastern originally called—I got that info the first time—and check that serial number against any mass purchases of phones in the greater DC area over, say, the past three months. If we get lucky, that serial number may pop up within a list of other serial numbers. That's a big if, but if we find it, then we've got all the other serial numbers I can run a program on, so if any of those become active, we'll know it immediately."

"That sounds like a long shot."

"It is, sir, but sometimes long shots bring a huge payoff. I have one other idea."

"Let's hear it."

"Well, I'm winging this a bit, but this is what I had in mind ..."

If one were watching, one would have seen the president visibly straighten as he listened to Darlene Phillips's idea. When she was finished, he whistled softly. "That might work; it just might work. You inform Starr and work out the details. This, if it's possible, takes priority over Russia. As important as Russia is, if this detail isn't dealt with, there may be no Russia."

"One question, sir. Should this idea pan out, how do you want us to continue?" Phillips asked.

"Phillips, your team has only one response. Respond."

"Yes, sir!" She hung up and immediately called Starr, bringing him up to speed on her conversation with the president. She had been dropped off less than half an hour earlier.

"You can make this work?" asked Starr.

"Won't know until I try. I think there's a chance. We gotta find this guy fast. He could blow the whole game."

"All right. We'll load up for anything and be back up to DC as quickly as possible. Get started, and keep me posted. I'll clue in the other two." With that, he ended the call. He went back and joined Styles. "The president talked to Phillips about that call from Global Eastern to the White House. She's got some kind of plan cooked up that might ferret out the weasel." Styles listened, never saying a word.

CHAPTER 66

PRESIDENT WILLIAMS CONVENED an emergency meeting of the heads of his security agencies. FBI Director Matt Sanderson was absent, as he was still in Indianapolis. He conveyed the sequence of events, from the discovery of the dirty bomb hidden at Madison Square Garden to the assassinations of the four suspects at the Holiday Inn. He did *not* reveal the discovered phone call from Global Eastern in Saudi Arabia to the White House. "Did I miss anything or leave anything out?" he asked.

The five men attending the president's meeting looked around, shaking their heads.

"That sounds correct, sir," Bernard Backersley of the CIA agreed. "Do we have any information on the shooter?"

"Not at this time. The FBI is scouring the area for any leads, but so far nothing."

"Who would want these men dead?" asked Charles Rockford, director of Homeland Security.

"You mean besides us?" retorted Backersley.

"I want each of you to utilize all your resources at hand to try to find who was responsible for this. Start to finish. Everyone coordinate your findings to Coverley Merritt," the president stated, referring to the man heading up the president's new Department of the Presidential Office. No one even bothered looking in his direction. "Work hard, gentlemen," he added, abruptly leaving the room

Darlene Phillips, back in her assigned office at Quantico, had all of her computers up and running, tracking cell phone transmissions, hoping desperately that she'd get a hit on one of the numbers she had discovered. The number that was originally used from the White House had come from within the purchase of half a dozen phones. That ID number was number two on the list of six. She had all six numbers programmed in, so the instant any of the phones were turned on, the computers would start recording and determine the location via a GPS fix. She felt confident that if the phones were used, she would find them.

Christman, Starr, and Styles had landed in Knoxville and driven back to the Ranch. All three went their separate ways, packing what they thought they would need: clothing, personal items—everything they could think of. Styles went to his armory and came back with three duffle bags. Neither Starr nor Christman asked him about their contents. Starr had whipped up some ham-and-cheese sandwiches, which they would eat back on the road to Knoxville.

With the Suburban packed up with all their gear, they headed once again to the airport.

Starr, driving, commented sarcastically, "Thanks, Starr, for the sandwiches."

Styles and Christman, as though they'd rehearsed, answered in unison, "Thanks Starr, for the sandwiches."

Starr chuckled and retorted, "Well, thank you, you're welcome."

The three men had spoken little since leaving Indianapolis. "Something on your mind, Marv?" Starr asked.

"Not really. Just thinking about that phone call. Bothering me," Styles replied.

"Me too. If anybody can track that call, though, it's Phillips."

"Yeah, she seems to know her shit all right."

"I'll say. That chick's a friggin' wizard on those computers," added Christman.

"If she doesn't find him fast, this whole deal could blow up in our faces."

"No one knows that better than the president, Marv," agreed Starr.

"Yep."

Halfway around the world, Nakhan Zazar went to Sheikh Ami al Hadid's office. "I received a call from our contact in America. Unfortunately, I was not able to take the call immediately and only received his voice mail. He says he has urgent news. He is to call back midafternoon. I will be expecting his call."

"Why were you not able to take the call?" Ami al Hadid demanded to know.

"I was busy with the financial aspects of our latest acquisition," Zazar lied. He dared not tell al Hadid he had been watching pornography on his computer.

"Understandable. Bring me this information after you speak with him." He waved Zazar away with his hand.

CHAPTER 67

NAKHAN ZAZAR HAD been waiting in his office, intently studying immoral images on his computer. *How can these infidel women enjoy themselves so much with a machine?* he thought as he watched the video for the fourth time. Then one of his many disposable cell phones rang. "Yes," he answered.

A voice with no name came over his cell phone. This was to be a private conversation.

"Have you seen the news?"

"Of what news do you speak?" Zazar demanded.

"The news on CNN, on half the cable news stations, on the websites," the voice continued.

"I have no time to watch such lies."

"Well, Zazar, these are no lies."

"Again, what is it that you speak?"

"Four men were killed in Indianapolis a few hours ago. The FBI is keeping it heavily under wraps, but I know what happened."

"How does this concern me?" Zazar responded, with irritation growing in his voice.

"Because the four men were Saheeb al Kazhed, Akbar al Hamid, and two unnamed men thought to be Afghanis. I believe you know these men."

Zazar gasped. *"What?"*

"You heard me, Zazar. The four are dead. Shot to death."

"How did this happen? Who did this?"

"I can tell you everything, Zazar. I can tell you how, I can tell you who, but it will cost you a lot of money."

"We have already paid you a lot of money for information. This is information. You will tell me now," Zazar insisted vehemently.

"This is new information, Zazar. Not what we previously discussed. I can give you every single detail, but it will cost more. Do you want the information or not?"

"How much money do you want?" Zazar asked, with outright anger in his voice.

"Ten million dollars."

Zazar's voice exploded into the phone. "That is outrageous. Impossible. We have paid you more than enough money for any information you provide. That was our agreement."

The voice replied calmly, "I'm changing the agreement. You have two hours to decide. If you want the details, call me within two hours. Otherwise, you will never hear from me again."

"I cannot authorize this myself. I must speak to al Hadid. He decides."

"Zazar, I don't care if you talk to his mother; you have two hours, and only two hours. One more thing—the money will be wired to my account before I tell you. I don't trust you."

Zazar started swearing at the voice in Arabic, which was not understood. Finally he was able to say, "I will call you in under two hours if al Hadid agrees." He slammed the cell phone shut. He was mad, and scared to approach al Hadid with this latest development. He was already in a foul mood, and this would certainly make it worse.

Half a world away, Darlene Phillips was smiling.

CHAPTER 68

STARR AND STYLES, with Christman piloting the aircraft, were on their way back to Washington, DC. They had grabbed some more food at a drive-through Arby's. Christman had complained the ham-and-cheese sandwiches just weren't enough. "I'm the pilot, and I don't take off unless I get some more to eat."

"Hell, J. C., you're starting to whine like Styles."

At that moment, Starr's satellite phone rang. Thinking it was the president, he was mildly surprised to see Phillips's name come up.

"Miss us already, Phillips?" Starr teased.

"Uh, no. Pay attention here, Starr. I called you first. I got a hit off one of those burn phone numbers. Short version, I was able to track the number used from the White House to Global Eastern, to one of six phones purchased together. I had a program tracking all six numbers, and one just hit. Called the same number at Global Eastern."

"Tell me you got the location."

"Oh yeah. Got that, and the person the location belongs to."

"Well, who the fuck is it?"

A long determined pause, then she answered, "None other than one Andrew Ladd. The call was made from his home."

"You're shittin' me."

"No, Starr, I'm not."

"Any way this could be wrong?" Starr could feel a frost come over the line. "Sorry, Phillips, no offense intended. It's just so damned hard to believe. He goes back a long ways with the president."

"Starr, is there any chance that his call might be for a valid reason?"

"Not that I would know, Phillips. I take it that you have not informed the president."

"Affirmative. I wanted to tell you first. Let you decide how to handle this."

"Gotta tell him; nothing else to do. We're forty-five minutes out of DC. I'll call you when we're back on the ground, sooner if something comes up." He clicked off.

Starr looked over at Styles and motioned for him to follow him. They went up to the cockpit, where Starr filled them both in. He relayed everything Phillips had just told him.

"*Son of a bitch*," Styles spit out.

"Yeah," agreed Christman.

Styles looked at Starr. "What're we gonna do here, Starr?"

"First I'm going to call the president and see if he has any specific instructions. Then we'll plan from there."

Styles nodded.

Starr went back to the rear of the plane and grabbed his satellite phone and dialed.

"Yes, Richard, what's up?"

"Sir, I've got something to tell you. It's going to be difficult."

"Richard, don't blow smoke, just lay it out."

"Phillips just called me. She got a hit off one of the phones, purchased as a group, that included the call from the White House to Global Eastern. She was able to pinpoint the location and from that identify who was making the call. By the time we land, which will be in about thirty-five minutes, she'll have a digital recording of the conversation. She can e-mail you a copy directly."

"Who is it?"

"Sir, it's Andrew Ladd."

Dead silence followed. Then, "There is no mistake?"

"No, sir. It's him. Once Phillips downloads the conversation, she can match his voice to a voice recognition program, and she'll know for sure. But we know Ladd lives alone, so it only makes sense. Plus I recognized his voice."

"Richard, call me the second that Phillips matches his voice. I don't want to instruct you on how to handle it until I'm one hundred percent certain. Is that clear?"

"Absolutely. I knew that was what you'd say." He heard the president hang up. *Can't even imagine what he's feeling right now*, Starr thought. He looked up and saw Styles walking toward him.

"What's the word?"

"Hold until Phillips matches his voice. Let him know the results. Take our directions."

Once more, Styles only nodded.

CHAPTER 69

T HE SPECIALIZED JET touched down outside of DC just after 11:00 p.m. Surprisingly, Phillips was there to greet them. As soon as the wheels stopped and the jet's stairway lowered, she bounded up inside.

"No doubt; it's Ladd," she exclaimed. "He's calling back in just over an hour. He's demanding ten million dollars for information detailing the deaths in Indianapolis. That alone absolutely confirms our suspicions about Global Eastern. That information is us. One thing in our favor is that he firmly demanded money first, information after. That should buy us a little time. If necessary, I can play with the routing of the money. But we need to find out how we handle this."

Starr nodded and went to the rear of the plane and called the president, again on the coded satellite phone.

After bringing the president up to speed on Phillips's analysis, he listened intently. Finally he said, "Yes, sir," and hung up. He turned to face the group.

"He wants us to take Ladd out, but not inside our borders. He wants Ladd to show up dead on Global Eastern's front door, if possible. Now we have to plan this mess."

Phillips came forward and tossed a large manila envelope on the conference table. "This is information on Ladd. Thought it might come in handy."

Starr grabbed it and emptied the contents on the table. He broke it up into four piles. Phillips looked at him and shook her head. "I need to stay on the computers. I've got my laptops with me." She turned away to retrieve them.

Styles spoke up. "Where does he live?"

Starr responded, "He lives on a four-acre estate outside of Fairfax, Virginia. Very private. Security on the property, including a guardhouse. Tough to get to him there."

Styles looked at him and stated evenly, "No, it won't be."

One hour and fifty-six minutes later, Nakhan Zazar dialed a phone number that he only knew as a voice and bank account number.

"You cut that very close, Zazar. I began to believe you were not interested in the information I can offer."

"I am not convinced it is worth the money you demand."

"It is worth much more, but I am not greedy. The information I sell, will not only explain the deaths I spoke of, but quite probably prevent others, perhaps your own. Now perhaps you understand why it is worth the amount I requested."

"I have spoken with Ami al Hadid. He agrees to pay the amount. It will be wired to your account tomorrow morning, when your Geneva bank opens."

"I have Internet access to my account, so I will know when it arrives. Then I will call you detailing all the information. This should transition smoothly, as long as you do not try to cheat me."

"I should be the one to worry about being cheated. I am giving you money for information you say is invaluable. I have no way of knowing that until I see for myself," Zazar snarled over the phone, making no attempt to hide his anger.

"Do not worry needlessly, Zazar. The information is what I say."

CHAPTER 70

S TYLES WAS OUTSIDE the estate of Andrew Ladd. Dressed entirely in black, including a full-concealment face mask, he was surveying the layout. The guard shack was a mere twenty yards to his left. He had a six-foot wrought-iron fence in front of him, behind a four-foot-high hedge. He was knelt down between the two. According to Phillips's scouting report, Ladd did not own a dog—something Styles was grateful for. She had pulled up the security schematic for the property, and it was surprisingly light: hardwired motion detectors at the doorways and garage, the usual hardware for window and door protection using magnetic strips, and, of course, the presence of two guards. This snatch-and-grab was not designed to be fancy. First the guards. Styles was equipped lightly for this job. He carried his Beretta, complete with sound suppressor, as a last resort only. He was determined not to have to use it.

He watched as the second patrol guard convened with the guard stationed in the guardhouse, at the end of the drive. They were both smoking cigarettes, paying no attention to the grounds. A bad habit developed by boredom. Styles reached up, grabbed hold of the top of the fence, and effortlessly pulled himself up and over in one easy motion. He dropped silently on the other side, crouched, and waited. Nothing. He quickly made his way up to a large maple tree, its leaves just beginning to open from the buds. Within five minutes, the second guard began his walk up the drive, less than three yards from Styles's position. As the guard walked past, Styles fell in behind him. He quickly closed the gap, grabbing the guard in a classic choke hold. "Relax, don't fight it. I'm only going to put you to sleep for a while," he whispered into the guard's ear. The guard continued to struggle but quickly weakened. Twelve seconds later he was completely unconscious. Styles turned him around, picked him up over his shoulder, walked him thirty feet away, and placed him behind a large bush. He quickly checked the man's pulse, finding it steady. He figured he had maybe twenty-five minutes before the guard came to. He would feel groggy for a bit. He quickly made his way back to the guard shack. He stood just outside the door, retrieved a small flashlight, turned it on, and tossed it out in front of the side window. He knew this ought to bring the guard out, turning him away from Styles, which is exactly what happened. The instant the guard was free of the doorway, Styles repeated the choke hold on this guard, with the same results. He picked up the guard and deposited him at the base of the exterior wall of the guard house, in the rear, well in the shadows.

He quickly made his way up to the front door. He saw no cameras. He knocked on the front door. He soon heard footsteps. When the footsteps stopped at the other side of the door, Styles called out, "Security, sir."

As the door opened he heard, "Yes, what is it?"

Styles pushed through the door. Andrew Ladd was in his pajamas. Styles spun him around and used the choke hold for the third time that night to render Ladd unconscious. He placed Ladd on the floor, retrieved a radio handset, and proceeded to hit the squelch button twice. He reached down, picked Ladd up, swinging him over his shoulder, and closed the door as he left. The event had lasted less than five minutes, from the time he'd put the first guard down. As he walked past the guardhouse, Starr drove up in a minivan. Styles wrenched open the side door, tossed Andrew Ladd inside, and followed. He closed the door, and then they were off. Styles quickly retrieved two large wire ties from his pocket. He rolled Ladd over onto his stomach, cuffed his hands behind his back, then put his ankles together, crossed, and cuffed those together. He then tore off a strip of Gorilla Tape and placed it over Ladd's mouth. He used his knife to make a small slit in the tape between Ladd's lips, to aid his breathing yet still keep him quiet.

Styles climbed up front to sit beside Starr, who asked, "What about the guards?"

"Sleeping. They should be waking up in a few minutes. Probably have a headache, but nothing more. They were just punching a clock."

"How'd you get into the house?"

"Didn't have to; he came out."

"How the hell you get him to do that?"

"I knocked on the door."

CHAPTER 71

T HE MINIVAN CONTAINING Starr, Styles, and Chief of Staff Andrew
Ladd drove inside the hangar that contained the DPO jet. The first
two were comfortable; the third was not.

"Phillips, I gotta admit I'd never guess you'd drive a minivan," Starr
quipped.

"And just what should I be driving?"

"I don't know, maybe a Bradley Fighting Vehicle."

"Funny, Starr."

"It worked," said Styles.

"Yes it did," Starr agreed.

Styles walked over to the minivan and hauled Andrew Ladd out.
He slung him over his shoulder and walked him up and into the jet. He
carried him to the rear and tossing him into one of the lounge chairs.
Ladd was now awake; his eyes alternated between glaring daggers at
Styles, and widening in outright fear. Starr joined them.

Styles stood over him and growled, "I'm going to remove the
tape from your mouth. You make any noise, I punch your lights out,
understand?"

Ladd nodded his head.

Styles reached over and ripped off the tape, taking some whiskers and skin with it.

"Damn," spat out Ladd.

"That's very close to noise, Ladd. Be very careful."

"Starr, what in the hell do you think you're doing?" Ladd demanded.

Starr snapped, "Ladd, shut up and listen very carefully. We know that you've had phone calls with Global Eastern from a burn phone. We've recorded those calls. We also know that the number you called at Global Eastern was also used for communication with Saheeb al Kazhed, a known terrorist who used Global Eastern as a front. That puts you in direct communication with a known terrorist group. That allows us to hold you indefinitely under the Homeland Security Act. Doesn't matter that we're not Homeland Security. The rules, or lack of, still apply."

Ladd was silent. Starr went on. "Ladd, I am not a trained interrogator; I only know what I've seen in the movies. But Styles here can cause you a great deal of pain if you don't tell me what I want to know. And just for the record, I'm acting under the direct authority of the president."

"I don't believe you," Ladd persisted.

"I don't care. We have you selling information to one Nakhan Zazar, for ten million dollars. Information that would reveal the president's latest plan on terrorism. Us."

Phillips joined the group, carrying a small satchel.

Right then Starr's satellite phone rang. Starr retrieved it, walking up toward the front of the plane for privacy. Seeing the call was from the president, he answered. "Yes, sir."

"Where do we stand?" inquired the president.

"We have the package," answered Starr.

"Good. See if you can learn anything from him. Terminate everyone he's connected with. I don't care if that's half of Saudi Arabia. Get it done." The president ended the conversation. Starr went back to the group.

"Ladd, that was the president. His only question was, do we have you? He also instructed us to see what else we might find out from you. Before."

"I don't know what the fuck you're talking about, Starr. Before? Before what?" Ladd persisted doggedly.

"Before Styles here shoots every fucking son of a bitch you've had contact with. So guess what; we don't need you." Starr looked at Phillips. "Put 'im out."

Phillips opened her satchel and took out a prepared injection. She removed the cap from the needle and approached Ladd.

"Don't worry, Ladd; this will only put you to sleep for about twelve hours. You'll wake up," offered Phillips.

Ladd started to struggle, but Styles reached over and held his head tightly against the seat back.

Phillips found the artery she was looking for, in his neck, and inserted the needle. Within seconds Ladd's eyelids began to flutter and then close.

"Pretty sorry fucking sight," Starr said, looking down at the figure still clad in his pajamas. Looking back at Phillips, he directed, "I need you to find Captain Petr Pevosky and Ivan Kovesky, his brother-in-law. That's our next destination."

Styles spoke. "Starr, there's a specialized piece of equipment I need. Who do we call?"

"What do you need?"

"A glide-chute."

"I'm on it."

Styles looked at Phillips and commented, "So you know about pharmaceuticals too?"

"Of course."

"Where'd you learn that?"

Phillips laughed. "The Internet, where else?"

Styles almost smiled.

CHAPTER 72

F BI DIRECTOR MATT Sanderson was back in DC, meeting one-on-one with the president.

"I don't have any concrete answers, sir. We believe that the shots were taken from quite a distance, probably over one thousand yards. We were also able to determine that the shots possibly could have come from an abandoned building, but we found no physical evidence. We did find two bodies of local gang members; looks like they were killed in a drug deal gone south. No reason to believe otherwise. Whoever killed those four was a hell of a shot; no doubt about that. The bullets were Lapua 6.5×47 sniper rounds. He was a pro. We're trying to figure out how he knew those four were there. Not many people were read in on this operation. We recovered cell phones, and our lab rats are tracking the calls made from the phones as we speak. At this point we simply don't know who did this. If I were to guess, I'd say Mossad is visiting us again."

"That's a conversation I intend to have with their director immediately. If Mossad is operating in our country, I damned well want to know about it," the president fumed. He had no intention of letting on that he already knew all the answers.

Sanderson continued. "The military took possession of the device. I was not told where they were taking it. Above my pay grade."

"Don't let it bother you, Matt; the military isn't going to tell any civilian. You know that."

The president stood, which signaled an end to the meeting. Sanderson immediately stood as well. The president offered his hand. "Matt, you've done a good job staying on top of this. Keep the DPO posted. I appreciate your effort."

"Thank you, sir, and I will." Sanderson turned and left the room.

President Williams reached for his phone and punched in a number.

"Yes, sir," Starr answered.

"Richard, just thought you should know I just met with Matt Sanderson. He had the FBI jet fly him back. He gave me what they'd found out. Looks like your guy got out clean. Sanderson suspects Mossad."

"Every time something happens and there's no clear-cut identity, it seems like Mossad gets the blame. Lucky for us."

"What is your status?"

"We are locating our Russian friends. Once that is established, we'll come up with our game plan. We may need some type of cover story, for whatever reason. I'll keep you posted."

"Sounds good, Richard. Tell your team job well done. I appreciate what they are putting on the line."

"No more than yourself, sir."

CHAPTER 73

THE NEW HANGAR that the DPO jet had pulled into was located at Ronald Reagan National Airport in Washington. It had been made exclusively available for Starr and his group. Its main feature was a small, but adequate, living and sleeping quarters for both male and female occupants. Starr, Styles, Phillips, and Christman were seated at the large conference table in the common area. This entire area was separate from the mechanical side of the hangar, offering complete privacy. Styles was going stir-crazy, Starr and Christman had been playing cards, and Phillips was the only one actually working. They had been inside now for twenty-four hours. Having to babysit Andrew Ladd was not helping Styles's disposition, though Ladd had been sedated much of the time. He had not set foot off the airplane.

"What are you going to do with me? Why haven't you asked me questions? I need to make a phone call," Ladd demanded during one of the times he was awake, allowed to eat, and use the bathroom. He never received any answers, just instructions to "eat."

Finally, Phillips got up from the table, went to the sink, and washed her face. She had been staring at computer screens for almost eighteen hours straight. "I think I've got something here." Immediately the other three joined her.

"What'd you find?" Starr queried.

"A couple of things. First, our friend on the jet just received ten million dollars in a Swiss bank account. One of his cell phones has been ringing off the hook. Calls are all from the same number, Global Eastern. Second, and this was harder, it appears that a shell company for Global Eastern just wired twenty million dollars into another Swiss account, which is held jointly by Captain Petr Pevosky and Ivan Kovesky. Unusual that people hold a joint Swiss account. Third, an additional ten million dollars was wired from the same shell company back into a Global Eastern account that is controlled solely by Sheikh Ami al Hadid. This thirty million was generated by five different accounts, all partners in Global Eastern. From what I've been able to put together, it appears the thirty million is an advance payment to the Russians for a device. The ten million was for that asshole on the plane to sell us out." She stopped to collect her thoughts. "There have been two first-class tickets purchased from Moscow to Frankfurt by Captain Pevosky. Name on the other ticket is Kovesky, and paid for from an account linked to Pevosky. Captain Pevosky has requested, and was granted, an emergency leave from the Russian Army. Death in the family. My guess is that these two Russians are going to run."

Starr was absolutely shocked. "You got into a Swiss bank's records?"

Phillips just nodded.

"I thought that was supposed to be impossible."

"For most," Phillips conceded.

"And the Soviet Army's system?" Starr asked in disbelief.

"Didn't have to. I got that intel from the flight information. He requested, but was denied, a bereavement package on the tickets. The rest is just adding two and two."

Starr was now visibly excited. "That means we can take those two in Germany and not have to fuck with Russia. That makes it easier, and a lot less dangerous for the president."

"Also means I don't get to jump from forty-thousand feet with a glide chute," deadpanned Styles.

Christman piped up. "Well, if it means so much, we can still climb up there for ya."

"I've got the Russians' itinerary ready to be printed out. Then we can make our plans," Phillips offered.

Christman asked, "What are we going to do with our friend?"

Styles answered immediately. "For now, he tags along. I've got something in mind."

Starr interjected, "The Secret Service and the FBI are looking for him. They've questioned his two security guards, but they don't know anything other than that they were grabbed from behind and blacked out. When they came to, Ladd was gone. The story is, they are expecting a ransom demand."

"Hope nobody holds their breath," Styles replied sarcastically.

Starr stepped away from the table and returned shortly with a cell phone. "Styles grabbed this from Ladd's house. He opened the phone and scanned the 'send' list. Seeing a number, he asked Phillips to check it against the list she'd compiled from her computer searches.

"Yeah, matches Global Eastern," answered Phillips, bringing a smile from Starr and a look of pure hatred from Styles.

CHAPTER 74

NAKHAN ZAZAR DIDN'T know whether to be concerned or not. He was confused. He had just received a text from the unknown voice stating that the voice's owner would be in Saudi Arabia in three days to personally deliver the information he held on the incident in Indianapolis. Zazar was irritated that he had to wait three days but pleased about a face-to-face meeting with the man. He went to find Sheikh Ari al Hadid.

Standing in front of al Hadid, he patiently explained the circumstances. He voiced his uneasiness yet focused on the positive note from the personal meeting that was to come. He hoped his voice hid his uncertainty.

Al Hadid looked at him solemnly for a minute, stroking his long, dark beard. "I am not sure what to think, Zazar. He has much of our money. What if he does not show?"

"I believe I have a way to track him."

"And how would you accomplish that?" al Hadid asked scornfully.

"I have bribed an official at the bank. He would give me information on this man, should I require it."

"What sort of information?"

"A name, a photograph, and any bank routing numbers should the money from our deposit be removed," Zazar informed him.

"How much money did this cost me?" al Hadid demanded.

"It cost you nothing; our brothers paid."

Al Hadid allowed himself a small smile. "Wise, Zazar, very wise."

"I am glad you approve. Allah Akbar."

"Allah Akbar."

President Williams was in a meeting with the head of his Secret Service detail, Jeff Loughton. "So no word on Andrew yet? What does Sanderson have to say?"

"No, sir. It looks like a kidnapping, but so far no ransom demand. There doesn't seem to be any other rational explanation," Loughton reasoned.

"This is not good. We cannot have our people being kidnapped. I want you to work closely with Sanderson and get to the bottom of this. Find him; find him now." He slammed his desk with his fist.

"Yes, sir!" Loughton left the room.

President Williams waited a few moments and then called Starr. "Richard, everybody is inside out with Ladd's absence."

"I'm sure, sir."

"You know what to do."

"Yes, sir. Styles has an idea. I don't even know yet. Right now Ladd's sleeping like a baby."

"He's in your hands, Richard. Do as you see fit under my instructions."

"You can be sure of that, sir."

CHAPTER 75

NAKHAN ZAZAR WAS back, conferring with Sheikh Ami al Hadid. "This meeting for the information has been changed. It is to take place in Frankfurt, Germany," he informed al Hadid, knowing he would be displeased.

"Why is this?" he snapped.

"This man will not want to come to Saudi Arabia; he is afraid, I believe. He suggested Frankfurt as neutral ground. I see no reason to argue the point. I will go myself."

"I do not like this, Zazar. I would prefer he come here."

"As do I, al Hadid; however, he refuses. He has our money. He has no reason to cheat us. As I have said before, he has never done so. I do not believe he has that intention now. If I were in his position, I would likely do the same." Zazar watched the sheikh, contemplating his suggestion.

Relenting, al Hadid gave his approval. "I do not like this, Zazar, but I trust your judgment. I want you to take Wazzuri with you."

Zazar cringed inside. He considered Wazzuri to be nothing more than a psychopath who lived for nothing but the pleasure of killing. "Al Hadid, why do you believe that necessary?"

"Zazar, it is not meant as disrespect toward you. However, should you find yourself in an unexpected situation, Wazzuri will provide assistance where you are not experienced. He will be ordered to follow your instructions, without question."

Zazar was not satisfied. "Al Hadid, you know I never question your wisdom, but I must speak. Wazzuri is a man who lives for the kill. He will say anything that he thinks you want to hear, but I fear greatly that he will kill anyone at any opportunity. I do not trust him; I have never trusted him. I do not believe he will follow my direction, despite what you may say."

An immediate chill enveloped al Hadid. "Zazar," he said angrily, "Wazzuri will go with you; he will do as you say. The discussion is closed."

"As you say, al Hadid. Allah Akbar."

Al Hadid merely nodded in return.

Darlene Phillips came out from her sleeping quarters yawning. She'd just finished with a four-hour nap and wanted to get back to her computers. "Any coffee?" she asked.

Starr answered her. "Yeah, I heard you up and stirring, so I made a fresh pot."

"Thanks. Where is everybody?"

"Our guest is aboard the plane, Christman is out picking up some food, and Styles is out running."

Phillips, over at the counter pouring her coffee, observed, "Starr, I've known some real physical fitness freaks in my life, but Styles is in a class of his own."

Starr agreed. "He's been like that all his life, from what I know. Too many times to count, his life has depended on his physical conditioning. If he ever gets tired of this, he could make a damned good living in a circus. That man is capable of doing shit that no pro athlete would ever even dream of. I've seen him hang by his knees, bend upward at his waist, and put three shots inside a two-inch group at eight hundred yards. Even I had a hard time believing that. If I hadn't seen it, I don't think I would

231

have. With him it's all about repetition. If you do something so many times, and don't stop, you'll always be able to do it. It's a religion with him. Take his fighting techniques, for example. He learned those years ago. They're ingrained in him. He doesn't have to practice the moves; more accurately, he has to maintain his ability to perform the moves."

Phillips had walked over to the table accommodating her computers and sat down. She sipped her coffee thoughtfully and continued. "He's a unique man. He definitely lives by his own moral code. I didn't like him when I met him; seemed like all the other arrogant self-absorbed assholes I've dealt with my entire life, but I was wrong. He's not. He believes in what he's doing. He thinks that he makes a difference. I respect him for that. There's a concept we both believe in—just because something is legal does not automatically make it right, and just because something is illegal does not mean that it is automatically wrong. He bases his moral code on his perception of right and wrong, not legal or illegal. I can't argue with that."

Starr couldn't help himself. "Phillips, you're not getting sweet on Styles are you?"

She answered with surprising candor. "No, I don't think so. He intrigues me. I'd like to have him as a friend. He's someone you can count on. People like that are few and far between in today's world."

"You are correct, Darlene. Marv doesn't have a lot of friends, by his own choice. He doesn't like most people. He's also the worst enemy on the planet Earth one could have. Word of advice: don't push him for friendship. Whatever it is, it is."

Phillips had been working at her computers for an hour when Styles came back into the hangar. He was scowling as he threw a heavy backpack onto the concrete floor.

"What are you pissed off about?" Starr asked.

"Not pissed, just annoyed. My time is off about seven seconds a mile right now. I've been slacking too much on training," he barked back.

"Not the first time, Marv, and probably not the last. Just do what you always do," Starr offered.

"Hey guys, I've got something here," Phillips said.

Both of them walked over. "Whatcha got?" Starr asked.

"Reservations. Two rooms at the Hilton Frankfort. Charged to the same card as the plane reservations. Funny though. One room has one occupant listed as Captain Petr Pevosky, and the second is Ivan Kovesky and guest. No second name listed. They arrive in three days. I've done a web search on the hotel; it has underground garage parking, lot of rooms have the walkway overlooking the lobby, theirs included, along with the usual shit. I'm printing out info on it now." The whir of the printer started.

Starr thought for a moment. "Phillips, book us two rooms. Use different cards, and be sure they haven't been used for anything before. Check in a day apart, same for departure. Bookend the reservations around theirs. Try the import/export business card for one and the antique appraisal card for the other. Try to get rooms across the lobby from theirs, one floor up and one floor down."

"Doing, sir," she responded.

Styles and Starr looked at each other and grinned.

CHAPTER 76

THE DPO JET was winging its way over the Atlantic, destination: Frankfurt, Germany. Starr was in the cockpit, shooting the shit with Christman, both of whom were wondering what in the hell Styles had in mind. He hadn't let anybody in on his plan yet. Phillips was back at the conference table, monitoring all of her computer screens, looking for any relevant information. Styles was working out as best he could in an airplane. He was just finishing up his routine of 2,500 push-ups. Since his exasperation two days earlier about being seven seconds slow on his pace per mile, he'd been a machine. Phillips, who was a fitness guru herself, could only shake her head in amazement at his overall routine. Just watching him made her own muscles hurt. He had even installed a bar across the overhead compartments so he could include his inverted sit-ups. When he finished that aspect of his routine, Phillips asked if she could try some.

"Sure," Styles said.

Phillips worked her feet around the vertical bars, then lowered herself into the hanging position. She focused for a moment, then raised herself at the waist, mimicking Styles. She did three, and that was it. She paused, then half fell to the floor. She got up, sat in a chair, and looked over at Styles.

"And you do *two hundred* of those?" she exclaimed.

Styles just nodded. "I can do more, but I lose flexibility in my abdominal area."

"*How?*" she demanded.

"Repetition."

Phillips just shook her head and stared at him. "You sure you're not a terminator?"

"Sometimes I wonder, Phillips. I've just been doing it so long I don't know how not to, I guess."

"Well, Styles, I'm impressed, and that's not easy."

"I don't do it to impress anybody; I do it to stay alive, 'cause of what I do."

"Yeah, I know, and I understand that. Listen, Styles, mind if I ask you a question?"

Styles looked at her somewhat suspiciously. "Guess not."

"I notice you don't seem to have any tats. I don't think I've seen any career soldiers who don't have tats."

"Tats can ID you. Might as well have a billboard on you. Lot of times I have to blend, and sometimes the best place to hide is out in plain view. Can't do that if you've got tats on you. Where I go, it'd be as bad as a neon sign around my neck."

She just nodded at him. "Makes damned good sense." She returned to her computers.

When Styles had finished his sit-ups, he got up and walked the plane a few times just stretching, then went up to the cockpit to confer with Christman and Starr. "How long before we get to Frankfurt?" he asked.

"Two hours, maybe a bit more. We're making good time. Got a forty-mile-per-hour tailwind, so our groundspeed is up around seven fifty or so," Christman answered. "Good. I'm going to go take a quick nap." He went back to an overstuffed lounge chair and stretched out, leaving those two talking together and Phillips busy at the computers.

Starr walked back and joined her. "Find out anything more?"

"Not really sure. I'm curious who this mystery guest is in Kovesky's room. So far no luck."

"Well, keep at it. If anybody can find something, it's you. I gotta say, you've done shit on that computer of yours that I didn't think possible."

She paused, looking up at him. "You got any idea what the plan is here?"

"Besides killing these bastards, no. Styles will let us in on that. That's what he's doing right now."

"What do you mean? The guy's sleeping."

"Only looks like that. He's planning; that's one of his ways. He goes into this zone that lets him get above everything that's going on. He just sorta looks down on it and imagines all the different scenarios and reacts accordingly. It's one of the reasons he worked alone on his assignments in the marines. Most of his COs couldn't understand that. Few of them even tried. The problem was, none of them could argue with his results. No one really knows just how many bad guys he took out. He won't say. You can bet your ass it was a shitload. He plays mind games with them. His version of psychological warfare. He scares the fuck outta them."

"How?" Phillips asked.

"That's something I'll never talk about, and I don't know all of it. He won't either, so don't piss him off by asking. When he went into the theater of these fanatics, he threw the rulebook away. Pay attention on this. Don't ever ask him about it."

"Yeah, don't," Styles agreed, startling both Starr and Phillips, as they had no clue he was behind them.

"Well, sonny boy," Starr said, changing the subject, "you have a nice nap?"

Styles just looked at him. "I'm hungry; anybody want a sandwich?"

Phillips spoke up. "Yeah, that'd be nice."

Starr just nodded.

Styles walked up front to see if Christman was hungry. "Yeah, and don't be so fucking chintzy on the ham this time."

"Okay, one lettuce sandwich for you, J. C.," Styles remarked. Ten minutes later he brought everyone the sandwiches, complete with chips, Diet Coke for J. C. and Phillips, and water for Starr and himself.

"I've got an idea," Styles said after sitting down at the table with Starr and Phillips. "Taking this from the point where you"—he glanced at Phillips—"faked the call from Ladd to this Zazar character to change the meet, I think it would be gracious of Ladd to book a room for him at the Hilton. That would put this cast of players at one location. Zazar shouldn't know that our Russian friends will be there. Put him in one of their most expensive suites. Have him check in the day after the Russians. Keep their meeting each other by chance to a minimum. We have to assume they know each other. That'll give me one day to take care of the Russians, which will eliminate the possibility of them seeing each other. Then it's Zazar's turn."

"That should be easy enough." Looking at her watch, she said, "I'll text the message now."

"Hold up just a second. While you're at it, be sure to have two rental cars waiting for us at the airport. J. C. knows the airport and says it won't be a problem stashing the plane. Make one a luxury sedan and the other a minivan. Tinted windows would be nice," Styles added.

"Got it. Anything else?" she asked.

"Not for the moment."

"Marv, how are we going to get the big guns through customs, since we don't have diplomatic status?" Starr asked.

"We won't need them. This is going to be up close and personal. J. C. says the plane won't be bothered, especially where he's going to park it. Once we get into the rooms, we'll have some shopping to do. It's a big help that Phillips speaks German. That won't draw undue attention to us, as Americans. J. C. will stay with the plane to take care of Ladd; you and I will be in one room, with Phillips in the second. I'll put the final pieces together when I recon the area."

Phillips interrupted them from the conference table. "We're all set. Got a Mercedes sedan and an SUV reserved. No minivans available. We pick them up at the airport. Texted Zazar and informed him of his accommodations, complete with room number. It wasn't cheap."

"Fighting a war never is," Starr interjected.

"This is what I've got so far," said Styles. "We probably won't need it, but our cover story is that Starr and I are in town to establish contacts for importation of California wines. Phillips, you are an antiques appraiser in town to research something for a museum. You figure it out what you're there for. I don't know shit about antiques. J. C. is going to remain at the plane at all times, to be sure Ladd is taken care of. Speaking of, when is he coming around again?"

Phillips looked at her watch again. "About an hour."

"Okay. If he gives you any trouble, smack him. If it was up to me, I'd throw his ass out over the water right now, but I need him."

Phillips addressed Styles. "What are you going to use him for?"

"He's going to be found where he shouldn't be."

CHAPTER 77

DARLENE PHILLIPS WAS the first to check into the Hilton Frankfort. Her room was located on the fifth floor, one floor above the two rooms the Russians had reserved, two floors below the room reserved for Nakhan Zazar. The Russians were across at her one o'clock position, Zazar above her. Captain Pevosky, Ivan Kovesky, and Kovesky's unnamed guest were due to arrive in two days. As agreed, her cover story was that she was an antiques appraiser. She had installed video surveillance on both rooms by placing micro cameras on the handrail system around the walkway that overlooked the huge lobby. Starr decided not to bug their rooms, for fear of the occupants checking for electronic listening devices. Christman had contacted an old friend who had a flight maintenance business located on the outer fringe of the Frankfurt Rhein Airport. He had directed Christman to a private hangar, which was normally leased out to a local business, but the plane that it usually housed was away for two more weeks.

Styles had spent the last twelve hours poring over all the facts they could retrieve on the Hilton Frankfort. Information downloaded from the Internet included their website, brochures that Phillips had brought them, and over two hundred digital photos she had downloaded to one of her laptops. He had chosen not to use firearms except as a last resort, wanting to draw the least attention possible during the physical operation of his part of this mission. Now he was putting the final touches on his plan.

Starr came over and sat down beside him. "You got it in your head yet?"

"Pretty much. I'm going to go out tonight and check the lighting outside. Get hold of Phillips and get her back here for dinner. There's a few things I need to know if she can do. That will play heavily on how I enter the building. I wish now that we had all of them coming in together. I'm going to take out the Russians, hoping they aren't discovered until after I take out this Zazar character. If the cops find the Russians, it'll fuck up the works. I want J. C. ready to roll on a half hour's notice. Advise him on that so he can do whatever he needs to do to be sure that can work. I don't know anything about air regulations, or whatever."

"What else?"

Styles pushed back away from the table and stretched. "We've got a good team here; first time I've ever really been part of one. Phillips has been a real help. You know, Starr, I wasn't happy when the Man told us about putting us all together. I gotta admit, though, I think we've done far more in this concept than you and I could ever have done on our own."

Starr looked at him. "Marv, sometimes you really surprise me. That's pretty big coming from you."

"I've changed a bit, Starr. Started when I smacked that idiot back in Afghanistan. That incident changed my perspective on a lot of shit. Not so much his stupidity, but the entire direction the military seems to be going in: fight but don't win. I'm really starting to think that all those conspiracy nuts who claim the only reason we're there is the money a select few are making just might be on to something. I know I'm not going to beat my head over it anymore; I'm just going to fight this war in the best way I know how. I've got the president and you to thank for that. I wasn't completely sold when you first told me of this idea you two came up with, but now I'm glad I'm on board."

"Well, let's just get done with what the president expects."

"We will, Starr, no doubt about it."

CHAPTER 78

T HE FOURSOME HAD finished dinner that evening and had cleared off the table. Phillips had found a good Italian restaurant and brought four large pizzas for everyone, as that seemed to have become the 'if all else fails' dinner. Now it was time for business.

Phillips started. "I've marked all the security camera locations on these diagrams. The coverage is good but can be avoided. I was able to remove Styles and your"—she glanced at Starr—"photographs from all the facial recognition programs that I'm aware of. It wasn't easy. I replaced them with composite photos I made up. Anyone who knows either of you will notice it, but they'll just think it's a glitch in the system. The exterior lighting of the building is not good from the third floor up. The lighting is designed to highlight the lower exterior decor and grounds, not the upper part of the building."

Styles nodded in approval.

She continued. "I picked up the items you requested, Styles; it's all in the back of the SUV."

Another nod of approval.

Then Styles spoke. "Phillips, how much access can you get with the hotel's different systems?"

"As to what in particular?" she inquired.

"Security video, any type of hotel communications, both ingoing and outgoing, elevators, lighting, anything at all you might think of. I'm more used to less urban combat situations, not big-city environments. I'm just trying to assess what information and control we might be able to get."

Phillips was quiet as she thought. "I'll know better later tonight, but probably just about everything. That's one of the good, and bad, elements of having everything run by computers. Makes it fair game." Right then one of her laptops gave off a signal. She went over to check.

Starr took the interruption as an opportunity to retrieve cold beers for everyone. Phillips remained at her computer for about five minutes, then her printer started up. She came back to the table three minutes later with paperwork, handing everyone a copy. "Well, we've got the identity of our mysterious guest of Zazar. His name is Wazzuri, an Iraqi. Ex-Republican Guard for Saddam. Appears he was the leader of a particularly nasty group. Murder, rape, in on the gassing incident—no telling how many people he's killed. Probably in the hundreds at the least. Big guy for an Iraqi. Stands six feet six inches tall and weighs almost three hundred pounds. Made it out of Iraq after the downfall of Saddam, showed up in Saudi Arabia two years later. Now is associated with Global Eastern, probably as an enforcer, or whatever you guys call that now. Definitely a sociopath. Undoubtedly a bodyguard for Zazar."

Styles smiled. "I've heard of him. Just missed him about ten years ago. He's a real butcher. Saddam Hussein suspected some poor guy of selling intel to the Brits, who claimed they'd never heard of him. Didn't matter. Hussein wanted answers, and this Wazzuri got them. Or tried anyway. Four of them rounded up his entire family, including grandparents. Then he grabbed this poor bastard and took him to a warehouse where every member of his family were suspended by their wrists. The story is Wazzuri told him he'd give him one chance to save his family. Of course he was lying. When the guy couldn't answer his questions, he took hemostats and pinned his eyelids open. Then, one by one, he disemboweled his entire family. Took hours for some of them to die. Then he took an acetylene torch and started cutting off his toes and feet. Every time he passed out, he got some kind of shot to wake him back up, and they continued. The heat cauterized the arteries and veins so he didn't bleed out. They had cut him apart up to his waist before he died. I was pissed I missed him."

Phillips just stared at him, face ashen. "Are you fucking serious?"

"Like I told you, Phillips, you have no clue of my world."

"I don't want any part of it."

"Like it or not, you're in it now. We're just fighting by more civilized standards—at least you three are. This part is *my* job."

Phillips just looked at Styles with a grim face. He didn't know if it was from aversion or repulsion. He wasn't sure he cared.

CHAPTER 79

THAT EVENING AFTER dinner, Styles accompanied Phillips back to the hotel. She had been quiet since the conversation about Wazzuri occurred. Styles was actually feeling a bit guilty about his candor, about what he knew of Wazzuri.

"Listen, Phillips, I didn't mean to freak you out back there."

"It's not you, Styles, really. It's just so damned hard to believe that in this day and age there are still people who can be that fucking cruel to another human being. I mean, it's not just having your guts ripped out, but my god, having to watch that happen to your family? That's the shit Hollywood producers stick on a screen."

"Still, I could have been a little less harsh."

She stopped and turned to face him. "I get it, you know. I get it, that this is as big a change for you as it is for me. Probably for all of us. We've all agreed to do something that's never been done, something that is highly illegal but necessary. If I didn't believe that what we were doing was right, I wouldn't be here. That you can be sure of."

Styles said, "I had a conversation with Starr earlier today. I wasn't thrilled about this team concept that the president put together. I also fully admit that Starr and I alone could never have accomplished what this team has. You and I got off on the wrong foot. There were valid reasons. As different as you and I are, there are also similarities. We were just two dogs sniffing each other out. Like I said, I'm not used to a team concept. I'm having to adjust. I realize that we have a good team here. You certainly have proven yourself."

"You can stop anytime now, Styles; you're starting to scare me a bit."

"You're welcome."

They spent the next hour walking the interior of the building. To anyone watching, they would have appeared to be just another tourist couple. Finally they found themselves back at Phillips's room.

"I need to see the inside of the room, particularly the balcony," Styles said.

"I thought you would."

Phillips used her electronic key card, and they went inside. Styles immediately did a complete study of the room. He then went to the balcony and studied the french doors, which opened up to a nice-sized balcony overlooking the city. He paid particular attention to the locking system. He went outside and studied the arrangement and proximity of the other guest balconies. Finally he came back inside and closed the door behind him. "Okay, I've seen what I need to see in here. Got some more to check out, and then I'll be back at the hangar."

"I think I'll take advantage of the pool. Been a while since I've been swimming, and it relaxes me," Phillips offered.

"Do me a favor. See what you can dig up on Zazar."

"Anything particular?"

"No, just maybe what he likes. You know, food, women, men, whatever. The more I know, the more choices I have to get to him."

"What about the bodyguard?"

"Won't be a problem."

"Right. I'll find out what I can. Let you know in the morning."

"That'll be fine. Enjoy your swim. Don't drown."

"Hell, Styles, that's as close to a joke as I've heard from you."

"Don't get too used to it."

CHAPTER 80

THE NEXT MORNING, Phillips came through the hangar door at six-thirty in the morning carrying breakfast, sans coffee, for everybody. Styles and Starr were sitting at the conference table while Christman was walking Andrew Ladd around.

She tossed three bags on the table.

"Get anything for Ladd?" Starr asked her.

"Yeah." She pulled up a chair beside Styles and sat down. "Zazar likes porn. I mean, *really* likes porn. I was able to pull up a list of the websites he browses—almost all of it porn. Everything except homosexuality. He's into bondage and machines. It was pretty disgusting."

Styles didn't say anything. He had opened the breakfast bags, stacking the different items so all of them could grab what they wanted. Everyone ate in silence. When they were through, Christman gathered up the trash and tossed it into a garbage can. He returned to the table.

Styles spoke. "I need to talk to Ladd. I need him coherent. When will that be?"

Starr answered, "He's pretty much there. I gave him his breakfast and coffee. He's still pitching a fit; that pretty much sums up how he is."

"Good," Styles replied. "You three stay here, no matter what you hear. I don't want to be interrupted." He got up, walked over, and boarded the jet. He walked back to where Ladd was handcuffed to a chair at a small table. He sat down across from him. He stared hard at him for a minute, then started speaking. "Ladd, I've only got one question for you. If I think you're lying, it will be the last thing you say, 'cause I'll reach across this table and snap your fucking neck like a matchstick. Do you understand?"

Ladd sputtered, "I am the chief of staff—" and was suddenly cut off as a hard slap across his cheek shut him up.

"Ladd, last warning. Only answer the question. Anything else comes out of your mouth and *snap*."

Ladd shut up, eyes wide and terrified.

"Now, here's the question. Have you ever met Nakhan Zazar? Has he ever seen you or seen a photograph of you? Does he know what you look like? Think very hard, and be absolutely sure. Your life depends on it."

Ladd answered immediately. "No, absolutely not. He doesn't even know me by any kind of name. Only by phone call. And banking information. I swear. No, he's never seen me."

Styles leaned closer to him, boring a hole through Ladd with his eyes. *"Are you absolutely sure?"*

"Yes."

Styles sat back. He was pretty damned sure Ladd was telling the truth. He had answered with no hesitation, with no time to think up a lie. Plus, he was scared out of his mind. He had reason to be. Styles stood up. Looking down at Ladd, he snarled, "If you're lying to me, I'll tie a rope around your feet and throw your ass out of this plane." He left the man sitting there shaking.

Styles went back to the conference table and sat down. "Ladd swears that he's never met Zazar, that he doesn't know his face. I believe him."

"How can you be sure, Styles?" Christman asked.

"Didn't hesitate a second, too scared to lie. He still thinks he might get out of this alive."

Starr looked at him in surprise. "That's not going to happen, is it?"

"Not a chance in fucking hell."

Phillips piped up. "What does that tell you?"

"It gives me access to their room. If necessary, I'm going to be Ladd."

"You think that will work?" Phillips asked.

Styles almost allowed himself a small smile. "Well, you'll like this plan better."

Phillips looked at him suspiciously. "What do you mean by that?"

"My first plan was to send you in as a hooker, courtesy of Ladd."

Starr and Christman immediately burst into laughter. Slowly Phillips joined them.

After the table had calmed a bit, Styles continued. "Here's what I'm going to need. J. C., sorry, I know it's getting boring, but you need to babysit Ladd. Starr, you need to be parked safely out of sight; be ready to follow our Russian friends should they decide to leave. Also, be sure to let me know as soon as they arrive. Try to ID who is with Kovesky. If they're getting ready to run, it's probably a significant other. That could change things a bit. Find out what you can as quickly as possible. Security cameras. Only ones I'm worried about are the cameras that cover the stair landings. They're mounted on the wall, opposite the door, and there's no way for me to avoid them. I've noticed people using the stairs for exercise, so the security staff is used to seeing people. Phillips, I need you to be able to 'freeze' and 'thaw' the images on the landings I call out. We can't just install a loop—too much chance security might wonder why they're not seeing anybody. Will that be a problem?"

"No, shouldn't be."

"Good. We'll all have our radio headsets like before. Everyone stay tuned. Same as in Indy. Starr, you keep a relaxed eye on those guys. Do *not* let them make you. Lose them first. The only thing I'm really interested in is how much they drink. Russians love their vodka, and it makes them stupid. I want to know if I'm dealing with stupid or not. I'm going to use the stairs to get to the roof, rappel down by rope to their balcony. I intend on being inside when they return from dinner if they go out. If not, I'll play it by ear. When I'm done, I go back up to the roof, change, and go back down the stairs to the lobby. If nothing's in the weeds, I'll go right out the front door. Everybody, be sure you have the channel schedule for the radios. Any comments or questions? Speak up; now's not the time to be bashful."

The other three looked at each other, then back at Styles, shaking their heads. Starr spoke first. "Sounds like a solid plan, Marv."

Phillips then added, "I'll keep an ear tuned for any hotel security chatter. That will be the first source should anything come up."

Christman said, "I'll keep a sharp ear out for anything you guys might need me for. Phillips, it might not be a bad idea to show me how to give our friend an injection to put him out, just in case I might have to leave for any reason. If he's asleep, we don't have to worry about him."

"Good idea, J. C.," Phillips agreed.

Starr ended the meeting by stating, "Okay, people, we've got our jobs; let's get to work."

CHAPTER 81

"POINT ONE, PARTY of three has arrived," Phillips stated over her radio headset.

"Copy, Point Three," Styles answered. He checked the time—just after four in the afternoon. "Point Two, confirm."

"Copy, Point One." That meant Starr knew the Russians had arrived, and he was in position.

"Point Two, did you sight arrival?"

"Negative, Point One, too many cabs."

"Copy, Point Two."

Styles was dressed in sweatpants and a sweatshirt. He had a gym bag with him containing black jeans, a black long-sleeved T-shirt, a black facemask, thin black leather gloves, 150 feet of black three-quarter-inch cotton rope, a bag of twenty-six-inch cable ties, and a roll of two-inch-wide Gorilla Tape. His silenced Beretta was strapped to the middle of his back, though he had no intention of using it unless absolutely necessary. His favorite knife was sheathed to the inside of his left calf. He figured he had about two hours to kill. "Point Three, ready on cameras?"

"Copy, Point One. Party of three in two rooms, third party confirmed as male."

That surprised Styles. He was just about to respond when "Point One, running facial recognition now" followed.

"Copy, Point Three. Time?"

"TBD, Point One."

"Copy, Point Three." Styles was annoyed. He knew Phillips was running the program as quickly as possible; he just wanted that information now.

"Point One, reservations for three, at seven, just made in the hotel restaurant."

"Copy, Point Three." *This should work out just fine*, Styles thought.

"Point One, identity confirmed. Mikhail Stovalasski. Russian. Born in St. Petersburg. Lifelong criminal. Robbery, suspected murder, loan sharking, smuggling. Believed to have killed his mother, but never confirmed or convicted. He's gay."

"Point Three, come back on last part."

"He's gay."

"Copy, Point Three." Styles had to stop to think about that. He hadn't seen that coming. In a way, though, he was relieved. He'd prefer not having a woman involved.

"All points, Point One in stage two." That was the prearranged code; Styles was going to go for a short run to loosen up. Everyone knew he would not go far and would have his radio with him.

All three acknowledged.

Styles got out of his parked car and stretched for a few minutes. He then spent the next hour and a half running. He wanted to be warmed up for the climbing that lay ahead, which would be different than waiting out a potential sniper's target.

Styles returned to his vehicle just as the sun was going down. He felt good. No radio contact had been established during his run. He took that as a good sign. "Point One, back on station."

All three acknowledged.

Styles picked up his gym bag and headed for the hotel's main entrance. The door was held for him as he approached. He gave a nod to the doorman and received the same in return.

"Point Three, freeze lobby stairwell landing."

"Copy."

Styles went over to the stairway as he might have done hundreds of times before and proceeded through. Halfway to the second landing, he stopped. "Point Three, freeze all remaining landing cameras in stairwell for the next three minutes."

"Copy, Point One."

Styles then hustled up to the roof entrance. He was through the door with twenty seconds to spare. He double-checked that the lockset would not automatically lock him out. It would have. He took out the Gorilla Tape and pulled off a strip, then affixed it to hold the lockset bolt inside the door edge to prevent it from extending into the doorjamb striker plate. Next he quickly changed out of his gym clothes and into his black attire. It was now just short of completely dark. There was only very discreet indirect lighting over the roof, coming from the lights over the city. He would have been extremely difficult to spot without a night scope. There was no reason to believe anyone would be utilizing one to watch this roof.

He walked over to the side of the building and looked down. He quickly identified the two balconies he was looking for. He retrieved his gym bag and pulled out the coil of black rope. He quickly tied one end around the base of the satellite dishes for the television and Internet feeds, then played the rest out over the roof. He tied a large knot in the free end, then lowered it between the two balconies two floors past where it needed to be. He took up the slack in the rope and tied that off to the rope already encircling the satellite dish base. He walked back over to the edge, studying the two balconies. They were both well bathed in light. He walked back to the wall of the stairwell access building and leaned down against the wall.

"Point One, ready to commence," Styles notified the group.

"Point Two copies that."

"Point Three copies that."

"Point Four, bored as shit." Christman said, extolling his thoughts.

Phillips replied, "Point One, three guests still home."

"Copy, Point Three," Styles confirmed. Walking back to the edge, he looked down and could see shadows occasionally appear across the balcony deck.

Ten minutes later Phillips said, "Point One, three guests departing."

"Copy, Point Three."

"Three guests entering elevator."

"Copy, Point Three."

"Three guests entering restaurant. Will visually confirm seated."

"Copy, Point Three. Don't be made."

"Copy, Point One."

Two minutes later Phillips spoke again. "Point One, confirmation of three guests seated."

"Copy, Point Three."

Styles pulled against the rope sharply and was satisfied. He donned his gloves, checked his gear, then went over the side, easily going hand over hand down the rope. When he reached the spot between his two target balconies, he walked the wall over to the one on his left, climbing over the railing. He pulled up the end of the rope with the knot in it and tied it around the base of a railing post. He then grabbed the rope coming from the roof and walked the wall twenty-five feet over to the second balcony. He tied the rope from the first balcony taut around the base of a railing post on this second balcony. Now he had easy access to either balcony. Neither balcony door had its shades pulled, so he could easily see into the rooms. This room had five suitcases in it while the first had only two. Kovesky and Stovalasski would be here. He tried the door and was surprised when it opened. He quickly stepped in and looked around. He checked out the bathroom and found it still steamy. He decided to take these two first, but he wanted to check out the second room. He quickly retreated to the balcony and lowered himself to the rope he had tied between the balconies. Seconds later he was hoisting himself up and over that balcony railing. He looked inside the room, double-checking it was clear, and tried that door. It was locked. He took a flexible, yet firm, strip of plastic from the pocket of his black jeans. It resembled a credit card. He quickly jimmied the bolt on the lockset and stepped inside. These locks were more for show than actual performance. How many people would be breaking in from this height?

Styles performed a quick tactical recon of this room. He noticed that the shower stall was unusual. The ceiling height was five feet higher than the rest of the bathroom. He stared at it for a second and couldn't really reason why that was. *Maybe ductwork or something*, he thought. Satisfied he'd seen enough, he returned to the first room, making sure that he had not disturbed anything.

"Point One, in position. Point Three, advise when our guests leave the restaurant."

"Copy, Point One," Phillips replied.

Now it was just a matter of waiting.

CHAPTER 82

NAKHAN ZAZAR WAS quite comfortable, jetting his way toward Frankfurt, Germany. Considering the circumstances, that is. He was pleased that he was being put up in one of the Hilton Frankfurt's suites, at no cost to him. He intended to spend an extra day, maybe even two, to enjoy the women Frankfurt had to offer. He was not pleased that he had that psycho Iraqi, Wazzuri, with him. The man was little more than an animal. All his speech was dismal, and he smelled as though he had never taken a bath. He was loyal to Sheikh Ami al Hadid and had been instructed by him, in front of Zazar, that he was to obey Zazar without question. Otherwise, Zazar would have been scared out of his wits in the company of this man. They had spoken fewer than ten words since they'd left the sheikh's compound to head for the airport. If Zazar had anything to do with it, they would speak still fewer words before their arrival back home. Unfortunately he knew that would be impossible.

Zazar had decided to get Wazzuri his own room and was more than willing to pay for it himself. The last thing he wanted was having him around to spoil his intended fun. When he had informed Wazzuri of this, he received only a grunt in return. To make matters worse, the man constantly belched. Zazar really wondered if he knew what soap was.

Considering their departure time, they would be in Frankfurt a bit early. He was not worried. He felt confident he would be able to talk the reservation desk into letting them into their rooms. He had money to bribe if necessary. He was quite eager to get away from the sand, from which there seemed to be no escape. The male steward onboard had brought them a well-prepared steak sandwich. An unusual dish, to be sure, but one Zazar craved. Global Eastern's main corporate jet, a privatized Boeing 727, had every imaginable convenience. It was appointed in a luxurious manner from its gourmet kitchen to its solid-gold bathroom fixtures. No expense had been spared. It may have well been the world's most expensive plane in its class.

After he finished his lunch, with tea, he informed Wazzuri that he had important business to complete on his computer and was not to be disturbed. Again he received only a grunt in return. He then retired to his private quarters and immersed himself in his graphic world of pornography.

President Robert Williams was meeting with the heads of the FBI, the CIA, the National Security Agency, and Homeland Security.

"So you are telling me that none of you have any idea of what might have happened to one of the most recognizable figures in this entire country? How can that be?" the president demanded. "We can read the classified ads from outer space, but we can't find Andrew Ladd?" He appeared to be steaming. The mood of this meeting was understandably tense.

Matt Sanderson of the FBI spoke first. "Sir, we all have been working with every resource we possess; we are just coming up empty. It's as though he's just disappeared from the planet. There have been no ransom demands; no group has taken responsibility—just nothing."

"Gentlemen, this is unacceptable. He's my chief of staff. He has information critical to the security of this country. *He must be found.*"

Bernard Backersley, of the CIA, was the next to address the president.

"Sir, I've been working everyone overseas; no one has seen him. We've covered every major access to all available transportation with facial recognition programs. He has not been seen."

Sanderson spoke again. "We've gone through his house top to bottom four times and haven't come up with a damned thing. Nothing. His security detail knew he was there; they were attacked from behind and choked out. When they came to, he was gone. I don't have anything else to say, except I have every available agent across the entire country looking for him."

The president was silent for a few moments before continuing. "I am not trying to assign blame, but I must tell you this situation is not inspiring confidence. You must do better. You must find him. Keep me informed." He stormed out of the room. The other four remained behind to confer among themselves.

Charles Rockford, the director of Homeland Security, spoke first. "I didn't want to bring this up in front of him, but does anyone else think that, just maybe, Ladd sold us out?"

"That was my first thought," Backersley replied. "At least after no ransom demands were made. I think we have to start looking at this more of an act of treason by Ladd, rather than a criminal act against him, at least among us."

Elliott Ragar, the director of the National Security Agency, agreed. "From what we know, or possibly more appropriately what we don't know, I believe that makes more sense. If he had been grabbed, I'm sure that something would have shown up somewhere. From the complete lack of any information, I have to believe that he planned this. As much as I don't like going behind *his* back, I think we need to keep this between ourselves for the moment, at least until we have some solid evidence to present." Everyone at the table looked around, nodding in agreement.

Matt Sanderson spoke. "Agreed then. We'll start looking from this new perspective, keeping it quiet for the time being. Well, gentlemen, let's see what we can find out." The four men got up from the table and left the room.

Down the hallway in another office, President Williams was watching a video monitor. He couldn't help but smile. *You're not the only one, Bernard.*

CHAPTER 83

"POINT ONE, GUESTS about to leave restaurant," Phillips announced. "Copy, Point Three," Styles answered.

Two minutes later Phillips stated, "Point One, couple headed toward elevator, single heading toward bar."

"Copy." Styles was in the correct room. He decided to wait out on the balcony, just off to the side of the door opening. Four minutes later the door to the room opened and two men entered. He could see their reflections clearly in a large mirror that was over a marble counter. He recognized Kovesky immediately from the pictures Phillips had downloaded. A dark, surly looking man. The other, Stovalasski, was a curly blond-haired "pretty boy." He would have looked perfectly natural styling hair in a high-priced salon. He did not look anything like the man Styles had pictured. Stovalasski turned on a sound system and tuned it to classical music.

In broken English Kovesky said, "Mikhail, the vodka, it should be cold. I go to piss," and walked into the bathroom, which was at the far end of the room.

Styles watched Stovalasski walk over to the other side of the room, where the bar and refrigerator were located, just outside the line of sight from the mirror. By the way he walked, Styles guessed that a fair amount of vodka had already been consumed. As Stovalasski opened the door to retrieve the bottle, Styles silently slid through the french door that he'd opened up enough to squeeze through. In four soundless strides he was behind him. Stovalasski closed the door and placed the bottle on the bar. He was just about to reach for two glasses when Styles cupped his left hand along the lower left part of his chin and placed his right hand at the top of his head, slightly above and behind his right ear. Styles violently snapped his head to the right, ripping his brain stem in half and snapping his neck. The man died instantly. Styles caught him and quickly laid him out on top of the bed.

He then hurried over to the bathroom, standing off to the side of the doorway. He heard the toilet flush. When Kovesky walked through, Styles grabbed him by the front of his throat, his fingers encompassing Kovesky's windpipe like a vise. He walked Kovesky over to a chair and sat him down. It happened so fast he never had a chance to react. Styles dug his thumb downward into a nerve center in the area between his neck and shoulder, which all but paralyzed him. He then removed his hand from Kovesky's throat. He eased up just enough so Kovesky could concentrate. And talk, barely.

"What do you want?" Kovesky managed to gasp out. "Who the fuck you are?"

Styles stared hard at him. Kovesky tried to struggle, but Styles just dug his thumb in deeper. "I want to know the answer to one question. Answer it and you live. Don't, and you die."

Kovesky noticed his friend on the bed. "Mikhail," he cried out.

"Relax, he's just sleeping," Styles lied.

"What do you want?"

"I'm only going to ask you once. How many bombs did you sell to the Saudis?"

"I do no such thing."

"Wrong answer, Ivan. The American president sends his regards." He stared hard into Kovesky's eyes for five long seconds, applying more pressure with his thumb all the time. He then drove a vicious front-knuckle strike directly through the man's Adam's apple that completely crushed his larynx and windpipe. He watched the man die retching. He waited about five minutes, then took a small razor-sharp pen knife out of his pocket. He carved "terrorist" into Kovesky's forehead. He walked over to Stovalasski and did the same. Styles didn't actually know if Stovalasski was a terrorist or not, *But what the hell*, he thought. *Couldn't hurt.*

He walked into the bathroom and used some toilet tissue to wipe the end of his knife blade clean, then flushed the tissue down the toilet. He marveled at the flexibility of the paper-thin leather gloves he wore. Putting the knife back in his pocket, he walked over to the entry door. He opened it slightly and placed the "Do Not Disturb" sign on the doorknob, then closed and locked the door. He then turned the lights down low, turned the music down a bit lower, pulled the shades on the french doors, and walked back out onto the balcony. He untied his rope from that railing, then walked the side of the building back to the second balcony. He untied the rope from the railing post and hitched it around the top rail.

Styles cautiously looked inside, finding the room to be just as it was. He squatted down next to the wall. "All Points, two guests down."

"Point One, single guest still at bar."

"Copy, Point Three." Styles decided to search Pevosky's room. A quick look didn't turn up anything out of the ordinary, with the exception of two laptop computers. Styles decided to hold on to those, so he took them out to the balcony and placed them up against the wall. There wasn't anything to do until Pevosky returned, so he decided to do some push-ups to keep loose. He had completed close to nine hundred when his headset came alive.

"Point One, single guest appears to be ready to leave."

"Acknowledged, Point Three."

"Point One, we have a problem. Guest appears to have company."

"Source?"

"Female, Point One. Looks like he picked her up. Advise."

Styles thought fast. He did not want anyone else involved. "Point Three, what is your location?"

"Lobby," Phillips replied.

"Point Three, you're about to become a field agent. Intercept him before he gets out of the restaurant. Come on to him hard. Do not let that female stay with him. *Whatever* is necessary. Accompany him to his room."

"Point One, suggestions?"

"Point Three, you're a woman; figure it out. Just get it done."

"Copy, Point One," Phillips said, a hard edge in her voice.

"Point One, is this a good course?" Starr asked.

"Point Two, following parameters as directed."

Phillips thought fast. She quickly made her way over to the restaurant entrance and literally bumped into Pevosky as he was approaching.

"Excuse me, sir," Phillips said in perfect Russian. "Oh, Petr, what are you doing here? It's *so* good to see you again." She stepped between Pevosky and the blonde woman he was with. *Hooker*, Phillips thought.

"Do I know you?" Pevosky inquired politely.

"Oh Petr, you hurt my feelings. If you don't remember me, you should certainly remember our room service bill in St. Petersburg last year. It took me three days to recover; I almost lost my job." With a twinkle in her eye, she said mischievously, "Petr, I was sore for days." She could see him searching his mind for some reference as to just what she was talking about. She moved closer and stroked his arm. "Petr, how can you not remember?"

"Obviously, you were not very good," the blonde interjected.

Phillips whirled around, eyes blazing. "Speak again and you will need new teeth, whore." Phillips continued to stare at her, daring her to speak. She turned back to Pevosky and told him, "Send this girl away. She is a waste of your time. And money," she added, her voice dripping with sarcasm. Phillips hooked her arm around Pevosky and began leading him out the door.

The blonde reached out, grabbing Phillips by the shoulder. "What are you doing?" she demanded.

In one motion, Phillips let go of Pevosky, spun on her left foot, and executed a perfect roundhouse kick to the blonde right in the mouth, sending her sprawling. "Go back to the gutter and fuck rats," she snarled at the woman on the floor. She turned back to Pevosky and, with her sexiest smile, said, "Now where were we?" She couldn't help but notice how much Pevosky was enjoying this entire incident.

"Back to my room to enjoy some ice-cold Stoli, if you wish," Pevosky suggested.

"I couldn't think of anything I'd rather do, Petr," Phillips responded, trying hard not to look ill. *Fuck you, Styles,* she thought, knowing he had heard everything and was probably laughing at her.

Several floors above, out on a balcony, Styles was doing just that.

"Point One, I believe Point Three will be rather pissed," Starr said, laughing.

"Point Two, focus on our assignment," Styles answered with a chuckle.

"Sounds like she handled it like a pro," Starr continued.

"Yeah, not bad. I'll say so to her if I'm not busy ducking."

They both heard over their headsets, ever so quietly, "Damned straight."

CHAPTER 85

AFTER FENDING OFF Captain Petr Pevosky's clumsy advances, Phillips arrived with him at the door to his hotel room. Passing in front of the door preceding his with the "Do Not Disturb" sign hanging on the doorknob, Pevosky commented under his breath, "Might as well fuck pigs."

"What was that, Petr?" Phillips asked, turning toward him.

"Nothing. Nothing to do with us."

You have no idea how wrong you are, Phillips thought to herself as Pevosky fumbled with the key card. Finally, he got the door open.

Trying to pass himself off as something other than a half-drunken slob, he stepped aside and, motioning her inward, said, "ladies first."

"Why thank you, Petr," she announced louder than necessary, to be sure Styles didn't mistake her for Pevosky. She didn't know what he had planned, but she did not want to be on the receiving end of anything. She stepped through the doorway, walking quickly to the center of the room. She kept her eyes straight ahead. Pevosky followed. He turned to close the door, and the instant it latched, he felt a searing, white-hot pain in his left knee. He did not realize that Styles had kicked him so hard the joint was reduced to bone shards. He didn't know why he was falling. His left wrist was caught, and he found himself flat on his back, staring up at a man with ice-cold eyes. He still could not grasp what had happened. The only thing he understood was that his left knee was on fire and it was bent at a very awkward angle. Instantaneously he felt his mouth being taped shut. He heard a voice. "You can leave now." It must have come from this man. Then he was yanked upward and deposited in a chair. Now, for the first time, he felt fear. He looked around for the woman, but all he saw was the door closing. He tried to talk but only mumbled low sounds. The man in front of him was dressed all in black. His first coherent thought was *Military*. His knee was screaming.

The man kneeled down in front of him. "Captain Petr Pevosky. The president of the United States sends his regrets that you decided to sell nuclear weapons to terrorists. He can't have that. So he sent me." Styles stared hard into the man's eyes for five seconds, then reached out, grabbed his head and chin, and violently twisted so hard he left him looking backward. Out came his pen knife, and once more he cut the word "terrorist" in his forehead. This time, he merely wiped the blade on the dead Russian's shirt. Styles walked over, opened the door carefully, and checked that no one would see him, then hung the "Do Not Disturb" sign on the exterior doorknob. After closing and locking the door, he surveyed the scene for a final time, then went back outside to the balcony, locking that door behind him. He quickly unhitched his rope from the railing, tossed the slack down, and hauled himself hand over hand back to the roof. He then pulled the rope up, coiling it as he did, then untied it from the satellite dish base. He stashed it back in his gym bag and changed back into his gym clothes.

Styles quickly descended the stairwell and strode out into the lobby. Scanning around, he found that it appeared no one had noticed him coming in from the stairs. He twisted and stretched as he walked toward the front door. When he walked through, a different doorman smiled and said, "Have a nice run, sir."

"I'll try." The doorman paid no attention to his gym bag. "All Points, primary assignment complete." Styles ran two miles, finding Starr waiting for him at the designated pickup point. He got in the front seat beside Starr.

"Any problems?" Starr asked.

"No."

Unfortunately, that answer was entirely incorrect.

Six minutes after Phillips had left the bar with Petr Pevosky and a cocktail waitress had helped the blonde hooker back out the door, a tall, well-dressed man entered. He walked straight to the bartender and engaged in a concise conversation. At one point the bartender walked back to his register and gathered some information. After writing it down, he returned and handed the note to the tall man. He received a generous cash tip in return. The tall man headed for the elevator. He was darkly tanned and looked older than his actual age because he had tinted his naturally light blond hair a shade of silver. Looking at him, someone might have taken him for a successful banker or perhaps investment broker. He wasn't. He was a pimp for the blonde hooker that Williams had just kicked, knocking out six of her teeth, and he was extremely angry.

Looking down at the paper he'd received, he proceeded to take the elevator to the floor of the room to which the woman who had attacked his girl and the Russian john had headed when they left the bar. As the door opened and he prepared to step off, he found himself staring at the very woman he was looking for. Thinking quickly he looked up at the number, mumbled to himself, smiled at the woman, and stepped backward, allowing her to enter. The scene had all the appearance of someone starting to get off on the wrong floor. Phillips gave him a slight nod, then turned to push the button that would return her to her own floor. Just as her finger approached the button, she was dealt a terrific jolt at the base of her neck. Then everything went black.

I love Tasers, the man thought to himself. He punched the button that would take the car straight to the basement. Phillips had not noticed the key inserted that locked the car out from any other stops.

When the door opened, the man easily carried Phillips over his shoulder to a waiting van. As he approached, the side door opened, and he unceremoniously tossed her inside. A man waiting within quickly bound her arms and feet with wire ties. Thirty seconds later the vehicle was blending into traffic and speeding away from the hotel.

CHAPTER 85

EVERYONE EXCEPT PHILLIPS had reconvened at the hangar. Christman was the first to speak. "What did you mean by 'primary' mission complete?"

Styles answered, "We still have to have our guest join his friends."

Starr asked, "What do you have in mind?"

"To have him found where he shouldn't be found."

"Anybody heard from Phillips?" asked Christman.

"Nope. She probably went back to her room," Starr offered.

"Okay."

Styles walked over and picked up his radio earpiece. He turned it on and put it in place. He could hear breathing but nothing else. "Strange," he said. "I can hear her breathing but nothing else."

"Maybe she's sleeping," Starr said.

"Phillips? At this hour? That doesn't sound like her," Christman stated flatly.

"No, it doesn't," Styles agreed. "Besides, why would she still have her earpiece? It doesn't make sense."

Starr got up and put in his own earpiece. "Yeah, I hear what you mean. No background noise at all."

"Point Three, you copy?" Styles asked.

No answer.

"Point Three, you copy?" Styles said louder.

Still no answer.

"Try the phone," directed Styles.

Starr grabbed his and dialed. "No answer."

"Something's wrong," growled Styles. "No way she wouldn't answer."

"Should I try the hotel?" asked Christman.

"No," Starr and Styles answered in unison.

"Never go through the hotel," Starr continued.

They looked at each other. "You go," Styles said. "Check her room. Everybody back on com. We've got a problem, and we need to deal with it fast."

Starr went out the door as Christman reached for his headset.

"What do you think happened?" Christman asked Styles.

"Don't know, but I'm starting to get an idea. Don't want to talk about it yet, though. J. C., I'm heading over toward the hotel. I want you to listen. Listen *hard*. Background noises, anything. I think there's a way you can run your earpiece through the computer and get more volume. I got no clue how. Talk to Starr if it helps. You hear *anything* else, be sure to tape it, and let us know straight away." Then he was gone.

"Great," he said aloud. "Like I'm a fucking computer geek." He walked over and started studying the task assigned him.

Darlene Phillips had regained consciousness but did not let on. She'd heard voices. First, she thought they were in her head, but she slowly realized her earpiece was still working. She became aware of other voices a short distance away. She kept her composure and made certain nothing changed to give away the fact that she was awake. She kept her breathing the same. Slowly her memory began to focus. The elevator. The tall man. Her neck feeling like it was going to explode. *Fucking Taser*, she thought.

269

"How much longer will she be out?" she heard a man's voice say in perfect German.

"I don't know. I gave her a good jolt. Probably harder than I needed to, but I was pissed."

Phillips didn't dare open her eyes to look but felt certain the second voice belonged to the tall man she had seen in the elevator.

"What are you going to do to her?" the first voice asked.

"Hold the fucking bitch until she makes up the money she's cost me. After that I'm not sure. If she's a problem, kill her. If not, well, she's just another whore."

Phillips was hoping desperately her cheeks were not turning red with anger. She had determined that she was tied. Her hands were lashed together at her stomach, and her knees and feet were bound together as well. She continued feigning unconsciousness.

"Fuck this, I'm going to get a drink," the first voice complained.

"I'll check the ties and join you. We'll come back in an hour."

Phillips felt her bonds being checked. She heard the men walking away, then a door opening and closing. She was certain she was alone. She had been terrified that captors would hear Starr screaming in her ear. She dared not answer just in case someone might hear her. She thought about coughing to let Starr know she was alive. She decided on making a soft clucking noise with her tongue against the roof of her mouth.

"Phillips, is that you? Can you hear me?" Starr yelled in her ear.

She clucked twice.

"Okay, if I understand you correctly, you can't talk. So make that noise once for yes, and twice for no," he said, purposely reversing what she had just done.

One cluck.

"Are you okay?"

One cluck.

"Obviously you're in trouble."

One cluck.

"Any idea where you are?"

Two clucks.

"Phillips, this is Styles. Does this have anything to do with the incident in the bar?"

One cluck. Two clucks. One cluck.

"Does that mean you don't know but you think so?" Star responded.

One cluck.

"Okay, we're on it. Hold on, I'll find you."

One cluck. Inside, Phillips smiled. She knew he would.

CHAPTER 86

S TYLES CONTACTED STARR, and they met a block away in the SUV Styles was driving.

"What do you think?" Starr asked, somewhat surprised by Styles's appearance. He was more cold and calculating as opposed to angry.

"I think whoever controls that hooker got to Phillips in retaliation for what Phillips did to her."

"How'd you come up with that?" Starr asked.

"Only plausible reason. Phillips hasn't pissed off anybody else."

"Makes sense," Starr agreed, nodding. "So how do we find her?"

"Start at the beginning. Somebody had to tell somebody who Phillips left with. That would be the logical way she was found. Realistically only one person would know who she was with and where they were going. Plus Phillips said that Pevosky was sitting at the bar. Bartenders do a shitload more than just pour drinks. They arrange: drugs, hookers, whatever a customer might want. All else fails, ask the bartender."

Again Starr nodded in agreement. "So what now?"

"We need to identify the head bartender and determine how he leaves the building."

"Marv, how do you know it's the head bartender? What if there's more than one?"

"Greed, Starr. No head bartender is going to stand for someone under him getting the action. I know of circumstances where a new guy has been killed for trying to horn in on someone else's business. It's a real pecking order, particularly outside of home."

"You got a plan?"

"Yeah, we go in and get a quick beer. Establish who's who. Find out if there's an employee entrance. We go in separate. Engage a conversation. Make up some shit about anything to try to find out what's what. Check for security cameras and let me know. I'll slip in, grab a table and observe." Styles looked at his watch. "It's almost midnight. We need to get Phillips back by dawn; otherwise, our timetable is going to get fucked up."

"You think we can get her back by then?"

"Either that or there're gonna be some body bags needed. Get going. Let me know about the cameras."

Without a word Starr got out of the SUV and headed toward the hotel. Reaching the entrance to the bar, he paused and casually looked around. He quickly spotted the security cameras. One was aimed at the cash register, and one was over the entrance; however, it appeared that if one were to stay tight to the right-hand side, he or she could probably stay out of view. Two more were scanning the seating area. The far-right rear looked like the best bet. He walked back outside into the lobby and found an area of privacy. He relayed the information to Styles.

"All right, go back in and grab a beer at the bar. You say there're two bartenders?"

"Yeah, pretty obvious who's the head guy. I'll stretch out my arm at him when you come in."

"I'm two minutes out."

Just 118 seconds later Styles came walking through the bar, staying hard right. Keeping his head down, he headed for the farthest table in the right rear of the bar. The cocktail waitress approached, and he ordered a draft. She left. Returning, she set the heavy stein down in front of him, and he merely nodded. She smiled and moved off to another table.

Styles studied the man that Starr had identified when he entered. In two minutes he'd learned all he needed to know. He grabbed a napkin and, looking around to be sure no one was paying any attention to him, poured his beer into a planter. He replaced the stein on the table and stuffed the napkin into his pocket. Using only the insides of his fingers, he left five Euros on the table. This manner, combined with the napkin, would leave no fingerprints. Then retracing his steps, he was out of the bar and back to the SUV.

Fifteen minutes later Starr joined him.

"What'd you get?" Styles demanded.

"Small employee parking lot out back. Single door. I'm guessing it locks automatically; probably have to buzz to get in. Guy's name is Gunnar. Way he was bitching, I'm guessing he's usually the last one out."

"Good job, Starr. Go back to the hangar with J. C. I'll keep you posted."

"One other thing. I asked about getting a woman for the night. He said he could call for one, or I could walk up toward the small park, just up the street, and I could take my pick. He also warned me about some guy named Clotaire. Told me not to get rough with any of his girls. I figure that's who you want."

Styles looked at his friend. "Damn good job, Starr. You might have just made this whole thing a lot easier. Get going."

Five seconds later Starr was out of sight.

CHAPTER 87

STYLES WAS STANDING just inside a hedgerow, surveying the rear parking area. Two streetlights were illuminating the area. Using his binoculars, he spotted three security cameras. No guards were visible. An electric chain link gate blocked the single entrance. A six-foot-high chain-link fence surrounded the entire lot. *Guess it keeps the honest people out*, he thought.

The area was not large, accommodating maybe twelve vehicles. Outside the secured area was a delivery entrance. Styles was unconcerned with that. Over the next hour he saw three people leave. None of them was Gunnar. Thirty minutes later, one more left. One car remained in the parking lot. *Gunnar's*, Styles thought.

He found a spot that was out of range of any of the cameras and climbed over the fence. He knelt down and drew his silenced Beretta. Taking aim, he shot out the streetlight closest to the building. That left an eerie glow to the area. Styles studied the scene. He decided there wasn't enough light for the cameras to pick up a recognizable picture. Staying low, he made his way over to a couple of large trash barrels. There was a commercial Dumpster, but it was located near the delivery entrance. Styles considered the ramifications of shooting out the nearest camera. Considering the hour, he thought that camera going down would not cause considerable consternation. A loud click later, only two cameras were working. No one came out to check.

Ten minutes later Gunnar emerged. He seemed to take no notice of the reduced light, stopping to light a cigarette, then turning to head toward his car. His walk was interrupted by what seemed to be a giant sledgehammer slamming into his chest and then into the back of the building. He was looking at only eyes, as the man who had grabbed him had donned a military-style mask.

Gunnar was held tight against the building as though he were glued. He opened his mouth to yell, but the aggressor merely shook his head no. Gunnar complied.

Finally the masked assailant spoke. "I'm going to ask you some questions. How you answer them will determine whether you live or die on the spot where you are now standing. Nod your head if you understand."

Gunnar nodded. He had no misunderstanding of the threat he was facing.

Quietly, the attacker continued. "Earlier this evening, there was a disturbance in your bar. It involved a friend of mine who is now missing. Listen carefully. If I think you are lying to me, I will *not* ask you again. I will crush your throat. Nod if you understand."

Once again, Gunnar gave a simple nod.

"Good. Now, very quietly, tell me about Clotaire."

Gunnar answered in a whisper. "He owns all the whores that work this area. All of them. If an independent tries the area, she is warned once to leave. If she doesn't, she is never seen again. Same with any other pimps. He is ruthless and has no compassion for anyone or anything. It is just business, and he lets nothing interfere with his business. His heart is so cold it would make a shark jealous."

"Did he take my friend?"

"I don't know for certain, but I would think so. He asked who she left with and what room number the gentleman was in."

"Where did he take her?"

"I don't know." Gunnar felt a hand grasp his throat. "I'm telling you I don't know. I've told you everything else, even offered you information you didn't ask. Why would I risk my life over this?"

Styles had to admit the man made sense. "How do I find this Clotaire?"

"Rough up one of his girls. He will find you immediately. All of his girls have cell phones that dial only his number. If any girl sees another girl in trouble and does not call in, she will feel his wrath. No one wants to feel Clotaire's wrath. Trust me. The man is a psychopath."

"Where do I find one of his girls?"

"Two blocks up the street. All the girls are his."

"What does he look like?"

"Tall and lanky. Silver hair. One more thing—he is an expert in karate."

"Gunnar, you have been very helpful. Usually, this is where I would put you to sleep in a chokehold, but I'm going to give you a choice. Toss your cell phone in the trash barrel. Walk over to your car, pop the trunk, get in, and close it firmly. If you do anything other than what I just said, I will shoot you. Now go."

Styles watched as Gunnar did exactly as he was told. "This was one for the books," Styles said to himself softly. Quickly he was outside the lot and on the phone to Starr. "I need you back at the hotel fast as you can get here without getting arrested. Park in the same place. Dress nice. Have J. C. follow you. Get here quick." He hung up.

CHAPTER 88

PHILLIPS WAS STILL pretending to be out when the door opened and then closed. She heard two sets of footsteps coming toward her.

"It looks like she's still out," said Clotaire.

"I think she is faking. Go get a bucket of ice water. That should wake her up."

"I'm awake, asshole," Phillips snarled in perfect Russian.

"Speak German, French, or English, but never speak Russian to me," Clotaire said in English.

"Fine. English. Why the hell have you kidnapped me?"

Clotaire brought a chair over and sat down next to the bed. "You have damaged my property. You must make restitution. When that is complete, I will decide your future."

"What property?"

"One of my girls. You will have to make up for her services plus pay for her medical requirements, including her teeth."

"So you're blackmailing me?"

"Oh no, that is not the case at all. You are simply going to make restitution."

"How much is that?"

"Yet to be determined, but I would estimate a minimum of seventy thousand dollars American."

"I am not a whore. Besides, that woman wouldn't bring seventy grand if there were three of her."

Clotaire just smiled at the girl tied on the bed. "You might not have been a whore, but you certainly are now. In case you haven't noticed, you have a new accessory to your wardrobe. That leather collar around your neck."

Inside, Phillips winced. She hadn't noticed it.

"That collar is locked in place electromagnetically. Only I have the code to unlock it. It is also an electrical shock device. I also control how hard it can jolt you. If necessary, it can kill, by explosion. Should any attempt be made to remove the collar, it will automatically kill you. You cause any problems—well, you should be able to figure it out. You will never be out of range because it uses the same technology as a cell phone. You could be halfway around the world, and I could still kill you. If you behave yourself and earn the money you owe me, I will consider releasing you."

Both of them knew that was a lie.

One very important fact that he was unaware of was that J. C. Christman had just heard every word over the computer-enhanced transmission from Phillips's earpiece. Housed in a very soft rubber compound designed to easily conform to an individual's ear canal, the earpiece's components had been protected by the electrical charge of the Taser. Instantly Christman was on the com detailing the information to Styles and Starr.

That information was not the only item that Clotaire did not know. He had no idea of the enemy that he had made.

CHAPTER 89

S TARR SLIPPED INTO Styles' SUV. Christman was about ten minutes behind. After a short discussion, Starr said, "Okay, think I've got it."

Styles said, "Starr, you realize that there's a good chance you might take some shots before this is over."

"I've taken shots before, Marv."

"Yeah, I know, just laying all the cards out."

Right then, Christman pulled up behind them. He parked and joined Styles and Starr.

They filled Christman in on the plan. "So, Styles, you gonna confront this guy straight off or follow him to Phillips?"

"Gotta play this by ear, J. C. Normally I'd deal with him right off, but because of this collar he's got strapped on Phillips, I gotta be careful."

"Sounds good to me. Let's go."

The three of them started toward the park. Styles separated himself and walked in. Starr drove up to where some of the escorts were congregated. He signaled toward a blonde, motioning her over.

"Hey there, handsome, I'm Natasha."

Starr smiled and said, "Of course you are."

She reached over and stroked the side of his face with her fingernails, gently. "What would you like to do?" she asked.

"How much?" Starr said.

"Depends on what you want."

"The works. Everything."

"Five hundred American would certainly make me happy. I can guarantee I'll make you happy."

"How would you like to make ten times that?"

She eyed him suspiciously. "What do you mean?"

"Natasha, this is going to sound crazy, but I swear it's legit. I want to pretend to rough you up a bit. Right out here in the open."

"You want to *what?*"

"I want to pretend that we are having an argument, make believe I shove you around a bit. It'll all be fake. I know this sounds nuts, but it's what I want. I'll give you five grand if you go along."

"That's the craziest thing I've ever heard. Besides, it will bring you great trouble."

"This is where it gets nuttier. That's what I'm counting on. You in? Money up front."

"What's to stop me from taking your money and running?"

"Trust me, Natasha, I have my reason, and you do *not* want to know what that is. You in?"

"Five thousand American, cash?"

"Yes. Right here, right now."

"Honey, for five thousand dollars, you can smack away. Make it real. Just not too real."

"Thanks, but I can't do that. We'll just fake it." He handed her the money.

She started. "Fuck you, asshole. I won't do that." She slapped Starr gently across his face.

"Fuck you, whore. You're not worth half that." He slapped her back. She pretended to stumble to the ground. Starr then made it look as though he were kicking her in the ribs, causing Natasha to scream violently. "Shut up, bitch," he yelled. Grabbing her hair, he acted as though he were slapping her across the face. He needed to stall for time.

"I'm going to take your purse and dump it. I need more time," he said quietly.

"Do whatever you must," she said.

"How much money have you conned men out of, whore?" he screamed at her, taking her purse and dumping it all over the ground. She had already stashed the money Starr had given her in her underwear.

Starr wasted more time pretending to rummage through her purse. He noticed that all the other girls were intently watching them.

He was just about to give up as he'd run out of ideas when a silver sedan came squealing up to the curb.

"That is Clotaire. He will be very bad trouble for you. You'd better start running."

"Thanks, Natasha. I slipped a phone number among your items. You need help, call that number. I owe you."

"You owe me nothing. What do I call you?"

Starr winked at her and said, "Call me John."

She stifled a laugh. "How original you Americans are." She immediately went back into character.

She looked over at the man getting out of the car that had just stopped. "Clotaire, help, help me. Please, Clotaire."

Starr started backing up over toward the edge of the park. There was a short stone wall surrounding it with a hedgerow growing behind it.

A tall man with silver hair was approaching Starr in an extremely menacing manner. "I teach you to fuck with my girls," he swore at Starr in German.

Starr, still retreating, placed his hands out to his sides and said, "I don't understand German, I only speak English."

"I teach you to fuck with my girls," he swore at Starr again, only this time in English.

"Hey, she was trying to rip me off. What am I supposed to do?"

"What I'm going to do. Rip your balls off and feed them to you," growled Clotaire, still advancing on Starr.

Starr's back was at the stone wall. He turned and hopped over it and pushed through the bush. "Look man, nothing personal but I'm not going to be ripped off by some whore."

282

Clotaire followed Starr into the park.

"Marv, now might be a good time," Starr said quietly. "Marv? Hello, Marv."

Clotaire was now within fifteen feet of Starr and had entered a fighter's stance.

Eight feet from Starr, just as he was about to launch an attack, came words with an ice-cold edge: "Your fight's with me."

Clotaire whirled toward the voice to see a man standing ten feet away from himself. He had no idea where this stranger had come from. A man dressed all in black, several inches shorter than himself. Clotaire immediately underestimated this new adversary. He turned back to look at Starr and was surprised to see him sitting comfortably on the ground.

Without waiting for Clotaire to say anything, Starr offered, "I just thought I'd get comfortable to watch the show."

"You get comfortable. When I'm done with him, I'll deal with you."

"If you say so," Starr shot right back.

The figure in black, including black face paint, advanced to within six feet of Clotaire and stopped. "Anytime," Styles said.

Clotaire instantly started into a classic karate combination of a side kick to the head, which Styles easily ducked, a roundhouse kick to Styles' head, which he easily dodged by stepping aside, and a three-punch combination, which Styles easily blocked. While most men would have become more cautious at this point, Clotaire only became more enraged. He tried a front jump kick to Styles' jaw, which missed, then tried a spinning back kick. Clotaire felt a hand grab hold of the front of his ankle as Styles stepped inside, then felt a tremendous pressure against his leg just below the back of his knee. Clotaire instantly found himself on the ground. Styles had used a combination of Clotaire's own force, by redirecting it, and simple leverage. Clotaire scrambled back to his feet. This time, however, he paused to study this opponent. He was not used to being bested. He changed techniques. He tried grappling. He dived headfirst at Styles' legs, trying to wrestle him to the ground but received a brutal elbow between his shoulder blades for his trouble, driving him to the ground. He got up again, although this time much slower. He intently looked at his enemy, hatred pouring from his eyes. He started to circle Styles.

Styles slowly moved, keeping Clotaire in front of him. "Maybe you haven't noticed, Clotaire, but so far I'm only being defensive. Care to guess how long you'll last if I go offensive?"

"I'm going to kill you," he snarled.

"Actually, no, you're not," replied Styles, his casual tone infuriating him even more.

Clotaire tried returning to the classic karate style featuring strikes and kicks. After three unsuccessful attempts, there was a fourth. He faked a punch and tried delivering a knee to Styles' face. Both of his feet were off the ground, in the spring required for a knee strike, when Styles struck. Styles stepped to one side and as Clotaire went past him, delivered a brutal punch to his left kidney. As he went down again, Styles caught Clotaire just under the arms with both his legs wrapped around him like a boa constrictor. He then placed Clotaire in a rear choke hold. They both stayed on the ground with Styles in complete control. He whispered into his ear, "Don't worry; I'm only going to put you to sleep for a little while."

J. C. Christman, staying very low, crept up on the driver of the silver sedan parked at the curb. The driver was smoking a cigarette and had his window down. Christman stuck the end of the silencer on his pistol against the driver's ear. The cigarette fell from the driver's hand.

"Don't even breathe hard, my friend, or your brains will be all over the windshield. Do you speak English?"

"Yes."

"Good. That's one strong point on your staying alive. Now, I'm going to climb into the backseat directly behind you. If you would be so kind as to unlock the doors." Christman heard the click of the locks releasing. "Don't even blink." He climbed in behind the driver. He said nothing.

"Now what?" asked the driver.

"We wait. Don't worry. It won't be long. Be sure to keep your hands on top of the steering wheel. I lose sight of one, I shoot. No warning."

Shortly two men emerged from the park. One man was carrying

a third over his shoulder. They walked up to the car and opened the curbside rear door. The unconscious man was thrown into the seat. One of the two men got in next to him, while the second man got into the front seat behind the driver. This man spoke. "Take us to where the girl is."

"What girl?"

His head bounced off the windowsill of the driver's door from the punch to the side of his head.

"Don't make me ask again."

The driver was bleeding from both sides of his face and only nodded. The trip took less than two minutes.

Christman spoke up. "You guys empty his pockets?"

"Yeah," Starr said. "We've got everything, including a fancy little electronic bracelet he was wearing."

Styles caught the look that came over the driver's face, and he grabbed him by the hair. "How many men inside? You lie, you die."

"None. Three other men are in a house behind this one. But none inside."

Styles looked at Christman. "You don't hear from me in five minutes, you shoot him in the head."

Starr got out, opened the rear door, and once again hoisted Clotaire up onto his shoulder. He hadn't stirred.

When Styles, carrying Clotaire, and Starr were out on the sidewalk, Starr said, "Phillips, you hear me okay?"

"Loud and clear, Starr. Where are you guys?"

"Look out the window, down on the street."

"I can't. I'm tied up on a bed on the second floor, I think."

Christman's voice cut in. "I'm not even gonna touch that one."

"Fuck you, J. C."

Everybody chuckled.

"Sorry, Phillips, couldn't resist."

"Yeah. I got an electric collar on me. Come get this fucking thing off."

CHAPTER 90

STYLES HAD CUT the wire ties from Phillips, who was up and stretching, trying to get the kinks out. Starr had shown her the electronic bracelet that controlled the collar that was attached to Phillips. She looked at it for fifteen seconds, turned on a power button, and hit another button with a downward pointing arrow on it, keeping it depressed until a zero appeared on a tiny screen. "Cut this fucking thing off me. No, wait a minute, don't. Wake that bastard up." Clotaire had started to show signs of starting to come around.

Starr walked back into the room and threw a glass of water in his face. That brought full consciousness back for Clotaire. He looked around the room, saw his predicament, and glowered at everyone.

Phillips walked up to him. "Tell me the code to release the lock. If anything else happens"—she looked over at Styles—"take your knife and castrate this fucking bastard. I mean it. Cut everything off."

Starr interrupted. "You sure? Why don't we just cut that damned collar off?"

Styles answered. "She's got her reasons." He walked over to Clotaire and yanked him to his feet. He looked straight into Clotaire's eyes. "You got my word on two things. One, you tell her straight, we leave and you live. You fuck up, and I will hack off your jewels. And it won't be fast. You decide."

Starr said, "Phillips ..." full of concern.

Clotaire looked at Styles, then at Phillips. "Punch both up and down buttons to the bottom. Then punch in 4-1-5-6. Punch both buttons back to the top. That releases the catch."

"*Phillips* ..." Starr said again.

Phillips punched in the code. She heard a click, and the collar fell off. She caught it before it hit the floor.

Styles spoke up. "Phillips, I took it easy on him; thought maybe you might want to have a go with him."

She stared laser beams through Clotaire. Without looking she said, "Thank you. Any other time I'd jump on that. I could hand this bastard his ass inside out. But I've got a better idea."

Styles smiled. He knew what was coming.

Phillips walked over to Clotaire and reattached the collar around the man's neck. She put the control bracelet into her own pocket.

"Remember what you told me, you motherfucker? Now I'm going to tell you something. I am *the world's best* computer hacker. *The fucking best*. I'll have this bracelet's code reprogrammed before the car gets out of sight of this fucking building. You understand what I'm saying here. So no matter who made this for you, they won't be able to control it. Only I can. So you spend whatever time you have left wondering when I'm going to call the code in. And I promise you this: at some point, when I've got nothing better to do, I'm gonna blow your head up. Look at me, you son of a bitch. I would say, 'Bet your life on it,' but that wouldn't be much of a bet." With that, Phillips drove her elbow right through the front of Clotaire's mouth, knocking out several teeth. "Have a nice life."

The ride back to the hangar was quiet. Upon arrival everyone went inside. The sky was beginning to lighten with the dawn.

Christman looked at the others and asked, "Coffee or beer?"

"Coffee," all three answered in unison.

"Coming up." Within seconds, the automatic coffee machine was gurgling, followed by the aroma of a fresh pot.

287

Within a couple of minutes, the foursome had their mugs and were sitting around the table. Phillips finally broke the ice. "How did you find me?"

Styles answered. "Went to the logical point. The bartender. He has a deal going with Clotaire and told him where to find you. I found him. He gave us a warning about not getting rough with his girls. So that was the plan, bring him to us. You know the rest."

Starr interjected. "That was quick thinking, Phillips, about that sound you made. If they'd caught on about the earpiece and moved you, we might not have gotten to you in time. Doubt if Clotaire would have kept you around these parts. Hell, the bastard might have even sold you."

"I'm surprised that the Taser that hit me didn't fry it."

"Lucky for us, electricity doesn't go through rubber."

"Lucky for me anyway," Phillips agreed.

Styles was looking uncomfortable. Phillips noticed it and guessed what was bothering him. She admired him for respecting her privacy, but she wanted to put him at ease, knowing he would never ask on his own. "Just for the record guys, they didn't hurt me. Well, there was the Taser, being tied up, being the butt of J. C.'s joke, and being kidnapped, but other than that, it was just another day at the office." That comment broke all the tension that everyone was trying to hide. Laughter surrounded the table, and it sounded good to everybody.

Phillips interjected. "Not to change the subject, but Styles, thanks a fucking lot for that little game change of yours." This immediately brought a smirk between Starr and Christman.

"Told ya," Starr joked, looking at Styles.

"Gotta be able to think and act on the fly, Phillips. We didn't have the time to react any differently. We had no contingency strategy in place that provided for Pevosky bringing a hooker back to his room. If you want to blame me for not allowing that possibility, then so be it. Bottom line is that in what we do, things don't always go according to plan. If it makes you feel any better, I once had to dress in drag, and no I'm *not* going to tell you about that. You did a damned good job, Darlene; let it go." The fact that Styles had referred to her by her first name did not go unnoticed by anyone.

"Thank you," she said coldly. "Let me be clear about one thing. I will *never, ever* sleep with anyone for this job. If that gets me bounced off this team, bounce me."

Styles gave her a look that would wilt a cactus. "Read me loud and clear. I am not a monster, and I damn sure wouldn't ask that of you. Even I have my limits. Most people might consider them twisted, but I respect you, Phillips, and I will *never* disrespect you."

The group was quiet for a moment, then Phillips spoke. "Thank you for that, Styles. Getting to know who you are—that probably means as much to me as anything anyone has ever said. And I've never thought of you as any kind of monster; you're just someone who does something few others do, or even can do. I also appreciate your confidence in me; I know that's something that has to be earned. Especially with you."

Starr spoke up. "Well, do we get back to what the fuck we're going to do now, or do we need a group hug."

"Fuck you," Styles and Phillips said in unison. That brought a chuckle from all.

"Okay, back to business," Styles stated. "We need to plan how we're going to get into Zazar's room after I've taken him and Wazzuri out. I've got two ideas. One, we wheel him up in a wheelchair; two, we carry him up like he's drunk. Any suggestions?"

Christman asked, "Which would cause the least attention?"

"Debatable," Starr offered. "Everyone is used to seeing the occasional drunk; same thing for a handicapped person. I would say more people would react with sympathy for someone in a wheelchair, which might cause them to pay more attention, than for a drunk, which most people are just going to look at and ignore."

Styles nodded in agreement. "I'll buy that."

Christman chipped in. "That makes more logical sense to me."

Styles got up, walked over to his gym bag, and then returned to the table. He unzipped it and brought out the two laptops he'd taken from Pevosky. "Here," he said to Phillips, handing her the computers. "See what you can get from these." Her eyes lit up. "Glad to." She carried them to another table in the room. She immediately opened them and started studying the contents.

It was approaching noon when Phillips finally got up from her table. She had eaten three slices of what had become the meal du jour. She had not even looked at the pizza, her eyes never leaving the two computer screens.

The decision had been made for Christman to make the room reservation early that afternoon. Starr's reasoning was that the checkouts would have taken place by then, increasing their chances of getting a room where they wanted. Everyone agreed.

Phillips sat back down at the conference table, and the other three joined her. "I've gotten some good information off that. Bank accounts, other weapons that have been stolen and sold, and to whom. It seems there are no more nuclear devices for sale, for the moment. At least not after this last one that's been offered. I'm not convinced there is one. I think Pevosky may have been bullshitting the Saudis just for the money. I've got a couple of encrypted files to open, but I can't do that without a different program. She yawned. "I'm heading back to the hotel. Any instructions?"

Styles said, "Casually check the 'Do Not Disturb' signs. Might not be a bad idea to stay clear of the bar. Be damned sure to watch your back. Probably best if you keep an eye on the doors in the morning too. Also for any radio chatter. We wait for Zazar to show. After he's taken care of, we'll bring up Ladd. Then we get the hell out of here. J. C., be ready to leave anytime after noon or so. It'll all depend on Zazar."

"I only need half an hour," Christman stated. "We're fueled and ready to go."

"Good," replied Styles. "Tomorrow we'll complete this end, and then on to Saudi Arabia." As a sarcastic afterthought, he said, "How I've missed the sand."

CHAPTER 91

AT SEVEN-THIRTY THE next morning, Phillips walked back inside the hangar. Starr and Christman were sitting at the smaller table, drinking coffee.

"Hey, what're you doing back here so soon?" Starr asked her.

Joining them at the table, she addressed Starr. "We might have a small problem. I double-checked a few items last night and discovered that I haven't been able to completely erase you from the systems."

Starr straightened up. "What do you mean?"

"You've had too many pictures taken that are public record, whereas Styles hasn't. I've been able to delete you from the official FRPs, but if someone really wants to do a hard-ass search, they'll be able to find you."

"So what does this mean?"

"We need to disguise you a bit when you haul Ladd through the hotel. Nothing serious. Facial recognition programs run like fingerprint programs. They concentrate on distinct facial features, such as eyes, nose, cheekbone, and chin. Change those, and an FRP will run right past you. There's no way you'll be able to avoid cameras, especially when you're at the reservation desk."

"So what do I do?"

Phillips tossed a bag she'd brought with her onto the table and emptied the contents. Starr just stared. A package of tampons was among the items.

"What the fuck am I supposed to do with those?" he asked incredulously.

Phillips couldn't help but laugh, with Christman joining her. "Easy. I want you to put a section of these between your cheeks and gums. That'll change your cheekbone appearance slightly. Be sure to have some bottled water with you; they'll dry your mouth out like you won't believe. Also be sure to wear sunglasses. Best I could do on short notice." She was unable to suppress a grin.

Starr just stared at her. "You want me to do *what*?"

"You heard me. Hell, it's not like they're used. Stop whining. It'll work."

Christman, still laughing, said, "Wait'll Styles gets a load of this."

Starr just buried his head in his hands.

"Where is Styles?" Phillips asked.

"Doing those sit-ups of his on the plane. He was doing push-ups when I woke up. He'd already made the coffee and was really gettin' it on," Christman answered, still chuckling.

"Well, Starr, you do what you want, but if you don't want to get recognized, do it. Wear a ball cap too. Trust me, when they find these guys, every agency in the world is going to be pouring over the security tapes."

"All right," Starr said, his head still down. After a few moments he got up and headed for the coffee machine. "Want some?" he asked Phillips.

"Sure. Nobody's been near the doors. Not to be morbid, but how long before those bodies might start to smell?"

"I'm sure Styles turned the AC thermostat as low as it would go. I would think twenty-four hours anyway, maybe a bit longer. Probably wadded up a bath towel along the bottom of the door just to help seal it."

"I intercepted a request from Zazar asking to check in a bit early. He expects to be there by one this afternoon. He also wanted to know if his suite had two bedrooms or if he could book a second room. The hotel has moved him to the floor above for two rooms that connect. Guess he doesn't want to be that close to his bodyguard," Phillips said.

"Maybe he has plans that he doesn't want Wazzuri to know about," Christman said, not snickering for once.

"Given his taste in websites, you're probably right," Phillips agreed. "What time should we put our ears on?"

"Noon, unless you hear different," Starr said.

Having finished her coffee, Phillips got up, walked over to the sink, washed the cup, and put it away. "I'm headed back to the hotel. Radio check at noon." With that, she left.

Thirty minutes later Styles exited the jet, immediately stood on his hands, and began walking around the hangar on his hands.

"Don't ask," Starr said to Christman.

After ten laps around the hangar, Styles flipped back to his feet, grabbed a towel, walked over, and sat down. He immediately noticed the package of tampons. "Do I even want to know?" he asked, which started Christman laughing again.

"No, you don't," Christman was barely able to spit out. Styles just shook his head.

Starr interjected. "Phillips was here; Zazar moved up one floor. Got two rooms that connect. Guess he doesn't want to be around Wazzuri all the time."

Styles got up and walked over to the conference table, where diagrams of the hotel were laid out. He studied them for a minute, then walked back. "Shouldn't be a problem."

"She also said Zazar told the hotel he'd be arriving around one, and got the go-ahead for the early check-in."

Styles only nodded.

CHAPTER 92

A T TWELVE-THIRTY, EVERYONE was in position and the radio check had been completed. Styles knew that as it was daylight, scaling the building was not an option. He had decided on a more direct approach.

Starr, dressed in casual business attire, had gone to the reservation desk and dropped off a set of car keys earmarked for Mr. Nakhan Zazar, compliments of his host. The car, the desk clerk was told, was already in the underground parking garage. "It's the silver BMW with the dark windows; can't miss it," the clerk was told.

Styles figured that Zazar would send Wazurri down to check it out, so that's where he intended to take him. "Point Three, ready on the parking cameras?" he asked Phillips, who was back in her room at her computers.

"Affirmative, Point One," she responded.

Styles was sitting with Starr, having just joined him inside the BMW. They had parked the car down near a corner, away from the elevator.

"Marv, where are you going to leave Wazzuri?"

"You'll see soon enough," Styles replied. Starr didn't push it.

Styles was dressed in his usual black attire, but this time, he had also blackened his entire face.

Fifteen minutes later they heard, "Point One, targets have arrived, headed for reservation desk."

"Copy, Point Three. Signal garage departure."

"Copy, Point One."

Styles looked at Starr. "As soon as you see me engage Wazzuri, take the Bimmer back and pick up J. C. and Ladd. Pull right up to the front like you own the place, and take Ladd up to Zazar's room. I'll be inside. As soon as you get him inside, go down and repark the Bimmer down here. I'll be down shortly. Be sure J. C. is on standby. This needs to be done ASAP."

"What about Phillips?"

"I'll send her out as soon as Zazar is in the elevator, which should be about now."

As if on cue, they heard "Point One, targets splitting up. One up, one down. Second target is big."

"Point Three, kill parking and stairwell cameras, and return to base immediately."

"Come back, Point One," Phillips requested.

"Point Three, get out now."

"Copy, Point One. Point Three gone."

"Okay, Starr, the show's about to start." Styles got out of the car, made his way over, and hid behind a concrete support column.

Thirty seconds later the elevator door opened and a very large Iraqi got off. He immediately started looking around. Then he slowly started walking toward the silver BMW. He had a quizzical look on his face. From where Styles was standing, Starr could see him, but Wazzuri could not. When Wazzuri was only about thirty feet from the car, Styles signaled with two fingers outward. Starr immediately started the car and left. Wazzuri, confused, just watched the car drive away.

Styles moved out from behind the column, as silent as a cat. He was six feet behind Wazzuri when his shadow was cast just off to Wazzuri's side by a fluorescent light mounted on the concrete ceiling. Wazzuri whirled around with a knife in his hand. The two men stared at each other, Wazzuri with a sneer of contempt on his face. He was looking at a man dressed in black that he knew he outweighed by close to a hundred pounds. He swore at the dark figure in Arabic. The dark figure stood perfectly still, at a slight angle toward Wazzuri. Suddenly Wazzuri made a couple of short thrusts toward the figure with his knife, but the figure didn't move. Wazzuri started to slowly circle his adversary, seeing only his eyes move with him. Now Wazzuri was openly smiling. "I gut you like a pig," he snarled at Styles.

No response, only his eyes moving.

Wazzuri stepped in quickly toward his target, thrusting his knife outward and up, only to have his hand blocked sharply at the wrist. He simultaneously felt a tremendous blow to his chest. He stumbled back two steps but did not go down. He was having trouble breathing. He was not sure what had just happened. Now the dark figure was slowly circling him. Wazzuri turned with him. Wazzuri made several slashing motions, the figure staying six inches out of range. Still Wazzuri sneered. He tried a feint with his knife, then swung a long, looping punch at the man's head, only to watch him easily duck under it. Before he could regain his stance, Wazzuri felt a blow to his liver that almost made him shit his pants. He had difficulty shaking off this latest strike. He backed up several strides, his opponent staying with him, just out of his reach.

Wazzuri was stalling for time, trying to get his insides back together. Never in his life had he been hit so hard. He was fighting waves of nausea. Still he sneered at this man, who appeared to be in no hurry. Wazzuri finally stepped forward, thrusting and lunging with his scimitar, a curved sword Middle Eastern warriors favored. On his fourth lunge, he found his wrist caught in what seemed like a vise, then turned over, and he heard the snap of the bone. Wazzuri growled in rage. With surprising speed, he was able to spin and catch the knife in his left hand, and he tried a back-swing thrust. The figure in black stepped aside, brought up his right foot, and proceeded to kick right through Wazzuri's left knee, shattering it. This brought a howl from Wazzuri, as much from pure fury as pain. Barely standing, he saw the man spin and deliver a spinning back kick directly into his left kidney, which put him on the ground. Wazzuri finally began to feel something unknown to him—fear. In his entire life, he'd never lost a fight, and he hadn't even touched this man. Before he could react, this man had him in a rear choke hold, which he knew he was not going to escape. Before he blacked out, he heard whispered in his ear "This is from the American president. If you are a terrorist, I will kill you." Wazzuri died on the spot, with a smile on his face. He was expecting paradise to receive him, but he found only darkness.

CHAPTER 93

STYLES WAS GOING up the stairwell toward the eighth floor. He stopped on the landing separating the eighth from the seventh.

"Point Three, you clear?"

"Confirmed, Point One."

"Did you verify which room target one is in?"

"Affirmative, Point One. Target one is in 828, which adjoins to 827. Door to 827 is unlocked. Repeat door 827 is unlocked."

"Copy, Point Three. Good job."

Styles went up to the eight floor landing, carefully opened the door, and scanned the area. He was too high up for anybody down on the lobby floor to notice him, and no one else appeared anywhere on the walkway. He knelt down and quickly crabbed his way over to door 827 and let himself in. He locked the door after entering. He went to the adjoining door and listened. He could hear Zazar speaking on the phone but couldn't decipher what was being said. No matter. He studied the door lock, finding it unengaged. This surprised him. He almost wondered if it was some type of trap. He opened it ever so slowly. When he had opened it approximately four inches, he could just see the back of Zazar in the mirror over the bar. He guessed

Zazar was fifteen feet in front of him, maybe six feet to his right. He closed the door just enough so it wouldn't latch and waited. Two minutes later Zazar ended the conversation and started swearing to himself.

Styles was through the door and on Zazar in a flash. Nothing fancy. He immediately placed Zazar in a rear choke hold. Zazar flailed wildly for a few moments, then began to weaken. Styles let up the pressure just enough so Zazar would not black out. "The American president sent me. If you are a terrorist, I will kill you." He then reapplied the pressure and proceeded to choke Zazar to death in the middle of his room. When he was dead, Styles carried him over to his bed and laid him out. He took out his penknife and carved "terrorist" into his forehead. He then retreated back into the adjoining room, locking the door behind him, walked out carefully scanning the walkway, and quickly made his way to the stairwell. He descended rapidly back down into the underground parking garage. He went behind the Dumpster where he had dragged Wazzuri's body. He took out his penknife, then carved "terrorist" into his forehead.

"Point Two, what's your position?" he said to Starr.

"Six minutes out, Point One, package on board."

"Change of plan. Bring package to parking spot in garage."

"Acknowledged, Point One."

Five minutes later Styles saw the silver BMW enter the garage area and proceed to where it had been before. Styles quickly walked over to it, opened the rear door, and grabbed Ladd. "I'll be right back," he told Starr.

Ladd was barely conscious. "Wha ... wha," was all he could mumble.

Styles carried him over beside the body of Wazzuri. Styles turned Ladd around to face him and slapped him a couple of times until his eyes opened a bit wider. "I don't know if you can understand me, you miserable fucking traitor, but I hope you know how much I'm going to enjoy this." He backed Ladd up against the concrete wall and, with his right hand, very slowly choked the man to death. Styles prolonged Ladd's agony. Finally the man expired. For the third time that day, out came his penknife, and he again cut the word "terrorist" into a forehead. When finished, he dragged Ladd's body and dumped it beside Wazzuri's. Finished, he went over, climbing in next to Starr. "All Points, phase two complete," he said. Then, to Starr, "Let's go."

299

CHAPTER 94

ALL FOUR WERE back aboard the DPO jet, awaiting the control tower's permission to taxi out to the runway. When Starr and Styles returned to the hangar, they found that Christman and Phillips had already cleared it out. All trash had been burned in a burn barrel just outside the building. The entire place had been wiped clean of any fingerprints, as had the two vehicles. With Christman at the controls, the other three were grouped around the conference table.

Starr asked, "Don't take this as an insult, Phillips, but you did wipe the hotel room for prints right?"

"Yeah, but I wore gloves whenever I was in there. I double-checked a couple of places just in case, but it's clean." Then she added, "Not too hard to understand why you changed the plan." She gave Styles an exaggerated wink.

Starr stared at her. "What do you mean?"

"Oh, my mistake," she said with a grin. "I figured you just didn't want a tampon in your mouth."

"Fuck the both of you," Starr snapped, and he furthered the conversation by stating, "I didn't change it; however, I admit that was a plus."

Styles and Phillips just grinned.

"Not to change the subject—much—but what do you have in mind now?" Starr inquired.

"Not quite sure yet," Styles replied. "First, Phillips, can you put together names and faces for me, for the guys who bankrolled Zazar and what's his name? The ones from Global Eastern who made up the money for the payment to the Russians."

"Shouldn't be a problem. I'll get right on it."

"Take a break, both of you," directed Starr. "We've been hard at it, and we've got a fairly long ride ahead of us."

Right then they heard Christman's voice coming over the intercom. "Time to buckle up back there. We're off." All three got up and moved.

"All set," Starr yelled. No one had buckled in.

After a two-hour catnap, all three gathered at the conference table. Phillips spoke first. "I've learned that Sheikh Ami al Hadid, the top dog of this little group fronted by Global Eastern, spends most of his time at a mosque just outside of Al Hair, which is about twenty-five miles southeast of the capital, Riyadh. The main airport into Riyadh is, as J. C. already knows, King Khalid International Airport. We are on our way there, posing as entrepreneurs in the import/export business looking for antique fabrics. That's our cover story. I've already set up a meet with some prospective high-end merchants. We're cleared as far as our flight route. We're vectored through Kuwait. I've arranged hangar space, but it's shared. Best I could do. Soon I'll have the names and photographs of the five men from Global Eastern who are involved with al Hadid. I've also been monitoring Zazar's cell phone, but no incoming calls have been tracked. I've also been monitoring the Frankfurt police, and so far it seems no one has been discovered. I can't even tell whether the hotel's security system realizes it's been compromised. Al Hair is a small town. Markets, gas stations, a few amenities, but it is not what anyone would consider modern. I'm going to download some satellite photos showing the layout. I should have all this info within the hour, maybe a bit longer."

Starr spoke up. "Sounds like you've been busy."

"Just trying to stay ahead of the curve."

"You're doing a damned good job of that."

Styles spoke up. "Once you get those satellite photos downloaded and printed out, let me know. Get as close as possible, with as much detail as you can. We'll have to rent a vehicle, obviously; two would be better. Make sure one is a four-wheel drive. Also, download some maps of the surrounding area if you would. I want to study it before I recon the region. Phillips, is there any way you can determine a schedule that al Hadid might keep? He's the main target; the other five are designated optional. Starr's right; you're definitely earning your keep here.

"Compliment me all you want, Styles, but you're going to make your own sandwich if you're hungry."

"That's not a bad idea. Who wants one?" Both Starr and Phillips nodded.

Styles walked up front and checked with Christman whether he wanted one. He replied yes.

Fifteen minutes later all were enjoying turkey, ham, cheese, and lettuce sandwiches. Phillips had returned to her computer station and was working while eating, leaving Starr and Styles to themselves.

"What you got in mind, Marv?"

"Not exactly sure, but probably a long-range shot. Love to get all six out in the open, but the chances of that are slim to none. I've got a couple of ideas, but I need to see the layout. Until then, there's no sense in wasting time planning."

"So what do we do?"

"Sit back and enjoy the ride."

Starr wandered up front and sat down next to Christman. "So what's our route?"

"Well, we flew over Austria; we're going to kiss the heel of Italy, cruise over the Mediterranean Sea, cross Kuwait, then go on to Riyadh. After that, it's up to you guys."

"I'll have Phillips get us into a hotel. At least this time you won't be stuck babysitting Ladd."

"That'll be nice. He tried to talk to me a couple of times, but I just said no. I can imagine a lot of shit I'd do for the kind of money he must've been getting, but selling out like he did—I couldn't do that."

"Luckily, J. C., most of us don't. Can you imagine what it would be like if more assholes did? Shit, we probably wouldn't be here."

"Ain't that the truth!"

They were flying over water now, and there wasn't anything to look at. "Think I'll go back and see what Phillips can do about a hotel for us. You need anything?"

"Nah, I'm good."

He returned to Phillips's computer station and sat down next to her. "What can you line us up for a hotel?" he asked.

"How long should I book us in for?" she asked back.

"A week. That should give us time to finish this mission, plus meet with these exporters to cover our story."

"Okay, Starr, give me a bit, and I'll have us in. Any prerequisites?"

"Close to the airport. Make sure it's a nice hotel, something that people in our storied position would be expected to stay in. At least a four-star, maybe a five. Book four rooms. Close proximity. Don't forget about the vehicles. Get three. Make two of 'em four-wheel drive, and maybe a luxury sedan. How's your knowledge of antique textiles, that kinda shit?"

"Probably almost as good as yours," she replied dryly.

"Okay, bone up on it. You speak the language, so you're point on this."

"Got it. Now go away."

"Bossy bitch," Starr said under his breath, with a wink. Phillips never looked up. He went and sat down next to Styles. "Phillips is getting us into a hotel—a good one. Booking us into four rooms for a week. She's point on the cover story. We're gonna get three vehicles, two four-wheel drives. That sound about right?"

Styles, turning away from the window, agreed. "Sounds good. I'm not up on the current Saudi political climate right now. It's still pretty calm, isn't it?"

"Yeah, we should be able to move about without any problems."

Styles continued. "It'll take me three, maybe four, days to set my end up. I'm going to need Phillips to see what she can learn about this sheikh's schedule. From what I know, some move around freely, some don't. I'm going to need to know what he does. I'm short of time on this setup, so the more we can find out, the better off I am."

Starr just nodded in agreement.

CHAPTER 95

J. C. CHRISTMAN ANNOUNCED they were about an hour out from Riyadh. "What a pile of fucking sand" came over the intercom.

Phillips called Styles and Starr over to her computer table. "Okay, here goes. I've got us booked into the Holiday Inn Riyadh Izdihar, four rooms all next to each other, for a week. It's costing us about sixteen hundred per room. It has all the amenities, including wireless, which I won't need; two restaurants; gym; pool; bar—all the usual shit. It's got private parking, and I've reserved three spaces for our vehicles—two Land Rovers and an Audi sedan. I've asked the concierge to arrange a meeting on the third day with two of our prospective clients. That'll give me time to know what I'm talking about."

Styles asked, "What about customs?"

"Washington is pulling some strings for us. We don't have full diplomatic status, but it's been made clear that we are representing a new area of the national museum, and our embassy here has greased some wheels. We shouldn't have to undergo full scrutiny. The plane won't be searched. We might be asked some questions when we pick up the vehicles, but it shouldn't be anything overboard. I'm the buyer, you two are my personal security, and J. C. is, obviously, the pilot. Let me do the talking; I'm fluent here, and that will make them much more comfortable. As you know, we're officially strong allies, though unofficially we've got a few problems to iron out. President Williams has made that clear. We should be okay. Embassy is supposed to get us some paperwork to keep in the vehicles stating we're on official government-approved business. Anybody asks us any questions, we show them that."

Starr asked, "Where do we pick up the vehicles?"

"They'll be at the hangar along with some government officials to check us in. The hotel is only fifteen minutes from the airport. Eleven point nine miles to be exact. When we land, like I said, let me do the talking. If they ask you any questions directly, just use your head and play along with what I've already said. They have no reason to be wary of us, so it should go smoothly."

Starr and Styles looked at each other and shrugged. "You gonna fill J. C. in?" Starr asked Phillips.

"Yeah, but that won't be anything. He's the pilot; he flies the fuckin' plane. Other than that, he don't have to know shit."

"You eat with that mouth?" Starr chided her.

"Hazards of being around you two," she retorted.

All three noticed the whine of the jet engines start to decrease. "Must be getting close," Starr commented.

Sheikh Ami al Hadid did not outwardly display it, but inside he was getting concerned. He had not heard from Nakhan Zazar for two days, and he did not like that. He was also too stubborn to pick up a cell phone and call him, firmly believing that Zazar should be the one to initiate communication. *I will wait one more day*, he thought. He busied himself with the ongoing construction of his new palace. He was getting older and was ready to take a step back, to let the younger set take more responsibility. This would also allow him to concentrate his focus on the destruction of the infidels. That was his burning desire, born of his hatred of America and its decadence. To the day he started his journey to paradise, he would bring war on America. He had the money to do it.

CHAPTER 96

ALL FOUR WERE tucked away in their hotel rooms. Landing, stowing the jet in the hangar, picking up the rental vehicles, and answering a few questions had all gone without incident. The hotel check-in had gone smoothly, and all of them had been shown to their rooms. Each found a brochure package detailing all of the amenities that the Holiday Inn offered. The rooms were nicer than expected. At four-thirty, all converged in Starr's room. Starr had checked the room for any listening devices, finding none.

They sat around the table in his room. Phillips spoke first. "The first meeting, for the antique tapestries, is set for ten in the morning, day after tomorrow. Starr, I'd like you to come along." He nodded. "What about you?" she said, addressing Styles.

"I'm going to take one of the Land Rovers and recon. I'm going to check out Al Hair first. I want to see the layout, what's around, everything."

Christman looked at Styles and asked, "You want company?"

"Not this time. I don't know what I'll see, and if something goes south, it's better if I'm alone."

"Probably right," Christman agreed.

"Phillips, what have you been able to learn about Sheikh Ari al Hamid?"

"Not as much as I'd like. He's building quite the palace ten miles southeast of Al Hair. From what I can tell, it's about halfway done. It's really the only place he travels outside of the mosque. He's a homebody. I'm still working on the names of the other money men. I hope to have that info tonight. If pictures are available, I'll have those too."

"That would be nice, but al Hamid is the main target. When he's down, that completes this primary assignment, but I'd like to take all of them, if possible, as long as it doesn't compromise us. Everything will depend on his timing, but I'm going to try to work this toward the end of the week. I'd love it if we didn't have to haul ass outta here, but that's almost too much to hope for. I need find out if there's some way we can jam cell phone communications here for maybe an hour or two."

"Besides blowing up the cell towers?" Starr asked.

"Yeah, besides that."

"I'll make some calls, but it'll probably be tough."

"See what you can do."

"I'll research that too," Phillips added.

Christman piped up. "What do you want from me?"

"J. C., you're going to be our runner. And make damned sure nobody fucks with the plane. Any Saudis find out what we're carrying, and we're gonna be in a world of shit."

"You want me to plan on sticking close to it?"

"I think you'd better. We can't afford not to. Anybody gives you any shit, get hold of Starr and Phillips, and lock it down tight. No matter what, don't let anyone on it."

Starr interjected. "I'll make a call; maybe somehow *he* can get us full diplomatic status. That'd definitely keep people out. Don't know if it can be done though."

"Try. That'd help," agreed Styles.

"You got it, sonny boy."

"Thanks, pappy," Styles popped back.

"Pappy—I like that," Christman stated.

"Yeah, I kinda like that too," Phillips said, grinning.

"Pappy this," Starr snapped.

Phillips, changing the subject, asked, "Do we want to get together for dinner tonight, or fend for ourselves?"

Starr thought for a moment and then said, "Let's get together, at least for this first night. Let's try that Al Luloa, it's both a buffet and à la carte. That work?"

Everyone nodded in agreement.

"Okay, let's figure seven. Meet at the entrance. Styles will take the stairs."

"Why's that?" Christman asked.

"Styles *always* takes the stairs."

Everyone met exactly on time. The food was much better than anyone had really expected. They had found that all too often, food in the Middle East seemed to taste the same. That could not be said for this particular restaurant. The conversation was light, no referencing the mission at hand. To anyone who might have been watching, they were just a group of Americans in town, probably on business of some type.

Finally Phillips broke the calm. She looked at Styles and quietly informed him, "I have some photographs you may find interesting."

"Is that right?"

"Yes. Several different locations. I've got them all marked, with references to a map I put together for you. Should give you a good idea of what's what. Hopefully, it'll save you some time."

Their manner suggested they might be speaking of ice cream.

"Security is not prevalent in the stairways. Looks to be only the main entrances, registration area, and by the elevators," Styles submitted. "I saw one in the pool area, but surprisingly not in the gym, unless it's hidden for whatever reason. None of the others seem to be, so I can't think of any reason it would be there."

"What time you headed out in the morning?" Starr asked Styles.

"First light. With Phillips's help, and some luck, I might have a plan in place by the time I get back."

"I'll keep working to try to come up with IDs and photos. These people are definitely camera shy," Phillips said.

"You come up with something, let me know, no matter the time," said Starr. "Everyone be sure to use your satellite phones. No cells, and damned sure no hotel phones. Except for any hotel business or whatever."

Christman and Starr decided to hit the dessert buffet.

"Phillips, I'd like to get those photos and maps now. I want to study 'em, then run.

"Sure. Okay to finish my coffee?"

"Yeah."

CHAPTER 97

THE NEXT MORNING found Styles up and running. He'd spent the evening before studying the map and photographs Phillips had given him. He now had a good image in his mind of what lay in relation to what in the area he wanted to look over. For his run he'd just spent an hour running up and down the stairwell. Then it was back to the map. He wanted to study the terrain that surrounded the mosque and then take a ride out to where Ami al Hadid was building his palace. Phillips was getting frustrated because she still had not come up with photographs for the other men involved. She did have three names though.

First up was the mosque. From the hotel, it had taken him about forty-five minutes to drive down to Al Hair. The sun had only been up for twenty minutes when he arrived on the outskirts of town. It was easy to spot the mosque, the largest building in Al Hair.

He was dressed like a typical tourist: blue jeans and light blue T-shirt. He had a tan windbreaker with him but it lay across the backseat of the Land Rover. Gray Reebok athletic shoes completed his ensemble. He purposely did not bring a gun on this trip. If for any reason he was questioned, he did not want to have to explain the presence of a weapon. That would lead to bad results, no matter what. He did have a folding lock knife in his right rear pocket. He had taken typical tourist maps along besides what he'd received from Phillips.

As soon as he turned off the main highway that led out of Riyadh, Route 500, all roads immediately turned to dirt. The roads were already filled with locals going about their business. No one seemed to give him a second glance. He pulled over and parked, pretending to look at one of his "tourist" maps. In reality, he knew exactly where he wanted to go. There was a slight hill on the western side of the mosque. A road, actually more like a trail, led up toward it. He pulled out of his parking spot and slowly headed that way. He made a big show of acting in the manner he thought a tourist would act. As he approached the trail, he shifted the Land Rover down into four-wheel drive and slowly started ascending the hill. He followed it to the top and then down the back side. He purposely drove five miles farther before turning around. He then retraced his route. He stopped before the crest of the hill and got out. He slipped on the tan windbreaker and slowly made his way on foot to where he could see the mosque. He had a pair of Nikon binoculars with him, and standing behind some brush, he was able to observe the activity below. He paid particular attention to several aspects and made strong mental notes. After returning to the Land Rover, he drove back the way he came, driving past the mosque. Turning, he followed another road, which led him to the opposite side he'd already observed. He found a place to pull off and park without being too conspicuous. He casually looked around at the buildings and noticed a three-story apartment building that looked as if it had been abandoned. He got out and walked around, seemingly in an aimless manner, with his maps in hand. He was now wearing a baseball cap with the brim pulled down low. Finding himself behind the building, he entered through a broken window. Stopping and listening, he decided no one else was inside. He quickly made his way to the top and found an apartment in ruins. He spotted what he was looking for—a window facing the mosque. Once again, he thoroughly looked it over, making several mental notes. Three figures emerged, and his attention was immediately drawn to the man in the center. *Hello, al Hadid, pleasure to see you*, Styles thought. It wasn't hard to pick him out; his robes were grander and his beard longer than those of the other two, but most important was the manner in which the other two men obviously deferred to him. Styles spent the next fifteen minutes watching his quarry. Finally, he alone retreated back inside. Styles made note of the time while quickly making his way back to the Land Rover.

Suddenly something caught his eye—a flash. He stopped and knelt down, pretending to tie his shoe. He caught the flash again, a quarter of a mile away. He knew it was the reflection off a lens—possibly a rifle scope, possibly binoculars. He got up and resumed walking, quickly getting to the Land Rover. No shots were fired, so Styles figured someone was only watching. He wanted to know who. He purposely drove the Land Rover in the direction of the two flashes, paying very close attention to every vehicle, every person. Nothing and no one stood out. When he passed the location that he thought the reflections had come from, he instantly noticed a Toyota Land Cruiser, a late seventies or early eighties model, parked a hundred feet down a side road. To Styles it stuck out like a sore thumb. *Not an official military vehicle—too old; probably some type of militia*, Styles thought. He could see three men in the vehicle. As Styles passed through the intersection, he noted the Toyota pulling away from the curb. The intent was clear. Styles had one thought—to get out and away from town before any type of confrontation occurred. He was sure one was coming. Styles picked up speed in his Land Rover. Being newer and more powerful, it pulled away from the older Toyota. Thanks to Phillips's map, he knew the road he was on would lead him nowhere, in a hurry. He kept the Toyota approximately three-quarters of a mile behind him for twenty minutes. When the Toyota would speed up, trying to close the gap, Styles would increase his speed to match, keeping the gap consistent. Styles noticed a slight hill with some scrub brush coming up and decided that would be a good place to stop. Two minutes later he pulled over and got out with his tourist map in his hand, acting as though the Land Cruiser were of no concern.

Forty-five seconds later the Toyota came sliding to a stop behind him. Styles had spread the tourist map across the hood of the Land Rover and appeared to be studying it with great intent. He wasn't even looking at it. Three men—one Styles guessed to be in his midthirties, the other two younger—piled out of the car, screaming at him in Arabic. Styles looked up, feigning surprise, and simply put his arms out to his sides. One of the men, the oldest, was holding an AK-47, an automatic assault rifle that could have come from either Russia or China. The yelling continued. Styles pretended not to understand what they were saying, but in fact he knew quite well. They were demanding to know why he was watching the mosque. Styles kept pointing to one ear and shaking his head. The other two men, who still had their pistols holstered at their sides, came up beside Styles, grabbing him by his arms. The man with the AK was still demanding why Styles had been watching the mosque. Stepping toward Styles, he brought the rifle up and back, preparing to strike Styles in the face with the butt of the gun. The instant the man's motion started forward, Styles kicked him brutally in his balls with his right foot, followed by his left foot kicking him in his forehead. Styles had used the two men holding him as leverage so that both of his feet were off the ground for a moment.

Helped by the other two men being caught completely off guard, as soon as his feet hit the ground, Styles used the men for assistance and was able to kick off and spin into a somersault, not only freeing himself from their grasp but also landing slightly behind them. Styles drove two fast and violent punches, one into each man's kidney. One of the men dropped down to his knees, though the other remained standing, barely, fumbling with his pistol strapped to his side. This man had turned toward Styles after the blow. He was in perfect position, and Styles delivered a vicious front-knuckle strike, catching the man squarely in his throat, completely crushing it. Styles hadn't even registered the man's last gurgling sound before he was on the third. This man was still down on his knees, facing away from Styles, desperately trying to regain his footing. Styles went directly into a half-jump into the air, coming down straddling his target. Backed by his own weight, Styles drove his right fist right at the base of the man's skull, breaking his neck and severing his brain stem. The man died never knowing he'd been struck.

The entire incident, which left three men dead, lasted less than five seconds. Styles turned in a slow circle, looking at everything, and saw nothing unusual, just scrub brush and sand. One at a time, he hoisted the three bodies into the Land Cruiser, and he then drove it into the middle of some scrub. He took out his knife and cut some other brush, and he did a good job of camouflaging the vehicle in a short time. He made sure to hide it from the air as well. He then took a final branch of the thick brush and swept away both his footprints and the tire tracks left by the Land Cruiser, right up to the point where it had parked and the three men had climbed out. Returning to his Land Rover, he again swept away his footprints. Then, after climbing inside, he leaned out the driver's door and eliminated the last of them.

Styles started up his SUV and drove onward down the road, and a quarter mile away he discarded the branch He continued for another five miles, then turned around and made his way back to the spot of the incident. He slowed considerably and carefully judged where he'd stashed the Toyota. He could not spot it. Satisfied, he continued on to check out Sheikh Ami al Hadid's palace.

CHAPTER 98

SHEIKH AMI AL Hadid was more angry than concerned. He had still not heard from Nakhan Zazar and was beginning to imagine that perhaps Zazar might be interested in more than what he'd been sent for. He had long held suspicions that Zazar was not completely true to their cause. He had never been able to prove it though. What really concerned him was the inability to contact Wazurri as well. His loyalty was without question, and while he'd instructed Wazurri to follow Zazar's instructions, he refused to believe that Wazurri would ignore him. Finally he'd had enough. He summoned Muhammad bin Kahlleb, husband of his eldest daughter, one whom he trusted without hesitation.

"Sit, Muhammad; I have something for you to do."

Sitting, Muhammad said, "How may I help?"

"I want you to travel to Germany. Find Zazar. Have him contact me immediately, in your presence. Wazzuri is with him. Wazzuri is to follow your orders as though they were my own. He may contact me for confirmation, but show him this." Ami al Hadid offered a sealed envelope to Muhammad. "Do what you must, but find him. Go now."

"As you wish," Muhammad bin Kahlleb said, and he was gone.

Sheikh Ami al Hadid sat at his desk, stroking his long beard. His eyes looked tired, a reflection of his inner being. He was ready to step aside; after all, he was three years past eighty and no longer had the strength, physically or mentally, that he'd enjoyed during his adult life.

Styles was headed toward the mosque, then on to the construction site of Sheikh Ami al Hadid's new palace. Four blocks away, he passed a long, new black Mercedes sedan. By reflex, he scanned the sedan's interior, and he saw a man in the rear with a displeased look on his face. This man stared openly at Styles with a look of pure hatred. It was only for an instant, but it was there. *Fuck you*, Styles thought as they passed each other.

Fifteen minutes later, descending a small hill, he saw what was obviously going to be one magnificent building. A fifteen-foot-high wall surrounded what Styles estimated to be a ten-acre property. He figured the building to be 75 percent complete, and the grounds were already well developed. He pulled over and parked. He spent ten minutes glassing the entire compound and guessed at least sixty workers were present. He also observed a separate construction entrance for the workers. The main entrance was already secured by stout, though decorative, iron gates, complete with a cinder block guardhouse, which was already staffed. He counted six guards patrolling the area, all armed with AK-47s. Styles burned the entire image into his mind, then turned the Land Rover around and headed back toward the hotel. He felt he had the information needed to complete his plan. This time, no one observed his presence.

CHAPTER 99

STYLES HAD JUST parked the Land Rover when his satellite phone rang.

"Yeah," he answered.

"Where are you?" Starr asked.

"Parking the truck."

"Get up to Phillips's room."

"On my way."

Two minutes later Styles knocked on her door. Christman let him in. Starr and Phillips were seated at the table in her room.

"Ladd and company have been found. The bodies were discovered late yesterday afternoon, but they just gave the official word. One of the ER techs let it out about your forehead carvings. The press is just eating that up. No identities have been released yet. Frankfurt is in an uproar; six dead, all at one hotel. Talk about a hornet's nest," Phillips said.

"Any word from DC?" Styles asked.

"No," said Starr.

"It's on all the cable news shows. Internet too," Phillips added.

Styles shrugged. "Not our problem."

Changing the subject, Styles addressed Phillips. "Can you get me a satellite photo of the palace that al Hadid is building? Close up as possible. This is where it is," he said, pointing to the spot on map he'd circled.

"Shouldn't be any trouble," she answered.

"So what did you find today?" Starr asked Styles.

"Pretty much all I need to know. I've got options on where to set up for a shot. I'd like to set up some kind of camera on the gate of that mosque and the entrance gate of the palace. There's a service entrance, but I'm only interested in that main gate. It's got a manned guardhouse, and six patrolling with AKs. About sixty workers in there. I saw al Hadid, with two others, outside the mosque for about fifteen minutes. Didn't recognize either of the other two." He was quiet for a moment, then added, "Had a run-in with some type of militia." He went on and described the incident in general, including that he'd wiped all his tracks clean. No one said anything.

"You don't think they'll be found?" Starr asked.

"Eventually. We'll be long gone."

Phillips spoke up. "CNN just broke the news that one of the bodies was Ladd. I'd hate to be the lead on *that* crime scene. Their on-scene reporter is going berserk trying to confirm whether he was carved up or not. White House has still not responded."

Starr asked, "Where do we go from here?"

"You and Phillips keep the business appointments. J. C. and I are going to set up some video gear. How many cameras we got?" Styles asked.

"Twelve, I think. All that gear's still on the plane."

"Okay. J. C., get ready to roll. We're going to set some cameras up. You drive. We'll be back in a while."

Right then, Starr's satellite phone rang. He picked it up, looked at the number, and nodded to Styles. "Yes, sir," he said into the phone as he walked over to the far end of the room.

"Let's go," Styles directed Christman.

Within an hour, they had returned from the airport with the equipment that Styles wanted. They brought it up to Styles's room and departed again.

"Where we off to ?" Christman wondered aloud.

"J. C., what do you notice on the sides of the secondary roads here?"

"Uh, not sure what you mean."

"Cars, J. C. Broken-down cars. We're going to go buy a couple of junkers and park them where we can place the security cameras. Nobody's gonna think twice about another car on the side of the road. At least not for a while."

"No shit. That's a hell of an idea."

Within ten minutes they were at a car lot. Styles did the talking. He had purposely changed into the most casual clothes he had, and he approached the small building as a salesman came out, smiling like the proverbial cat who ate the canary.

Styles spoke in purposely broken English. "I wish to buy two cars. Cheap. I won't haggle on price. Do you wish to make this sale?"

"Yes, yes, I sell cars, I have family to feed. I have seven children. I sell you cars."

Styles walked around the lot and picked out two older Toyota sedans. "These two will do. How much?"

"Very fine choice, very fine. You can have both for only four thousand American."

"I'll give you two."

"Please, sir, I have family; I must have four."

Styles turned away and started for the Land Rover. He had gotten to within ten feet of it when he heard, "Wait, wait." He turned around.

The salesman was motioning him toward the building. "All right, two, but you are robbing me."

"Then don't sell the cars," Styles retorted.

"Follow please."

Styles followed him into the building.

"Please fill out these papers."

Styles put three thousand dollars on his desk. "How about three thousand, and just forget the paperwork."

The salesman's eyes went wide, but with caution. "I don't know if I can do that."

Styles reached over and picked up the extra thousand. "It's up to you."

The salesman smiled and said, "I will just say the paperwork must have gotten lost."

"Works for me. Give me the keys. I'll be back for them tonight."

Styles and J. C. left the car dealership and drove down to Al Hair. It was dusk, as the sun had set. Within an hour, Styles had marked where he wanted to place the vehicles. They returned to the hotel. Styles ran up, grabbed the video cameras, and found Starr. "Need you now." Starr followed without a word. They both joined Christman back down in the parking area. Upon returning to the Land Rover, they climbed in. "Back to the car lot, J. C."

Twenty minutes later they formed a three-car caravan, heading toward Al Hair. Styles had filled Starr in on the plan of driving over to pick up the two junk cars. They dropped the first car two hundred yards from the mosque. Styles affixed three cameras. They were then off toward the palace. He followed the same routine upon his arrival there. Then the three returned to the Holiday Inn.

CHAPTER 100

M UHAMMAD BIN KAHLLEB arrived at the Hilton Frankfurt only to
find more police than he'd ever seen in one place. He instinctively
felt severe apprehension. He had taken a cab from the Frankfurt Rhein
Airport and was deposited at the front entrance. He thought it would
be too obvious to turn away, so he gathered his wits and proceeded to
register.

"What is all this excitement?" he asked the desk clerk nervously.

"You don't read the newspapers, watch the news?"

"No, I don't believe the Western propaganda. I am here to meet
someone on holiday."

"There were six men killed here. All believed to be terrorists. We
have asked the officials to try to lower their visibility, but unfortunately
they are ignoring us. If you wish to find a different hotel, I understand."

"It is of no concern to me. I will take the room."

"Very good, sir. The hotel would be pleased to discount your rate
because of the uproar."

"That would be good," Kahlleb exclaimed. After the check-in process
was completed, he grabbed his one bag and headed for his room. After

stepping inside, the first thing he did was open his laptop computer and start researching what was happening. It was not hard to figure it out. His blood ran cold as he read the account. He was instantly on the phone to Sheikh Ami al Hadid, who answered wearily on the fourth ring.

"Yes."

"Al Hadid, Zazar and Wazzuri are dead. Wazzuri was found alongside the chief of staff of the American president. Three Russians are also dead. All had 'terrorist' carved in their foreheads. The police are everywhere. What should I do?"

Silence.

"Al Hadid, what should I do?"

"You can find out no more? What about our money?"

"Al Hadid, the police are everywhere. I have no way to find out any information. I am scared even having this conversation. The authorities suspect there must be some type of connection between the Russians, this chief of staff, and Zazar, but I do not believe they know. At least, that has not been made public. I do not believe there is anything I can do here. You sent me to find Zazar. I have done so. He is in their morgue. What else can I do?"

Ami al Hadid answered, with anger. "Nothing. Zazar has failed us, failed our purpose. Come home. I need to think."

Kahlleb spoke up. "I shall stay the night and return tomorrow. I do not wish to draw attention to myself."

"Do what you think best, Kahlleb. I am not angry with you."

"Thank you, al Hadid," he said before realizing he was speaking to a broken connection.

The foursome had been observing the images from the video cameras overlooking the mosque and the lavish palace Sheikh Ami al Hadid was building for himself. They had discovered no distinct patterns during the three days of surveillance. Phillips and Starr had kept their appointments with the textile merchants who specialized in antique tapestries. Phillips had shown an amazing knowledge of the subject, especially considering she'd studied it for only three days via the

Internet. Styles had been working out intensely, Christman had logged a great deal of monitor time, along with Starr, and Phillips was still concentrating on photographs. She had finally been able to produce two. She was visibly upset regarding her inability to account for all five.

"Phillips, let it go," insisted Styles. "You've more than done your job. You can't reproduce what is not there."

Phillips just looked at him, glaring, then returned to her computers. There was no quit in this girl. Styles admired that.

"So you got a plan yet?" Starr asked Styles.

"Yeah, gonna happen tomorrow. At least the first half of it. J. C., we're going to head out before dawn. You'll drop me off and return here. When I want a pickup, I'll call. Be ready to leave at zero three thirty. We'll both take the stairwell. I'll have my gear already aboard."

"You got it. I'll be ready."

CHAPTER 101

S UNUP THE FOLLOWING morning found former sergeant Marvin Styles firmly encamped in the spot of his choosing. He had placed himself at the midway point of a small knoll in the middle of the scrub brush that was so frequent in the area. He was virtually invisible. He was in his desert ghillie suit, a sand-colored net tent over him, lying on a blanket that matched the color as well. He was exactly 1,252 meters from the open area of the mosque he was watching. Armed with his specialized M40A3 sniper rifle, complete with the big Leopold scope, and shooting the 6.5 × 47 Lapua round, he was easily within his kill range. He also had a spotter's scope set up beside him, along with his binoculars. He had two spare magazines at his ready as well, but he doubted he would need them. Now it was just a waiting game, something he excelled at. The weather could not have cooperated better; there was little to no wind. Styles was in his prone position and was watching everything within the compound.

Over his radio headset he heard, "Point One, just intercepted a call from someone named Kahlleb to Ami al Hadid. I caught a break from the word recognition program. Kahlleb informed al Hadid he was returning home. He reported police all over the Hilton Frankfurt. Best guess is he was sent to find Zazar," Phillips reported.

"Copy, Point Three."

Styles continued waiting. Shortly after eleven he noticed a similar Toyota Land Cruiser arrive at the mosque. Two older men got out and went inside. Fifteen minutes later they returned outside and left. *Must be missing those three*, Styles thought. He wasn't the least bit concerned they would be found anytime soon. Finally, at two in the afternoon, the main door opened and four men came out. Styles instantly recognized Sheikh Ami al Hadid. He studied the other three men closely and decided two were the same as those in the photographs Phillips had worked so hard to obtain. Although he had no direct evidence placing the fourth man in the group he was after, he decided it stood to reason that the chances were greater that he was part of the group rather than not. He made his choice.

Ami al Hadid was by far the oldest of the four. Normally Styles would take him out first. However, it made perfect sense he would be the slowest to react. Al Hadid was second from the left, so Styles made his mind up to shoot from right to left. He double-checked the wind—virtually nonexistent. He had the scope set for the distance. He carefully brought the crosshairs onto the target farthest to the right, settling on the middle of the man's forehead. He gently squeezed the trigger. His eyes never wavered from the scene. Racking the bolt action as smoothly as breathing, the result of thousands of repetitions, he targeted the second man. Same place, same result. He immediately swung the rifle slightly to his left and found the third target, who had just turned to run. He centered between the man's shoulder blades and squeezed. He then targeted Sheikh Ami al Hadid. The look on his face was more resigned than surprised. He hadn't even turned. He seemed to be looking straight at Styles, but because Styles was using his suppressed rifle, there was no way the sheikh could locate his position. He brought the crosshairs up slightly, to right between his eyes. He squeezed the trigger. Four shots, four targets down. People were starting to run around, most ducking, or just trying to hide. No one had any idea where the shots had come from; they had heard nothing. All people saw were four large sprays of blood, three of them including brain matter. None of the men ever felt what hit them.

Styles checked his watch. It was 1415. Styles had decided to make a tactical retreat from the immediate area. He was going to cross thirty-two miles of desert, which would bring him to a secondary road he had marked on a map for Christman. "All Points, target plus three down. Point Four, pick up at 1830 hours. Copy and confirm."

"Point One, copy and confirmed," Christman replied.

Styles quickly packed his gear, leaving the sand netting folded up at the top of his pack. His rifle was slung across his back. He crawled on his hands and knees backward, up and over the crest of the knoll behind him, again brushing his tracks away with a branch. Once he was past the small peak, he stood up and started running, keeping low. He would have been extremely hard to spot unless his moving profile was picked up. The path he'd picked made this a low probability, as he had chosen to be in the middle of nowhere. There was a slight chance he could be spotted by his tracks from the air, but he felt that chance was remote. The worst-case scenario was if any aircraft flew slowly enough to spot his tracks, but he was confident he could shoot them down. He strapped a small GPS unit to his wrist and started running at a steady, easy pace, averaging nine minutes or so per mile. Over hard ground, he could average seven or less, but this was sand. Every half hour, he hydrated from his canteen, and he just kept running. He saw no one and heard nothing other than the sound of his own footsteps and breathing. He was constantly alert of his surroundings. Ten miles into the trek, he saw a man herding goats a mile directly ahead of him. He instantly lowered his stance, and swung wide to the left, giving the man a wide berth. He was able to slip past him, never being noticed, and then realigned himself back on his original course. The side step had cost him approximately twenty minutes. He was still within his original timetable.

Running at his steady pace, and constantly on alert, the distance dwindled easily. He had not seen any sign of life since the goatherd. The run was uneventful, his legs working in synergy. He arrived at his destination point, pulled up a few hundred yards short, and walked the rest of the way. He continuously watched for traffic, as he was now in view of the road. He was heading for a small rock pile to hide behind. He arrived ten minutes before his scheduled time. Eight minutes later he saw a set of headlights approaching in the distance. "Point Four, flash your high beams." Styles watched as the approaching vehicle flashed its lights. "Point Four, you're ninety seconds out. Styles waited, and Christman stopped twenty feet from his position. "Point Four, Point One approaching."

"Copy, Point One."

Fifteen seconds later Styles opened the rear door of the Land Rover and climbed in. Christman immediately pulled away.

"I'm going to change," said Styles. After stowing his gear in the rear of the Land Rover, Styles climbed over into the front seat, stashing his silenced Beretta under his seat.

"Any problems?" Christman asked.

"Nah. Ran across a goatherd, but I just swung around him. Don't tell Starr this, but if I never had to run in this fucking sand again, it wouldn't hurt my feelings. Seems I've been running in this shit half my life."

"Yeah, but this is where the bad guys are."

"Another reason I hate these bastards."

"I got the route back to the hotel plotted into the GPS. We're going way around the picnic ground and coming in north of the airport. Ought to avoid any unnecessary local LEOs that way," Christman offered.

"Good."

"What's next?"

"Group talk. Might have to call the Man. That'll be Starr's decision."

"You hungry?"

"Yeah, I am actually."

"Think we'll pass by some drive-throughs. I'll hit one."

"Thanks, J. C. Got any water?"

"Small cooler behind you."

"Good thinking, my man." Styles helped himself.

Two hours later they were fed and back at the Holiday Inn.

CHAPTER 102

P HILLIPS, STYLES, AND Christman were all seated around the table
in Starr's room.

"Cops are going nuts about this sheikh's death. Sounds like they're
bringing in the military. This guy had major juice. The other three have
all been confirmed as board members of Global Eastern. I think your
hunch about the third guy was right," Phillips commented, addressing
Styles. "That leaves two left unaccounted for. One problem we might
have is that the government's going over all foreign visitors with a fine-
tooth comb. Anyone that is even questionable will probably be held. No
foreign planes can even file a flight plan without specific government
approval. We can't ask Washington for help on this, 'cause that'll raise
red flags all over the place. We're on our own."

J. C. interjected. "Well, we knew that going into this. Anybody got
any ideas?"

Phillips asked, "What if we just try to wait it out? Starr and I've had
those two meetings. Hell, I even placed an order. Doesn't that justify
our presence?"

Starr responded, "In our country, probably yes. Not here. Things don't work normal in this part of the world. The military's gonna want somebody's head on a platter, and they won't stop until they get it. Whether it's the right head or not don't mean shit."

Styles had been quiet all this time. Finally, he weighed in. "J. C., how fast can that plane of ours get us to Kuwait?"

"Wheels up to the border, probably forty minutes. Quicker if we can handle the afterburners."

"Phillips, is there any way you can fake a government approval for a flight plan?"

"I think so. It won't last all day, but I think I can upload to the airport computers long enough for us to get airborne. Somebody will catch it soon enough, but it ought to buy us enough time."

"All right. Do what you need to do. I think we're short of time here. All the government has to do is place just one of our faces and we're in the shit. Originally, I was going to discuss whether it was worth trying to find, and take out, the other two, but now I think we need to get outta Dodge."

Christman joined in again. "I've been through crap like this before. It wouldn't surprise me if they had soldiers guarding every foreign-registered plane at the airport."

Styles said, "Then what we need is a diversion. A big one."

Starr just shook his head. "I was afraid of this. What do you have in mind?"

"A diversion."

"What kind of a diversion?"

"Oh, I don't know. Maybe blow up a refinery or something. That should keep 'em busy for a few minutes."

"Christ, Styles," Starr exploded. "A *refinery*? You want to blow up a fucking *refinery*?"

"Just one of the little ones. Don't want gas prices back home to go up. I saw one north of the airport when J. C. and I were coming back just now. That'll work."

Starr was incredulous. "Just how are you going to do that?"

"Incendiary rounds in Bertha. Just one problem, though; Bertha and those rounds are still on the plane."

"Great," exclaimed Starr.

"Not that big a deal. Timing on this will be everything. Everybody take everything except the clothes on your back—and of course your computers, Phillips—and get rid of it. Away from the hotel. Throw it out. While you guys are doing that, I'm going after the rounds. When I get back, we meet back here. Starr, you and Phillips will take a vehicle and head toward, but not to, the airport. Find someplace to hole up no more than ten minutes away. J. C., you're going to drive the Land Rover. Make damn sure you've got something to cover your ears with. This rifle is not suppressed, and it's *loud*. We're going to have to do this on the move. We'll lower or bust out the rear window. Then J. C. will drive us past the refinery. A few well-placed shots, and we've got a fireball. Starr, you and Phillips will be able to see and hear it. It's only ten minutes past the airport. When you hear it go up, time it so you're at the plane in fifteen minutes. Don't stop for anybody or anything. If you have to come in hot, come in hot. I'll already be at the hangar, covering you, in case anybody's chasing you. That Barrett will stop anything that could possibly be after you. Phillips, this whole plan depends on your phony authorization. If that doesn't go through, be damned sure to let me know before I blow the refinery. Everybody understand?"

Everybody nodded.

"Okay, let's get at it," Styles snapped.

While everyone else went in different directions, Styles returned to his room and dressed in black. Then he retrieved the Land Rover and headed to the airport. He parked about a half mile away from the hangar, which housed their plane. He easily made his way up to the large open door that led in from the tarmac, and sure enough, two soldiers were watching the aircraft. Styles was able to slip inside and took a few minutes to observe them. They were not taking the job seriously, speaking and joking about women. The light was coming from the far end of the hangar, and he had no trouble making his way toward them without being seen. He didn't want to leave any blood to be found. He heard one of the men tell the other that he needed to take a piss, and that man walked toward the far wall, where the bathrooms were. That soldier wasn't even halfway there when Styles had crept up to within ten feet behind the soldier who had been left behind. Styles was crouching down, hidden behind the landing gear. As soon as the first soldier went through the door, Styles moved. The soldier was small in stature. His sidearm was holstered. Styles couldn't see any other weaponry. He silently moved behind the man and drove a straight-knuckle strike directly to the base of his skull. Before he could fall, Styles placed him in a rear choke. Styles was certain the man was already dead, but he wanted to be sure. He dragged him over to the back side of the hanger, next to a large trash barrel, then dumped him in. He ran over next to the bathroom door. A minute later the second soldier came out. As he walked past Styles, he never saw the blow that caught him square in the throat. He gurgled once and keeled over. Styles caught him, checked for a pulse, found none, dragged him over, and tossed him atop the first soldier. He spotted an old tarp and tossed it over the two bodies. Three minutes later he was in and out of the jet with Bertha and the ammo he wanted. Then it was back to the Holiday Inn.

CHAPTER 103

STYLES HAD THE floor. "Okay, everybody set?" All nodded in return. "How long do we have on the flight plan authorization?" he asked Phillips.

"Once I hit send, it'll be entered within seconds. From there, it's anybody's guess. It'll depend on who is watching, and how hard. Could be as little as ten, fifteen minutes; could be hours. No way to know. I tried to upload an encryption code to block anyone trying to remove it, but their system isn't sophisticated enough to accept it. My cell phone is more advanced. For all the money this country has, some of their systems are barely above waxed string and cans."

"Okay, let's hit it." Everyone headed toward the parking area separately after placing "Do Not Disturb" placards on their doors.

The group rolled out in the two Land Rovers, leaving the Audi sedan behind.

Starr and Phillips found a strip mall six minutes away from the airport, parked, and waited.

Styles, with Christman driving, headed past the airport, toward the oil refinery. He'd smashed out the rear window, which allowed excellent positioning of the big Barrett when mounted on its bipod. "Make sure all the windows are down, J. C.; the concussion is gonna be strong. Cram as much tissue in your ears as you can. We'll make a pass by, and then hit it on the return."

"Gotcha," he hollered back.

All the windows came down. They drove past the airport and soon were upon the refinery.

"Slow down; let me check it out," Styles directed, and Christman complied.

Styles saw what he needed to see. "Okay, go up a mile or so and turn around. When I give the signal, slow to about thirty. Steer with your knees and put your hands over your ears. This is gonna be *real fucking loud.*"

Christman got the Land Rover turned around and started back. Styles had his targets picked out. Three separate large circular oil containers. *This is gonna be a clusterfuck if they're empty*, he thought. He chambered the first round, sighted in on his first target, and squeezed the trigger. Even Styles was shocked at the concussion felt inside the vehicle. Had the windows been closed, they would have been blown out. A second and a half later he saw a flash against the side of the storage tank. A giant *whoomph* followed, and flames shot skyward. They were then hit by a shockwave that almost caused Christman to lose control of the vehicle. "Hold her steady, J. C." He sighted in the second tank and squeezed the trigger, with the same results. Then the third. Same action, same results. In less than ten seconds, the oil refinery was a boiling inferno. "Let's get the hell outta here."

Eight minutes later they were back at the airport. "Let's hope Phillips's plan works," Christman said.

They pulled up to the hangar. Nothing seemed out of the ordinary. In a flash, Styles was out of the Land Rover and set up at the hangar door with the big Barrett, just in case. Four minutes later Starr and Phillips came rolling up. Styles motioned them inside and pointed for Starr to park alongside a far wall. The vehicle had barely stopped when Starr and Phillips came rolling out, each holding one of Phillips's computers.

"Everybody on board," Styles yelled.

334

The three scampered up the flight stairs with Styles raising the steps and closing the door behind them.

"How we lookin', J. C.?" Starr hollered up to him.

"Just got clearance from the tower, but they sound confused. I'll bet somebody is checking that flight plan authorization right now. We gotta get outta here."

"Once we're off the ground, can they call us back?" Phillips asked.

"Long as we're in Saudi airspace, they can call us back, but if the radio is off, we can't hear them," Christman said, grinning as he reached up, pretending to turn it off. He made short work of the taxi to the runway, paused, and hit the throttles, sending the plane hurtling down the runway. Twelve seconds later they were lifting off, with the lights below falling away quickly.

"Starr, get up here," Christman yelled. When Starr sat down next to him, Christman pointed out a large dial, with a lighted sweeping hand rotating within it. "If any dots show up on that screen, let me know. Do not take your eyes off of it. Phillips, get on your computers. See if you can monitor any kind of communication between the airport and the military. Styles, there's a manual in the cabinet right there—blue cover, no writing. Get it out and familiarize yourself with it. And pray we don't have to use it."

All of a sudden, the control tower from King Khalid made an announcement over the radio. First in Arabic. Then English. They were being ordered to return to the airport immediately.

"What do we do?" demanded Starr.

"Watch that dial, and hold the fuck on. *Everybody*, hold the fuck on," Christman yelled at the top of his lungs.

He put the jet into a steep dive, leveling off at three hundred feet.

"What're you doing?" yelled Starr.

"Getting under their radar. Make it harder for them to find us," he said as he reached over, and the turned off the plane's transponder, a device used for location purposes.

"Styles, get up here," Christman screamed.

"Yeah, whaddya need?"

"You watch that radar screen. That shows the ground. Let me know if any humps show up. We're going down to two hundred feet. In the dark I can't see if we're gonna hit anything. Watch that thing like a hawk. If *anything*—and I mean *anything*—shows on that screen, let me know. It's reading about ten miles ahead of us. I've got it in sensitive mode, so it'll pick up anything. At this speed, that gives me about forty seconds to react. If we have to hit the afterburners, that'll go down to about twenty-five seconds, maybe less."

Phillips came running up. "I think the military is scrambling fighter jets to intercept us."

The scene in the cockpit was almost surreal. Here they were flying around 730 miles per hour, two hundred feet off the ground. You could cut the tension with a Popsicle stick.

"Starr, anything on your radar?"

"Negative, J. C."

"Slight rise ahead, J. C.," Styles advised.

Christman stole a quick look at his screen and climbed fifty feet in altitude.

Phillips spoke. "The fighter jets are reporting they have us on the edge of their radar screen."

"Thought we were under their radar?" Starr said.

"Ground based, not a fighter jet's."

"How far are we from Kuwait?"

"Close, but not close enough. Not for comfort anyway. Okay everybody, get ready. Styles, keep your eyes *glued* to that radar screen. Starr, you watch too. I don't care about the fighters anymore. I care about a hill. Or anything. Hold on to your hats, sports fans." Christman lit off the afterburners. The thrust forward was inconceivably strong. The whole plane shook and seemed to explode as they broke the sound barrier. Sooner than anyone thought possible, the plane had rocketed up to over just under 1,200 miles per hour—twice as fast as the plane was originally built to fly.

"Let's hope it holds together," yelled Christman.

"Fighter pilots are reporting they lost us," Phillips informed everyone.

"We caught 'em with their pants down. They never expected us to fly this fast. They didn't have time to react. They won't be able to close on us now to reacquire us. We should be in Kuwait airspace in eight minutes. Starr, call whoever you need to call and have them inform Kuwait we're coming in hot and low and we're not military. Otherwise, we'll probably get shot down."

Starr returned in four minutes. "We are vectored through Kuwait; however, they are insisting we climb to thirty-five thousand feet upon entering their airspace. We are also not to exceed normal civilian jet flight speeds. The pilot is to report his heading and follow it explicitly. We are not authorized to land anywhere."

"Christ, a fucking speed limit in the fucking sky," Styles swore aloud.

"Ladies and gentlemen, Flight Shityerbritches hopes you've genuinely enjoyed your flying experience and hopes you will travel with us again," deadpanned Christman.

Once again, laughter broke the tension.

CHAPTER 104

THE DPO JET containing Starr, Styles, and Phillips, with Christman piloting the craft, was halfway across the Atlantic Ocean, headed for Knoxville, Tennessee. Styles and Phillips had assisted Starr in writing up a complete report, beginning with their departure from DC headed to Indianapolis. That already seemed like a long time ago. The report was stored, in a heavily encrypted file, in Phillips's computer. She had surprised everyone by picking up some magnificent steaks and was preparing a well-deserved dinner for everyone in the plane's kitchenette. Christman, with the plane on autopilot, was turned around in his seat, with everyone engaging in conversation. They were lightly discussing the mission, dissecting it and wondering what they might have done differently. In the end, they all agreed that for a first assignment, they had done well. Phillips was still miffed about her inability to obtain positive identification and photographs for the last two men, but they all seemed certain that they were probably board members of Global Eastern. It only made sense.

With dinner finally made, they all enjoyed a meal that at the time felt and tasted as if it was fit for royalty. Phillips was the star of the hour.

When dinner had been cleaned up, the discussion returned to their assignment. Phillips had also been notified that the computer equipment she had requested had been delivered to Knoxville and was ready to be picked up. She had insisted on setting it up herself. She had planned on dividing her time between the Ranch and her apartment outside of Fairfax, Virginia. Starr and Styles were returning to the Ranch, full-time of course, and Christman was a little undecided. He knew there was always a cabin for him at the Ranch.

Starr and Styles were relaxing with an ice-cold Molson Red Ale, Phillips was enjoying a glass of wine she had picked up in Germany, and Christman was bitching about drinking water.

"We all have our crosses to bear, J. C.," Starr razzed him.

Once they were out over the Atlantic, the group relaxed considerably. Though it remained unspoken between them, they all felt good about putting down some very bad men. Styles particularly. He hated terrorists, hated everything they stood for. To him they were cowards who hid behind women and children, too afraid to even wear a uniform. Given the chance, Styles would kill every single one of them that crawled the earth. His time in the Marine Corp had left a bitter hatred in him for these jihadists. In his mind, they were not worthy of being called "soldier."

"It's all over the Internet about Ami al Hadid being assassinated along with three members of his board of directors at Global Eastern," Phillips announced. The woman seemed tied to her computers.

Styles raised his beer. "To four more of those bastards we've put down; may they rot in hell."

"Cheers," answered the other three in unison.

Then Starr's satellite phone rang. He looked at it, nodded at everybody, and went toward the rear of the plane. Styles and Phillips heard him say, "Yes, sir."

Starr was quiet. He just listened intently. After two minutes he hung up without speaking another word. He got up and motioned for Phillips to follow. He joined Styles toward the front of the plane.

"That was the President. A radiation detector just went off less than an hour ago. Caught it coming into Texas from Mexico."

The sound of the jet engines increased.

CPSIA information can be obtained at www.ICGtesting.com
Printed in the USA
LVOW10s0224130715

445983LV00002B/128/P